In Praise of Northern Heat Series

"These authors sure know how to turn up the heat and what a delightfully hot read this was." — *Coffee Time Romance*

"Honestly, I knew we had talented authors who lived in Canada since I've read them before, but somehow having their writing displayed under one cover just amps up the wow factor." — *Just Erotic Romance*

In Praise of

Opal Carew

"Opal Carew has done a great job in developing a well-written story about the healing power of love. The passion they share and the love that is built between them is very romantic as well as heart-warming. This book is for all the hopeless romantics. I know they will enjoy this as much as I did." — *Cupid's Library Reviews*

Lauren Hawkeye

"Tantalizingly sensual and shockingly intense, Lauren Hawkeye combines the erotic and the artistic … making this story feel original and daring, providing a hero whose moments of self-doubt make him increasingly sympathetic and a scarred heroine whose courage can break down any resistance." — *Romantic Times Book Reviews*

Eve Langlais

"Lexie is one fantastic heroine. She is tough and doesn't apologize for it. These characters are so engaging that I honestly believe they could have carried the story without interaction with anyone else or added elements, but the action was so compelling that the story just flew by." — *Night Owl Romance*

Cynthia Sax

"No matter which genre Cynthia Sax writes in, her engaging and graceful writing style always shines through and pulls the reader into her highly entertaining stories. Sax crafts a steamy chemistry between a hot, protective, and controlling boss and an organized, efficient, yet lonely, assistant. This enticing love story filled with sexy shenanigans will leave readers absolutely breathless."
— *Lusty Penguin Reviews*

turn up the heat
Best Erotic Romance Novellas

Edited by
Opal Carew

Northern Heat Series 2

QUARRY
PRESS

ISBN 978-1-5502-406-3

Cataloging in Publication Data is available at the Library and Archives Canada and the Library of Congress.

Quarry Press acknowledges the financial support of the Government of Canada through the Canada Book Fund (CBF) for this project.

Publisher: Bob Hilderley
Designers: Susan Hannah and Laura Brady
Typesetter: Laura Brady

Poem in the Introduction: Marissa Caldwell and Laurie Cooper, Creative Consultants at Pub-Craft

Printed and bound in Canada.

Published by Quarry Press, Inc., PO Box 1061, Kingston, Ontario K7L 4Y5
www.quarrypress.com

MIX
Paper from
responsible sources
FSC
www.fsc.org   FSC® C107923

Contents

Introduction

Northern Heat continues to burn red-hot here in Canada, and we intend to carry on that steamy trend with the release of *Turn Up the Heat*, this second anthology of Canadian erotic romance.

These stories have been widely celebrated at home and abroad. As one of the first Canadian anthologies of erotic romance, *Northern Heat* has been praised as "emotionally compelling, sexy, contemporary romance" (*Publisher's Weekly*), a "delightfully hot read" (*Coffee Time Romance*), and "simply deliciously naughty fun" (*Romance Junkie*). *Romance Junkie* goes on to say, "It seems we're constantly bombarded with news about Canadian celebrities, but amongst the movie stars, singers, and sports icons are a whole other grouping that has gone mostly unmentioned... until now."

Despite the frigid winters we've had the past few years, the world of erotic romance is blossoming in the Great White North. The end of the year saw the rise of many Canadian romance authors to the forefront of the genre. These include the talented authors published in *Northern Heat* and now *Turn Up the Heat*.

Readers seem to love collections. Last fall, I was invited to become involved in a collaborative project with several other authors. The invitation came from *New York Times* bestselling author Sara Fawkes. I jumped at the opportunity and was delighted to find that six of the eight authors involved were Canadian, including Cathryn Fox, whom I'd worked with on *Northern Heat*. As often happens with these things, I found myself drawn into other similar projects. I have since contributed to five of these collaborative anthologies (or as they are popularly known, boxed sets) and almost all of them were dominated by Canadian authors. Four of the five hit the *USA Today* bestsellers list, and two hit the *New York Times* list!

That means that Cathryn Fox and Sharon Page (both in *Northern Heat*), as well as Lauren Hawkeye (in *Turn Up the Heat*) and I have all become *New York Times* and *USA Today* bestselling authors, which is every author's dream. To top it off, we are all listed among the Amazon Top 100 Achievers. Clearly, Canadian erotic romance authors have become stars in their galaxy.

Northern Heat was our chance to show that, contrary to popular belief, Canadian winters are not all snow and ice. We were so excited with the success of *Northern Heat* that we just had to do it again! In *Northern Heat*, we brought you 12 tales of love and lust. In *Turn Up the Heat*, instead of short and fast, we go long and deep, with four much lengthier stories, featuring contemporary, paranormal, and futuristic romance genres. You may have encountered some of these erotic romance genres, but others may be virgin territory.

Contemporary erotic romance involves modern characters and true-to-life situations. *50 Shades of Grey* has made this genre mainstream. This is where you find stories that really could be yours! You will find characters struggling with love and lust as we do from day to day. (Alas, I have never found myself swept off my feet to an exotic paradise by a billionaire, but stories like these make it easier to dream!) Look to Lauren Hawkeye's novella "Sex & Love" and Cynthia Sax's "The Good Assistant" in this anthology for two masterful contemporary romance stories.

The paranormal genre focuses on supernatural romantic

characters, such as werewolves, vampires, faeries, and shape-shifters. Vampires have long been popular with romance readers, and this genre became even more popular with the widespread success of *Twilight* that brought sexy paranormal men into the mainstream. This genre goes far beyond sparkly vampires, however. The stories can include any better-than-normal features such as time-travel, superpowers, and (often sexy) super-humans. Who doesn't love their hero to be a little 'larger than life' anyway? Have fun reading the paranormal story by Eve Langlais in this collection.

Similar to the paranormal genre, the futuristic and fantastic style focuses on not-quite-everyday romances. Taking place in the near (or very distant) future, these stories tell us of love and sex in the world of science fiction. We're not just talking about *Star Trek* here, although there would be nothing wrong with a little romp on the USS Enterprise. The futuristic genre takes us to another time and place with imaginative science, technology, and travel—even taking us to other planets or parallel universes—and certainly providing us with another way to escape our winters. My fantastic tale of "Slaves of Sex" is designed to leave you longing for more than this world can offer.

Not all erotic romance is so intense. We are not above laughing at ourselves, true deprecating Canadians that we are. Here is a poem we received from two fans of *Northern Heat* and *Turn Up the Heat* that should take your mind off your desires for the moment.

A Tribute to Canadian Erotic Romance
You have probably heard of "Canadian things,"
But you still may not know of our hot sexy flings.
The truth is, we really don't all live in igloos,
And not all of us get to make love in canoes.

It is true we lose our minds when we win hockey Gold –
And quite honestly, most of the year it's too cold.
But some erotic romance can provide us with heat!
With snowsuits, or no suits, we do great sex-feats.

Billionaires, bikers, and extraterrestrial beings:
These men are why we don't spend all our time skiing.
Some of our heroes even take different forms –
We've got to have something around to keep warm!

From sci-fi, to hist'ry, to the sweet here-and-now,
Our snow's not the only thing we know how to plow.
Our stories are passionate, and steamy, and fun!
      Stay away from another Canadian pun...

All sexy Great-White-North winter joking aside,
Our Canuck romance authors are a point of pride!
When it comes to romance, we set quite the buffet.
And I'm just going to say it – we're better than Grey.

We may be polite – Sorry! – and show some respect,
But we won't be sorry for how well we write sex.
There's no time to waste – open the pages of this book!
Inside you'll find much less word-play (plus much more fore-play).

Now that you've seen how hot it can get in the Great White North,
it's time to Turn up the Heat!

Opal Carew

Sex & Love

Lauren Hawkeye

chapter one

I have to start this story by telling you that love is a complicated thing. It runs each of our lives, really: the people we love, the people we don't. The people who love us. The ones we love who don't love us in return. And then, to complicate matters even further, there are so many different kinds of love. I love my mother, my dog, even my ex-husband, yet I love them all so differently. It's a good thing, I think, that all of this love is so innate to us humans, because if we all stopped to think about it, to analyze and dissect, we'd go collectively crazy.

Three of the people I love most in the world are my best friends from college. They've been in and out of my life since I was 18, have been loved by me and have loved me in return. And, though I love them all equally, again, my feelings for each are different.

First, there's Megan, Megan Jolie. After collecting degrees in business, psychology, and engineering because she didn't want to join the rest of us in the drudgery of the day-to-day work force, or so she says, at any rate, she has settled nicely into running a small company that sells things on eBay. Secretly, I think that this job pleases her so much more than all of the others did because of the huge discounts on her beloved designer merchandise, but I figure, hey, whatever gets her through the day. I have to say that her impeccable style works for her, too. As what is politely referred to in society these days as a "big woman," Megan makes no apologies for her five-and-a-half-foot, size-20 frame; she never has, and she flaunts it accordingly in the Dolce and Gabbana and Christian Dior garments that find their way into her mailbox almost every morning.

When I first met Megan, back on that first day of English 101, she was actually quite thin, and was pretty, I guess, in an average sort of way. You know the type — long, sunshine-colored waves, cornflower blue eyes, cute nose, and a pert butt. The girl next door. But somewhere along the line, she decided life was too short to subsist solely on rice cakes and greens, and that was when she became really, truly, enviably gorgeous. That kind of flesh on another woman might just look puffy and pale, but on Megan it's ... decadent. Succulent. Kind of makes you want to just take a great big bite.

One of my other best friends has done just exactly that; he dated Megan for precisely one year and seven months, a long, long time ago, back when her idea of a great meal was a grilled chicken breast on top of her dressing-free salad. Jude has expressed his regret many a time that he never got to ... well ... *know* her, you know, in the Biblical sense, since she has become large and in charge. Truth be told, I think he's still kind of hung up on her, at least he certainly was during the short but sweet two weeks he dated me, once upon a time. Since my track record with men has been something short of stellar ever since, I've long suspected that Jude, sexy, sexy Jude, has spoiled me for all other men.

It's not so much that Jude is gorgeous, though he definitely is easy on the eyes with that rangy build, tight behind, tousled caramel hair, and the intense, dark, dark green eyes. But I think it's more the conflicting images of his personality that make him irresistible. You know, the classic bad-boy thing, what with his ever-present motorbike, the tight jeans that perfectly mold his impressive package and the aforementioned butt, the thin scar that slices through his left eyebrow, which is the result of a scramble out the bedroom window of a much older, very married woman with whom he was having an affair.

He was all of 19 at the time.

The other side of Jude is the surprising one, the soft heart in the tough shell. Jude works with young adults afflicted with Down Syndrome and has more care and compassion in his big toe than I do in my entire body. Usually when he tells people what he does for a living they laugh in disbelief; rude though it is, and even after knowing him for ten whole years, I sometimes have difficulty assimilating the two images in my head. Still, it works for him, and I've never met a man so successful, both in business and in his personal life.

Aah. Successful in one's personal life. That's where my final best friend, Trevor, fails painfully, I must admit. A self-confessed computer geek, Trev would much rather stay home playing World of Warcraft than go out and socialize with real people, with in-the-flesh people. And I can hardly blame him because, while around us, those he's comfortable with, he is one of the wittiest, most intelligent people you could possibly imagine. Around strangers, he is a clam, one of those stubborn ones that will open only the tiniest slit with a squishy, soft center that so wants to open up and somehow, somehow just can't. Trevor gives new meaning to the label "wallflower" at the few parties we manage to drag him to, though really, I guess, he doesn't so much flower as wilt, the wall holding him up instead of the other way around.

He's not a bad-looking guy, really. He's gone from skinny to wiry over the years, despite his disgusting diet of McDonald's, Pizza Hut, and KFC, and he has a pleasant face beneath his reddish brown hair; a face made cute, almost, with its spattering of toasty freckles; and deep chocolate truffle eyes. His horn-rimmed glasses are even kind of sexy, *I* think, anyways; it's just his social skills that need some work. But like I've said, around us, the "Core Four," as we call ourselves, he's witty and wonderful, one of my favorite people. And, just like the other two, I love him dearly.

And me? Well, I'm not all that exciting, I don't think; not like the others. My name is Desi, and if I had to describe myself in three words, I'd say that I'm neurotic, offbeat, and creative. I'm an artist, you see. A damn good one, if I do say so myself. I work in a medium called gouache, which in simpler terms, is a specific kind of paint I love for its bright, true colors. Mostly I do landscapes, but instead of putting them on canvas exactly as I see them, I apply what I like to think of as the "Desi Twist"; that is, I switch around the colors. The sky might be pink, the mountains orange, and the trees blue. Sounds odd, I know, but it works for me, and for a lot of other people as well, it seems, because while sales of my actual canvas works are few and far between, I make a killing on greeting cards. And for those art snobs out there, no, I don't consider manufacturing greeting cards to be selling out. I want to share my art with the world, and until I become the next Andy Warhol, which I have no doubt I will someday, what better way is there?

Color is important to me. So important, in fact, that three years ago I started running my life by it. I've been through a green phase and an orange phase already; right now, I'm into red, where I'll stay until the mood strikes me to change again. I love red; it's such a passionate, energetic color. In fact, it kind of makes me horny, sometimes; it's so vibrant and full of life, and I think that being constantly surrounded by sexual energy improves my art tenfold. I feel very connected to the color. I think maybe because my hair is red naturally, though right now I have my long, sassy layers dyed a shade closer to a campfire flame, a shade I think sets off my deep blue eyes more wonderfully than the burnished copper of my natural hue. Fire and water; can't get a much more intense combination than that.

Jude likes to make fun of me for my color phases, but I don't really care. If I want to wear a red dress and red shoes and eat red apples and red meat, I'm not hurting anyone, am I? And it makes me feel noticeable, special even, which is no easy feat around Ms. Plus-Size-Model Megan, Jude the hunk, and witty, brainy Trevor. I sometimes think that maybe that's why I started it, so I could have my own "thing," my own way to make my tiny, less than spectacularly figured self stand out in a crowd.

Well, whatever the reasons, I like myself, and I like my friends. No, wait — I *love* them. And myself, of course. And this love for each other is what has, in large part, propelled our lives for so long.

And that, dear people, is where our story begins.

Sitting back on the cushy leather couch at Megan's house — we were all there for our monthly dinner together — I sipped at my drink (a red strawberry margarita, of course) and studied my friends, enjoying the warm feeling that comes about by just being around the three of them. And maybe, just maybe, from the tequila in my drink, as well.

"... Every fucking night!" Trevor was complaining about his room-mate again, a girl named Lily whose lack of brains was more than made up for with her bust size. I always found it amusing that it was her personality that so irritated him because most men wouldn't give two hoots *what* she did, so long as she did it in the too small T-shirts and Band Aid-size skirts of which she was so fond.

After popping the lid off of a sweating bottle of amber ale, Trevor took a long, satisfying-looking chug before slamming the heavy steel bottle opener on the coffee table to demonstrate his frustration. Jude studied Trevor's hand on the heavy metal object before speaking.

"I still don't see why it's such a big deal, Trevor." Jude couldn't quite control his smirk as he said it. I figured that, if Jude were in Trevor's position, he'd know exactly what to do, and then some, a thought that made my mouth twist up a bit, like I'd just eaten a ripe, juicy lemon. "Can't you just hide in your room, or something? That is, if you're really dead set on not enjoying the show."

"I'd still know she was doing it," Trevor muttered and took another, smaller sip of his beer. "I'd still be uncomfortable."

Megan neatly laid the spoon with which she had been stirring the spaghetti sauce on its little ceramic spoon rest. Reaching for the glass of white wine, a chardonnay that, knowing Meg, was crisp, buttery, and delicious, that sat at her elbow, she said, "Well, Trev, you really don't have a lot of options here. Ask her nicely to stop, ignore it, or move. That's pretty much it."

"I can't ask her to stop." Dejected, Trevor crunched loudly on a rice cracker covered in creamy cheese and herbs from the platter of hors d'oeuvres that was sitting on the coffee table. "She lives there, too."

We were all silent for a moment; there wasn't much else to say. Trevor had his knickers in a twist because Lily, the aforementioned big-breasted, little-brained roommate, liked to walk around naked after her evening bath. He said that, yes, it was great that she was so comfortable with her body and all, but the fact that he was being forced to get comfortable with it himself, through no fault of his own, made him kind of queasy.

Again, see the lack of social skills there? Most men would take Lily's naked prancing as an invitation into her pants, or lack thereof, I guess, and would make a pass, but Trev just kept fumbling the ball. Truthfully, I didn't think he was lying; he seemed genuinely distressed at his situation, and I felt for him, as I'm sure we all did, even as we poked fun at what we assumed was just a prudish reaction.

What are friends for, after all?

"Oh, I don't know." Trevor had lost some of his verve. He stroked the neck of his beer bottle thoughtfully. I watched his hands as he did so, the artist in me suddenly twitching to sketch the long, tapered fingers; the wide, smooth palm; the bony wrist as they all moved, flowed in a graceful dance. It wasn't the first time I had admired his limbs, and I thought, again, of what a shame it was that those gorgeous digits did nothing but tap away at a keyboard all day when by rights they should have been composing symphonies or some other bloody piano thing, because they were just that damn beautiful.

"What do you think she means by it?" Trevor's eyes were suddenly dark and deep, piercing us each in turn, daring us, and just daring us, to lie to him. Megan and I remained silent. Jude, however, guffawed loudly, pounding his thigh, and I had the fleeting thought he might shoot pilsner right out of his nose.

"Jesus, Trev, what kind of world do you live in?" Jude calmed himself, mostly, and tried, really tried, to sober up when he saw Trevor's irate expression. But he couldn't quite control one last snicker from slipping out, a snicker wrought, I'm sure, by that intense drive that all men have, the one that must be stored in their dicks, that causes insults about testosterone and virility to pour out of their mouths the second one of their buddies mentions sex. It was just something

I noticed guys do, and that was why we were all shocked when calm, mild Trevor stood up straight and hurled his beer bottle across the room while shouting, in the loudest voice that I'd ever heard him use, "A virgin one! That's what kind of world I love in, you asshole! A goddamn virgin one!"

Stunned, we all looked from Trevor to the wall and watched the pale, foamy ale slowly trickle down, down the pale green paint to drip, with agonizing slowness, onto the shattered remnants of the amber-colored glass.

As one, we returned our eyes to Trevor. Defiantly, he thrust his chin into the air, though his eyes remained fixated on the wall, at the visual display of his frustration. Not one of us said a word; it was as if he had told us he had cancer or something equally awful, though obviously, while odd, a grown man's state of virginity was not nearly so serious.

"Go on; make fun of me," Trev muttered, fidgeting with a brown rubber band from the bowl of knickknacks that was, as always, in the center of the coffee table. "The twenty-eight-year-old virgin. What a fucking joke. I wouldn't even know what to do with Lily, even if that's what I wanted. Which it isn't." Obviously needing some space after this bombshell, he turned on his heel and marched down the hall to the bathroom, away from the living room where we three sat, shell-shocked, blinking stupidly like the proverbial deer in the headlights.

"Aren't you going to say anything?" Trevor surprised us all with his silent return, and I heard something in his voice besides the anger and apart from the defiance, something fragile and so delicate that it might break if one of us so much as exhaled too loudly. The others must have heard it, too, for in that moment, though I knew, with the knowledge that comes from long-term friendships, that none of us would dare to hurt Trevor with casual words, I could all but feel a warmth extending from each of us to where Trevor stood, quiet and awkward, on the spot where the beige carpeting and the dark slate tile met in a thick, solid stripe.

It was Megan who finally broke the silence, the silence that, while long, was somehow not as awkward as it could have been.

Crossing the room to where Trevor stood, she placed a fleshy, curvy arm around his shoulders, squeezed gently, and released before asking the room in general, "So who's hungry?"

* * *

Megan Jolie. Jude Hawke. Trevor Schimel. And me, Desi, short for Desdemona, Sinclair. Friends for a decade, best friends who have met for dinner religiously on the second Tuesday of every month for as long as any of us can remember, no matter what, though we all certainly saw each other at other times during the month as well. We took it in turns to host, rotating between my red hued one bedroom loft, Jude's surprisingly cozy, fifty-year-old house; Megan's posh apartment; and the streamlined condo that Trevor shared with the big-breasted Lily. We all brought food and booze and tales of our lives and celebrated our friendship, the love we had for each other, for hours, hours, and hours until one of us would realize the time and begin to distribute shoes and coats and to herd everyone toward the door. It never mattered that we had to leave because we all knew that any of us could pick up the phone, or stop by, at any time and continue on.

chapter two

I was stuffed, absolutely stuffed full of Megan's incredible spaghetti; her gooey, homemade cheese bread; and the tomato, basil, and Gouda salad she had thrown together at the last minute. Still, I couldn't help but continue to dip crumbly little bits of warm flatbread into the sun dried tomato pesto that sat in a glass dish in the middle of the kitchen table, and I refused to feel guilty about it, since it was a red food after all. No matter how good it tasted, though, I really just looked to prolong the moment, the sappy, Hallmark card-esque feel-good moment, as the four of us sat, or in Jude's case sprawled, around Megan's antique oak kitchen table. The sandalwood-infused candles flickered, and the cloying but not unpleasant scents of garlic and oregano still thick in the air. It was during those times I was happiest, on the second Tuesday of every month, when those that I loved more than anything in the world surrounded me.

I nibbled another morsel of pesto as I listened with a cocked ear to the continuation of Trevor's story.

"Well, I don't want to have sex with her, so I need a solution," he said as he played with the pit of a Greek olive left on his plate after the meal. "There has to be a way to make her understand it's not appropriate."

"I'm not sure it's considered inappropriate to walk around nude in your own home." Megan gestured gently with her wineglass, its iridescence reflecting the gleam of the candlelight.

"And really, Trev, how can you say you don't want to have sex with her? She's a fucking Playboy's wet dream, that one. You must want to, unless you've gone blind." Jude leaned back in his chair, comfortable as always with his own masculinity. Since he was usually so sensitive, I thought maybe he just knew Trevor too well and was too comfortable with him to realize he rubbed salt into a sore.

Trevor's eyes remained fixated on his almost empty plate, and he squirmed in his chair a bit. "It's not that I don't want to have sex with her, ever," he continued. A bit of a flush that I didn't think had anything to do with the wine crept up his neck. "It's more that I just don't want to have sex with her, right now."

"Aah." I got it, even if Jude looked completely confused, and Megan showed no expression at all as she calmly sipped at her wine. It was simple really. He didn't want to give his virginity to some blonde bimbo who had plastic tits and the IQ of a chimpanzee, one who would likely have been hard-pressed to spell his name correctly, or maybe even hers. Not that hard to understand, actually; I wouldn't either. But I wasn't in this situation, since I gave away my virginity to Tad, my high school sweetheart, a big, burly football player I really didn't think would understand me and my colors at all if we were to meet now.

Even if I was the only one who understood Trev's rationale, it wasn't my place to explain it. That night, the poor guy went through quite enough already, what with the unintentional outing of his sexual status and all. Not that any of us thought being a twenty-eight-year-old virgin was a bad thing at all, if it was his decision. But I knew, and the others knew, it wasn't from lack of trying, and *that's* what made the situation so delicate.

As I watched the dynamics play out, the light bulb went on for Jude. I always found his face fascinating. The way the long, lean planes reflected everything that went on in his head, which was surprising, because his badass image looked like it held a lot of secrets.

It occurred to me that the fascination might stem from feelings I didn't want to acknowledge, but I chose never to dwell on those, focusing instead on his physical beauty. Beauty that was enhanced at that moment in the face that so easily traveled, visually, from consternation to comprehension to confusion, all within the blink of an eye. Finally, he got it, and Trevor saw the light bulb lodged in Jude's frontal lobe blink on.

"I just wish I could get it over with,"Trev muttered, and my heart experienced that going- through-the-blender sensation as I watched my friend's face, my awkward, incredibly loveable friend, and saw the frustration and shame mirrored there. "I just wish I could just do it, you know, just so it can be done, and then I can go and fuck Lily, and Barbie, and freaking Betty and Veronica and anyone else I can get my hands on!" He laughed at his outburst and finally looked up from the table, the dark wood, which had held his gaze all night. I was struck by a thought that had tickled at me for years, the one that told me that, if Trev could just get the right moves down around the opposite sex, you know, like if he could train with Will Smith in the movie *Hitch* or something, he'd be beating off women with a stick. In fact, as I studied his face in profile as he ruefully laughed at himself, at the sardonic smirk displayed over sharp white teeth, the tasty, toasty skin, even the appealing way his earlobe stuck out, just a bit, I thought that, right now, I wouldn't mind relieving him of his problem myself.

I wondered, briefly, how he was hung, and the thought brought an extra bit of moisture both to my mouth and to my cunt, even as I chastised myself. This was Trevor I was thinking about there. *Trevor*, the twenty-eight-year-old virgin, who probably couldn't find a vagina with a neon arrow pointing the way and a crowd of people shouting encouraging directions.

Just as I took a moment to think that that was a bit of an uncharitable thought on my part, Trevor said, deadpan, "I don't suppose either of you girls want the job, huh?" He chuckled, and I felt my face flamed into a shade of scarlet I would probably have found quite fetching if it hadn't been on my face and the result of the dirty track my filthy, little mind took.

It took a moment for me to realize the table had fallen silent, and the three of us, Megan, probably myself, and, good Lord, even Jude, were all flushed the same rosy color. Trevor looked at each of us in turn, puzzlement written all over his face, because our quartet routinely joked about sex, all the time, raunchy, nasty conversations that could make even the most jaded lady of the night raise her eyebrows in surprise. So why, at Trevor's innocent little comment, were we all acting so weird?

"Guys?" His eyes found mine and held steady. "What do you think?"

chapter three

You know that feeling, the one that appears after you've downed one cocktail too many and the world around you seems to move at warp speed and at the same time in slow motion? Well, I wouldn't say I was drunk, exactly, as I perched on the edge of the lake-sized, opulent bed in Megan's immaculate bedroom, but that was the feeling I had right at that moment, nonetheless.

I didn't feel like a participant in the event that was about to take place, either; instead, it was as if I was on the outside looking in, the view distorted as if seen through a layer of undulating water, and as much as I blinked, it wouldn't come clear. Still, I saw a pretty picture, distorted though it was, and since I had no idea what to do, at any rate, I took a moment to just look.

The artist in me couldn't help but admire the way the light of the sandalwood and jasmine scented candles Megan had carried in from the kitchen played over the hard dips and lean planes of Jude's face. As he stood against the dusky blue of the bedroom wall with his dark eyes intent on the triad composed of Megan, Trevor, and me as we sat, somewhat awkwardly, on the deep, forest-hued spread of the bed. When he turned his head, and his features moved from light to shadow, I was put in mind of an angel, one who had fallen from grace. It took me back, made me remember the two weeks we once spent together, weeks in which that hard, rangy body was mine to do with as I wished. The thought had me shifting restlessly on the crisp, Egyptian cotton duvet.

The movement caught Jude's eye; he turned to me, and the touch of hunger, which played over the corners of his lips, made me feel as if I was about to be eaten alive. He didn't move, though, even though I felt myself lean in his direction a bit. A magnetic force pulled me closer. I watched as his eyes flicked to Trevor, and then back to me, and I wondered if he was uncomfortable with the idea of getting naked around another man. Although, with the behavior reported from men's locker rooms, I wouldn't have thought that to be the case. Still, maybe this was different, with the sexual edge that had been added, I mused. Then it hit me. No, I realized, his shift in limbs wasn't intended as an entrance to our frozen tableau, but rather to observe and direct, as if the scene was part of a naughty film. *Trevor's First Time*, or something like that. Despite the hilarity that edged into my consciousness, I found I was more than glad for the direction, though I was disappointed that he wouldn't be joining in.

Jude, I knew, had done … well, *this*, before. I, no matter what my reputation would have others believe, had not. In fact, the wildest time of my life, sexually speaking, of course, peaked when I was with Jude himself, so long ago. No joke, it's been all downhill from there.

When Jude signaled for Megan and Trevor to kiss, though, I knew that all might be about to change.

Their first kiss was tender, a tentative exploration that demonstrated the love they felt for one another. I smirked a bit at the frothy little giggle that bubbled up, out of Megan's throat. Both closed their eyes as their lips met. Megan's shiny mauve lipstick smeared onto the stubble that shadowed Trevor's face. It was brief and sweet, the way a first kiss should be. Although I knew I had the implicit invitation to watch, I had to admit I felt a bit odd, a bit outside the circle of warmth surrounding the two, as if I shouldn't be there. Still I stared, as the pink bows of their lips met, again and again, sipping almost politely at the first juice of lust.

"Do you want to kiss Trevor, Desi?" Jude asked, his gravelly voice edging into the dense soup of my thoughts.

I didn't answer at first, needing, somehow, a moment to turn the notion over in my mind, to examine it from all angles, though I knew, ultimately, what the answer would be. "Yes." I breathed, and nodded acquiescence; before I fully realized the implications of my answer, Trevor had a lean hand at the back of my head and held me in place as his lips, hot, wet and much fuller than I had ever expected them to be, fed on mine hungrily, as if he hadn't just eaten himself almost sick at the amazing feast Megan had prepared. I kissed him back, the sexual frustration incited by Jude pouring out in a torrential storm, and we nipped at each other's flesh, tangled our tongues together, gulped sensations like a fast-food meal. When after what seemed an hour we pulled away, breathless, my mouth felt bruised and well used. I flicked out my tongue to lap at it, to soothe it, and I panted like a wild animal in heat.

For those of you who may be criticizing how it was I could be so turned on by Trevor, when I openly admitted my continuing attraction for Jude, I say bollocks to you. There was no rule that said a woman could only have sexual thoughts about one mate at a time. Ask any woman who's ever been in a long term relationship.

And Jude *was* there, after all, watching. Always watching.

"Desi, kiss Megan now," Jude commanded, and for a moment I thought of telling him to get real. It's such a cliché male fantasy, really, watching two girls make out, and after all, Megan and I were there to help Trevor lose his virginity in a warm, loving environment, not to get it on with each other. But the hunger and naked excitement in Trevor's eyes gave me pause; it was obviously something he wanted so badly to see he could almost taste the sweet flavor on the rough surface of his tongue. And though I couldn't see Jude from where I knelt, in Trevor's lap, I'm sure his expression was just the same.

Tentatively, I crawled across the bed, the fabric of my red dress pulling tightly against the breasts that had never needed the restraint of a bra, and the material chafed at my nipples, causing them to pebble, small and tight. Megan did the same, and when the matching cupid's bows of our mouths met, I heard muffled groans from deep in the throats of both men.

It turned me on.

I could hear the breath of both men, as my mouth played over Megan's, as my fingers tangled in the long fall of her golden hair. I couldn't say I found kissing her sexually exciting in itself, but the power it allowed us to wield made me feel like Aphrodite, like a geisha, like a highly cherished courtesan. So I threw myself into it, nipping and stroking, our tongues mating, and was rewarded with the unmistakable sounds of clothing falling to the floor. The rasp of a zipper, the soft whispers made by cloth on skin. Not being able to see, sound was the only sense engaged and gave the scene a dreamlike quality, a sweet floating sensation. And even hearing it, knowing it, a frisson of shock jolted through my system when hard male flesh, hot enough to melt my candy-colored dress, grasped me around my waist and covered me from behind.

Although it had been so long since I had seen his body, I knew instantly that it wasn't Jude touching me, not his anxious fingers tugging at the dozens of frustrating buttons that traveled the length of my spine. I allowed Trevor to undress me, and inexperience made his fingers falter. I was slightly surprised at the tiny, very tiny, yet intense trickle of disappointment that wound its way through my bloodstream, blood that pumped hot and hard regardless. I supposed Jude was with Megan, touching her in all of the plump, generous places he always admired so openly, but when I yanked the ropy coils of my red tresses from the tangle of Trevor's fingers to look, I saw Megan alone on the bed, a Rubenesque vision of beauty in the soft light, her soft linen blouse open to reveal generous breasts encased in swatches of pale pink lace, breasts that seemed to be quivering for the touch of a hand, of a mouth, of anything.

Gingerly, not sure how I was going to feel about it, I leaned over and took one of the rosy crests into my mouth, suckling gently through the lace.

Megan groaned, and I thought that it wasn't so bad. Though it made me feel like a baby suckling at the breast of the earth mother, an odd thought, I think, to have when in the midst of a menage, I decided that, if it brought such joy to a man, it was definitely something to tuck away into the back of my mind.

I fell forward suddenly, my somewhat pointed chin disappearing into the succulent folds of Megan's flesh, when I was entered roughly from behind. Once I righted myself, my weight braced on my hands and knees, I discovered it wasn't the expected cock impaling me, but rather fingers, three of them, I thought, as I could feel each digit moving separately within my pulsating walls. The exploration was anything but elegant. I even winced when the hand delved a little too deep. Once I was wet, slick and shiny from the bumps against my clit that I was sure were accidental, it felt good, really good. I felt the familiar trembling of my thighs that always accompanies sexual arousal for me.

I turned over, flopping onto my back the second I was free. Panting slightly, wanting an orgasm but feeling, somehow, that being too greedy for it wasn't proper menage etiquette, I placed Trevor's hands on Megan, urged him to undress her, not wanting anyone in the room to feel left out. I didn't feel the same worry for Jude, as I gazed over the mass of trembling flesh and entwined limbs to meet his eyes, aching with something I couldn't understand. His hand was wrapped firmly around his erection, thrusting forward from the thick thatch of curling black hair, and stroked up and down in firm, even motions. My eyes caressed the sight, the thin, pale skin lined with blue veins. The need to taste him overcame me, to feel the flavors of salt and tang spread over my tongue as I sucked. But when I moved to get off the bed, to cross the room and take him in my mouth, Jude shook his head at me, and his face told me he wouldn't be dissuaded.

"Stay," he said, and I obeyed, though obedience had never been one of my finer points. I didn't have much time to think about doing otherwise, however, because Trevor suddenly spread my legs, and the scent of latex from a condom intensified as it rubbed against my flesh. I had a short but cranky moment at being torn away from the intense moment with Jude, but Trevor's incredible and somehow sweet awkwardness reminded me of the reason we were all there, after all. Poor guy. After a few unsuccessful attempts on his part to enter me, to finally feel the sensation of a woman's pussy milking him dry, I reached a hand down between our bodies to guide Trevor's cock into my cunt, desperate for something I couldn't identify. I didn't think, however, it was related to Trev and the overeager thrusts of his cock.

I was granted a moment of clarity as Trevor thrust into me. The thought crossed my mind that I was okay with Jude not touching me, as long as Megan was in the same boat. It wasn't a rational thought for sure. Megan was one of my best friends, as was Jude, and what he and I had was over long ago. But any woman would tell you that there was nothing rational about the mix of sex and emotion, so I wasn't overly worried at the direction my thoughts took. Certain they'd pass with the flare of heat consuming us all. Still, I did my best to clear my mind and to enjoy the body I was permitted to touch, to sample and to feast upon. For otherwise, I knew I'd be doing Trevor a grave disservice.

It wasn't hard to do, really, when Trevor took a moment to brush my hair off my face, to smile and assure me he knew it was me he was inside. To demonstrate the gratitude he felt to me, and to all of us, for letting him experience this momentous occasion with us, the people he loved most in the world.

Reaching out with my right hand, I laced my fingers with those of Megan's left; she shifted to her side and used her right hand to trace the contours of Trevor's backside as he moved inside me, making us a circle, a ring, the universal symbol of love and devotion. I began to enjoy the feel of Trevor's cock inside me. While not long, it was thick and stretched my thin inner walls, forcing them to absorb the little shockwaves of sensation that accompany intercourse. Since I wanted the night to be about him, and not me, I held back my moan of disappointment when the building tension between my thighs stuttered and went silent. Instead, I gently shoved him off me and onto Megan, who had waited so patiently and was likely ready, more than ready, to have Trevor to herself.

I shifted on the bed, getting out of the way of the two bodies moving as one beside me. Looking up, I found Jude staring at me, licking his lips. His gaze pinned me, and I couldn't breathe. Where had these feelings come from, I wondered. Had they been dormant for all of these years, waiting for this one evening to spring free? Or were they new, tiny buds eagerly looking for their place in the sun?

Maybe it didn't matter. Maybe they were rooted only in the situation, in this one unreal night, but I wasn't sure I cared. Because as I stared back at him, our very deepest selves caught in a contest of wills, while the air thickened and grew heavy around us with the scent of sex. I knew at that moment, I would give anything to be with him.

I heard the noises made behind me, the soft, pretty little sighs and the deeper, satisfied grunts. I felt the tug of the sheets under my bottom as the movements picked up the pace, as Trevor learned, truly learned, the meaning of the word *fuck*. But I couldn't bring myself to look, to watch the erotic scene played out so close to me that the occasional limb grazed my flesh, because to look would be to break the hypnotic trance between Jude and myself. I was so caught up, punch drunk by the throbbing between my legs Trevor had been unable to assuage, I felt sure I would die if the connection broke.

I crawled to the foot of the bed, which was so high my tippy toes could barely reach the floor. Jude's expression warned me, still, not to touch, and a perverse part of me thought I'd be damned if I'd let him know how much the denial of that touch pained me. Fine, I thought. Fine. I wouldn't touch him, wouldn't lift a finger to stroke over that smooth golden skin, not even if it killed me. But I vowed that, before I was done, he'd feel the intense craving just as much as I had.

Bracing the cheeks of my ass against the slippery bed linens, I spread my legs wide, and then my cunt wider still, my artist's fingers exposing my pink secrets like the inside of a ripe, juicy fruit. I heard his breath hitch, saw his cock jerk, and felt a swell of smug satisfaction as he swallowed with a dry mouth at the visual I presented him.

Like I mentioned, I'm a natural redhead, and the truth of this can be seen every time I strip down. I painted, in my mind's eye, the blend of reds swirling in front of Jude's irises, the rosy flesh of my finger, the soft blush of my inner lips, the bright pink of my hard, tight clitoris. And surrounding it all, the wealth of silky copper, exploding in a series of tight curls, like fireworks in a night sky. I like to picture things like this, to know what other people see when they look at me. In this case, the passionate swirl of red, the color of my life, making my pussy tingle and my nipples pebble tightly, and urging me to give him more.

Licking the index finger of my right hand, even as the fingers of my left framed my tender spot, I slowly trailed it down my body, grazing the valley between my breasts, the slight swell of my belly, and the edge of the glistening curls between my legs. When I slowly rubbed that same finger over my clitoris, causing my breath to come faster and the jiggling globes of my breasts to sway, I heard Jude moan, watched him pump faster, faster, the tip of his hard cock turning a ripe shade of purple and becoming shiny and slick with precum.

I licked that finger, sampling my own flavor, then returned it to its busy work. Tasted again, savoring the taste of my own sweet cream as it spread over my tongue. Even as I felt the swell of orgasm begin for me, which my own sure fingers could bring so much more easily than Trevor's thrusting cock ever could, I saw Jude's muscles give a telltale quiver, one I knew from experience signaled his impending orgasm. As I came, the blood rushing through my cunt like a red waterfall, I slid off the bed and dropped to my knees in front of Jude, guiding his quivering dick low with hands that had never been more sure; the thick, salty come of his release spilled over the flesh of my breasts, such as they were, a reminder to him that it was me who had turned him on so, who had given him his release.

Jude and I remained as still as statues in that odd state of desire so sweet I wanted to lap it up like honey, gooey and good. My thoughts became a riptide, pulling me under, threatening to drown me, and squeezing out every breath.

Behind me I heard Megan's voice begin a series of soft, pretty little cries, a rising crescendo that signaled her impending release. Mixing with her moans in a grand symphony were the frenzied grunts issuing from Trevor's lips — an excitement I'd never before sensed from him. It reminded me that Jude and I weren't alone, though it took some effort to release myself from the spell that he had woven around me.

The moment was drawing to a close. Trevor was the happiest I'd ever seen him. But the spell wasn't broken, not for me anyway, disproving my theory that my attraction to Jude was merely physical. An awkwardness as foreign to me as all of the lands I had yet to visit fell between us, though relations with each of us and the other two seemed fine. But as we dressed and moved toward the door to say our respective good nights, I noticed a distinct awkwardness between Jude and me, born of the odd direction the night took. Being the woman who dislikes anything uncomfortable, I bid good night to a sated Megan and a jubilant Trevor and walked down the stairs of the building alone. In the parking lot, shivering a bit, I waited for Jude to follow me through the front glass doors. Once he had, without asking, I hitched up my skirt to climb onto the back of his motorbike. I had no intention of allowing the stilted awkwardness between us to continue on, especially not when feelings intense and unexpected, whirled around within me so brightly I couldn't think straight.

He looked at me questioningly, cocking his head to one side, arching an eyebrow. In response, I told him, simply, "Take me home with you."

chapter four

Some of our usual comfort returned by the time we were cozily ensconced in Jude's surprisingly welcoming home. The spacious, half-century-old bungalow had been inherited from his mother's sister, and many of the furnishings and other household items remained the same, fussy florals and chintzy fabrics should've made the badass man living with them look ridiculous, but somehow, they didn't. I doubted anything made Jude look ridiculous, cursed as he was with physical perfection.

We curled up on one of the floral couches, one at each end, our feet tangled beneath an insanely colored, hand-crocheted blanket. We'd sat this way millions of times before, but I was surprised at Jude's initiation of the position tonight. I expected something more along the lines of relieving the sexual tension still humming along my goose-bumped skin by fucking against the front door or something. Now, as I lay in what to me felt like a distinctly platonic position, a glass of Bailey's, a drink that to me tasted like liquid sex, in my hand, I wondered if I had imagined the whole thing. But I had a feeling, an odd one rolled around in the pit of my stomach, which wasn't entirely normal; something was up, that was for sure.

Well, if I had imagined it, and we were just friends as always, then

I saw no need to pussyfoot around. "Why didn't you join in?" The words flew out of my mouth before I fully thought them through, but I wasn't overly concerned. We'd talked about sex millions of times over the years. His physical recoil at my question surprised me, though, and I found that I, too, was a bit wary of the answer, wondering if, somehow, there was a deeper meaning behind his standoffishness, an answer other than the one I expected to hear.

Or maybe not, I thought, as I leaned forward, the swells of my breasts rising out of the low neck of my dress, which Jude's eyes fastened on immediately. Deliberately, I took a deep breath, causing them to rise and fall, and nearly cackled with glee at his sharp intake of breath.

Hmm. Maybe that heated moment earlier, during which I felt as if Jude and I were the only two people in the world, wasn't as imaginary as I feared.

Still, he blinked, though, when I nudged at him with my foot, reminding him he hadn't answered my question. Blink, blink. Blink. I was perversely gratified to find satisfaction in his shock. I hadn't recognized the feeling swirling around in the pit of my stomach as anger until now. How could he have subjected us, Megan, Trevor, and I, to such an intimate, revealing state and not join in, effectively placing us in his control? And why had he been so reluctant to let me touch him? Another control game? Watching me want him, revealing a desire so hidden I hadn't even known it was there, all the while keeping his under control?

It felt good to say it, to get it out. I just realized how vulnerable I had felt, even though the sex had been undeniably good, with someone watching and yet holding back.

Yes, I fully realize I can be classified as moody, as emotional. Call me what you will, it doesn't bother me.

"What are you talking about? What we did ... "

I cut him off. "*We* didn't do anything," I reminded him, sitting up straight on the couch, the creamy goodness in my glass sloshing over to land with a wet splat on my arm. "You didn't let me to touch you, except at the very end. And you wanted me to; I know it. I want to know why." A blotchy column of red crept up Jude's neck and stained his face. I had never seen him blush before and wondered what the blood coursing rapidly through his veins meant.

He was silent for a moment, and I couldn't read the planes of his face in the late-night darkness of the room. When he said, "I don't know," I had no choice but to believe him, as I always had. Although, I wondered if my suspicions were simply in overdrive when I suspected he was holding something back. But I was distracted by the light, by the butterfly touch of his fingers on my foot, by the fingers tracing the high arch with exquisite delicacy with a touch just firm enough to keep me from screeching with laughter at the tickle.

Was he trying to distract me, I wondered? Something still felt off. But here and now, I was being offered what it seemed I had wanted for a long time, and I would be a fool not to take it.

He shackled my ankle with his fingers, holding me tight. He sat forward slid his other hand up the inside of my thigh, and any other questions I might have asked were lost in the tornado of sensations, which tumbled down on my head like the house on the wicked witch in the *Wizard of Oz*.

A beam of light from a car passing by outside caught his face. Our eyes met and held, even when the light passed, and we were in the dark again. I felt his gaze struggle to see me clearly, even through the hot summer night air hung a curtain as thick as velvet between us.

Then the curtain parted, and Jude was on top of me with his weight pressing me so far into the worn squishiness of the ancient couch that I felt as if I was about to be swallowed alive. As his avid mouth slid sweetly over mine, tasting of sugar and liquor, smoke and man, I decided I wouldn't mind a bit if it did, if it swallowed me whole so I could stay here, just like this, forever.

I would later discover that this craving, this need had made its extraordinary appearance at the very ordinary dinner hosted by Megan was going to cause me a lot of trouble, but at that moment, with what I wanted held tightly in my grasp, I couldn't have known and probably wouldn't have cared.

"You still don't wear underwear," Jude whispered into my neck. I shivered at the realization that this was real. I could smell the sweat on him, caused by his earlier orgasm, and it brought back memories of the times we'd fucked all night long, allowing each other only brief snatches of sleep, catnaps just long enough to revive our insatiable sexual appetites.

I wondered, even as his lips trailed down to lay light, fluttering kisses over my collarbone, if he smelled the same to Megan, who'd had such a hold on the heart that lay beneath the prickles even then, the hold that had eventually come between the intense heat that Jude and I had shared. I hadn't minded at the time, apart from the loss of rights to that spectacular body, since he and I hadn't much of a chance to develop an emotional connection. But tonight, as my skin absorbed the sensations caused by his roaming fingers and his avid mouth, I felt a flush of triumph. I felt as if I was getting some of my own back, and again, this may not have been the most rational thought but, as I've said, women and sex do not make for a rational equation.

"Close your eyes," he told me, and I grumbled at the order. I like to look, I like to see; given what I do for a living I think that's obvious. And I wanted to look at him, to see his eyes fog as my hands stroked his length, I wanted to see his jaw tense at the sight of my flesh.

Seeing the argument on my face, tasting it on my lips, he pressed a finger to each of my eyes, stroked a calloused pad over my fluttering lashes. "Close your eyes, Desi," he repeated. Those featherlight flickers of sensation over my brow were so soothing that, eventually, I obeyed.

It was a struggle to keep them closed, though, as new sensations assaulted my body. I squeezed them tightly shut at first, so focused on keeping my promise that I tuned out my own pleasure. But gradually, I understood that without sight all the other senses were heightened. The sound of Jude's breath, raspy and deep, and his murmurs of approval as he undressed me slowly. The unique taste of the flesh he offered, the press of crisply curling hairs on my tongue. That sweaty smell that turned me on so, and the dense odor of sex rising into the air as it wafted off of our skin. The feel of those lean muscles, tensing before again becoming fluid under my inquisitive hands.

My nipples spiked as my dress was pulled down, the air icy cold in contrast to the fevered heat of our skin. Wet warmth surrounded first one, and then the other, causing me to cry out in surprise. His fingers skated, featherlight, in the valley between my tits; I arched my back, cramming my flesh into his mouth. I may not have had much for him to sample on, but he seemed more than content with the mouthful he had, sucking so hard on my right peak I felt the answering tug all the way down through my womb.

He kissed my stomach, the smooth dip of it. "This is new," he commented as fingers traced the tattoo of an artist's palette, a rainbow of colors instead of just my favored red, colors that danced over the tight skin of my left hip.

"Jude ... " I didn't actually have anything I wanted to say, the name simply slipped off my tongue like chocolate melting in the hot sun. In response, he settled between my legs, pushing them apart, the rasp of his seven o'clock shadow burning the tender skin of my inner thighs. I sneaked a peek through slit in my eyelids, and savored the image of his golden skin, so dark against the milky paleness of my own. Shadows were absorbed, it seemed, by his hair, his eyes, his mouth, turning him into something dark, a creature of the night, a demon of lust.

The thought made me shiver, and even as his teeth found the sensitive skin that joined my legs to my belly, he caught me peeking, saw me watching him, watching him pleasure me and driving me wild. He grinned in response and, with his eyes fastened tightly to mine, slid a finger over the pulse between my legs. My back arched, and my heels dug for purpose into the slippery fabric of the sofa, trying to gain ground, but the finger had moved on from the burning bud to discover and trace the small, silky curls of my outer lips and the tight, wet skin of the inner ones. One more teasing brush over my clit, and the questing finger slid into me, much surer than Trevor's had earlier, twisting and turning until it found the small sponge of flesh that resided high in my cunt, a spot so sensitive that I writhed beneath the weight pinning me down, not sure if I wanted to get closer and feel more, or to run away and remove myself from pleasure so intense it caused pain.

I came hard and fast from that pressure deep in my vagina, hard and fast with no warning. It's hard to explain, but an orgasm centered on a woman's G-spot is different than one from the clit, not less and not more. It didn't leave me shaking, like the pressure on the hard nub of my sweet spot would have, but I was still weak, weak and wrecked and clawing my way up for breath, the responding surge of liquid between my thighs pulling me under like a riptide and threatening to drown me.

When Jude dipped his head and lapped at that cream, lapped at it like a kitten at a saucer full of milk, I screamed, thrashing my head from side to side. Sobbing as he fastened his mouth tightly to my clit, sucking it into that wet, willing cave, I came again, the pulse flooding my body; he pressed the heel of his hand against my pubic bone, staunching the flow before it lost control.

When I came to and looked into his eyes, I thought he'd stand, remove his clothes, then cover me once more and sheath himself in my waiting heat. I was right about the first part, at least. I allowed a low growl to escape my throat as the black T-shirt was cast aside, exposing a muscled chest densely matted with black hair, and tight denim was worked down over those narrow hips and that tight butt until they fell to the floor.

Instead of settling himself back between my legs and thrusting deep to ease the ache in my cunt that the orgasms had only exacerbated, he wrapped arms, ropy and hard, around my waist and rearranged my position, rolling me with smooth movements until my naked belly quivered against the prickly upholstery of the couch. Then all was still.

Pushing myself up onto my elbows, I twisted and craned my neck to see. Jude stared at my rear, at the curved mounds of flesh, with an intentness I didn't understand but made me shiver all the same. When I moved he jolted from his reverie and gently pressed me back down, down to sink into the waiting softness.

I sniffed the night air, cold and crisp, as my body tensed in anticipation, of what I wasn't sure. I found out when a finger, one of those fingers of his that I decided had to be magic, slowly, moved its way down my spine. It veered off its path to teasingly trace the jutting bones of my shoulder blades, bones softened by plush skin pulled tight. Then it resumed its path, tickling lower and lower until the curve of my spine swelled up, just a bit, and became a valley that divided the curving hills of my ass. I thought his hand would stop there when it reached that intimate crack, but it didn't; instead, it delved into the mounds of flesh and nuzzled through the tight channel to explore.

When the pressure stilled and at the same time increased right against the pucker hidden deep, I let out a startled, somewhat strangled noise. Jude's hand froze, and I knew he'd remove it if I asked him to, but the sensation wasn't unpleasant, really, just ... different. And very unexpected. After a still, thick moment though, I relaxed again and, knowing he'd wait for permission, murmured my assent.

The pressure began again, thickening until the tight, stubborn skin gave way, and the foreign flesh intruded into what I had always considered a deep, dark secret. I'd never really understood the male sex's obsession with the ass, with placing their sex ... well ... *there*, but I had to admit I was slightly intrigued. So I refrained from pulling away.

I focused on the finger invading my flesh, rotating slightly, loosening the tightly clenched muscles. I decided it was pleasant enough, felt good even, but it was never going to be enough. Squirming a bit, since my clit, which had become cool from lack of attention, protested, I hoped he'd get the hint, and he did, sliding his free hand over my hip, across my belly, through the tangle of curls, and finally onto the small bump, where he rubbed. I sighed in pleasure.

Funny, I'd always been a staunch advocate of women taking charge of their own sex lives, of asking for what they wanted without fear. And I'd found that, in general, men enjoyed this; it took a load of pressure off them, since they aren't and never would be mind readers. But with Jude, I felt unaccountably shy, relying on the very mind reading skills I didn't believe even existed. Perhaps it was a twisted test on my part to see how attuned he was with me, how much, essentially, he loved me. And as he finally answered my prayers and sheathed himself to the hilt, after rolling that familiar tube of latex down the length of his dick with clever fingers that he cruelly removed from their teasing caress over my skin. Of course, I sighed and decided he passed the test. Of course, it's likely that his expertise, the seemingly psychic ability of his to touch me exactly where I most wanted was a consciousness gleaned from the scores of lovers I knew he'd had, but right then, at that moment, I indulged myself and pretended it was all about me.

I stopped thinking, became nothing but sensation when, finally, the pace quickened, my hips were gripped and my legs forced apart to allow him in deeper. I dug my fingers without purchase into the undulating layers of cloth and foam, trying to hold steady as each hard, deliberate thrust nearly knocked me down, flat. I wanted to thrust, to push backward as he moved ahead, to greaten the friction as our flesh pounded together, but found myself instead doing all that I could to just hold on for dear life.

His movements became frantic against me, and our flesh slapped loudly every time it connected. I cried out, not in pain but with need. In response, my cunt was cupped and pressed hard in the sensitive place where we joined. My world went bright; colors danced behind my closed lids. My muscles trembled before coming to a full, satisfied stop. Jude wasn't far behind, emptying himself into me with a final, violent thrust and a great shout. Then he stilled and became silent, too.

Later that night, as we spooned, limbs entwined, in his oddly ornate, wooden four-poster bed, I felt at peace. Every cell of my being was sated and full. Exhausted, we slid together toward sleep with Jude's hands tangled in the startlingly bright mass of my hair. Just before I slid over the edge into sleepy oblivion, I heard him murmur a name; too tired to do anything but hum a sound between my lips, I figured it was mine.

chapter five

"So, is it love, then?" Megan swept a ridiculous-looking, rhinestone-encrusted fuchsia feather duster over the shelves of the bookcase that was already, to my eye, immaculately clean. I didn't answer immediately, not because I had nothing to say, but rather because my mouth was full. In preparation for the cocktail party she hosted that evening, Megan had gone to town preparing fancy, savory little hors d'oeuvres, baking pita chips and flatbread from scratch, and whirling together spices with creamy goodness to make succulent dips that likely carried a week's worth of calories in every bite. I was at her apartment hours before the party was scheduled to help, supposedly, but as usual, my assistance consisted of stuffing my face with the intended offerings, though I preferred to call it quality control, giving my abject approval over every one. So, since my mouth was crammed with bits of crispy, spiced bread; cream cheese; and spinach, I took my time in replying, which the ever-efficient Megan took as hedging.

"It's not that hard a question, Desi," she said as she moved about the room. "Do you love him, or don't you?"

"Of course, I love him," I replied, and my conscience was saved from the fiery pit of hell because this was true. But there, you see, was where those different kinds of love come into play again. I loved Jude, sure I did, and had for almost ten years. But was I in love with him? After a month of togetherness, of sex so intense it made me delirious, of dinner dates and pillow talk, and the exchange of house keys, I still wasn't sure. I mean, having loved him for so long already, was falling *in love* with him really going to feel any different? The only woman I felt comfortable dissecting the topic with was Megan, but it still struck me as ... well ... inappropriate, somehow, to discuss my lovey-dovey feelings about Jude with his ex.

Truth be told, this change in the dynamics of our little group of four had caused a thin wall to slide into the space, which had once been wide open and free, between Megan and me. That is, I should say, I felt the presence of this wall, of this barrier tangible to me. Although I longed to discuss it, to talk it through until like the KOOL-AID Man I burst through it and reestablished a connection, I was afraid that talking about it, acknowledging it with words, would confirm its presence that might at that moment exist only in my head.

Chewing contemplatively on a bundle of cranberries and cheese wrapped in flaky phyllo, I was startled to find Megan in the room with me across the island, slathering some kind of herby-looking thing onto a cracker. She popped it into her mouth, chewed, and swallowed. She dusted her hands off on the thighs of her blue jeans, which likely cost her three times more than what a normal person would've paid. She tucked a loose strand of blonde hair behind her ear, then rubbed a finger over the bridge of her nose. Finally, she lifted those startlingly blue eyes of hers to meet mine.

"Does he love you?" Her gaze steady and true. I didn't know what to say, so I stuffed a handful of breaded carrots into my mouth. Didn't know what to say, because I didn't know the answer myself. Did Jude love me? Well, of course he did, and he had for a long, long time; I knew that, certainly. But was he *in* love with me? I didn't know, couldn't answer that any more than I could the reciprocal question. But what I really wanted to know was, why did Megan care? *Did* she, in fact, care? The thought that she might threw me for a bit of a loop.

I knew, beyond the shadow of a doubt, that once upon a time,

Megan and Jude had, indeed, been *in* love with one another. But, while their connection had lasted significantly longer than mine with Jude had, it had still seemed to burn fast and bright and had been extinguished just as quickly. And *she* had done the ending, if I recalled correctly, so was it really possible that a torch might still burn in her heart?

The answer seemed to lie in her eyes, which were dark with interest disguised as casual concern. I wanted to say something, anything, to remove the curtain of awkwardness, but nothing, not a thing, flowed off of my tongue. I stared at her helplessly with my hands full of crudités that with my appetite gone, I knew I wouldn't eat. My mouth opened wide, and then closed. I wished for a drink of icy water that could and would unglue my tongue from the roof of my mouth but found myself rooted to the spot, frozen in place, able to do nothing more than breathe and stare.

Slowly, awkwardly, Megan reached across the island to lay a hand on my shoulder. "Just … be careful," she told me, her expression deadly serious.

"I will," I replied automatically and with the silence broken busied myself with peeling cello wrap from the platters and hauling them into the living room. As I did, my thoughts were consumed with wonder over what on earth she meant.

It was later that night that I found out.

chapter six

I stood in a corner of the room with Jude, a glass of red wine in one hand with my eyes glued to the gorgeous sight of Megan as she twirled about her living room, doing a sexy cha-cha to something with a hot and heavy Latin beat and the hands of a very handsome man I didn't recognize upon her. I smiled, happy she was having such a good time; I, however, wasn't. Our conversation from earlier in the day threw me out of sorts in the worst possible way and straight into a funk the likes of which hadn't come over me since the disturbing days of my teen angst. And Jude wasn't much help, running off as he kept doing to chat with someone else, to munch from the table full of appetizing morsels I had eaten myself sick on earlier in the day, or to fetch yet another drink. I could tell he edged past tipsy and toward full-blown drunk from the pungent fumes on the breath that blew hot and ripe on the back of my neck. True, he stayed put, dutifully, after I snapped at him for leaving me yet again. The last time he had gone off somewhere, playing the social butterfly. In my disgruntled state, I resented his presence if it was going to be offered reluctantly.

Sulking into my wine, I thought sarcastically to myself that it was shame I wasted my new dress on my undeserving boyfriend. A mere slip of fabric, red silk and black lace, it was one of the most daring things I'd ever worn, and I had envisioned Jude mentally taking it off me with his eyes even as I slipped it on. But, even when combined with black fishnets and four-inch fuck-me heels, it had solicited a simple, "You look very nice, Desi," from him, and I hadn't been in the mood to tease a bigger compliment from him.

The music changed to an old Michael Jackson number, a cheesy one but one that nonetheless filled the dance floor. "C'mon, let's dance," Jude said as he tugged on my arm. I tugged back, not sure he'd be able to even stand up unaccompanied by the wall for a whole five minutes, but sometimes when you're small, you find yourself maneuvered more easily than you would if you were six feet instead of barely five. The long stem of my glass was removed from my hand, and I was all but carried into the middle of the throng of people. I wondered if Megan even knew all of the people who were currently tromping around her apartment, but she seemed singularly unconcerned, so I let the thought go. And my frosted layer of pure bitch thawed, a tiny little bit, when Jude pulled me close and nuzzled my neck.

"I love you, babe," he said. "You know that, don't you?" I tried to rationalize away the instantaneous flipping of my stomach at his words, telling myself it wasn't anything I hadn't heard before from him, but a small trickle of girlish pleasure made its way through. I allowed a smile, foolish and bright, to cross my face.

I caught Megan's eye as Jude and I swayed, surrounded by bodies, and was upset when she frowned at me. While I doubted it was a frown of jealousy or of discontent at my happiness, and it was merely a further expression of the concern she had shown me earlier, I still took it harshly, pissed off that any bad vibes intruded on the moment. Deliberately, I turned my face inward so it pressed against the good-smelling flesh of Jude's chest, which laid beneath the ever-present black T-shirt, and thought that maybe, if I could get him alone later, the dress wouldn't be such a waste after all.

I felt his hands lower to my hips, pulling me into a sensuous bump-and-grind he led. One hand slipped between the heat of our bellies and tickled at the soft swell of flesh, and I enjoyed the intimacy of the gesture, the closeness it brought even in the midst of so many souls. When his hand dipped lower, and those clever fingers of his sampled the moisture of my center through the thin silk of my dress, I stiffened, shocked he dared to touch me so intimately in such a public place. Don't get me wrong. I was no prude, and I'd never been averse to the occasional display of public affection, but this was ... kind of weird. What if someone saw? It was completely inappropriate, to my way of thinking, anyways, and especially rude to Megan, our hostess, who was the ex-girlfriend, for goodness sake, of the man who currently touched me in places best meant for a dark room and candlelight.

I shifted against him, trying to move his fingers to a safer, less intimate zone, and as I did so I felt the press of his full-fledged erection, right into the curves of my soft belly. I opened my mouth to protest but managed only a weak squeak when he began his work in earnest, rubbing his fingers hard and fast over my clit, through the soft silk, which added an extra layer of pressure, in an unmistakably concerted effort to get me off. I felt like I should leave, push my way out of the throng of dancing bodies, to make my views on the matter known, but it seemed that my views became less and less concrete as the seconds ticked by. The pulse between my legs came faster, and my world narrowed to that one hot, bright point. I ceased trying to shove away and instead ground my hips against his clever fingers, begging for more, more heat, more pressure, more everything. Unconsciously, the rest of my body joined in the dance, writhing and rubbing against Jude shamelessly, a straight-up fuck with our clothes on. And I ceased to care who saw, desiring only that Jude continued what he did, continued fucking me with his hand, continued without stopping, until I came. I don't know if it was the thrill that accompanied the naughtiness of what we did that helped me over the edge so quickly, or if I was merely ripe and ready through no conscious effort of my own. Instead of the long, slow climb to orgasm I normally experienced, I came quickly in a rush against the firm pressure of Jude's hand as we rocked our bodies to the sound of Michael Jackson. Stunned, I stumbled, and Jude caught me in his arms and held me still. Looking up to see the crystal-clear triumph in his eyes, I wondered if he was as drunk as he'd seemed. He looked so pleased with himself that I had to smile, but felt oddly exposed still, shocked at what I had done, and terrified someone saw. I excused myself to run to the washroom.

I bypassed the main toilet, which had a lineup three deep, and slipped through Megan's bedroom to the smaller chamber in the back. I didn't actually have to pee; I merely wanted to survey the damage caused by sex on the dance floor, to see if I had that unmistakable just-fucked look.

I did, and I took my time repairing it, relieved to have a moment away from the press of people. The smell of perfume, food, and human flesh. Oddly, the illicit orgasm had relieved me of the black mood I'd been trapped in. After a long, cool drink of water from the ceramic cup at the side of the brass sink, I deemed myself refreshed enough to rejoin the party, to rejoin my boyfriend, and to bask in the light of the words of love he'd spoken to me.

As I stepped out of Megan's bedroom and into the long, narrow hall the light faded somewhat though, as I saw them, standing together at the back of a group of people that had joined the line for the toilets. Turned toward each other, they were mirror images, each with a shoulder and hip against the cool green paint and another hand in the matching jeans pocket. It was nothing new, really, seeing Trevor and Jude stand together, which I had seen them do millions of times before. What gave me pause, what had me halting for a startled moment in the doorway of Megan's bedroom, was the *way* in which they stood together. Hips cocked, toes turned inwards. Heads tilted. From here, it looked ... well, it looked distinctly flirtatious, like they were coming on to each other, though I knew that couldn't possibly be true. It must just be the angle at which I stood, I told myself; that was all. But still, I held back a breath, making myself dizzy. When Jude leaned in to murmur something in Trevor's ear, I waited for the touch of their lips.

It didn't happen. Even as relief, heady enough to make me dizzy, shot through me, something about the scene dredged up a stream of something thick, thick and sickly, which coiled slowly in my stomach like viscous molasses being poured from its small paper carton. Since I had no other place to go, I squeezed by them in the crowded hall, pretending not to have seen their very male figures standing so intimately, and made my way into the kitchen, hoping for another glass of water, one that I contemplated pouring right over my head. As I stood at the sink, gazing out into the night of the city from six floors up, I saw the reflection of my boyfriend, my boyfriend I knew so well, or at least I thought I knew, approaching me from behind.

"Hey," he said, rubbing a caring hand over the nape of my neck. "How's it going?" I stiffened a bit before forcing myself to relax, wondering … well, just wondering. I turned to face him, and buried my face again into his familiar smell. "You okay?" I didn't want to lie, but I couldn't honestly say that I was, either.

"I'm feeling a bit off," I told him in complete truth. "I think I might book it, head home for a bath." Was I imagining the wicked light that came into his eyes, the light that overshadowed his concern? Was this just female paranoia, feeding off of the two very large glasses of wine that had joined the other fluids of my body in the course of the last hour, or was it something else, something real?

"Want me to go with you?" The offer relieved some of the pressure in my belly. My spirits lifting a tad, I shook my head ruefully and offered up a small smile. "No, I'm okay, but thanks." I stood on my tippy toes for a kiss good-bye, and the one he offered was deep and delicious, long and soothing, instead of the quick peck I expected. With a full-fledged smile this time, I squeezed his butt, hard, once, before leaving to find my jacket. I just couldn't muster up the energy to wind my way through more bodies than I had to, to retrieve it from the spare room.

I eagerly anticipated the fresh air of the cool night outside on my face, thinking it'd clear my head and help me to get a handle on the dredges of my foul mood. Instead, the contrast of the cold from the fevered heat of inside brought greasy nausea roiling into my belly. Fearing I'd empty the contents of my stomach into my surroundings, I opted to walk the ten blocks rather than ruin some poor cabbie's night by adding the fragrance of eau de vomit to his vehicle.

I looked up as I started walking and picked out Megan's window from the dozens surrounding it by counting up and over. It showed the silhouette of the mass of undulating bodies that writhed away behind its screen, looking for all the world like the secret to life was hidden there, in that room, that room filled with joy. But I knew that it was a pretense, that not every person there could possibly being having as much fun as the perfect party in a beer commercial suggested; I knew somewhere in the mass of flesh, someone else was likely feeling just as outcast as I was. The realization, the suspicion that I wasn't in it alone, didn't help to remove any of my misery because, as I walked away from the party and my heels clicking sharply on the pavement was the only noise that could be heard, I felt, somehow, that I still was.

Alone.

chapter seven

S omething was wrong.

I couldn't put a finger on it, couldn't tell you how I knew, but my woman's intuition told me something was up. And since it was Jude who kept popping into my head, I figured it had to do with him. I'd never been the kind of woman to create trouble where it didn't exist, to pick a fight over something that didn't need to get fought over. But something about this evening, about Jude's frequent disappearances, about his odd exhibitionist behavior on the dance floor, about his all-around strangeness had an army of little cowboys two-stepping their way around my already queasy stomach.

Of course, that moment in the hallway. That moment I did my best to forget, but it kept creeping into my mind unawares, mockingly, to announce that there was something I missed, something big, along the way.

I stripped off my now-irritating dress the second I walked through the front door into my haven and padded barefoot and naked into my kitchen. I swung open the fridge door and inspected the contents, searching for something to settle my stomach. The only thing that looked even mildly appealing was the nearly empty jug of skim milk that, after a quick whiff, seemed safe enough. I poured myself a tall glass and rested its chill against my slightly sticky forehead before taking a sip.

Oh, ugh. No, no, no. That was worse. The wine in my system curdled the milk, causing me to gag. I poured it slowly down the drain, anxiety building as I watched the viscous white liquid swirl, around and around and around in a dizzying swirl.

Bracing my hands on the edge of the counter, I tried once again to tell myself I was being ridiculous. But I knew myself well, better, I think, that most women could say for themselves, and knew that the only way I was going to rest was if I took an action to prove my own thoughts. So, I grabbed up the set of keys I had carelessly tossed into the ceramic bowl on the counter, the heavily glossed one left over from my orange phase I still quite liked, and headed for the door. I took a moment to sneer at the tiny scrap of red cloth that had done me no good whatsoever before deciding to forgo it, instead pulling a long, tan raincoat over my slight frame and belting it tightly.

No need to give anyone an unexpected thrill, after all.

I forwent the high heels, too, since my feet, which has just suffered through ten blocks in their aching height, protested vehemently at the very thought. I opted instead for rubber flip flops, red ones, of course, with silly cloth flowers attached to the toes. Feeling much more myself than I had all night, I went through the open door and out into the night with my thoughts turned toward Jude's house.

I took a cab this time, since even the flat flip-flops couldn't salvage the damage already done to my poor, tender arches. I was lucky to find a driver who would take me such a short distance, since Jude lived only a five-minute drive away from my apartment building. The way my evening had gone, I hadn't been hopeful. But there indeed was one, and he even gave me a deal on my fare, though I think it was more because I didn't protest when he ogled my legs than because he felt charitable. Lights were on in the cozy little row house, so I knew Jude was home. This surprised me and ruined my plans a bit, since I had intended to be lying naked in his bed when he came home. I figured arriving in nothing, but a trench coat just might make his evening anyway and would go a long way toward making up for my odd behavior earlier that night.

I didn't feel bad about entering the house unannounced, either. After all, he gave me a key. Wanting him to get the full effect of my outfit, or lack thereof, I kicked off my sandals and tiptoed barefoot down the hall with anticipation humming pleasantly through my veins as I approached the bedroom, the opening of my coat clenched tightly together in my fingers. I saw from a crack that the door remained open and the room was lit from within.

Now, for those of you who think that this sounds like a horrid little farce of a movie, I won't tell you you're wrong. Perhaps if I had realized the clichéd nature of the scene, I wouldn't have gone in, but then I wouldn't have known. Then, where would I be? I think it was much better to know, to have seen the sight that played out before my eyes, distasteful though it was to my senses that had anticipated a night of love.

Through the crack in the door, I saw Jude lying naked, spread full length on the bright red comforter I had given him as a gift. I wondered if he had maybe stripped down for a shower then, too drunk to continue, passed out on the bed. His body was such a familiar sight that I almost moved toward it automatically with my hands reaching to stroke in all the familiar ways, but he wasn't alone, which I saw when another half naked body enter the picture, a body clad only in worn denim pants. Yes, that was sarcasm you heard. Had he been naked with someone a bit more ... well, expected, such as the big-breasted, empty-headed doll named Lily, Trevor's roommate, I could have at least experienced the expected emotions, the rage, the sickness that came with unfaithfulness. But since it wasn't Lily, nor a Lily clone, pressed against Jude, but Trevor himself, I think the indescribable nature of the emotions that washed over my body in a cold shower were completely understandable.

What. The. Fuck.

My mind told me to run away, to get as far away from the image as I could, but my legs stubbornly remained in place, frozen to the spot, as did my eyes. You know how, when you drive by the scene of a really bad accident, and it makes you feel sick to your stomach, you don't want to look, but you do anyway? You keep right on looking until you can't look anymore, even though you know the horrific visual is going to stay with you long after you've gone.

This felt exactly the same. Exactly. I couldn't even make a noise that would alert them to my presence and would stop the madness happening before my eyes. My mouth was glued shut, and no amount of pressure would separate the jaws packing as much tension as a pit bull's. And my heart insisted that the way my mind processed the visual was wrong, that I should stay until it changed, until I understood.

But I knew, even as I stayed, lurking in the shadows, it wasn't going to change. That what I saw was real. My boyfriend, instead of enjoying the naked body under my trench coat, was making love to a man. And not just any man, it seemed, but to *Trevor* of all people. Trevor, who until a month ago was a virgin. Trevor, one of my best friends. Two people I never thought would betray me at all, let alone together.

I hope you understand why this had me feeling rather mixed up.

Still, emotions aside, I stayed right where I was, and I watched. Before my eyes, Trevor's jeans dropped to the floor to join the slightly more faded ones I knew belonged to Jude. Next came his shirt, and then, he wore nothing. Jude reached out with his ropy, muscled arm I knew so well and drew him down to where he waited on the bed.

I heard the rumble of low male voices but couldn't make out individual words. The tone, however, the unabashed sensuousness of it, came across loud and clear, and I was shocked down to the soles of my bare feet as they lay, cool and naked, against the dark hardwood of the floor.

After the next few minutes, I decided nothing would shock me ever again.

Jude rolled onto his side, his dark gold skin full of dusty shadows in the dark. I made out the sight of his cock, though, long, hard, and undeniably aroused. Aroused by being naked with Trevor, I thought, though the idea still seemed laughable. Jude, who had been a ladies' man for as long as I knew him, aroused by the sight of another's cock. Was this the first time?

As Trevor kissed his way down Jude's chest, tangling his fingers in the whorls of hair there, much as I liked to do, my mind flashed to another time, not so long ago, when the two men had been naked together. The night Trevor lost his virginity, the night we all fucked together. Well, almost all of us; Jude hadn't joined. Was this why? Had he been scared of letting Megan and I know his true feelings, his true kink?

I felt completely, utterly stupid. Jude hadn't been turned on by me at all. It had been Trevor all this time, and I had simply trotted along, blissfully unaware while all the while I made a complete fool of myself.

At that point I probably could have left, but I felt the perverse need to stay. Maybe if I stayed to the end, something would click, and I'd understand. Or maybe I'd wake up and find it was all a dream.

But as Trev's mouth edged ever closer to the jutting flesh of Jude's prick, I realized neither option was likely. Yet, I remained, watching as Jude reached down to stroke a hand over the abs lining Trevor's stomach. When Jude brushed his hand lower and made his way through the light curls feathered over Trevor's low-hanging sac, I broke out in a sweat at first I thought was from stress. But when Trevor's head dipped lower, and his surprisingly soft looking, bowed pink lips wrapped around the pulsing head of Jude's cock, I realized the sensations firing through my veins were from lust, not disgust.

The sensuality of the two men making love, two pricks competing for attention, two sets of strong, masculine hands wasn't lost on me. My poor, confused sense of self wondered what was wrong with me that I stayed and watched something so painful to my heart, but I obtained some perverse measure of pleasure from it.

I ordered myself to stop thinking, since it had gotten me nowhere that night. Emptying my head, I simply watched as the two men I loved discovered the magic of each other's bodies.

From where I stood, I could almost smell the testosterone mixing with the unmistakably musky aroma of sex, as Jude turned his face to the side and nuzzled his cheek against the pillow. Tremors rolled along his body, muscle by muscle; the copper coins of his nipples were pebbled, hard and tight. His hips twitched, forcing his cock deeper into Trevor's mouth, and he groped his way through the jungle of the sheets, searching for something, anything, to secure himself on. I saw a light dew of perspiration break out all along his skin and waited for him to moan, as he always did when the two of us were naked together with his dick shoved as far into my mouth as it could get and the stiff hairs that surrounded his member tickled my lips. It didn't come, though. Instead, he stilled, and his cock appeared to soften, a bit, between the pursed lips of the other man.

As if to distract everyone, even himself, from that fact, Jude reached around and flipped Trevor over, rolling him onto his belly with a smoothness as familiar to me as the tight ass now facing my way. As Trevor raised himself up onto his knees, stilling in anticipation, and Jude frantically worked his own cock, up and down, up and down, and the sight made me itch to touch. I'd always been entranced by the perfection of his male organ, the way it stood up, perfectly straight, when aroused; the way the deep purples and greens of the thick veins that wound their way around the stalk could be seen through the translucent outer skin. His prick wasn't circumcised, and I loved to move the extra flap of skin up and down with my teeth, increasing sensation and taking it away as I pleased. As such, the sight of his strong hands, which knew how to make me scream, rubbing all over that gorgeous piece of anatomy, had juice pooling between my naked thighs and trickling down the soft curves of my sex.

When the thick length of his cock was hard enough to please him, Jude reached for the jeans on the floor, taking out a little foil packet I knew contained a Durex "ribbed for your pleasure" condom. He tore open the foil and rolled it over his member, then spat into his hands and rubbed them along his dick.

No. He wasn't going to ... was he?

It appeared he was. I thought, possibly, there was a moment of hesitation when he leaned forward and his dick stroked the quivering line divided the cheeks of Trevor's behind, but hesitating or not, he continued to advance, and I couldn't hold back my squeal of dismay as it slowly, jerkily, pressed itself into Trevor's waiting anus.

The men both stilled, deer caught in the headlights, at my high keening. Recognizing my voice, Jude bounded off the bed and crossed the room in two long strides, leaving Trevor frozen in the middle of the bed. The door opened to reveal my sorry self, a hard-tipped breast hanging out of the trench coat, which came partially undone; my hair mussed from the fingers that wrung through it in agony; vulnerable bare feet announcing that I, too, had once belonged here. Jude's dark eyes held mine, and I'm fairly certain there was an anguished look deep within them, but I would never be sure because I turned on my heel and ran out the door, leaving my flip-flops, and a part of my heart, behind.

I heard my name called over and over until I was out of earshot. But I didn't look back, since there was no way either of them could have talked his way out of the situation. I saw enough to know that the sickness I had carried around in my belly earlier in the evening had been a foreshadowing; it was replaced now with something heavier, thicker, and darker unlike anything I'd ever felt before.

My feet carried me forward over rocks, old gum, and other shrapnel until I reached my home, locked myself in, and collapsed against the door in a boneless heap, crying hard enough to shake my body.

The night solved one question, though, I understood as I curled into a tight, miserable ball on the prickly red welcome mat I collapsed upon. However, I certainly no longer wanted to hear the truth of the answer. Still, it remained, and I knew without a doubt my love for Jude was of the capital *L* variety.

Effectively, I was screwed.

chapter eight

Wiping the last vestiges of sickness from my mouth, I sat back on my heels and rested the sticky heat of my forehead against the cool porcelain of the toilet. My body felt cold and weak like I'd never be able to stand again. This might have seemed melodramatic, but for anyone who'd ever had their heart broken, they knew that this was not an exaggeration.

And that was what this was, I finally concluded. Heartbreak. I didn't know when I fell in love with Jude, or if I'd been in love with him since the day he came into my life, but the feelings were there, clear as day. I found it ironic and somewhat laughable it took something as tragic as the events of the evening to force me to admit them, even to myself.

What went wrong? I admitted to having jealous moments, several of them, over Jude's relationship with Megan, but they never bothered me overmuch; I trusted them both. That trust was misplaced, it seemed, on Jude's behalf, at any rate. But I never thought, not in a million years, that the person he'd betray me with would be a man. And not just any man, but Trevor, geeky, gawky, and new to the whole sex thing. Trevor, someone nearly as dear to my heart as Jude himself.

Crawling to the bedroom, across the multitude of brightly hued rag rugs I'd placed there years ago, I pulled the plug from the wall of the phone, ringing off the hook. The sudden silence was deafening. The only noise was the thud of my hands and knees as I made my painful way back to the bathroom.

It was too quiet, this severing of connection. So, just to have some noise, I turned the hot tap in the tub on full and the cold on a quarter. The resulting torrential gush into the smooth porcelain of the old claw-foot tub soothed me, as did the curling tendrils of steam that rose from the rapidly pooling water. As I winced at the heat that cleansed away the dirt and grime from the cuts on my feet, shredded during my barefoot run from Jude's house, I thought I heard, in the distance, a frantic pounding on my door. Having reached a state of blissful numbness, however, I no longer cared. Jude had a key, true, but I was secure in the knowledge that the thick brass security chain I engaged would ensure my privacy. So I ignored, or at least made a semblance of ignoring, the person who so desperately wanted admission to my home, while really keeping my ears cocked to better determine the length he tried. The amount, really, he deemed I was worth trying for.

When I turned off the taps, fifteen minutes later, all was quiet.

I was truly alone.

And, alone, I gave into the searing rage built bit by bit, since I saw Jude and Trevor standing so close in the hallway at Megan's. The rage that I hoped, if embraced, would carry me through the sorrow and the pain, until my heart healed and hopefully once again be whole.

As I let loose with a primal, *I-am-woman, hear-me-roar* wail, I threw the item nearest to my hand at the wall. It happened to be a bar of soap, one of Jude's milky green ovals of Irish Spring. Harmless enough, really, that soft crescent that was swollen with water. But it hit the framed picture of my three best friends and I, the one hanging on the wall above my tub, with a force the likes of which I hadn't thought myself capable. Good, I thought, I'd never much liked it there, anyways, but never got around to moving it. As I watched, the frame, dislodged from the nail on which it hung, slid quickly and loudly down the wall and landed with a large *crack* on the ceramic lip of the tub. From there, it slipped, in slow motion, into the tub along with me, slicing into the flesh of my calf painfully, though the cut couldn't have been more than an inch long. Still, those seemingly small wounds are the ones that bleed the most, and as the red gushed out into the water, I saw that the glass of the frame had, instead of shattering, broken into four relatively even sized pieces. One for each of us, I thought, which was appropriate. Because not only had Jude broken my heart, the in-love part of my heart, but I knew that nothing between the four of us, the "Core Four," would ever be the same again.

chapter nine

Desi,

I'm worried about you. Trevor and Jude won't tell me what happened. Please call me, or I will be forced to break down your door — and you know that, unlike you, my little pipsqueak, I am big enough to do it, too.

Love,
Megan

* * *

Desi,

I don't know how to say sorry to you, so I won't, though you know I am. It just ... happened, I guess. I'd also say I'd never do anything to hurt you, but that's a crock, as you well know, because I did. But ... I want you to know that I'd take it back if I could. I hope you can forgive me. Because if you can't, I don't know if I'll be able to forgive myself.

I love you to bits, babe, though I know this wasn't a good way of showing it.

Trev

PS: As you've probably guessed, I think I'm gay. But Jude's not. So ... I don't know. Maybe you should listen to what he has to say.

* * *

Desi

I'm sorry.

I know I could say it a thousand times and not have you believe it, but I truly am sorry, with all my heart.

And my heart, incidentally, belongs to you.

I fucked up big time. There's no other way to put it. And I'm not going to give you a bunch of lame excuses, either. I did it; I can't deny that, obviously. And I can't even tell you why. I can only say I had to know, had to experience that, to make sure you were the one. I wish I could have found a way to know without hurting you, and above all, I wish I had a better reason. But I don't. I know that you, of all people, don't want to hear a bunch of bull crap, so I won't give you any flowery, simpering excuses or convoluted explanations you'd have to peer too deeply into.

So here it is, plain and simple, and I hope you can find it within yourself to forgive me.

Because, as I've said, my heart is yours. Whether you take it or leave it to rot, it's yours.

And now you know.

Love, from the bottom of my heart,

Jude

Jude was right; I didn't want to hear a bunch of crap. And I did appreciate the truth — the stark, unrelenting white light of it.

But it didn't change what I had come to know in my heart. That, in order for me to be happy again, for all of us to be happy again, I had to let it all go. The concerned notes from my friends helped with this. I knew they all meant what they said. But, apart from a brief, tear-filled fest with Megan over lunch one day, I wasn't ready to face the starkness of that reality, not just yet, at any rate.

But every day I was a little bit stronger and knew the time was coming. The time it would all be let loose to float into the world and be dispersed by the universe. The time I would again be free.

But that time wasn't now, or rather, not yet. But I knew, deep within myself, all would be well again.

For me, at any rate.

Medley of plants.

chapter ten

When I stepped, tentatively, through the door to Megan's apartment, it looked as if I never left. It had been three months, though, since that first night, the night that everything changed. Now, the round-robin scheduling of our monthly dinners was back to Megan.

They skipped me for obvious reasons.

This was a big step for me. But it wasn't because I harbored any anger; no, the fury that initially shook my small frame, justified though it had been, had long since faded. The human state pretty much demands we make mistakes, all of us, and, through the twisted machinations of our emotions and relations with one another, traps us into situations guaranteed to trip us up. The only way I could stay mad about the mistake Jude and Trevor made, the big-ass, nasty mistake I was sure I'd still whip out during future arguments, was if I never made one myself ... and let me assure you, I have. Plenty of them. I'd been the "other woman" once or twice, and I'd been forgiven for that, then far be it for me to cast that forgiveness back in anyone's face. Cast the first stone, and all that.

No, the hugeness of my appearance tonight had more to do with my decision regarding my future with Jude. I tried, numerous times over the past week, to pick up the phone when his number flashed over the call display, not to ask him why, since he'd already told me, and not to demand an apology; I'd received that, too. No, the reason I wanted to pick up the phone was simply to hear his voice, because the truth of the matter was I missed it. Missed him. And the phone remained on the cradle only because, alone, I didn't have the strength to say what I needed to say.

Here, at Megan's, I wasn't alone. Would never have to be alone. And the feeling was good.

Ignoring them all for a moment, I looked around the room. Saw the spot on the wall where Trevor smashed a beer bottle months ago while announcing his virginal state, a spot that looked a bit brighter than the rest of the soft green. I thought maybe Megan had repainted it to cover the stain with something fresh and new or if she'd simply scrubbed so hard at the residue that clung, sticky and dark, the result was a brighter, cleaner green than the original.

Food was laid out on the dark coffee table; this, too, was typical. I saw a gleaming bottle of red strawberry margarita mix sitting beside a platter of something crispy that smelled divine, and smiled inwardly; Megan, my friend knew I'd come.

And behind the bottle, clad true to type in tight, faded denim, was the lean length of a leg I knew the shape of so well that it might have been mine. And, actually, it was my own, in a way, as was the rest of the man it was attached to, the man whose face I looked at for the first time in months as my gaze slowly traveled upward from his knee.

I told you earlier in this story I never saw Jude blush. Well, it appeared there were a lot of firsts here, because I had never seen him cry before, either. Not that burst into sobs at the sight of me or anything; no, he was too much of an alpha for that. But the slick wetness that shimmered over the clear, deep green of his irises was enough for me and confirmed my decision.

As did the subtle shift of his hips on the couch, which moved him just an inch further away from Trevor, next to whom he sat. That inch told me volumes about their story. Even if I was worried, the presence of the skinny, red-haired man seated next to Trevor, on his other side, would have assuaged the despair.

It seemed things were different all around, and the realization warmed me all over. I took a full step into the living room, and before I could take a second was enveloped in the arms of Megan, pressed against her soft, sweet smelling flesh, and comfort oozed from her skin into mine. As she scurried off to mix me a drink, a fuzzy navel, by my own request, I continued to force my legs forward, bit by bit, until I stood in front of Jude.

This was it; I had to make sure I made the right choice. But, as I leaned over and touched my lips to his in a soft, sweet expression of love, my heart swelled, and I wondered how I considered anything else.

When I pulled away, his hands reached blindly for mine and clasped tight. His face was the one, this time, full of uncertainty; in response, I shot him a cocky grin and dropped into his lap, the purple wool sweater I wore leaving a trail of fuzz in its wake. As Trevor and Megan cheered, and an icy cold yellow drink was urged into my hand, I pressed my lips up to Jude's ear and nuzzled.

"I'm still not wearing any underwear," I whispered.

The look on his face was more than enough for me.

epilogue

"I think I liked it better when everything in your life matched," Jude grumbled as, muscles straining, he pulled the new sofa, bit by bit, across the hardwood of his living room floor. I appreciated the view of his arms as they strained and the sweat that dampened his T-shirt, making it cling to the hard muscles of his chest. I felt bad for him, a tiny bit, that he did all of the heavy lifting.

But I still wanted the red couch under the window, instead of beneath the orange, blue, and gold painted canvas, one of my own, hung, slightly haphazard for the moment, on the north wall.

"It still matches," I told him, offering up a sweet smile that I knew he'd appreciate, even as he moved the couch to the third place I'd tried. "It's just not all the same color anymore."

Inching the hulking piece of furniture over one last fraction of a foot, Jude dusted off his hands on the thighs of his jeans, and then peeled his tight top up and over his head with eyes fastened on me when he mopped his brow with the soft cotton. I knew what it was he saw. A small woman, with long, curly hair back to its natural copper color. Small breasts and curvy hips covered by a bright blue cotton dress. Feet bare with each toenail painted a shocking pink.

And, most importantly, a face softened, a bit, from the wary expression it had worn over the years. Softened with smiles, laughter, and good things.

And, most of all, with love.

Slaves of Love

Opal Carew

chapter one

Shena stood totally naked on the high rock ledge overlooking her favorite pond. Her scratchy tunic and loose-fitting *taygha* pants sat in a heap on the grass by the water, her plain white bra and panties tucked underneath. Two crimson *garals* glided over the water on delicate, feathered wings. Others trilled in the trees, and a light breeze set the leaves aflutter, the gentle rustle soothing to her soul.

This lovely spot had been her mother's favorite place. Her mother had died from an outbreak of *Gahdagha* flu, which had claimed the lives of several people in the county when Shena was only a year old. Coming here helped her ground her emotions after dealing with her father's foul moods.

She swallowed hard as she stared over the glittering water, barely seeing it. Her face still smarted from his smack when she'd dropped a plate while clearing the table after the midday meal. What bothered her most was that he'd come at her with his fist clenched but, at the last minute, hesitated, then slapped her with the flat of his hand. A blow from his fist would have left a black eye or split lip.

She'd noticed the trader ship — the second this week — arrive this morning and couldn't help thinking a mark on her face would make her a less desirable commodity for the traders. Maybe her father intended to carry out his threat this time. She had dashed out of the house as soon as she'd had a chance, hoping if she kept out of sight, he would forget how much she displeased him.

For others, the arrival of a trader ship raised great excitement. The marketplace would swell with exotic goods from many worlds, alongside staples necessary for the inhabitants of this small planet, Tarun, to survive. Shena, however, had lived with her father's threats far too long. One day, if she wasn't terribly careful, he might actually carry out his threat to sell her to the traders. Although slavery had been banned on most of the planets in the coalition — including Tarun — E'Le'Dor, only a few star systems away, still had a thriving slave trade.

Shena closed her eyes and sucked in a deep breath, allowing the sweet, delicate fragrance of *caulila* blossoms to wash through her. The sun warmed her body, and a soft breath of air brushed across her skin. She smiled. This was what heaven must be like. Sweat trickled between her breasts as she gazed on the rippling water below, sunlight glistening off the surface. It heartened her to know that such beauty existed in the world, even though everyday life was so lacking in it.

She leaped headfirst from the rock, arms outstretched in front of her. The coolness flowed across her naked body as she cut through the water, the grime of sweat and apprehension sluicing from her. Her breasts tightened and her nipples puckered into tight buds. She angled upward. Her head broke through the surface of the water, and she drew in a lungful of fresh air. She floated on her back, the tips of her breasts poking up through the water. The sun felt glorious on her face, and she closed her eyes and emptied her mind, enjoying the only real freedom she knew.

A snap startled her to alertness. Her eyes flicked open, and she shifted to a vertical position in the water, keeping her arms close as she treaded water, attempting to cover herself. She searched the water's edge with thorough, sweeping glances, but saw no one along the sandy edge or within the trees and bushes beyond the rocky shore.

At a rustling sound, her gaze snapped to the left. A *dealla* stepped from between two trees and peered at her with wide brown eyes, then dashed away on its long, lanky legs.

That's all it had been, she chided herself, still quivering. Just a timid grazer. Not one of her father's soldiers. She swam to the opposite shore and pulled herself from the pool. Beads of water trickled down her limbs and torso.

She dropped onto the small, secluded strip of beach and stretched out on the warm sand. Her skin felt fresh and alive. It even glowed a healthy pink. The decadence of the sun dancing across her body excited her. Her breasts peaked, and her thighs felt deliciously warm. Her fingers slid across her rib cage, over the curve of a breast to her nipple, tight and aching, longing to be touched. She dragged her fingertip over the pebbly areola, then across the tight nub, which felt like a round, soft bead. She loved how it hardened when she touched it, the sharp pangs of excitement that jolted through her, connecting straight to her lower regions. The inner muscles of her vagina tightened and ached. The pace of her breathing increased.

She shouldn't be doing this, but the intensity of the feelings in her body, the need those feelings aroused, was too overwhelming to ignore. Who would know, or care, what she did?

She cupped her breast, exulting in the feel of the nipple pressing into the sensitive palm of her hand. Her other hand slid across her belly and downward, pausing at the silky feel of her pubic hair. She stroked it, smiling. Soft.

She cupped her other breast and felt her face flush. Her other hand continued downward, across her inner thigh, then around the fleshy fold, spiraling inward. Her muscles tightened as she focused on the intense sensations.

Her finger slid up to the small, hard button cradled in the folds. She dabbed at it, then stroked once and almost cried out at the intense pleasure it gave. The world faded around her as she settled deeply inside herself, experiencing the stroking of her finger, the building of the heat within her, the pleasure flooding through her.

Stronger and stronger. Higher and higher. It rushed through her like white water in a torrential river. Her breathing, labored and harsh, rushed through her lungs. She felt, rather than heard, the moan start in her throat, then build to a crescendo as she exploded in a burst of pleasure.

She dropped back onto the sand, feeling the air flooding in and out of her lungs, loving the languorous feeling of her body, replete, satisfied in a pleasure of her own making. She stretched, then pushed herself to her feet, knowing she should head home, but reluctant to leave.

* * *

Keern sat beyond the bushes, watching the beautiful wood nymph, his eyes glazed over and his breathing slowly returning to normal.

He'd left the small space port in Dudane five long, hot hours ago. The tedious trip had given him ample time to remember all the reasons he'd left this backwater, technology-barren planet in the first place. He'd begun to reconsider his sketchy plans to turn this visit for his brother's wedding into a permanent stay.

About an hour ago, he'd stopped at the secluded pond to fill his canteen. When he'd heard a splash in the water, he'd cautiously approached to see who was about and had spotted this lovely young woman swimming naked in the pool. Suddenly, this outdated planet brightened with exciting possibilities.

He hadn't been able to drag his gaze from her. The sunlight had glistened on her long golden hair as it floated around her, and he could see her creamy, naked shoulders and the swell of her breasts above the water. His cock had leapt to attention immediately, confined painfully within his black leather trousers. *Shet'ra,* what did he expect? He hadn't been with a woman since Kolanna, the last in a long line of shallow, manipulative women looking to him for excitement. His distinct, sexy accent — as women described it — developed over 15 years of travel across a myriad of worlds, stirred their imaginations. They hoped for exotic gifts and travel to far-off places, but their idea of luxurious, pampered trips did not match the reality of his more basic lifestyle.

His knowledge and understanding of extreme environments put him in high demand across the sector. Anything from frozen tundra to desert inferno, if it was within the range of human endurance, he could survive and navigate it. Most of his jobs involved rescue and recovery. Sometimes training. Clients ranged from rich thrill-seekers to troop commanders wanting him to lead survival courses.

Certainly, he knew how to move through unfamiliar terrain quietly, yet when he'd seen the naked woman in the water, his hormones had flared and he'd missed his footing and tramped on a twig. She must have heard it snap because she'd glanced about, searching for an intruder. Never shifting his gaze from her captivating form, he'd sat down on a rock, ensuring he did not make another sound.

He didn't usually spy on naked women swimming in pools, but she was so beautiful he couldn't help himself. He'd held his breath as she'd pulled herself from the water, revealing the full length of her totally naked body. Her breasts, generously proportioned, curved upward, tipped by small areolas with tight, hard nipples. His gaze had drifted to the golden thatch of hair at the top of her thighs, and his throat had gone dry.

When she'd started exploring her sexy, round breasts with her hands, pleasuring herself, he'd almost groaned out loud. He'd had to hold himself down with a steel will to stop himself from leaping from the bushes and joining her in pleasuring that gorgeous body. He'd wanted to hear her moan from his touches.

When she'd reached down to her private folds and stroked her damp crevice, he had almost burst at the seams. In fact, he had taken out his cock, long and hard in a full erection, and stroked it, trembling with the longing to drive it into her glistening opening. He closed his hand around it, stroking back and forth as he watched her, feeling the skin gliding over the hard muscle beneath, excruciating need building within him. He wanted to take her, to fill her up and explode within her in a mind-numbing ejaculation of pleasure.

But he had no right to intrude on her privacy. He had no way of knowing if she would welcome him or flee from him. His instincts told him she would flee. Although she looked open and uninhibited, he somehow knew it was only because she was sure she was alone.

This pond belonged to his family, but they rarely visited here because it was on undeveloped land on the outskirts of their property, far from the house and the fields, and the other landowners respected the boundaries of their neighbors.

The last thing he wanted to do was cut short her incredible performance, but more importantly, he didn't want to frighten her. So he moved his hand to the rhythm of hers, imagined himself plunging into her as she moaned in pleasure, and burst in a fierce ejaculation just as she cried out in climax.

Now he slumped back on the ground, exhausted.

Once his breathing calmed down, he put his wilted member away and pulled himself to his feet. He really should be on his way, but as he watched her extend her arms in a long, languorous stretch, then push herself to her feet, he decided to stay and see if she would dive into the water again. The beauty of her agile, curvaceous form cutting through the water was sheer poetry.

Suddenly, the hair at the back of his neck prickled. Had he heard horses? Quietly, he pushed through the underbrush, leaving the lovely nymph behind as he headed toward the road. He raced to the peak of the hill leading to the quiet spot and saw a wagon of soldiers heading this way. *Darg'ra*, what were they doing here? At this distance, he couldn't make out the crest on their uniforms, not that he would necessarily recognize which of the landholders it represented after more than a decade away.

The pond was not obvious from the road, secluded behind trees and brush, so they weren't coming here by accident. Why would they be trespassing on his land? Did they know about the young woman?

These soldiers didn't look like the type who would watch her quietly from a distance, and he couldn't stand the thought of these oafs catching sight of his lovely maiden, let alone touching her with their large, rough hands.

He had to get back to his wood nymph. He had to protect her.

* * *

Shena felt a hand slide around her naked body and pull her backwards against a hard male chest. At the same time, another hand clamped over her mouth, cutting off her scream.

"I won't hurt you," a strange male voice promised. The hint of an unfamiliar accent tinged his words. Off-world and educated.

She froze in absolute terror at being held in a man's grasp while naked and vulnerable. Yet at the same time, the feel of his body against hers set off some very strange feelings. Arousing feelings. Her throat constricted painfully, and she clawed at the steel arm fastened around her waist, desperate to free herself.

His grip tightened, pulling her more firmly against his body.

"Listen to me." His words rasped in her ear. "There's a group of soldiers heading this way, so stay still and don't make any noise. You don't want to draw their attention."

Soldiers? She froze in terror.

"They won't be content to just watch politely, like I did. If I remove my hand from your mouth, do you promise not to scream?"

She nodded. Whether he spoke the truth or not, she didn't know, but she was too terrified to chance it. He released her mouth, but not her body.

"Let me go," she demanded, her voice a harsh whisper.

"I don't think so, *neisha.*"

His light, teasing tone sent her off balance, and his use of the endearment confused her. *Neisha* was not a term an off-worlder would use. In fact, with the slight drag on the last syllable ... Could he be a local?

"If I see your luscious body again, I may not be able to control myself." His words melted through her.

She became aware of her nipples tightening, her vagina contracting. He'd watched her swim. Oh, God, he'd seen her taking pleasure.

Memories of the pleasure rippled through her body, but this time she imagined his gaze as a tangible feeling caressing her body as her fingers caressed her intimate self. Images superimposed on her memory, of him leaving his hiding place, of his strong, tanned hands touching her body.

He loosened his hold on her slightly as he used one hand to remove his cape, then eased her away from him just enough to slide it around her shoulders. She grasped it and pulled it close around her, fastening it at the neck. The rich, smooth feel of the fabric, unmistakably *ancula,* a Tarun fiber, surrounded her with warmth and an odd sense of security. The heady, male scent enveloped her.

He gripped her arm with a gentle but resolute hold and guided her with him into the wooded area overlooking the pond. She struggled, trying to free herself from his grip, desperate to get away from him, her insides shuddering uncontrollably at the powerful and unfamiliar feelings of attraction to him.

His hair, dark brown and wavy, curled around his ears and neck. His warm bronze eyes watched her as he effortlessly guided her along, yet she didn't feel threatened by his gaze, not like she always did with her father's men. Their stares, which seemed to strip her of dignity, always frightened her.

"We'll stay here until they pass," he said.

"Let me go," she insisted.

"No. You don't believe I'm telling the truth about the soldiers. Until you see them with your own eyes, which should be in about five minutes, I'm going to hold tight."

She was far too conscious of his arm around her waist. His other arm slid around her, and then his hand flattened on her upper chest just below her collarbone, pressing her tight against his strong, broad chest. His leather belt and metal buckle pressed into her lower back, and his pelvis pressed against her buttocks. Only fabric lay between her bare bottom and his ... She felt a blush flame across her face, and she struggled against him. Oh, God, she felt a bulge grow against her. Her movements were arousing him. Blinding fear lanced through her, challenged by a powerful desire to experience the tender loving of a man.

Drawn back to the memory of him watching her earlier, it was far too easy to imagine his chest naked against her swollen breasts, to imagine him moving his pelvis against hers in a forbidden act.

Five minutes in his arms. She didn't think she'd survive the conflicting feelings wreaking havoc on her sanity. She would find a way out of this. Maybe if she gave him false confidence in her submission ...

"Fine," she said tightly and slumped against him. As she'd hoped, his hold relaxed a little, and she thrust her elbow into his solar plexus, then pushed back with all her might. He stepped back, regaining his balance, then caught his heel on a rock. They both fell, but she ducked and rolled out of his grasp, then darted into the woods.

She dashed through the trees, intending to retrieve her clothes and race home. Under ordinary circumstances, it was much simpler to swim across the pond, but she couldn't do that without being spotted by the stranger; he'd catch her for sure. It was a longer, harder route, but after ten minutes, she spotted the burgundy-leafed blazing fire bush alongside the grey-green bark of the two *elra* trees near where she'd left her things. Her gaze locked to the spot where her clothes *should* have been. God, they were gone!

Had the stranger taken them? As she stepped from between the trees, searching the ground for any sign of her tunic and *tayghas*, a leering voice froze her in her tracks.

"Look, fellows. What have we here?" A burly man with a straggly, sand-colored beard grinned at her, exposing grey, crooked teeth. His grubby uniform jacket hung open, exposing a sweat-stained shirt beneath.

His lurid gaze traveled down the black cape to her feet. She was conscious of the grass between her toes, which reminded her that her feet were bare. What would he think? His focus shifted from her feet to the opening of the cape, which she clung to in a desperate effort to keep it closed.

"I suppose you're looking for those." He pointed to where another man held up her plain white bra and panties.

"Well, well, men. It seems the lass must be naked under that cloak."

Sandy-Beard stepped toward her and she backed up, bumping against a tree. A bitter taste filled her mouth as adrenaline flooded her system. Her whole body trembled uncontrollably.

"I bet she's up for a bit of fun." His voice lowered to a gritty huskiness. "And I'd sure be willing to show you a bit of fun, lass."

Suddenly, three other men began to crowd around her, and terror squeezed the breath from her.

"Aye, and we would, too, Clancy."

He shoved them back. "One at a time, lads." His sneering lips curled into a caricature of a smile. "Or maybe two. But not 'til I've had my go."

Dizziness overwhelmed her, but she fought it as she tried to ease sideways to use the same trick as she had on the tall, dark stranger — funny, she hadn't felt the same kind of fear with him — and escape to the side, but the man's hand shot out to rest against the tree on her right, trapping that escape route. The other soldiers loomed on the left so she'd have nowhere to run.

As he reached for her, terror built within her like an inferno. He clamped his hand around her shoulder, his bony fingers digging into her flesh, and grasped the clasp at her neck.

She felt faint as she tried to stifle memories that still haunted her nightmares. Memories of the young woman who used to keep house for her father. The image of the woman, hands fastened above her head, clothes stripped from her body. She had screamed as the soldiers rammed into her, over and over again. Those screams still echoed through Shena's body.

"Remove your hand from her, or you'll lose it."

The stranger's voice! She turned her gaze to see him standing at the edge of the clearing. Tall. Dark. Ominous-looking.

"Who the 'ell are you?" her captor demanded.

The dark stranger stepped forward, bringing his hand to the hilt of his sword. All the soldiers backed away except the man holding her.

"I said, remove your hand." The words came out as a low warning, but an undercurrent of rage carried clearly in his tone.

Her captor hesitated, but he reluctantly pulled his hand from her shoulder. "What's it to you, stranger?"

chapter two

K eern had to use all the control he could muster not to strike down the man holding the frightened woman in his grip.

He reached for her arm and drew her away from her captor. To his surprise, she flung herself against his side and wrapped her arms around his waist. As she buried her face against his chest, he allowed his left arm to circle her waist, tucking her tightly against him.

"She's my woman," he lied, wishing it were so.

The man's eyes narrowed, but he stepped back. "You shouldn't let her go running around tempting a man to distraction like that. After all, if a man sees a naked ankle, can a naked thigh be far behind?"

"You are trespassing. This land belongs to my family."

The man narrowed his eyes.

"No, this land rightfully belongs to Henry Wakefield. He gave us permission to be here."

Anger simmered through him. Will would never give up this beautiful place.

"He has no right to give you permission. My name is Herrington, and this land has been in my family for five generations. I do not take lightly to being called a liar."

The woman pressed to his side stiffened. He stroked her back reassuringly. If not for her, he'd take these lying, undisciplined oafs, but he didn't want to do anything to frighten her more.

Uncertainty flickered in his opponent's eyes.

"I suggest you take your leave."

The soldiers grumbled, but mounted their horses and left.

Keern vaguely remembered his brother complaining about a greedy neighbor with an eye on their land. Could this Wakefield be telling others this pond belonged to him, giving them permission to use it as a way to solidify his claim? Would he keep whittling away at the edges of their property, expanding his own in the process?

"They're gone," he said to the woman still clinging to him. The feel of her soft and pliant against him, the delicate floral smell of her hair as it wisped across her cheek, sent his hormones soaring. He hooked his finger beneath her chin and lifted until she looked into his face.

Her eyes were glazed with terror, and he wished he'd skewered the bastard who'd torn away her peaceful bliss. Better yet, he wished he'd had his laser pistol and been able to fry every last one of them, but technology was forbidden here. The coalition had designated this planet as a conservation area, to be kept untouched by industry, pollution, and chemicals. Anything high-tech was deemed a threat to the natural balance of the world. Keern used to hate that policy, until he'd traveled to other worlds and seen how technology had changed society, damned near destroying many.

Less than a half-hour ago, he'd watched this lovely woman bathing in the sparkling water, carefree as a creature of nature in her glorious nakedness. He'd felt a little guilty spying on her, but how could he resist? Her beauty surpassed that of any woman he'd ever seen. He could almost believe her to be a mythical being straight from one of the storybooks his mother used to read him when he was a boy.

She gazed up at him, her blue eyes soft and dewy.

"Thank you."

The words, like delicate petals, drifted from her lips. She looked like a woman wanting to be kissed. He slid his other arm around her and drew her body close to his. The memory of her pressed against him earlier, naked and dripping wet, tightened his body in arousal. He couldn't help remembering that she was still naked beneath his black cloak.

"Why don't you thank me with a kiss?" he murmured.

* * *

Shena wanted to grant him more than a kiss. She'd never felt this way with a man before. Safe. Protected. She wanted to burrow into his arms and stay there forever.

At her hesitation, he smiled encouragingly. "Surely you can grant me one kiss?"

One kiss. Yes, at least that. She drew her tongue around her lips to moisten them, then parted them slightly as she raised her hands to hold his face. His cheeks scratched slightly with the new growth of his beard, but she didn't mind. The very masculinity of it stimulated her, made her feel more feminine. His eyes, the color of sun-gilt bronze, darkened as he watched her. She pushed herself onto her tiptoes to reach him, and he waited for her. When her lips touched his, she felt as if she would faint, the feeling was so painfully exciting. As though he sensed her weakness, his hands slid up her back and he pulled her closer to his body. She moved her lips on his, and he followed her lead, though she sensed he carefully controlled his movements.

She felt the tip of his tongue slip across the seam of her mouth, then nudge with a delicate pressure. She opened, granting him access. His tongue slid inside her mouth, then caressed the inside of her lips. The delicate yet powerful sensation caught her breath. He pulled her tighter to him. Her breasts, crushed against the hardness of his well-muscled chest, swelled, the nipples tightening to hard buds. She longed to feel bare skin against hers.

As though reading her mind, he skimmed his hand over her, then slipped it inside the cloak to cup her breast, and a choked sound of pleasure escaped her. His other hand pushed her cloak aside and cupped her bottom. He pulled her pelvis close to his body, and she felt the bulge of his arousal. She tensed, and he immediately loosened his hold, but his hand remained on her breast, warm, exciting, her nipple thrusting into his palm. As he parted from their kiss to gaze down at her, his hand shifted slightly on her breast, sending arrows of pleasure shimmering through her body. She knew she should pull away, should be frightened of him touching her, but his warm bronze eyes, filled with compassion and kindness, soothed her frazzled spirit.

"I won't do anything you don't want me to."

She couldn't utter a word under the primal need raging through her, so she just nodded, then slipped her arms around his neck and pulled him into another kiss. His hands danced the length of her body as he eased her onto the soft grass beneath their feet. He untied the cloak and slowly peeled it back, holding her gaze the whole time. He smiled as he looked at her naked body, his gaze like liquid fire across the length of her.

"My God, you're beautiful."

She smiled back at him. No one had ever told her that.

He kissed her lips, dipping his tongue inside her mouth, then moved to the crook of her neck. Slowly, he kissed down her chest and over the swell of her breast. She melted as his mouth captured her rigid nipple. Her eyelids fell closed as his hand found her other nipple and nurtured it to heightened arousal. Both her breasts wanted more. She wanted more. Had she said it out loud? She didn't know or care.

All that existed for her was the rise and fall of her breathing, the rigid need of her breasts, the overwhelming desire for something more. She just didn't know what. He stroked her breasts, and she undulated to press more firmly into his hands. The rhythm of her labored breathing, the odd, whimpering sounds she made, only skimmed the edges of her consciousness.

"It's all right, sweetheart."

His calming words sluiced through the heated fever overtaking her. His hands fell away from her breasts, but his lips claimed hers, capturing the tiny sound of disappointment. Their only contact now was his mouth on hers, but his tongue sweeping across hers, and the ardent pressure of his lips, demanded her full attention. Her heated body longed for more, and an instant later she felt his body return. Naked now. She opened her eyes to look at him. His arms, thick and corded with muscle, settled on either side of her, suspending him over her. Her nipples peaked as the light coating of coarse hair sprinkled across his tanned chest stimulated those sensitized nubs. She dragged her hands across his strong, broad shoulders, awed by the feel of his steel-hard muscles rippling under her fingertips.

Then, with a flash of frigid water through her veins, she froze at the feel of his hard shaft falling across her belly. Her eyes shot wide open. He eased his pelvis away from her and placed the tip of his cock against the moist opening of her vagina.

She sucked in a breath as panic tore through her, and she planted her hands firmly on his chest.

"No." The word, choked out, was hardly audible.

He paused. "What is it, *neisha?*" The tip of his immense cock sat cradled in the soft folds of her, waiting for entry. One shift of his huge, muscular body and he'd be inside her.

Open, a voice inside her screamed. *Pull him in. Feel the power of a man inside you.*

He kissed her temple, still poised to fill her. Fear churned through her insides. Oh God, what if he didn't stop?

"Tell me."

The word her father had used so many times to describe this act, the word the soldiers around her always seemed to use with such relish, the word she had come to fear so completely, came unbidden to her mind.

"Don't fuck me," she choked out.

His thick brown eyebrows lowered, darkening his expression, and he eased away, then settled beside her. He stroked her hair behind her ear.

"I prefer to call it making love. Where did you hear a word like that?"

She closed her eyes and shook her head.

"I would never *fuck* you, my little wood nymph." He kissed her gently, the tender brush of his lips warming her. "And I won't *make love* to you unless you want me to."

He deepened the kiss, and heat flooded through her

"Even though I feel I might die of need." He smiled in an attempt to reassure her.

"Is it okay if I do this?" He stroked her breast.

She nodded at the exquisite pleasure.

"And this?" He flicked her other nipple with his tongue, and she moaned.

"How much do you know about making love?"

"I know that it means pain. When a man ... enters a woman, she screams and bleeds."

Shena remembered when her father had decided to punish the young housekeeper. He had tied her hands above her head and fastened the rope to a large hook on the ceiling, then given her to the soldiers. He'd made Shena watch, telling her that would be her punishment if she ever allowed a man to take her virginity. She remembered how, afterward, the girl had hung from the rope, her feet dangling loosely, blood streaming down her thighs.

"You're trembling." His voice brought her back to the moment. He gathered her in his arms and held her close. "You know, it doesn't have to be like that."

"I ... I can't. My father told me ... if I ever let a man ..." She sobbed.

He stroked her hair. "It's all right. I told you I wouldn't do anything you didn't want me to." He folded her in his arms and rocked her.

"Do you trust me?" He whispered the question in her ear, setting the fine hairs along the side of her neck on end.

"Yes," she breathed. It was strange, but she knew she did trust him.

"Then let me show you another way to take pleasure."

He eased her back and stroked the length of her body, from nape to hip. Very slowly, he moved his hand to her down-covered mound.

"Will you let me? I promise I won't do anything to harm your maidenhead."

She nodded. He stroked her fur, then slid his finger between her intimate folds, skimming the surface. The exquisite feel of it nearly overcame her. He stroked again, and her breath caught. He kissed her belly, then dipped his tongue into her navel. His kisses drifted lower until she felt his tongue slide through her curls, then lick the moist slit between her thighs. His tongue entered her, twirling and cajoling, licking and thrusting. His mouth shifted, covering the rigid nub of her clitoris.

She cried out in pleasure. He dabbed and flicked as his fingers slipped to her slit, stroking until the pressure building within her threatened to explode.

"Do you like this, *neisha?*" he paused to ask.

"Yes."

His mouth claimed her again, and she cried out. Heat raged through every part of her, inundating her senses with burning pleasure, building to an impossible level, then bursting into ecstatic flames.

Her body, which had been clenched tight, relaxed.

He stroked her hair. She gazed up at him.

"That was incredible."

His smile widened. "I'm glad you approve."

He kissed her, gentle and sweet. He tasted of her, and that excited her.

He had given her so much pleasure, but she had done nothing for him. She noticed his cock still stood tall, swollen with need.

"What about you?"

He followed her gaze and grinned. "You *have* left me in a state, *neisha.*" He nuzzled her neck. "But don't worry about it. I'll deal with it. Just give me a minute." He lay back on the grass and wrapped his hand around his erection and pumped.

That wasn't good enough for her.

chapter three

Keern watched her inquisitive expression turn to one of determination. She rolled and pushed herself to her knees. Her
breasts shifted enticingly as she reached for his wrist and stilled his
movement.

"I want to do something for you now."

She drew his hand to her mouth and planted a delicate kiss in
his palm. Her gentle, moist lips brushed him where his penis had
just been. His groin tightened at the thought of her lips brushing
against his oh-so-ready cock, her mouth surrounding his rigid member and sucking it deep within. Of course, she wouldn't do that, and
he wouldn't ask her to.

She reached out with a tentative finger and touched his huge
erection, then stroked the length of him with her fingertip. Her delicate, inexperienced touch sent jolting, almost painful need through
Keern. And the way she looked at it! Her wide, intent gaze filled with
curiosity. He almost burst on the spot. Clenching his groin muscles,
he held back, determined to experience the full pleasure of her
exploration.

"What can I do?"

You can put it in your mouth.

He smiled. "Well, you can touch it like you are now. You can stroke it."

She shifted to a kneeling position and curled her fingers around him. He drew in a deep, calming breath.

"Like this?"

He nodded, then guided her hand the length of him, showing her how to stroke, back and forth.

* * *

Shena reveled in the feel of the skin, soft as kid leather, sliding over rock-hard muscle. It felt so powerful, and she was in control of it. She stroked, listening to his breath quicken. His eyes fell closed and she watched him, stretched out on the ground, totally naked, responding to her touch. This strong, powerful, incredibly handsome man seemed to be totally at the mercy of her touch.

She was giving him pleasure. It made her want to climb on top of him and drive his shaft deep inside her. To move up and down on him, like her hand did now, but using intimate muscles to squeeze and pleasure him.

His hand stilled hers.

"Sweetheart, it's not a race. The longer it lasts, the longer we enjoy the pleasure."

She smiled and drew her hand away, loving how he teased her. She'd never known a man to be playful or show a gentle nature. She touched him with the tip of her finger and dragged it the length of him, then over the head and back down, loving the way his breath caught as she touched the tip.

She had never seen a penis close up, had certainly never wanted to touch one, but with this man, she felt safe. She wanted to take this opportunity to satisfy her curiosity, to touch it, explore it.

And she wanted to give him pleasure.

She touched the tip again, spiraled down and traced the lower ridge around the head, then stroked underneath. From his broken breaths and the little spasms of his body, she could tell he enjoyed it immensely. She licked the tip of her finger and dragged it over his tip again. His eyes flipped open.

"Oh, for a moment I thought ..."

He shook his head, smiling, but his eyes remained open, watching her.

She licked her finger again and dragged it around the tip of him. His eyelids drifted half closed.

"You know," he said, his voice husky, "some women ..." He trailed off, as if he had a suggestion he was hesitant to make.

"Yes, what is it?" she asked eagerly.

"Some women like to touch it with their mouth."

He paused, watching her reaction with hopeful anticipation. He had touched her with his mouth and it had brought her exquisite pleasure. She wanted to do that for him.

She leaned forward and kissed the tip of him, then moved down to the fur-covered sacks at the base, then back up. With the tip of her tongue, she dabbed at the small opening, tracing it with tiny circles. Encouraged by his soft moans, she licked him like a stick of candy, lapping at every part of his cock. The head, the shaft, the sacks. She loved the feel of his contours under her tongue and his reaction when she licked the ridge under the head. She teased him by tracing around and around, until his breathing was ragged.

"I promised myself I wouldn't ask you this, but ..."

"What is it?" She wanted to please him.

"I would love it if you took it inside your mouth," he murmured, his voice rough with passion.

She smiled and licked the tip of him, opened her mouth, and eased him inside slowly. With the entire head inside her mouth, she lapped her tongue around him, then wiggled it over the tip. He groaned.

"Sweetheart, at some point I'm going to explode." His breath caught as she sucked on him, pulling him in deeper. His hands captured her head, stilling her. "I'll release an ... emission. If you don't want that in your mouth ..."

She wrapped her hands around the base of him and stroked

upward, following her mouth as she released him, keeping as much of him as she could in the warm, wet prison of her hands.

"You mean your seed, don't you?"

He stroked her cheek with the tip of his finger. "That's right."

"It won't hurt me. Right?"

"That's right. You could swallow it if you wanted."

She smiled. "Fine." She slipped over him again and moved, up and down, licking and cajoling, watching his face contort in pleasure.

She squeezed and sucked while she gently grasped his furred balls in her hands. He groaned, and she moved faster, squeezed more firmly, drawing him deeper and deeper inside her mouth.

"Oh, God, sweetheart. Now."

He grunted and moaned deeply. She felt warm liquid spurt inside her mouth, warming and exciting her. She sucked and swallowed, continuing to stroke his balls. Finally, his taut, clenching muscles relaxed, and his huge rod stilled and slowly diminished in size. She eased it from her mouth and laid it on his belly, enjoying the sated expression on his face. He drew her to his side, and she curled up next to him as he held her close and kissed her forehead.

"*That* was incredible."

She loved that he echoed her words. As if the pleasure she'd given him matched what he'd given her. She hoped it was true.

She had never felt as safe as she did right then in his arms. Never again would she know such bliss.

But right now, she would enjoy it with every part of her being.

After several long, languorous moments, he rolled to his side and propped his head on his elbow, gazing down at her. His roguish smile and the glint in his eyes sent warmth shimmering through her.

"I don't even know your name."

"Shena."

"That's a lovely name." He stroked her hair behind her ear. "Shena, I want to get to know you better."

Warmth curled through her belly at his words.

"I'm returning to my family home after several years of traveling, and I can't think of a better way to settle in than to court a lovely young woman like you. Especially since I am so overwhelmingly attracted to you."

A gentle flush of pleasure traveled across her cheeks.

"I want to meet your family and state my intentions to your father."

His words jolted her like a slap across the face. Panic overwhelmed her at the thought of him meeting her father. She tried to gather her thoughts, muddled by the closeness of his hard, male body and the soft, loving look in his eyes.

When she was sixteen, a young man had shown interest in her. His name had been Jonediah. One evening, she had met him by the river, and he'd held her hand while they'd enjoyed a pleasant walk together. He had been about to kiss her when her father found them. Horrified, she had watched while her father beat Jonediah senseless, almost killing him. Afterward, he'd told her if she ever showed interest in a man again, other than one he'd chosen for her, he would kill him.

Keern leaned forward and kissed along her jaw, then murmured into her ear, "If things go as well as I expect they will, I can see us exploring more pleasures of the body ... in our wedding bed."

She stiffened and pulled away from him, then pushed herself to her feet. She would not allow him to be hurt because of her, but if she explained what had happened to Jonediah, he would probably try to rescue her from her father. Such recklessness would cost him his life. She needed a reason why she couldn't see him.

"What's wrong, Shena?"

She gathered her clothes and pulled them on. "What is your name?" she asked.

He stood up and retrieved his own clothing. He smiled. "Keern."

"And your last name is Herrington." Her throat tight, Shena watched as he tugged on his pants, hiding his magnificent maleness.

"Yes, that's right." He pulled on his shirt, hiding his broad, muscled chest from view.

She turned away. "I am a Wakefield. My father would never accept you."

"Ah, is that it." He reached for her, but she slid away. "If it's about this pond, I'd gladly give it to him if it would help win your hand."

"It's not about a stupid pond," she grated. "If my father knew what we had done here today, he would kill you. Just forget about me."

"I won't forget you," he said with determination. "And you won't forget this." He stepped forward and pulled her into his arms, then kissed her. Her ragged breathing revealed all too clearly how he affected her.

Staring at his fierce expression, she knew he would not listen. He would chase her — to his death. At the thought of him skewered by her father's sword, his life seeping away, agony sliced through her.

She had to stop him. She settled her weight evenly on her feet and slowed her breathing, feeling it move through her. Sometimes, when she was very afraid, she could reach within, to a strength deep inside herself, and, distancing herself from reality, draw on calm she did not feel. She thought about her father and the cold visage he displayed to the world, and she emulated it. She had to drive Keern away.

* * *

Keern watched her expression change. Calm, poised, sharp as a dagger. She had transformed from his beautiful wood nymph to a cold, manipulative woman.

"Did you really believe the role I played this afternoon?" The mockery in her words astonished him.

His eyes narrowed. "What do you mean?"

"I enjoy a romp with a stranger every now and again, and you were very good, but it was for one afternoon. That's all."

"You're telling me that what we shared was all a lie?"

"Of course. I enjoy playing the helpless virgin sometimes. I didn't think you'd really fallen for it. I thought you knew we were playacting."

His gut clenched. "I don't believe you."

How could he? She had enchanted him. Her sweetness had melted through him, totally claiming his heart.

The memory of Kolanna and how she had fooled him with her sweet, loving act stormed through his thoughts. Hadn't that agonizing incident taught him that he couldn't trust a woman? Any woman.

She raised her eyebrows. "I don't care if you believe me, or not. I'm tired of this game. And I'm tired of you." She shot him a look of disdain. "Stay away from me, or I'll tell my father you took me against my will." Her clipped, indifferent words cut through him. "Then he'll find you and kill you."

He grabbed her arm. "Why would you do that?"

She glared at his hand around her arm and jerked it away. "Because I don't want you to come near me again."

* * *

Keern rode toward his family home still seething at the memory of Shena and her trickery. Her transformation had shocked him.

How had he been so completely fooled by her act? Why hadn't he wondered at her willingness to do the things they'd done together? Of course, he'd not been thinking with his head so much as with his groin. She had backed off on the idea of intercourse, but then, she'd be shrewd enough to avoid pregnancy.

When he'd received the announcement of Jordan's wedding, nostalgia had started within him and along with it a desire to return to his place of birth and settle down like his two brothers, to find a gentle woman to marry, to start a family. Shena's sweet innocence had been so appealing. He had seen in her what he'd wanted to see in a woman.

As he rode toward the iron gates of his home, he heard the horn sound and whoops from the guards. His name sounded on their lips, along with shouts and hurrahs. He smiled as his gaze drifted along the gravel path curving through the meadow of wildflowers to the large stone-and-timber house about a half-kilometer up the hill.

It was good to be home.

The gates opened, and as he rode through, people rushed to the gate to greet him.

"Keern, you've finally arrived."

"Will." It had been a long time since he'd seen his older brother. A few more lines crinkled around Will's eyes, but other than that he hadn't changed.

Keern dismounted his horse, handing the reins to an eager pair of hands. He strode toward Will and held out his hand in the offer of a handshake, but his brother scoffed and dragged him into a bear hug, pounding his back for good measure.

"Come, the women want to see you."

"And what about Jordan?"

A huge grin split Will's face. "Yes, him, too."

They walked toward their family home, built with their father's own hands.

"He's not too busy dreaming of his wife-to-be?"

"Oh, I think he can spare a few moments for his older brother."

Jordan, their younger brother, was to wed four days hence. Keern had made the trip to join in the festivities. He hadn't told them yet that he intended to stay, not wanting to disappoint them if he changed his mind.

"We leave on the morrow to Chamberlan. Kristinna's family is looking forward to meeting you."

"Brother, here you are." At Jordan's voice, Keern spun around.

He smiled at the sight of his younger brother. He stood as tall as Keern himself, a man now. Keern had known the lad must have grown, but with the reality staring him in the face, he felt sadness at having missed so much.

Jordan threw his arms around Keern in the same bear hug as Will's. "So, the star-traveler returns."

"As if I'd miss my favorite brother's wedding."

"That's what you said when you came for mine!" Will cut in.

Keern flung his arms around both their shoulders, laughing. "Of course. You're both my favorite."

At the house, the women greeted him with exuberance. Will's wife, Jenna, a tall, graceful woman, gave him a warm hug. Their cousin, Helena, pleasantly round and ever-smiling, gave him a kiss on the cheek, and her husband, Jacob, shook his hand.

Entering the house triggered a plethora of painful memories.

Their father had died when Keern was six years old. Will had become the head of the household at a young age, and they had all pulled together as a family, becoming closer than most.

Despite that closeness, Keern had withdrawn after his mother's death.

Where Will's job was to run the family, Keern had decided his was to protect their mother. He was determined he could protect her from anything, if he tried hard enough — and he put his heart and soul into doing just that. The illness, however, had slipped right past him, stealing her away with a finality that had devastated Keern.

After her death, everything around him had reminded him of her. The rocking chair where she'd rocked him in her arms as a child, the woods where they'd gone for long walks and talks about life, the fields where they'd worked together, shoulder to shoulder, alongside his brothers.

He had felt strangely betrayed by her. Abandoned. Although he knew logically she'd had no choice, his heart had known nothing of logic.

So once he'd turned 16, he left the family and traveled — partly to escape his pain, partly to understand the universe around him. In that universe, he'd found new experiences, new worlds, and excitement beyond measure. What he hadn't found was love, nor anything that could replace the sense of belonging that he felt when he was with his family.

Returning to this place now, after all these years, still prodded him with painful memories, but they were dulled. He intended to dredge up the happy memories and heap them on top. To embrace his family and move forward with his life.

To finally heal the wounds.

The women had arranged a wonderful feast to welcome Keern.

He spent the evening in the glow of warm family conversation.

As the hour grew late and the fire warmed his outside while the wine warmed his insides, his thoughts turned back to Shena. Another painful memory.

He'd never see her again, if fate was kind, but somehow he knew he'd never forget her. He remembered the sweet scent of her hair, the softness of her skin, the delicate taste of her body.

"That is my wife's favorite goblet, so I think I shall retrieve it from you before you snap it in two."

At Will's words, Keern shifted his gaze from the fire to the glass he held, his hand clenched tightly around it. He allowed Will to take it and set it gently on the rough wood table in front of him.

Will settled in the chair beside him. "Where were your thoughts, brother?"

"On a woman."

Will chuckled. "I see. Anyone in particular?"

Keern scowled. "Do you know Shena Wakefield?"

chapter four

Will's brows rose. "Wakefield, eh? I know Henry Wakefield has a daughter." He swirled the wine in his goblet.

"That's right," Jordan chimed in. "In her twenties. Pretty thing, from what I've heard, but he pretty much keeps her under wraps. Planning to make a profitable marriage, I'll wager."

"How do you know of her?" Will asked.

"I stopped for water at Sersa's pond, and I saw her there."

The memory of her naked, glistening body flashed into his mind. Need pulsed through him, impossible to ignore. His jaw clenched.

"She obviously had an effect on you."

Keern's glance darted to Will, but relaxed at his brother's amused expression.

"The woman is lovely to look upon, but she has the disposition of a devil," Keern responded.

"That's a Wakefield, all right." Jenna poured more wine in his goblet and sat down across from him.

"The father's a mean one," Helena chimed in. "He treats his servants more like slaves, and we've heard of terrible cruelties."

"Plus, he hates us," Will added.

Keern glanced across at him. "Why?"

"Because he wants our land," Jordan answered. "He'd love any excuse to wipe us off the face of the planet. But he knows the other landowners would band against him. He's got far too hungry an eye as it is."

"He's always been hungry for land, 'tis true," Helena said. "But you know, the reason he hates us is more personal. His wife used to come here a lot, needin' to get away from his foul moods. Theirs was an arranged marriage, you know?"

"That's right." Jenna poured some more wine, then sat down beside Will. "The rumor is, he fell in love with her at first sight, and *his* father, who gave his son anything he asked for, arranged the marriage. Young Wakefield must have believed the woman would fall madly in love with him, but in truth, he frightened her with his aggressive ways."

Will tipped his glass to his lips, then set it on the table. "I remember how, when I was young, she'd come to visit with her baby daughter."

"Why don't I remember any of this?" Keern asked.

Will leaned forward, a wide smile on his face, and tousled Keern's hair as if he were a little boy. "Because, brother, you were barely three years old."

Keern ran his fingers through his hair to smooth it back in place. "I still don't see why he hates us."

"Because," Jenna said, "he believed she and your uncle were having an affair."

Keern's gaze jolted back to Will, who nodded.

"Uncle Jeb?" Keern could scarcely believe it. He didn't remember his uncle well — he'd disappeared when Keern was very young — but from everything he'd ever heard about him, he'd believed his uncle to be an honorable man. Certainly not someone Keern would suspect of having an affair with another man's wife.

Keern had always admired Uncle Jeb, especially his sense of adventure. Keern had followed his uncle's example when choosing to travel across the stars, undaunted by the fact that everyone assumed Jeb had died on some exotic planet, since no one had ever heard from him again.

"I'm not saying he actually had an affair with her," Will said. "Wakefield was jealous, domineering, and extremely possessive of his wife. She was actually afraid of him." Anger flared in his eyes.

Jenna placed a hand on her husband's arm and stroked gently. "Realize he loved this woman and she didn't return his love. His ego would demand he find a reason to justify her not loving him. Another man was a simple solution."

"And Uncle Jeb actually did love her." At Will's quiet words, everyone turned to stare at him. "He didn't act on it, but I overheard our mother and father talking. They were convinced he loved her. I'm sure that's why he left. He couldn't bear to be so close to her and not be with her."

"She died of *Gahdagha* flu soon after that," Jenna added.

Helena leaned forward conspiratorially. "Or so they say."

"Helena." Jenna shook her head. "Those are just rumors."

"True." Helena's fingers toyed with the stem of her goblet. "Some rumors say that Wakefield killed her. Others say that he sold her to the traders."

Keern leaned back in his chair, disturbed by the turn of the conversation. "That doesn't make sense. How could a man do that to his own wife?"

Jacob sighed heavily. "You really don't know Henry Wakefield, cousin."

The others nodded their heads. Keern's gut twisted inside. With a father like that, no wonder Shena had learned to be so callous.

Will grinned, in contrast to the long faces around the table.

"I must admit, it would be a lovely irony if you and his daughter had taken a shine to each other and wound up in wedlock. Then our two lands would be joined, but not in the way he had hoped."

Keern swallowed some wine, pushing aside heart-rending images of Shena joining hands with him in front of a flower-veiled altar, a delicate blush on her cheeks as she leaned toward him for the wedding kiss. A more vivid blush covering her entire body as they joined in the wedding bed. His body tightened, and he longed to feel her gentle curves again, but this time while thrusting into her body. He longed to make her completely and forever his.

Slamming those thoughts into the dark recesses of his mind, he plunked his glass onto the table.

"Talking about wedlock, shouldn't we be discussing Jordan's impending doom — I mean, joining?"

The men roared in laughter under the glares of the women, then began a hearty discussion of the events to come.

* * *

Keern awoke with a start. Actually, with a jolting release. He became aware of a warm stickiness on his stomach.

Dehn'ra, another dream about that witch of a woman.

He flung aside the covers and stormed to the window. Moonlight illuminated the rolling hills of unfamiliar land surrounding the manor of Jordan's new family.

He raked his fingers through his hair.

Over the past four days, Keern had tried to keep his focus on his family and the wedding of his brother. There was much to keep him busy, but still he couldn't keep visions of his beautiful wood nymph from his mind. How could she have turned out to be such a brittle, scheming woman?

Night after night, in the depths of his dreams, he felt her soft, white skin beneath his fingers, heard her delicious moans of pleasure, and he exploded in passion. And every morning, he awoke to wet evidence of his folly.

He had started to hate her, as much for his primal, loathsome longing as for her callous actions.

He would forget her. With time.

Today had been Jordan's wedding day. Tomorrow, they'd be back on the road. Once he was home again, he would find a way to get Shena out of his mind.

* * *

Shena awoke with a start as someone ripped back her covers and hauled her out of bed. As her bleary vision focused, she realized the rough-handed man dragging her along the cold marble floor, barely waiting for her stumbling feet to keep up, was Bahrd, the most brutal of her father's men. He always leered at her as though waiting for the opportunity to strip her naked and violate her. The skin on her arms pebbled in goose bumps, and her chest constricted so tightly she could barely breathe. Oh, God, had that opportunity arrived?

A semi-toothless grin claimed his face as his gaze raked across her, as though he read her thoughts.

"Yer father wants te see ye."

Her anxiety did not diminish at that revelation. As he dragged her down the corridor, she wondered if this had anything to do with Keern.

Four painful days ago, she had left Keern with that dreadful, but necessary, lie. She'd felt violently ill as she'd raced home. She'd stolen up to her room and curled into a ball on her bed, sobbing.

Over the next few days, the image of Keern's handsome face, filled with loathing, remained burned in her memory.

Yet in her dreams, he bound her in a web of sexual desire and took out his anger in beautiful bouts of passion.

Bahrd pushed open the door to her father's study, and she cringed as he shoved her inside.

"There you are, daughter."

Her father sat in the tall brown leather chair behind his shiny ebony desk. He removed his glasses and placed them on the book he'd been reading. A fire blazed in the marble fireplace, radiating a warm glow. He rubbed his well-trimmed beard, then tapped his long, elegant fingers on the desktop as he watched her, light dancing across the navy silk of his vest.

His composure didn't fool her. In his ice-grey eyes, she saw danger. He hid it well from others, but she had learned to read the intensity of his anger within the calm depths.

"I've heard you've been meeting with a man."

She remained silent, unable to utter a word. How had he found out about Keern?

He pushed himself to his feet and strode toward her. "You were seen at Sersa's pond with a man who claimed you were his woman. Is this true?"

She glanced at the floor.

He struck her swiftly, a bone-jarring blow to the jaw, knocking her off her feet. Pain jolted through her hands as they hit the hard stone floor, breaking her fall.

"Is it true?" The tone of his words, strung taut as a tightrope, demanded an answer.

She straightened her arms, pushing herself onto her hip, legs curled to one side.

"No, not exactly. I — "

He kicked her in the ribs, knocking her to the ground again. Blinding pain shot through her, and she could barely suck in enough air to keep from passing out.

"Not exactly?" he sneered. "Does that mean you're *not exactly* a virgin anymore?"

"I am," she choked, then coughed, trying to catch her breath. "I am still a virgin."

His eyes narrowed as he glared down at her. "Even if you are, Drakemont doesn't believe it. He'll never wed you now."

Her father had been intending to marry her off to Reginald Drakemont? He was a foul-smelling miser of a man. Cruel and demanding. He frightened her almost as much as her father.

He kicked her again. Tears welled in her eyes from the exploding pain in her chest.

He grabbed her hair and pulled her head back, forcing her to look into his eyes. Into torrents of rage.

"I wanted that marriage. I wanted the platinum he offered for you and the alliance between our families. Our combined forces could have dominated the entire region."

He released her with such force, her face smacked against the cold, hard floor. Pain lanced through her cheekbone, and she shuddered as she suppressed a sob.

"Now you've ruined it." He strode away from her, then stood

staring out the window, his hands clasped behind his back. "I'm told the man you were with was a Herrington. Is that also true, daughter?"

She pushed herself to her knees. "I'd never seen him before, but he protected me from some soldiers who came along."

"Drakemont's soldiers. Who I'm sure you had no reason to fear."

So that's how he knew. One of them must have recognized her.

"Was his name Herrington?" he demanded.

"I don't know."

"Don't lie to me. Right now, your usefulness to me is close to nil since everyone believes you are soiled. If you lie to me about this, then I must believe you're lying to me about being a virgin."

His voice grew very quiet. "That means I have no choice but to follow through on my promise."

He glanced toward Bahrd, who stood at the door, grinning at her. She trembled, remembering the young housekeeper. Remembering Bahrd violently thrusting into her. Remembering her father's promise that she would suffer the same fate should she ever lose her virginity — and her usefulness to him.

"You have one more chance to answer truthfully. Was his name Herrington?"

She hesitated, and he dragged her to her feet and propelled her toward the door and the sneering lout. Oh, God, no. The thought of those rough brutes and what they'd do to her ... She couldn't ...

"Yes," she cried, hating herself for her weakness. "His name was Herrington."

He released her arm and she fell to the floor.

"Those *dehn'rad* Herringtons will pay dearly for this."

She quivered at his words. Saying anything to try to help Keern would only make matters worse. If her father suspected she had feelings for the man, he would relish the revenge even more. She could only pray Keern would survive her father's wrath.

He shoved her at Bahrd. "Keep an eye on her until I get back. I don't want her talking to anyone."

Bahrd wrenched her arm from her father's grasp and dragged her through the door.

* * *

"For heaven's sake, Keern. Go ride ahead. Your restlessness is unsettling the horses."

Keern glanced at the carriage carrying the women, then back to Will riding horseback beside him. What if thieves attacked?

"But if there's trouble — "

"There won't be. Even if there were, we could handle it."

Keern nodded to Will, thankful for his brother's instincts. His brothers and cousin, the carriage driver, and the five soldiers accompanying them should be able to handle any danger that came their way.

Keeping pace with the carriage was a difficult task today. He wanted to feel speed, to allow the wind to sweep his brain clean of unwanted memories. If he'd been on Kulasta, the planet he'd called home for the past two years, he'd have climbed into his air car and sped up to two hundred kilometers per hour, letting the landscape fly past in a blur.

"I'll ride as far as the hill, then wait for you."

"Go." Will waved him away. "As far as you need."

Keern rode and rode, forgetting about time and distance. When he reached the valley, he stopped and dismounted, then sat on a rock and listened to the *garals* twittering and warbling in the trees. A cacophony of sound surrounded him.

But a distant noise drew his attention. Listening intently, he thought he heard shouts, then a scream. He bounded onto his horse and rode up the hill. At the top, his heart lunged to his throat as he saw the carriage halted, surrounded by armed men. Swords clacked against each other as men battled.

Keern rode at top speed, returning to protect his family. These men didn't look like thieves. Why in the world were they attacking?

Two of Will's soldiers were down, and he saw one of the enemy thrust his sword through the driver. Quickly, Keern took down two of the attackers as he fought his way to his family. His heart leaped as he saw the man who appeared to be the leader lunge a sword into Will's chest.

"No!" Keern raced toward the man, sword raised.

The man jerked aside in time to dodge Keern's blade, then turned his horse and fled. The others followed. Keern realized there were only three of them left, to their five still standing.

"Jordan, stay with Will and the women. Men, follow me," Keern commanded, then galloped after the retreating figures. The soldiers followed his lead.

The fleeing men scattered.

"I'll follow the leader; you men get the others," Keern directed.

After a few miles, he caught up with the leader and swung his sword, wounding the man's left arm and driving him off his horse. He ran, but Keern leaped from his horse, knocking the man to the ground.

"Who the hell are you, and why did you attack us?" Keern demanded.

"I am Henry Wakefield." He pushed himself to his feet, throwing a look of disdain Keern's way. "One of you Herrington devils defiled my daughter."

Wakefield. Shena's father.

"Why do you believe that?"

"My daughter told me."

Shena had lied about their encounter, just as she'd threatened. That witch had caused Will's death!

Wakefield's eyes narrowed, and he raised his sword. "It was you, wasn't it?"

His eyes filled with rage and he lunged at Keern, swinging wildly. Keern easily countered, forcing the man backward.

They fought hard for several minutes, but Keern dodged Wakefield's final thrust and sank his sword squarely into the man's chest.

Keern gained no satisfaction from Wakefield's death. It wouldn't bring Will back. Nothing would bring Will back. Despair gripped him in an awful, frigid hold. His brother was dead.

And Shena had been the cause. He would never forgive her for what she'd done. And somehow, he would find a way to make her pay.

chapter five

Keern slung Wakefield's body over the back of his horse, tied it down, and raced back to his family. The women sat weeping in the back of the carriage, with Will's body across Jenna's lap. One of the soldiers had already returned, one of Wakefield's men still draped over the back of his horse, and was helping their cousin Jacob lay the bodies out along the side of the road. A few minutes later, the others returned.

Keern desperately wanted to ride ahead, to take Wakefield's body and dump it on the chief constable, then race to Wakefield's house and drag Shena to prison. He wasn't sure what the charges would be, but there must be some way to punish her for causing Will's death.

But Keern wouldn't leave his family now. Thoughts of Shena had sent him riding ahead a mere hour ago, taking him away when he was most needed.

If he hadn't gone ahead, maybe Will would still be alive.

* * *

Keern slammed his fist on the official's desk.

"Chief Constable Murray, Shena Wakefield is responsible for Will's death."

The man leaned forward in his chair, his steel-blue eyes clashing with Keern's. "Mr. Herrington, if she didn't wield the sword, then I don't see how I can arrest her."

Jacob clutched Keern's arm. Keern eased back at the gentle pressure from his cousin's hold. The constable knew Jacob. Maybe he could get somewhere.

"Wade, can you at least bring her in for questioning?"

The man's flashing eyes lost their edge as they shifted to Jacob. Chief Constable Murray took a deep breath.

Keern lowered himself into one of the leather chairs facing the desk, then glanced out the large windows on the adjacent wall. The sun had disappeared behind the trees, and the clouds above them were lined in pink and purple.

"Jacob, look, I've got to ride out and tell the girl about her father. You and your cousin can ride with me, as long as you keep him in line."

Keern fumed, but knew it wasn't really directed at this man, but at Shena. The woman who had betrayed him and cost him his brother.

Keern, Jacob, and Chief Constable Murray arrived at the Wakefield house after nightfall. A guard let them in the front gate, and they rode on to the house.

In the light of Aos, the largest moon circling Tarun, the place appeared cold and sinister. The branches of the large *agoba* trees arched outward, casting looming shadows across the enormous house and the stone pathway leading to it.

They approached the huge, curved wooden doors, and Murray grabbed the brass knocker, rapping it against the door, sharp and loud.

A long time passed, and he rapped again.

Finally, the large door creaked open, revealing a burly man almost two meters in height, with a straggly brown beard and equally straggly, shoulder-length hair.

"Bahrd, I've come with bad news," Murray said. "Henry Wakefield is dead."

The man's eyes darkened as he scowled.

"I've come to talk to his daughter," Murray continued.

The man's face closed up. "Can't say I know where she be."

"Then you'd better find her," Keern demanded.

The man's shoulders squared and he leaned forward. "And who's going to make me?"

Keern started forward, but Jacob grabbed his arm.

"Bahrd," Murray interjected, "I need to speak with her. Go find her."

The man glared at Keern, then glanced back to Murray. "I don't think lookin'll turn her up, Chief."

"Do you think she'll turn up by tomorrow morning?"

Bahrd shrugged.

"I see. Let's put it this way. I want her at the courthouse by nine tomorrow morning, or I'll come out looking for her. Got it?"

The large man shrugged again. "Whatever ye say, Chief."

Keern itched to plow past the man and search the house room by room until he found the lying bitch, but that wouldn't get him anywhere right now. He followed the chief constable and Jacob away from the Wakefield house.

Tomorrow, he would see Shena again. His heart stumbled a little at the thought, an image of her sweet, smiling face swirling through his head, which just cranked his anger up a notch.

Shena had been awakened by the loud knocking, not that she'd been sleeping very heavily, with Bahrd hanging around her door, watching her. She heard men's voices outside, but couldn't hear their words. At the thunderous sound of Bahrd's boots on the wooden stairs, she clung to her covers, watching the door.

He appeared in the doorway, a gigantic, looming shape backlit by the moonlight from the large window over the stairs.

"Looks like yer an orphan, lass." He stepped toward her and dragged the covers from her body. She lay on the bed, shivering in her light cotton nightgown. His gaze raked over her.

"I been wantin' a piece o' that for a longen now." His hand rested on her thigh and slowly slid upward.

She scrambled up the bed, leaving his hand behind. He grabbed her ankles and dragged her back down, then flung his arms wide, opening her legs. The feral gleam in his eyes jabbed at the deepest fears squirming inside her.

"What do you mean, I'm an orphan?"

"What do ye think I mean, girl? Yer father is dead. Killed by one of them Herringtons. But not afore he killed the one he was after, I'd wager."

Shock pummeled through her. Her father was dead.

Was Keern dead, too? Her heart constricted, and sharp pain lanced through her.

Bahrd's grunt dragged her back to her current situation. With her father gone, she would be at the mercy of the soldiers. Legally, she now owned her father's holdings, but she knew as soon as her father's soldiers heard of his death, they'd strip the property bare and take off. She was sure they wouldn't hesitate to take their pleasure from her before they left.

Bahrd released one of her ankles, then tugged his belt strap and released it from the buckle.

Her heart hammered wildly in her chest. Her only chance was to appeal to Bahrd's greed.

"Do you really want to do this?"

"Oh, yeah." He tugged the zipper down on his pants. "I want to do it every way possible, then watch while the others do it."

"You know, the slavers will pay a lot more for me as a virgin. My father always told me so." She made her voice as persuasive as she could.

"Eh?" He paused and rubbed his chin. "The slavers?"

"You are going to sell me, right? I mean, if you don't, one of the others will, but you're here first. If you can sell me as a virgin ..."

"You're just sayin' this 'cause you don't want to get fucked."

"Of course." A tinge of anger colored her voice, hard as she tried to conceal it. "But it's also true. You and I will both do better if you leave me untouched and take me to the slavers."

Never in her wildest dreams had she ever thought she'd be begging to be taken to the slavers, but right now, that threat was a lot more distant than the leering Bahrd and the prospect of her father's men climbing on top of her one after another.

Bahrd grunted, staring at her, his gaze sliding up her legs and pinning on the crotch of her white panties, fully exposed. She held her breath, watching him.

"You know, with the money you get for me, you can enjoy a lot of women at the brothel."

Finally, he grunted and grabbed her wrist, then dragged her through the house, out the back door to the closed wagon. He pushed aside the tarp covering the door and shoved her through, then bound her wrists and ankles. He wrapped a gag around her mouth.

He disappeared back into the house and reappeared about a half-hour later to fling a large cloth bag beside her. It made a loud clunk when it hit the wagon floor. Probably filled with all kinds of treasures and whatever money he'd found in her father's office. She heard him attaching the horse to the wagon, and a few moments later, the wagon jerked forward.

Hours passed and she must have dozed off, but a sudden lurch of the wagon jolted her wide awake. Nightmares of men pawing at her, their large, rough hands touching every intimate part of her, left her in a sweat. The rope around her wrists and ankles cut into her skin. The gag was damp with saliva.

Outside, the throng of a city market sounded around them. Vendors calling out to attract buyers, carts rumbling past the main road, horses snorting. The smells of fruits, spices, and cooked meat assailed her.

They were close. She cringed, her whole body rigid with fear. Her shaky stomach quaked, almost to the point of vomiting.

The noise reached a crescendo, then slowly diminished as the cart continued and finally stopped. They would be at the back corner of the market, away from the buyers. Her father had pointed out the place to her many times. This was where the slavers made their deals for new stock. It was illegal on Turan to buy or sell slaves, but the authorities looked the other way as long as the dealings were discreet and the right people were paid off.

Moonlight glinted in her face as Bahrd slung back the tarp over the back of the wagon. His knife blade flashed, grazing her skin as he sliced through the ropes around her ankles. Blood oozed from the small nick he'd made on her foot, and it stung sharply, but she hardly noticed as he hauled her to her feet and out of the cart. Her legs ached from lying immobile on the wagon floor for so many hours, but she hobbled to keep up with him as he dragged her forward, his meaty hand tightly wrapped around her forearm.

The sky was black and studded with stars, but unnatural light shone all around them. They approached a large metallic wagon, rounded and shiny, the likes of which Shena had never seen before. By rights, it should not be allowed here, nor should their artificial lights, given that technology was banned from Tarun, but the slavers took a great many liberties with the law.

Several hooded figures stood outside the wagon, interacting with locals. All the slavers wore long, tan, hooded cloaks. Sometimes a flash of rust-colored leather clothing and dark brown boots and gloves could be seen as they moved. One of the slavers glanced toward them as they approached.

"I'm bringin' this lass to ye for sale. She's Wakefield's daughter. A virgin. He's talked to ye about price before."

Below the hood, piercing eyes flashed, locking on her. Then the man nodded. "Follow me."

He opened the door of the metal wagon and led them inside. Two men glanced up from their conversation. They wore the same garb as the other slavers, but their hoods were down, draped over their shoulders and backs. One had dark, shoulder-length hair and a moustache and beard, while the other had fine, short blond hair and was clean-shaven. The dark-haired one stood up and approached them. The man who'd led them inside spoke to the other two in a language Shena didn't understand, and then Dark Hair grabbed her arm and tugged her forward.

"Wait a minute. I ain't been paid yet," Bahrd complained.

"We must verify that she's a virgin."

A chill started along Shena's neck and shivered down her spine.

Bahrd started forward to follow, but the hooded man stepped in front of him.

"Out of my way. I want to watch."

Dark Hair stopped and glanced back. So did Shena.

Bahrd shoved the man in front of him, smaller by at least a head. The man touched Bahrd with one gloved hand, and he lurched backward, clearly in pain.

"You will sit and wait," the slaver stated with authority.

Shena continued staring behind her as Dark Hair dragged her forward again, through a doorway, toward one of her greatest fears. He closed the door behind her, and she glanced around to see a large chair-like thing made of long pipes or rods of some sort.

"Sit," the man commanded.

She glanced at the contraption, uncertain. Dark Hair grabbed her arms and spun her around, then backed her into the thing, pushing her downward. A strap slung under her thighs about six inches from her knees caught her weight, and another hugged her back at her waist. He grabbed her right wrist, positioned it above her head, and strapped it to the vertical rod on the right side of the chair thing, then took her left wrist and attached it to the left rod. Next, he tugged her leg forward, parallel to a horizontal rod extending straight out in front of her, and strapped her ankle to the hard metal. Similarly, he restrained her other ankle.

He stepped toward a high table jutting out from the wall, where he tapped on buttons and stared at some kind of changing display. With a whirring sound, the rods started to move, flattening out, positioning her in a stretched-out, horizontal position; then the ones at her ankles separated, opening her legs.

chapter six

Shena's breaths became short and hollow. The man stepped toward her, scissors in his hand, and pushed up her gown, exposing her underwear. She gasped as he slipped his finger under the white cotton at the crotch and tugged the garment away from her body, then clipped the cloth with the scissors, exposing her most private flesh. Her face burned.

Oh, God, this is really happening.

He slid his hand away, his fingers grazing her pubic curls. What was almost more frightening than his touch was the total look of indifference on his face. He returned to his controls and tapped at the buttons. A movement near her ankles drew her attention. A silver device moved toward her, a long, slender oval, like a fat cigar, moving upward between her knees. She tried to close her legs, but the straps held her firm. In fact, she realized that she couldn't move her lower body at all. Panic roared within her. Her wrists strained against the straps as she tried to kick her legs, but nothing happened.

The device continued moving higher, now between her thighs. She sucked in deep breaths as it came closer, zeroing in on her womanhood, and her breath caught as the cold, hard metal nudged against her.

Her vision blurred and she felt faint.

Oh, God ... Oh, God ... Oh, God.

Was it going to thrust inside her?

Thoughts spun wildly through her head, but the device stopped when it firmly pressed against her soft flesh, slightly parting the folds.

She released the air from her lungs, then drew in another breath. They were checking if she was a virgin, she reminded herself. It wouldn't be very useful if the test itself broke her maidenhead.

Every muscle tensed, she waited for what would happen next. Her shallow breathing left her feeling light-headed. Suddenly, nausea rolled through her stomach as something — or things — seemed to crawl into her, like the legs of some giant spider. They crept up the walls of her vagina, then continued moving deep inside her, probably into her womb. She lay stiff and shaking as the things prodded her insides. She had never known a moment so long or filled with such dread as she now experienced. It seemed like hours as the tendrils swirled inside her. Then painfully, slowly, they withdrew. The cold device eased away from her.

Her head flopped back, her neck resting on another strap. At least that was over. The whirring began again, but this time, the rods drew her upright and folded her forward, her backside thrust behind her, her legs still held wide apart. She couldn't see it, but she could feel a cold metal device brush against her buttocks, then settle firmly against her anus. It pushed forward a fraction more, opening her a little, and then the tendrils invaded her again. Tears prickled at her eyes as the device squirmed within her, fluttering against her insides, torturing her with an almost intangible touch. A few moments later, the tendrils slipped out, and the device drew away.

This time, the whirring rods returned her to a sitting position, but another device approached her face. When she tried to jerk away, she found she couldn't move her shoulders, neck, or head.

The device pushed between her lips, and the tendrils explored the inside of her mouth, then slid down her throat. She felt the need to gag, but her body did not obey. She felt sick at the invasion of her body, but she wondered if the butterflies in her stomach were nausea, or the legs of the device swirling inside her.

The tendrils withdrew, and Shena, once again able to move, immediately threw up all over the sterile-looking white floor. Her captor didn't even look up as the foul smell of her vomit filled the room. A small, round device on wheels, about a foot around and three inches high, scurried across the floor and disposed of the mess, leaving the floor gleaming white once again.

A few moments later, after tapping on his buttons and staring at his device, the man released the straps at her wrists and ankles. She immediately shoved her gown down to cover herself. He pulled her to her feet and led her back to the other room, then pushed her into a chair. A regular one this time, although not like the wooden ones Shena was used to.

Bahrd stared at her as if she might have found a way to cheat him; then he turned to the slavers. The original man who'd brought her and Bahrd to the wagon had left.

"Well? Where's my money?"

"In good time." The blond man wrapped a thin, black cord around her wrist. "We must take her statement next."

"Her statement? And why do ye think she'll tell the truth?"

"Because this device will tell us if she's lying." The blond slaver turned to Shena. "Have you ever had vaginal intercourse with a man?"

She dropped her gaze and shook her head.

"I need you to answer me out loud. Have you ever had vaginal intercourse with a man?"

"No." The word barely came out audible from her tense, dry throat.

"Have you ever had anal intercourse with a man?"

"He's askin' if a man ever stuck his dick up yer ass," Bahrd leered.

Her already flaming cheeks flared hotter. "N-no."

Good God, why would they ask such a thing?

"Have you ever had oral intercourse with a man?"

Her eyes widened, and she locked gazes with the indifferent gray eyes of her interrogator for a split second before shifting to stare at her hands. "No."

"Why don't you try that answer again?" Blond Hair said, voice matter-of-fact.

"He's askin' if you ever sucked a man's prick," Bahrd interjected. He leaned forward, his mud-brown gaze intense. "Have you?"

She remembered the feel of Keern's rigid cock in her mouth, the way she had lovingly stroked it with her tongue.

"I ... But that's not sex. I'm still a virgin."

Bahrd's hawk-eyes locked on her with keen interest.

"Yes or no," Blond Hair asked.

She nodded.

"I need you to — "

"Yes," she said out loud.

"With how many men?"

Her hands clenched around the arms of the chair. "One."

"How many times?"

"Once. Only once."

"So? What does this mean?" Bahrd demanded.

"Technically, it means she's a level-two-B virgin."

"What's that?"

"Level-three means all three orifices are virgin. Two means two are; one means only one. Level-two-B means only the mouth is not virgin, and level-two-A means the anus."

Bahrd lurched to his feet and started unbuckling his pants as he moved toward Shena. He pulled his dangling prick out of his pants and pushed it at Shena's mouth.

Shena cringed in revulsion.

Dark Hair grabbed Bahrd's arms before he could push it against her lips.

"What do you think you're doing?"

"Well, I ain't been paid yet, and since she sucked cock before, I'm aimin' to get my share before she's sold."

"Not a wise business move."

"Eh?"

"I said she is *technically* a level-two-B," Blond Hair explained. "In cases like this, we have some leeway. Given only one incident, we don't have to disclose that information and can sell her as a full virgin."

Bahrd lurched forward again.

"If one's okay, two won't make a difference."

Blond Hair shoved Bahrd back into his chair.

"When buying a virgin, our patrons desire a woman who is naïve in the ways of sex," Blond Hair said. "Two times can very well make a difference, but more importantly, it will put us outside our regulated tolerance level. We have a clear understanding with Mr. Wakefield. He is entitled to the full amount for this virgin. If you wish to have her perform oral sex on you, you will be required to pay the difference."

He eyed Shena. "How much?"

Shena knew he'd be reluctant to admit that her father was dead. They'd probably buy her anyway, but the weight of her father's status behind the deal gave him a better bargaining position.

"One thousand local credits."

"A thousand?" His fists clenched. "No woman is worth that."

Shena gulped a sigh of relief as he shoved his limp member away and zipped up.

"Look, you're not leaving for a few days," Bahrd continued. "How 'bout I bring back a few friends, maybe twenty or so. We'll split the thou'. A lot of 'em would love to fuck her face. Fifty each wouldn't be so bad."

Shena shuddered at the thought, her already queasy stomach lurching.

"Out of the question," Dark Hair responded. "If you paid the thousand and used her, she would then be officially classified as level-two-B, and we'd make her available in the brothel while we're here. In that case, we would keep the thousand plus the fifty per man."

Shena shuddered again. Her father had told her the slavers often put their slaves into the local brothels. A big attraction was the night they made the locally purchased slaves available. The men seemed to love the opportunity to be with women they knew and couldn't have had before.

Bahrd's expression turned sour. "Fine. Just give me the money."

Several moments later, with the exchange of money and a bill of sale declaring payment for a full virgin, Bahrd was on his way.

Shena glanced around, wondering what would come next. She didn't have long to wait. Dark Hair grasped her arm at the wrist and elbow, and before she had a chance to pull away, Blond Hair pressed a metal rod against her skin. Searing pain and the smell of burning flesh assaulted her at the same time. She cried out, tears prickling at her eyes. When he removed the rod, she saw a circle about an inch in diameter burned into the tender white flesh about three inches from her wrist. A single line radiated from the centre of the circle to the edge.

Dark Hair exclaimed in some foreign language, then yelled at Blond Hair. He disappeared into the other room and returned a moment later, holding a metal device. When he brought it near her, Shena cringed, but Blond Hair held out her arm while the other held the device to the branded skin. Seconds later, the mark, along with the lingering pain, disappeared.

What an amazing healing device. But why in the world had they inflicted the brand on her, only to remove it? Blond Hair continued to hold her arm, and Dark Hair put the healing device down, then grabbed the rod again. He fiddled with a lever on the end of it, then pressed it into her flesh once again. She cried out, then whimpered as they branded her once again. This time the mark was a simple circle.

Dazed, she stared at the angry red skin as the men placed metal bands, connected by a chain, around her wrists. One of them led her out the door and around the back to a truck. She'd heard the word in reference to the self-powered vehicles the slavers, and some of the other rich merchants, used to transport goods from the space-port to the market. Another transgression allowed to the wealthy off-worlders who could buy themselves past the law.

The door on the back of the truck creaked open, revealing twenty or more women packed inside, sitting along each side of the truck or on the floor. Her captor pushed her inside and closed the door behind her. A little light entered the dismal space from a small window in the door. No one said a word. Shena continued to stand, uncomfortable with so many bodies so close.

About twenty minutes later, the door opened again and two

more dazed women were pushed into the truck. The door closed behind them.

A rumbling started, and the vehicle lurched forward, slamming Shena against one of the newcomers, who hit the door with a thud. The floor bounced below them. Shena pressed her hand against the door and eased herself to the floor, as did the other two women.

About a half-hour later, the truck stopped and the door opened.

Four hooded slavers stood outside.

"Get out."

Shena was glad of the breeze across her face as she pushed herself from the truck and the heavy closeness of the air inside.

The slaver ship lay about a hundred meters ahead. Big, flat, dull silver. The hull, which had always appeared smooth from a distance, was made up of all kinds of panels with handles and devices jutting out. The ships had always looked so tiny up in the sky, but this one seemed gigantic, with its yawning door and the darkness within.

The guards herded the women onto the ramp leading to the door. Shena's knees almost buckled as she realized her father's nightmare threat had finally become a reality.

She had been sold to the slavers.

The large hatch closed behind them, blocking out the setting sun and probably her last view of her world.

Shena and the others were led to a large open area just inside the ship's entrance. One by one, their chains were removed, and they were left standing there for a long time. Finally, a tall, bearded man followed by two guards came and led them into a narrow corridor. After a few turns left and right, one of the guards opened a door to an empty room about fifteen feet square. The women plodded inside, glancing around. In the walls, there were niches about six feet long and two feet high. They were stacked six high, about twenty-four in all. Shena did a quick count of the women. Twenty-two including herself.

"I think that's where we sleep," one woman whispered.

"Silence." The tall, bearded man strode into the center of the room. A guard closed the door.

"Most of you will be taken to E'Le'Dor, where you will be sold as slaves. Along the way, we will stop at two more worlds, where we will pick up more slaves. When we are on planet, many of you will be loaned to the local brothels."

"What happens to the ones who aren't taken to E'Le'Dor?" a woman to his right asked.

Shena didn't see exactly what happened, but she did see the woman fall to the floor, writhing in pain, one of the guards standing over her.

Ignoring the woman's wails, the speaker continued. "I didn't say you could ask questions."

He paced a few feet, then back again.

"Once you are sold, your new owner can do anything he wants to you. He can touch you anywhere. He can fuck you anywhere. He can make you suffer in any way he likes. He can even kill you."

He stared at them with steely eyes. "Get used to the fact that your body is his. Learn to pleasure him, and you may survive longer."

He paced again. "Never make eye contact with a normal person. As a slave, you must keep your eyes downcast at all times."

He pointed to Shena. "You. Come here."

Butterflies swarmed through her stomach as she stepped forward.

"Sit."

She glanced around. There was nowhere to sit down.

He pointed at her with a black rod about six inches long. Intense, rippling pain shot through her, frying every nerve-end.

"I said sit!"

She crumpled to the ground, then sat cross-legged.

He nodded. "Better. Now, look at this."

She glanced up at the black rod he held in front of him. He shifted it in front of his face, stopping in front of his eyes. Her gaze met his for a brief instant.

"I told you never to make eye contact!" he snapped.

He pointed the rod at her again. This time, the pain became completely immobilizing. She fell to the floor, writhing. Her limbs flung outward and her body twitched involuntarily as every nerve-end, every muscle, every organ felt as though it would explode. She prayed for anything, even death, to end the excruciating torture.

Finally, the pain released her body, and she sucked in air, lying on the floor like a wounded animal, unable to move.

"I hope this demonstration will help you all remember the basic rules. Now, all of you, get into the bed slots and sleep."

He walked away. She felt soft hands lift her. Two of the other slaves hooked Shena's arms over their shoulders

"Can you walk?" one asked.

Shena tried to move the muscles of her legs, but they did not respond.

"No." The sound released from her mouth on a breath of air, barely audible.

The women carried her to the nearest column of niches and laid her onto the floor, then slid her into the lowest bed slot.

Shena's heart thumped loudly as she glanced at the close walls around her. She felt like she was in a coffin. Could it get any worse than this?

A few moments later, the lights went out, leaving her in pitch-black darkness. She felt as though she'd been buried alive.

chapter seven

The next morning, Shena awoke exhausted, but relieved to climb out of the tiny sleeping space and thankful to find her limbs working fine again, if a little stiff. Most of the night she'd lain awake, despair coursing through her at the thought of Keern's death.

She and the other women were handed bowls of warm, tasteless food that didn't quite fill their stomachs. Then they were led outside the ship to a large, fenced area with over a hundred women inside. Shena's group consisted of the women taken in yesterday. The other women had been with the slavers longer, she realized, as evidenced by their downcast eyes and dirty, bedraggled appearance.

Once inside the pen, Shena stayed away from the fences. There were several men in the area, some loading and unloading wagons or performing various other tasks and some just milling about. One was reading a newspaper, and the word "Herrington" caught her eye. It was in the front-page headline. She stared, trying to make out the rest, but with the way he had it folded, the only parts she could make out were "Herrington" and "Wak." The man shifted the paper, and the word "Dead" became visible.

Her heart thundered in her chest. The paper held the answer to the question she so desperately wanted answered. Was Keern still alive?

She grasped the wire of the fence and strained to read more, but the man with the paper was too far away.

"What is it, honey?" one of the other women, a tall brunette, asked.

"That newspaper." She pointed at the man. "It has the name of ... someone I know. I think he might have been killed."

"You're new, right? Well, you could ask the guy to give you the paper."

"You think he'd just give it to me?"

The woman laughed. "Not for free. Just show him your assets."

Shena stared at her, wide-eyed.

"You might as well get used to using them to your advantage."

Shena tightened her hands around the wire.

"Oh, sweetie, I didn't see the mark." The woman's gaze had come to rest on the circle on Shena's arm. "You'd get in big trouble for that."

The woman glanced at the man with the paper. "Is it really important to you?"

Shena nodded.

The woman called out to the guy. "Hey, you. With the newspaper." The man glanced toward her. "I'd love a little news. How 'bout you give me that paper?"

He raised an eyebrow. "What'll ye give me for it?"

She ran her hands over her breasts. "I could show you these."

He stepped closer, chewing a toothpick.

"I can see lots of those for free when the *graebers* come bribin' ye with food."

One of the other women whispered in Shena's ear. "Part of the payoff to the local police for the slavers to operate here is that they let them come and offer food in exchange for favors from the women." She pointed to places in the fence with holes large enough for things to be passed in and out.

Shena's new friend opened the buttons of her top, slowly, then parted the fabric enough to show a little cleavage. The man's gaze locked on her fleshy curves.

"So you don't want to see them?"

"As I said, I'll see 'em later for free."

"Maybe. But you won't get to touch them." The woman made her voice sultry and low.

His gaze remained riveted on her hand as she slid it inside and stroked herself.

"It's just a little newspaper," she continued in that silky tone. "You can buy yourself another."

"Come over here," he said as he moved to one of the openings in the fence.

She stepped close, but not too close. "Do we have a deal?"

"I don't know. Let me see what I'll get."

The woman pulled the fabric further apart, just short of revealing her nipples.

One of the other women who had overheard Shena's desire to see the paper leaned close to him and said in a muffled whisper that Shena could just barely hear, "She only wants the fashion section. Give her a page at a time."

He smiled, then said, "Show me all of 'em, and I'll give you the first page."

The dark-haired woman pulled open her top, and his jaw dropped. She had the largest breasts Shena had ever seen. He shoved the first page through the bars. The woman who'd whispered grabbed the page and carried it over to Shena.

"Now come over here so I can touch them," he demanded.

The brunette buttoned up her top and turned away.

"Hey, I thought you wanted this?" He waved the paper, clutched tightly in his hand.

He grabbed one of the women through the bars and dragged her against the fence, but one of the guards pushed him away. The women laughed, which made the guy angrier, but the guards prodded him on his way.

Shena pulled the page open and began to read the article, which revealed that her father had gone after the Herringtons and killed one of them. Her heart lurched as she read the words, until she saw the first name.

Will. Not Keern.

She relaxed, relieved, yet knowing Keern must be suffering the loss of his brother. The words blurred as she read how her father had killed him and the eldest remaining brother, Keern, had killed her father.

Her father was dead, and she felt nothing for him. Only a coldness deep inside.

The article went on to say Keern blamed the daughter for his brother's death because she'd lied about an encounter between them, after which, according to the reporter, she'd claimed Keern had raped her.

She remembered his tender touch and the way he'd brought her exquisite pleasure. He must feel mortally wounded believing she would call such a thing rape.

The words at the bottom of the page indicated that the article continued on a later page, which Shena did not have. The paper dropped from her hands.

A fist tightened around her heart as she thought about the pain Keern must be in.

He blamed her for his brother's death. And rightly so. Although she hadn't told her father Keern had raped her, she had verified his identity to her father. Maybe if she had lied ... Maybe if she had held her tongue ...

If only she could change things so that she and Keern had never met.

Her soul ached as she could almost feel his hatred gripping her.

* * *

Two days after Will's funeral, Keern and his family sat in court. He and the chief constable had gone back to the Wakefield house and tried to find Shena, but no one knew her whereabouts, or so they had claimed. As the judge entered the courtroom and sat at his desk, Keern glanced around. Still no Shena.

After listening to all the statements from Keern's family and their men, the chief constable had agreed they had acted in self-defense, but with so many rumors bouncing around about the reason for Wakefield's attack, this hearing was being held to determine if Keern would be tried for the rape of Shena Wakefield and possibly the murder of Henry Wakefield. Since Shena was the key witness, Keern was amazed she wasn't here.

As the proceedings progressed, he kept an eye on the door and another on the clock, wondering when she would make her entrance. As the minutes ticked away, he began to realize she wasn't coming. His gut twisted as he wondered if something had happened to her — and cursed himself for caring.

The judge glanced through his glasses at the papers on his desk. He cleared his throat, the sound reverberating through the large wood-paneled room.

"Mr. Herrington, in your statement, you say that Mr. Wakefield attacked your family and killed your elder brother, Will, and in turn, you killed Wakefield. Since he was the one who instigated the attack, you claim you acted in self-defense and the defense of your family."

"That is correct, Your Honor."

The judge lifted the paper in front of him, then shifted it sideways, examining another.

"It seems, however, that Mr. Wakefield attacked your family because he believed you, Keern Herrington, raped his daughter."

Anger rocketed through Keern at Shena's vicious lie, but he kept it tightly hidden.

"I did not, Your Honor."

The judge leaned forward, his eyes dark and forbidding, and held up a sheaf of papers.

"I have signed statements from a number of people in Mr. Wakefield's employ who say that when Wakefield heard rumors of the alleged rape from a neighbor, Wakefield confronted his daughter and she claimed you *did.*"

"She lied," Keern stated calmly, although he felt anything but calm.

The judge glanced around the courtroom and scowled.

"Well, since Miss Wakefield is not available for questioning at the moment, I have no way to verify that."

"Your Honor, we have evidence to support Mr. Herrington's claim."

Keern glanced at his lawyer, and the man nodded back, a sure smile gripping his face. The lawyer had told Keern as they stepped into court this morning that he had new evidence that would prove Keern's innocence, but had refused to tell him what it was. The man loved the dramatic.

"Well, bring it here, man," the judge ordered.

The lawyer approached the judge and handed him a large, flat envelope. The judge opened the flap, tugged out a piece of paper, and examined it. He shook his head, his mouth a grim, straight line.

"Well, that explains why the young woman's not here," he muttered.

Keern's heart froze. Was Shena dead?

The judge raised his gaze to the courtroom. "It seems that the young woman has been sold to the slavers. I have a photograph here that shows her in the slavers' camp, and the brand on her wrist verifies she was a virgin. She's holding a newspaper showing the date as two days ago. The claim she made to her father about Mr. Herrington was obviously false."

He turned his gaze to Keern. "Well, Mr. Herrington, it seems you were telling the truth. This hearing is adjourned."

His gavel cracked against his desk, and joyful voices erupted around Keern.

But Keern hardly heard them, or felt the slaps on his back from his brother and cousin.

Shena had been sold to the slavers?

He approached the judge and reached for the photograph. The judge handed it to him, and he stared at the image of Shena, wearing a plain white gown, a circle branded into the soft, pale flesh of her inner arm, visible as she held a newspaper. The article she read was about her father's attack on Keern's family.

A slaver ship had left yesterday. That was probably the one she'd been on. His stomach twisted. Protective urges swarmed through him at the thought of the slavers touching her, pushing their devices into her, at the pain she would have felt when she'd been branded, but he slammed back those urges. That witch had been the cause of Will's death and she deserved every foul experience fate seemed eager to give her.

As a virgin, she would not suffer a great deal on the way to the slave market, but she would be trained. That would not be pleasant. No, where she would truly receive her just punishment for her treachery would be at the hands of her master.

If only he could be the one to administer that punishment.

* * *

Keern pulled his pack from the back of the wagon.

"Are you sure you want to do this, Keern?" Jacob asked. "You know we could really use your help, with Will gone and all."

"I have to do this. Jordan is more than ready to take over the household."

"Well, if I can't talk you out of leaving, can I accompany you while you find transport?"

"No need. I'll manage."

Jacob nodded and shook his hand firmly. "I hope I'll be seeing you again, cousin."

Keern smiled. "I'm sure you will. Take care of them for me, Jacob."

Keern turned and walked away, hearing the creaky wheels of the wagon and the clomping of the horses' hooves as Jacob left.

Keern knew the slavers would be heading for E'Le'Dor, the only planet in the coalition that still allowed slavery. Not many passenger ships serviced Tarun, but he negotiated passage on a small trade ship. Luckily, E'Le'Dor was a prime location on the trade route.

chapter eight

Shena followed the woman in front of her, prodded forward by the guard. The door of the ship slid open, revealing an alien landscape beyond. A sea of sand. A wavy horizon. An amber sky.

The planet E'Le'Dor.

She plodded forward, sixth in a long line of women, her ankles and wrists weighed down with chains. The skinny, vacant-eyed young woman ahead of her stumbled as she passed through the doorway. Shena felt the dense, stifling air blast in her face. Her dwindling reserve of energy seared away as she concentrated on moving one foot at a time down the ramp.

Setting foot on an alien planet sent a tremor through her. She squinted against the blazing light of an unfamiliar sun. Her stomach twisted at the thought that soon she would be sold to some brute whose only interest in her was claiming her virginity.

Who would buy her and how she would be treated, she didn't know, but she was sure it would be a horrendous experience. Some of the other women speculated about rich men buying them and lavishing them with jewels and fine silks, but Shena knew better than to fill her mind with such fancy.

These men wanted fresh virgin bodies, and more than likely once their hymens were spent, the women would be discarded, replaced with new virgin meat. Then they'd probably be sold to brothels. Or for labor. Or just put to death.

Keern watched as Shena was led to the block. He was shocked at the emptiness in her eyes.

After hearing of Wakefield's death, one of his soldiers must have sold her to the slavers. Keern was surprised she hadn't been raped by such a despicable man, but it seemed he was more interested in platinum than lust, because Shena was listed as a prime virgin, and interest in her at the market was high.

Keern had arrived on the planet several days before the slavers. His friend Jakmerah was very influential and had accompanied him today to bid on Shena.

The guard shoved Shena's bound hands over a large, dangling hook. Then another man pulled a chain, hauling the hook and Shena's arms upward, until she held herself on her tiptoes. She barely seemed to have the strength to do that.

The auctioneer regaled Shena's attributes in a dialect Keern could barely understand. He heard words like "stunning beauty" and "hair like golden sunshine." Then the man tore open her rag of a garment, exposing her naked body to the whole marketplace. A protective instinct shot through Keern and he jerked forward, but his companion grabbed his arm.

"Easy, Keern. There is nothing you can do for her now. Leave this to me."

Keern froze, then nodded. He trusted Jakmerah. He had to leave this in his hands.

The auctioneer slid his hand under Shena's left breast, lifting it slightly, saying words Keern couldn't hear through the red-hot rage slicing through him. He swore to himself he would tear the man's hands off if he ever got close to him. Shena just stood there, like a lifeless statue. The man gestured and the hook rose higher, until she hung from her wrists. He spun her around, lifting her garment to run his hand along her round, firm derriere. Then he spun her back and lifted her ankles, starting to spread her legs.

"*Darg'ra,* Jakmerah," Keern muttered under his breath. "Do something to stop this, or I will!"

Keern hated the protective urges compressing his insides. He despised this woman. What did he care if she was humiliated? Of course, he was disgusted at the thought of any woman being put through such degradation. It wasn't stronger because it was Shena, he assured himself.

Jakmerah nodded and did a throat-cutting gesture to one of his guards. The guard signaled to the auctioneer, who glanced at Jakmerah, then nodded and stepped away from Shena. She hung now, motionless, eyes closed.

The auctioneer started the bidding. Eager men called out their bids, the numbers going higher and impossibly higher. Keern glanced at Jakmerah, wondering if they'd lost her.

After another minute of bidding, Jakmerah lifted one finger. The auctioneer nodded and announced the bidding closed.

Jakmerah drew a horizontal circle with his finger, and the auctioneer rushed to Shena to release her and throw a rough blanket around her shoulders. Keern's taut nerves eased a little once Shena was covered.

"What happened?" Keern asked.

"One of the advantages of social standing," Jakmerah responded. "If I see a woman I want, I get her. Courtesy is to let the bidding rise, to see what price she would have brought, and that is considered their tribute to me. I rarely take advantage of such privilege, so they will feel highly honored by this transaction."

"And how will I repay you, my old friend?"

"With your continued friendship. That is, after all, the true measure of a man's wealth."

Keern slapped him on the back and nodded his thanks. He turned to see Shena being led from the stage, clutching at the blanket, just like she had clung to his cape after he'd swung it around her shoulders the first time they'd met. He slammed that memory aside, knowing images of the blood-boiling passion that followed would overtake him otherwise.

Keern watched as two of Jakmerah's guards went to fetch Shena. She would be transported in the utility vehicle flown by the guards, while Keern rode with Jakmerah in his luxury air car.

When they arrived at Jakmerah's palatial estate, the guards parked at the back entry with Shena while Keern and Jakmerah stepped out of the comfort of Jakmerah's air-conditioned car at the front steps of the huge stone home. The oppressive heat of the day had cooled a little as the sun sank toward the horizon.

"Do you want me to send her to your room, or would you like a special suite?" Jakmerah asked.

The guest room Jakmerah had provided was a suite by anyone else's standards, comprising a sitting room with two adjacent bedrooms, each with adjoining bathrooms. By a special suite, Keern knew he meant a sumptuous room set up for seduction.

"My room," Keern answered.

"I know you said you wanted her brought to you this evening, but I wish you would reconsider. The woman has endured a terrible ordeal. I'm sure she is exhausted and frightened. Why don't you let me send her to the women of my household? They will bathe her and give her clean clothing and a good meal. Let her rest tonight, and she will be much more enjoyable tomorrow, I promise you."

"Jak," Keern said, through clenched teeth, "it is vengeance I seek, not a passionate romp."

"So you say, but I saw the way you looked at her, the way you strained to protect her. What has she done to deserve your need for vengeance?"

"She killed my brother."

Jakmerah's black brows rose. "This small woman wielded a sword against your brother?"

"Her father actually drove the sword into Will, but it was her intentional lies that forced the act."

"What form will this vengeance of yours take?"

Jakmerah's intent gaze unsettled Keern. They both knew Keern had total control over Shena now that she belonged to him, a gift from Jakmerah. Keern could do anything to her, according to the laws of this planet, including torture, mutilation, even death. She was his property.

Jakmerah squeezed Keern's shoulder. "I know you, old friend. It is not like you to take vengeance on the helpless."

"You *knew* me, old friend. Before the wounds inflicted by that witch. Anything I do to her is a reflection of what she did to me."

Jakmerah sighed. "It is your business, Keern."

A servant opened the heavy, rounded oak door, and they strolled inside. The marble floors and a fountain splashing in the centre of the foyer added to the cool, pleasant feel of the room.

"You will send her this evening?" Keern asked Jakmerah.

"Will you agree to a bath and a meal?"

"Yes. Whatever."

"And something to wear?" Her garment had been shredded on the auction block.

"Fine. But no fancy clothing."

"Agreed. Something simple, but clean."

* * *

Shena followed the guard through the long marble hallways, preparing to meet her fate. Thank heavens some sort of wonderful technology kept the air cool inside this place.

When she'd arrived here, some women had brought her a clean gown and some food, then led her to a bath where she could wash off the sweat that had clung to her ever since arriving on this oven of a planet. After her bath, the women had warned her that the man who'd bought her hated her and wanted to hurt her. It seemed he had known her father. Probably one of his many enemies. Apparently, her new owner had decided to exact revenge on her for whatever wrongdoing her father had wrought.

As if being sold into slavery wasn't bad enough, she had to be bought by some merciless man just like her father.

The two guards led her through a sumptuous palace, which she hardly saw. They led her up a grand staircase and along a stately hallway, then another, until they reached a double doorway at the end of the corridor. They knocked, then opened the door and led her into a sitting room. The guards turned and left. She heard the click of the lock after they closed the door.

She stood in the center of the finely appointed room, feeling a little faint. Two leather chairs sat facing a large window, the drawn curtains hiding whatever view lay beyond. She longed to sink into one of the chairs and fall into a deep, peaceful sleep, but she knew she wouldn't be able to sleep even if she dared to sit. Which she did not.

Over the weeks aboard the trader ship, she had learned very well what happened when she disobeyed whatever man happened to be master at the time. Her back still stung from the lashes she'd received, a punishment she'd been told many slave owners preferred, probably for its entertainment value. Just like her father had. She preferred to avoid any more, and she felt certain sitting without being given permission would be considered disobedient.

A door opened, not the one through which she'd entered. She did not look at the man. That would be a sign of insolence. She kept her gaze cast downward.

"Look at me."

She glanced up at him with unfocused eyes, making out the vague image of a tall, bearded man with dark, piercing eyes.

Keern stared at her, acutely aware of the hollows at the base of her neck and the gaunt look of her face. She had lost weight.

She stared up at him with eyes dull and lifeless, until her gaze caught on his — and held. A glimmer of fear and possibly ... pain? ... rippled across the placid blue pools, but no recognition.

He strode toward her and grabbed her chin, a little too roughly, and locked gazes with her.

"Look at my face. Do you remember me?"

Confusion washed across her features, and then recognition sparked in her eyes.

"Keern." His name shuddered from her. Her voice, trembling with torment, quavered slightly.

chapter nine

He savored the effect, committing it to memory, tucked away in a place he could retrieve it often to soothe the vivid recall of pain too long subdued. Inflicted by her. Of a heart too long shattered. Broken by her.

"What are you doing here?" she asked.

His gaze locked on hers and held tight. She shrank slightly.

"I own you, and I intend to make you pay for the death of my brother."

She stood trembling.

"You lied to your father. You told him I'd stolen your virginity. He and his men attacked my family. He killed my brother, thinking it was me."

She shook her head, her eyes wide and liquid. "I know, Keern. I'm so sorry. I — "

"Shut up!" he barked.

She flinched at his harsh words, and he pressed toward her.

"There is one reason, and one reason only, why you are here. So I can punish you for the pain you have caused." His jaw clenched around the words.

"But I didn't — "

"Shut up! I don't want to hear your lies."

"You won't let me explain?"

"Why should I? I remember all too well how good you are at deceit."

He stepped toward her. Her back stiffened, and she refused to step back, but she couldn't quite hide the flicker of trepidation in her eyes.

"Are you afraid of me?" he asked.

She held up her chained hands, eyes glittering with defiance. The chain clinked together, swinging back and forth in an arc.

"You hold the key to my destiny. You decide if I live or die. I'd be a fool not to fear you."

Unwanted admiration flickered through him.

He took another step toward her, putting his chest within an inch of the tips of her breasts.

Keern expected her to retreat, to step back from his looming presence, but she stood firm, claiming a small piece of ground as her own.

Surveying her with a cool sweep of his eyes, intending to shake her damnable calm, he felt his body tense with anticipation of what was to come. Her simple white gown followed the curves of her body in an alluring fashion — and only two thin straps held it up.

He'd waited so long. He'd imagined his revenge a thousand times. Now he could barely restrain himself. But he would. He planned to enjoy this to the fullest. He would linger over every step. Her breasts rose and fell in an unsteady rhythm, though she held her head high and didn't flinch at his perusal.

He could wait. To feel her body writhe beneath his own as her vulnerable flesh succumbed to his strength. To taste her sweet flesh with his tongue, especially the honey-tipped nipples that remained in his dreams, perpetually glazed with shimmering droplets of water. To smell the womanly scent of her as she responded to him with the slippery glaze of feminine readiness. To see her face, tilted back in the agony of blissful passion, overwhelmed into vibrant submission. To hear her beg for the release only he could provide, as he was so sure she would, then the strangled moan of pleasure as she slipped from this reality to the "little death" of orgasm.

Yes, he would enjoy this. But if his desire was for revenge, why did his fantasy include her pleasure? Perhaps it was simply the male need to know he could satisfy his woman.

He grabbed her wrist and dragged her into his bedroom. "Are you going to fight me?"

Fear sparked in her eyes, but she jerked her head up defiantly, her tumultuous mane of golden hair tumbling over her shoulders.

"No," she stated simply.

Proud and beautiful. But also deadly, he reminded himself, pushing aside the reluctant admiration.

"Really?"

He grabbed her, dragging her into his arms. Her bound hands jerked up between them, sweeping across his groin, triggering a pulsing heat through him. Her palms jammed against his ribs, and she shoved against him, hard, but her struggles were insignificant against his greater strength. He loosened his hold on her, pleased to see the scarlet anger coloring her face as she realized she'd lost control of her composure and belied her claim.

He brought his teeth to her neck and nipped.

"I don't mind if you fight. It'll be all the more challenging. On the other hand, a quiet submission on your part could provide its own reward — to us both." His hand skimmed her form from her hip to the side swell of her breast.

"If you actually participate, we might both enjoy this."

The stiffening of her spine gave him his answer — the answer he wanted. She would not willingly enjoy this — did not intend to give him the satisfaction. That would make his revenge even sweeter. Because she would enjoy it, making her humiliation more complete.

"I won't fight you. And I won't enjoy this. If you prefer taking defenseless women against their will, that's your weakness, not mine."

She glared into his eyes with a fierceness of utter strength, of spirit if not of body. Anger prodded him at his growing admiration of her, but he pushed it aside, not allowing anything to spoil this experience.

"It's no weakness to carry a battle through to completion. You started the war. I am simply finishing the fight. If I am victorious, you have no right to complain."

She sucked in a breath, seemed ready to say something, then shook her head and looked away. He stepped forward and tore the straps of her gown, shoved the fabric down her body until it slid to the floor. She stood before him, tall and proud, even with brief white panties her only protection from his eyes. The only sign of her trepidation was her averted gaze. Her breasts, as full and tempting as he remembered, swept forward in a graceful curve, the taut nipples beckoning to him. He covered her firm white breasts with his hands, pressing against the soft flesh, feeling her nipples peak in automatic response to his touch. The feel of her sent tremors of need thundering through him.

He wanted her. More than he'd ever wanted any woman before. Once again he tried to convince himself it was because he wanted to hurt her, to make her pay for Will's death. He wouldn't take her life — though as her master, he could do so legally — but he could take her innocence. With one as strong as her, that would be worse than losing her life. Still, the pulsing need within him threatened to make him slave to her, not the other way around. It would be so easy to succumb to the desire to hold her close, to whisper sweet words of love in her ear, to beg her to love him with all the gentleness he knew she had inside her. Something deep inside him wanted to hear her speak words of loving encouragement, wanted her to want him in the most basic of ways. He wanted her to invite him inside her body, to beg for his love, not because he wanted her to submit, but because he wanted to fulfill her wish with loving intent.

Anger flared as he realized how vulnerable he'd become to her. If she were a man, this would be simple. They would battle with weapons until only one remained standing.

With a conniving woman like this one, things were far more complicated.

Thrusting away the unwanted feelings she'd aroused in him, he similarly thrust her onto the bed. He flung her hands over her head, pinning them with one of his while he claimed one taut nipple with his mouth. He savored the feel of her soft skin pebbling under his tongue, the thrust of the nub hardening in his moist warmth. His teeth nipped gently, and she cried out in distress, though more imagined than real, since he'd been careful not to hurt her. Though she may deserve it, he would not hurt a woman as part of love play. He might enjoy her trepidation, but he would not inflict real pain. Turning his head sideways while he stroked her other nipple with his index finger, he watched as the flesh puckered erect. Her chest rose and fell in an unsteady rhythm under his cheek, and her heartbeat sounded erratic. Lifting his head to stare at her face, he saw her eyes scrunched tightly closed, as though she were undergoing some unbearable agony. Searing pain slashed through his chest.

His whole world seemed to tilt beneath him, sending him off kilter. He had wanted her to fear him, had needed it for what seemed like forever, but now ... but now he needed her to want him. Needed it so desperately, it almost consumed him.

As though his gaze touched her like a physical caress, her eyelids flipped open and she stared at him. He released her wrists.

"Put your arms around me," he commanded.

She failed to comply, and he glared at her.

"Do it!" he commanded tightly.

She shook her head. The clinking of the chain as she shifted her hands drew his attention, and he snatched the key to her cuffs from the shelf at the head of his bed. She flinched, shielding her face with her linked hands. Clearly, she'd thought he'd intended to strike her. His protective instincts lurched to the surface, unwanted and dangerous.

"My God, you really are afraid of me." The realization flashed like ice water through his veins.

He grabbed her wrists and unlocked the bonds.

"Isn't that what you wanted?" She rubbed at the red, raw marks left on her wrists from the iron bands.

It was. But now ...

Darg'ra! He couldn't let her get to him. On the other hand, he couldn't look into those blue eyes — calm surfaces that hinted at levels of pain so intense, he dared not allow himself to be drawn into them — without wondering what had caused that intensity. He jerked to his feet, desperate to get away from her.

"Yes, but I've tired of the game for now." He strode across the room, toward the door. "Sleep. You'll need your strength later."

He hazarded one last glance at the bed, to see her curled into a ball, her back toward him.

Snaky red lines marred the surface of her soft white flesh. Most were the fresh markings of the lash, a result of discipline inflicted during her captivity with the slavers. As he moved closer, barely aware he'd changed direction, drawn to her like a mother grizzly to a wounded cub, he noticed older scars, healed over, but a map of previous ill-treatment. They were faint enough that he had not noticed them when he'd first seen her, but now, highlighted by the new scars, they stood out clearly.

chapter ten

Shena felt his overwhelming presence behind her. She hugged her knees tight to her chest.

Why didn't he leave? He'd just told her he'd tired of her for now. Why didn't he just leave her in peace? Give her time to build up her immunity? She felt herself weakening. She had caused him pain, and he needed to strike out at her. She felt his pain, like a hideous weight crushing her body.

He wanted her to fear him, but what she feared most was her need for him. Could she survive this with her heart intact?

The bed compressed under his weight as he sat behind her. His finger traced a crooked line down her back, probably following one of her scars. She flinched at the remembered pain.

The searing heat of the lash cracking against her skin. Barely able to stop herself from crying out, she lay rigid and still, waiting for him to leave. A moment later, he rose, and she heard his footsteps as he left the room. Sighing, she relaxed a little, wondering when he'd return and what he would do then. She had little time for such contemplation, as he returned moments later. She felt him apply a thick ointment to her back with gentle strokes of his fingers.

"With one as bold as you, I assume you were beaten to force submission."

"No worse than the others," she replied, remembering the tawny redhead who'd lain battered on the cell floor beside her. The girl, no more than seventeen, had died in her arms.

She'd been an example to the others, the guard had told them.

"I fared better than some."

"I find that hard to believe, with your insolence."

She could almost believe he was teasing her, if it weren't for the hatred she'd seen in his bronze eyes. She remained silent, allowing herself to enjoy the gentle flow of his fingers along her back, the soothing feel of ointment relieving the stinging pain of her wounds.

"What about these old ones?" he asked. "There are scars that have been here some time."

Oh, God, why did he ask about those? Did her humiliation have to be so complete? Too exhausted to face the prolonged questioning she was sure he'd put her through, she answered.

"I was a selfish, unworthy daughter." She repeated the words her father had flung at her so many times that she accepted them as unquestioned truth.

His fingers stopped moving on her back. He must hate the thought of touching someone as vile as she.

"Unworthy? In what way?"

"I ... I displeased my father in many ways."

"So he beat you?" His voice rose in mild interest.

"Yes, he ... he had to teach me proper discipline."

"By whipping you? What grave sins did you commit for such a punishment? Did he find you with a man?"

"Oh, no," she cried, horrified at the very thought. "I told you that my father threatened dire consequences if ever I gave myself to a man."

Realizing her current situation and what would soon happen between them, she spun her head around to stare at him, eyes wide, then quickly turned away once she'd met his fierce, angry stare. Of course, he'd be angry assuming the auctioneer had lied about her.

"I ... I am still a virgin."

"Never mind that. You don't think being given lashes is dire consequences? Especially from your father?"

She didn't know what to say. What did he expect? She refused to think about what her father had threatened, what she'd seen him do to others.

"Answer me."

His voice grated against her raw nerves, and she felt incredibly vulnerable. She couldn't find her own voice and refused to remember the threats and the agony her father had inflicted.

His hand clamped down on her shoulder, and he urged her onto her back.

"I want you to ..." His words started off angry and sharp, but trailed off as he stared down at her, his dark eyes narrowing. She knew she'd gone pale; her cheeks felt cold and empty. Maybe he was afraid she'd be ill if he pushed her. Or could he be showing her some kind of mercy? The thought quickly dissipated as he tugged the sheet from her naked body.

"Are there scars anywhere else?" he asked, his voice flat.

Her eyelids closed for a moment, to head off a flow of tears she refused to shed. Of course, he'd be worried about having bought damaged goods.

"No."

Her father had been careful to limit scars to her back, in case, as he'd often threatened, he ever decided to send her to the auctioneer's block. How ironic, she thought, not for the first time, that she had wound up on that block after all, and yet her father had not been able to enjoy the profit from it.

His fingers trailed down the center of her chest, traced the lower line of her ribcage, then back up her side. Her breasts swelled to the feel of his fingers so close, and she tried to deny to herself that she wanted his large, warm hands to capture them, draw them into his mouth. She remembered his gentle touch by the lake, the way he had made her feel special and wanted. How safe she had felt in his arms. She wanted to feel that again.

"Why the hell are you looking at me like that?"

At his sharp words, her gaze jerked into focus on his face. She'd been seeing him as he'd been that first day they'd met, remembering his roguish grin, his debonair demeanor. At this moment, a scowl marred his finely featured face.

"I ..." Shaking her head, she averted her gaze, not sure what to say, not sure what he wanted to hear.

"*Shet'ra*, you're driving me to distraction with your wide, innocent eyes and your helpless act. Remember, I know how good an actress you are. Do you think that because I showed you some compassion, I've forgotten why I brought you here and what I intend to do with you?"

His hands slid across her shoulders and down over her chest to cup each breast in a firm hold. He kneaded them with a pulsing rhythm. Like two pebbles tossed in a pond, waves of arousal radiated from them in mounting need. His hands slid under her breasts, supporting the weight of them, and his thumbs circled over her nipples. Jagged spikes of need shot through her, and she sucked in a ragged breath. He flung his leg over her, straddling her, holding his weight on his knees. He tore off his robe and balled it up before tossing it across the room to fall haphazardly across the settee.

He was fully aroused, and his erection fell across her belly. The heat of his huge cock burned into her flesh, and she wanted to shift and swivel her hips to capture him inside her, to let the heat of it melt the cold that had held her frozen for so long. He leaned over her and licked her nipple, and she thought she'd go insane with wanting. Involuntarily, she arched beneath him, and he pushed her down with his body, his swollen flesh so close to where she wanted it to be.

He tugged her nipple deep into his mouth and suckled, while his hand caressed her other breast, keeping it swollen with need. Switching, he warmed the other with his mouth, then slid his hands down her sides, over her hips. His fingers slid inside her panties, and she felt the slick wetness lubricate his touch. Unerringly, he found the small point of pleasure within her fold and stroked it with the tip of his finger, lightly at first, then more firmly until she could barely catch her breath.

She caught sight of his face once, in her hazy cocoon of need, and his cold, calculating look sent shivers of trepidation through her.

She clamped her eyes shut against that cruel glare.

Images flung themselves against her closed eyelids, dragging her into the agony of memory. She remembered the housekeeper, two years older than her at the time, chained, her clothes torn from her body, a scream tearing from her throat as the first man thrust into her, the sound of his flesh smacking against hers as he took his pleasure at the cost of her pain. Her screams tore through the night, haunting Shena, turning dreams to nightmares.

His cock nudged at her sensitive, womanly flesh, and ice tore through her insides. In a moment he would plunge into her, causing unbearable pain and blood.

"No!" The sound wailed from her own throat, drawing her back to now.

At his sharp expletive, her eyes snapped open and the evil memories were replaced by the reality of her current situation. Would Keern hurt her like that? Everything she'd learned about him told her he wouldn't, even in anger, even hating her as he did.

"*Dehn'ra!*" He flung himself away from her and strode from the room, this time without looking back.

* * *

Curled into a tight ball, Shena sobbed herself to sleep. A fitful sleep full of ominous shadows and fear. She awoke with a start, slipping out of the nightmare world into the darkness of reality.

She slid from under the covers and pulled on the remnants of her gown, then moved to the window. The shimmering light of two moons caressed the courtyard below the window. Where had Keern gone? Fear started deep inside her, building up to a steady thrum. What if he'd decided he didn't want her? He was her only link to her home. If he left her here, she would be stranded on this strange world, destined to live life as a slave. Even with the horrendous memories of her past, she suffered a gnawing desire to return home.

And she wanted to see Keern again. Even if he hated her. Even if he wanted to punish her.

Of course, Keern probably didn't intend to take her back to Tarun. What did he intend to do with her after he exorcised his need for revenge?

She slipped to the door and slowly turned the knob, being careful not to draw attention from anyone on the other side. She heard men's voices in the next room as she pushed the door open a crack. One was definitely Keern's. She peered out the crack and saw Keern and another man sitting in the leather chairs, talking. Keern's back was to her, but the dark eyes of the stranger shifted, and she thought he stared right at her. She froze, terrified she had revealed herself. Her lungs tightened painfully, and she waited for him to punish her in some way. Would he call the guards and have her dragged away, or simply banish her into the room again?

But his gaze simply returned to Keern. Maybe he hadn't seen her after all.

"What do I do with her now?" Keern asked.

"Take her home and marry her," the other man answered.

"That's insane. I told you, she's responsible for Will's death."

"So punish her by making her keep your house and bear your children."

"You're no help, Jak."

"I am trying, my friend, but you don't make this easy. You obviously love the woman. I'm trying to help you realize it."

Shena's heart thudded. Could it be true?

chapter eleven

Keern glared at Jakmerah. The man was a good friend, but did he have to be so overbearing in his opinions?

"I don't love her."

Jakmerah made a scoffing sound. "Look, you keep saying she's responsible for your brother's death, but she did not wield the sword — her father did. And you do not know what she told her father because you have not asked her."

Keern slapped his hands on the arms of the chair and pushed himself to his feet. "She will only lie." He paced across the room.

"Even if she did tell her father you defiled her, he must not have believed it, because she was sold to the slavers as a virgin, and it is widely known that they verify this. If he believed you stole her innocence, why would he, or anyone in his household, still believe she was pure?"

"Maybe whoever sold her tried to ..."

A vivid picture slammed across his vision of some ham-handed oaf laying his hands on her ... tearing her clothes ... touching her soft skin ... hurting her.

Just like he himself had. *Shet'ra!*

"Do you think if a man 'tried to' with a woman like that, he would stop just because he came into contact with her maidenhead?"

"One greedy for money might."

"You have eyes. No matter how greedy the man, faced with her beauty, he would not stop."

"*I* did."

"That, my friend, is because you love her."

His fists clenched. "I don't love her."

"Fine, you don't love her. So what do you intend to do with her?"

Keern paced some more, rubbing his chin. "Her father is dead, so she has no family or home to go back to. Would you keep her here?"

Jakmerah nodded. "If you wish it, my friend." He sat back in his chair, scratching his chin, a thoughtful look in his eye. "My brother is looking for a concubine to add to his collection. She would be well-treated there, and loved often. He ensures that he visits each of his women several times every month."

The muscles in Keern's jaw tensed painfully.

"Or perhaps I will keep her myself. I have not had a virgin in a very long time." Jakmerah raised an eyebrow. "She is still a virgin?"

"Yes," Keern grated, hating the thought of any man touching her, even his good friend Jakmerah.

Especially his good friend Jakmerah. Keern was sure he kept his women well satisfied, and the thought of Shena stretched out on Jak's bed, moaning his name, begging for his hands and body to pleasure her, tore at his insides.

"Good. I could always give her to my brother afterward. I don't need an addition to my harem, and my brother will be honored if I break her in for him."

"Maybe this isn't such a good idea."

"I see. Would you like me to keep her as a harem slave, where no man will ever see her? Keep her a virgin forever?"

Keern scowled. "I'm tired of this conversation. It's been a long day. I'm turning in."

"Fine, we'll talk again tomorrow." Jakmerah took a sip of his wine. "You go ahead and sleep. I'll let myself out after I finish my wine."

Keern nodded and strode to the second bedroom of the suite.

Shena watched Keern disappear behind another door. As soon as the door closed, the man named Jak stood up and strolled toward her room. Her eyes widened as she realized he had to have seen her. She backed away. He pushed the door open and stared right at her.

"Tell me one thing," he said. "Do you love Keern?"

Dumbfounded, she didn't know what to say.

"Don't think about it. Just answer."

"Yes." Astounded, she knew absolutely it was the truth.

He smiled. "Good." He sat down. "Then let me give you some advice."

* * *

Shena sat listening to the young women with fascination. They were here at Jakmerah's bidding, to teach her the secrets of seducing a man.

"I think we need to show her," Gheni told her companion, Dania.

Dania giggled and dropped her robe to the floor, then tugged off her bejeweled bra, revealing large, round breasts. Her areolas were as big around as daisies, and her breasts were firm. As she slipped her skirt down over her hips, Gheni shed her own clothing. Her breasts were a little smaller, and the areolas were the size of small buttercups.

"If you want to drive a man to distraction," Gheni said, "then touch yourself. Like this." She ran her fingers across her nipples, and they pebbled immediately. She plucked at them, and they tightened and thrust out.

"The only thing that gets them more aroused is if you touch another woman," Dania said, dropping her panties onto the floor.

Both women stood naked.

"That's right," Gheni said as she approached Dania from behind.

Gheni slid her arms around Dania and stroked up her ribcage, then cupped the woman's breasts. Dania leaned back against Gheni, resting her head on Gheni's shoulder, eyes falling closed as Gheni stroked and tweaked her breasts until they thrust forward in obvious excitement. She slid her left hand down Dania's stomach as she cupped one breast with her right hand.

Dania sighed as Gheni slid her fingers between Dania's legs.

"Dania, you're already wet," she crooned.

"What do you expect? You know exactly how to touch me." Dania sighed.

"Gheni. Dania. You're supposed to be helping Shena, not your-selves."

Shena's gaze shot to the door, her cheeks flaring with heat at the sight of Jakmerah standing in the doorway. He did not look angry — in fact, he smiled indulgently at the two women. As a testament to the truth of what the women had been telling her about arousing a man, she could see proof of his arousal by a growing bulge along the seam of his trousers.

The women giggled and stepped toward Shena.

"Come on. We'll show you."

One woman started to lift the hem of Shena's gown.

"No." Shena skittered back.

"Stop," Jakmerah commanded. "She will not be comfortable. And if you undress her in front of me, I will not be comfortable. Not and leave her for Keern."

The women stepped away from Shena, and she relaxed a little.

"What would you like us to do now?" Gheni asked Jakmerah.

"Stay focused on showing her what to do to enamor her man. Remember, she will not have another woman to tempt him with." He raised a hand as if to stave off offers from them. "And I'm sure she will not want one. Now, proceed with her lessons."

He made no move to leave.

The women smiled, and Gheni lay down on the bed. "I will be the man, and Dania will be you, Shena."

Dania stood in front of Gheni and swayed her hips back and forth, running her hands up her body, cupping her breasts, then run-ning down again. She stroked her fingers over her nipples, pinching them lightly. They puckered and thrust outward. She sashayed toward the bed and crawled over Gheni, settling over her hips. She leaned forward, cupping one of her breasts and offering it to Gheni, who smiled and leaned forward to suck the nipple into her mouth, making Dania gasp.

"Oh, yes," Dania cried.

Gheni slid her fingers to Dania's dark curls, and Dania cried out again.

"Oh, Gheni, touch me. Slide your fingers inside me."

"Ladies, this is a truly wonderful spectacle, but I think you need to give Shena some specific techniques she can use." Jakmerah's voice was slightly hoarse, and his bulge had grown.

Dania stood up and retrieved a banana from the table. She pulled back the peel slowly, deliberately.

"Maybe I should show her how to please a man with her mouth." She discarded the peel and licked the banana from one end to the other, then sucked the end into her mouth. She sucked with a rapid pulsing rhythm, her cheeks hollowing.

Jakmerah's eyes glazed.

"Dania, bring that over here." Dania followed Gheni's instructions, and Gheni slipped the end of the banana into her vagina. It curved upward, looking like an erect penis.

"Yum." Dania climbed on top of Gheni and licked, starting at Gheni's curls, eliciting a groan, then sliding the length of the fruit. She slipped her mouth over the end of the banana, drawing it inside. She took it deeper and deeper. She stopped about two inches from Gheni, and then her eyes lit up and she slid off again. She pushed on the banana, easing it into Gheni a couple of inches.

"Oh, yes," Gheni moaned.

Dania covered the banana with her mouth again and took it in until she reached Gheni's curls. Then she twirled around the fruit and her tongue flicked out, stroking Gheni's clitoris.

Then the banana broke.

Dania chewed it and swallowed, then licked Gheni, sucking until she'd drawn the rest of the banana partway out. She licked around it, sucked, licked, sucked, munched. Gheni arched and moaned. Dania thrust her tongue inside, her hands sliding up to grasp Gheni's breasts. Gheni bucked and gasped as Dania continued to pleasure her. Her groans increased until she screamed in ecstasy. Dania smiled and kissed her companion on the lips. They embraced for several moments, then turned to Jakmerah.

"Our banana is broken. Whatever will we do now?" Dania pouted.

"Yes, poor Dania is left unsatisfied," Gheni added.

Both women looked at Jakmerah with big eyes.

"Well, you two were being so creative, I didn't have the opportunity to give you this. I thought it might be a useful teaching aid."

From a pouch at his hip, he pulled out a cucumber, about fifteen inches long.

"Ohhhh." Gheni grabbed it and shoved Dania onto the bed.

Gently, she parted Dania's legs and stroked her vagina, then eased the cucumber inside. She eased it out a little, then in again, out and in, going further inside each time. She stopped at about eight inches, then climbed on top of Dania and slid the other end of the cucumber inside her own vagina. Gheni started moving on top of Dania, sliding the cucumber deeper inside herself until their two vaginas met, joined by the long green cylinder. Shena could see a small band of the green vegetable between their two bodies as they moved. Gheni tilted her pelvis and spiraled it around. Dania shifted up and down. They both started to moan. Dania licked Gheni's breasts, and Gheni stroked Dania's. Their moans increased until they both cried out in climax.

They both lay back on the bed, laughing.

"Jakmerah, you naughty man. You distracted us even more. Shena won't need to know how to do that."

"Maybe not that exactly," he answered, his voice hoarse, "but she is learning about being uninhibited and creative."

Both women got up and approached Jakmerah.

"I think what she needs to see," Gheni said as she and Dania stripped away his clothing, "is a demonstration on a real man."

chapter twelve

Each woman took one of Jakmerah's hands and led him to the bed. He lay back and let Dania stroke his fully extended cock.

"You see how beautiful it is?" Dania asked Shena. "Would you like to touch it?"

Shena shook her head vehemently, staying close to the wall, as far from the bed as she could get.

Dania stroked the very tip of Jakmerah's erect penis and showed Shena a clear drop of liquid on her fingertip, then took it on her tongue.

"Your man will love it when you taste him. And he will love to taste you."

Jakmerah gestured for Gheni to approach him. She crawled over his face. He wrapped his hands around her thighs and thrust out his long tongue to lick her.

Dania wrapped her hands around Jakmerah's slender but very long cock. She worked her hand up and down, sliding along his length.

"The head is very sensitive. Gliding your tongue around the tip is a wonderful way to start." She illustrated her point, her pink tongue curling around the bulbous end of his penis.

Gheni shifted back and forth in an increasing rhythm over Jakmerah's face as Dania stroked his cock with her tongue.

"Cover him with your mouth and slowly work deeper." She took Jakmerah's erection in her mouth, sliding up and down on it, taking it deeper each time.

Gheni started moaning.

"He'll like to be sucked on. Suck hard and deep, but sometimes gentle, and sometimes just lick him."

Gheni's moans came faster, and Dania drew his cock deep into her mouth, her cheeks hollowing as she sucked hard and fast.

"Oh, yes, Jakmerah. Yes!" Gheni cried.

Shena could see Jakmerah's mouth moving busily on Gheni as she gasped, then stiffened.

"Ohhh," she wailed, her cry intensifying until finally she moaned loud and long. Her climax seemed to vibrate through everyone in the room.

Finally, she slumped. Jakmerah released her thighs, and she sank down beside him on the bed. She leaned over and kissed him, long and lingering, her hair streaming over his face. She smiled and lay back on the bed, watching Dania's head bob up and down on his cock.

"Dania, come here." Jakmerah opened his arms to her, and she released his erection from her mouth.

She climbed on top of him, and Shena sucked in a breath as Dania impaled herself on his raging-red cock. Jakmerah grasped her hips as she bounced up and down. Two, three, four times, and then they both groaned. Jakmerah's face tensed. Shena could see the base of his penis every time Dania shifted upwards before grinding down. They picked up their pace, her body thrusting down on him, swallowing him, over and over again. Faster and faster. Dania's voice rose in a wail of intense release.

Shena could feel the wetness between her own legs. She ached for a man inside her. Her breasts swelled with the need for a man's hands on her. Keern's hands. Keern's hard, rigid cock. She wanted it in her mouth, then inside her, thrusting like Jakmerah was doing with Dania.

Dania's moan trailed away, and Jakmerah let out a loud guttural sound. Dania smiled down at Jakmerah. She kissed him tenderly, their tongues entwining, then eased herself off his cock and stood up. She gathered her clothes and pulled them on, then approached Shena. Dania gestured Shena to the chairs at the table in the corner, where they had a view of the couple still on the bed.

Gheni sat up and licked Jakmerah's not-so-rigid cock.

"Mmm. You taste of Dania."

His cock hardened quickly as she sucked him.

"You can't see very well from here," Dania said to Shena, "but she's stroking his testicles. She cups them gently in her hands as she sucks on his penis. She's probably swirling her tongue around him while he's in her mouth, too."

"Now, my love." Jakmerah's loving words signaled Gheni to release his cock from her mouth. He rolled her onto her back and climbed over her, then placed the tip of his penis at her opening.

Shena felt her body stiffen.

"What's wrong?" Dania asked.

"Won't this hurt her?"

Dania smiled. "No, of course not. This isn't her first time, but even if it was, when the man is gentle and loving, it doesn't hurt."

Jakmerah eased away from Gheni and looked at Shena. "You're afraid, aren't you? Because you're a virgin?"

His gentle, compassionate questions let loose the fear and horror she'd kept locked inside her for so long.

"Yes. My father ..." She swallowed, searching for words. "He gave a young woman to his soldiers ..." The ghastly scene flashed through her mind again, and tears streamed from her eyes. "He made me watch as they ... as they ..." Her throat choked up and she couldn't continue.

Jakmerah spat sharp words in a language Shena didn't understand, as Dania took Shena in her arms and held her, patting her back.

"It's all right. Go ahead and cry. It's all right."

Shena sobbed in her arms for a few moments. Another hand stroked her back, and she looked up to see Jakmerah standing beside her, still fully naked. She couldn't help but stare at his long, stiff cock jutting out over his belly.

"Shena, that is not how it should be between a woman and a man. Your father was a very sick man. He allowed those men to brutally rape that girl."

He stroked her hair. "That is not how it will be between you and Keern. He will not hurt you."

She wrapped her arms around herself. "This afternoon, he wanted to hurt me."

"But he didn't. He won't hurt you." He stroked her cheek. "Trust me. I've known him a long time. He is an honorable man."

She nodded, appreciating his reassurance, but uncomfortable with his nudity.

"Now, let Gheni and me show you how it should be between a man and a woman."

He smiled and returned to Gheni. He knelt beside her and drew her into a warm embrace, kissing her tenderly. She curled her fingers through his hair and pressed her breasts against his chest. He eased her back onto the bed and climbed over her, then stroked her between her legs.

"You're ready for me, my love."

"Oh, yes. I'm very ready. Make love to me, Jakmerah. Let me sing with the stars."

He eased his cock inside her. Slowly. Shena watched the woman's face as her tender smile turned to one of pure bliss.

"Oh, Jakmerah, that feels so wonderful."

He pushed in all the way, then eased back and pushed forward again. Gheni moved to meet him. He thrust forward, drew back, thrust forward, drew back.

Gheni's breaths came faster, and she made little moans and sighs. Their volume increased as he quickened his pace.

* * *

Keern breathed deeply, sucking in the warm night air. He'd taken a long walk to try to clear his head, but he still didn't know what to do about Shena. He'd been walking for hours. Time for some sleep, if sleep would have him.

He entered the palace and strode to his suite. As he entered the sitting room, he heard some disturbing sounds. Sounds of pleasure. Coming from Shena's room.

What the hell?

He strode to the door and flung it open. Shock chilled him as his *friend* Jakmerah happily fucked Keern's woman.

"What the hell do you think you're doing?"

Jakmerah didn't even look up. He just kept pumping into Shena until she screamed loudly. In abandon and release.

Keern strode across the room, ready to drag Jakmerah off her.

Jakmerah eased away from Shena and whispered something in her ear. She rolled away and drew the covers tightly around herself, her tawny hair cascading over the white sheets.

Jakmerah stood up, naked, his cock still hard and glistening with Shena's moisture.

Keern's stomach contracted. He couldn't decide whether to slug Jakmerah, or to throw up and then slug him.

"Keern, you gave Shena to me, remember?"

Keern's fists clenched. "No, I didn't."

"You asked me to take her off your hands."

"*Darg'ra,* I said I wouldn't decide until tomorrow."

"Does that mean you've decided you want her?"

"I didn't want you to have her."

He stared at Shena's naked shoulder, barely showing beyond the white sheets. He had blown it. Jakmerah had relieved her of her virginity. Keern wished he had it to do over. He wanted to be her first one. In fact, he wanted to be her only one. Ever.

But it was too late now.

"Keern, do you want Shena?"

"Yes," he hissed. "I want her."

Jakmerah gestured across the room. "Then have her. She's still yours."

Keern jerked around to see Shena sitting beside another woman in the corner of the room.

"What the hell?" Relief washed through him.

"We were instructing her on how to please a man."

Keern seethed. She seemed willing enough to learn from Jakmerah. Keern had a feeling that as soon as Jakmerah had finished demonstrating lovemaking with another woman, he would have given Shena direct experience.

"She doesn't require any further instruction, thanks."

Jakmerah inclined his head. "As you wish."

The woman sitting beside Shena gathered the clothing strewn on the floor and followed Jakmerah and the other woman from the room. Keern slammed the door behind them.

"Did you enjoy that?" he demanded of Shena.

"It was very instructive." She kept her head down.

He remembered the fear in her eyes earlier and hated himself for it. No matter what she had done in the past, no matter what her part in Will's death, he did not want her to fear him. In fact, he wanted her to look at him like she had that first day he'd met her. With wide-eyed innocence and pure adoration. Maybe it had been only a lie, but he longed for it again because at that time, he had believed she could love him.

He tucked his hand under her chin and tipped it upward.

His heart compressed when he saw the red puffiness of her eyes. She'd been crying.

"Did Jakmerah force you to witness that?" he asked gently.

"No, not exactly. He wanted to help me."

Keern's insides churned. Wanted to help her fit in here, where her role would be one of concubine, of pleasing her man. Some man other than Keern.

If Keern left her here.

"You don't have to learn those things, Shena."

"Then what do I have to learn, Keern?"

He scowled. At himself, not her. Because he didn't know what to tell her. "Never mind that for now. It's late. We both need to sleep."

He stripped off his shirt and tossed it onto a chair. "Don't worry. I'm not going to touch you. We'll just sleep." He dropped his trousers onto the floor, then climbed into bed.

"No, I don't think we're just going to sleep," she said, her voice strong with determination.

"What?"

Shena tugged open her gown and let it drop to the floor. The sight of her glorious, firm, round breasts sent his pulse skyrocketing. Her nipples were already swollen and rigid. Watching Jakmerah and his woman had obviously excited her.

chapter thirteen

Shena wanted Keern, and she wanted him now. Whatever happened tomorrow or the next day didn't matter. She needed him, even if she could only have him for tonight.

Gheni, Dania, and Jakmerah had provided her with some powerful tools, and she intended to use them.

He watched, his bronze eyes intent, as she climbed onto the foot of the bed and prowled toward him. Slowly, she dragged the covers from his body, noting with satisfaction his fully aroused state. She tucked her fingers into his underwear and eased them down ... slowly ... revealing by inches his enormous cock. She locked gazes with him and licked her lips, slid his briefs down his long, lean thighs, and tossed them over the end of the bed.

Leaning over him, she lowered her mouth to the base of his erection and licked the length of his rigid cock, swirling her tongue around the ridge of the swollen tip. He sucked in a quick breath, but remained motionless.

A tiny, clear drop of liquid oozed from the opening, and she captured it on the tip of her tongue. She cupped his chin in one hand while she parted his lips with her fingers, then swept her tongue into his mouth to share his taste with him.

Still he didn't move, so she took his hands in hers and guided them to her breasts, planting his palms on her hard, sensitive nipples. She sucked in a breath at the exquisite feel of his hot hands cupping her breasts.

She eased one of his hands downward and tucked it into the intimate folds between her legs, then dipped his finger into the thick moistness pooling there. Pulling his damp finger to her mouth, she dragged her tongue along its length as she had his cock, then drew his finger inside and sucked with a rapid pulsing rhythm, as Dania had shown her. His breathing accelerated, but he still refused to react. So she dipped his finger into her dampness again and used his finger to circle her nipples, glazing each one with her own moisture, then leaned toward him, offering an erect pink bud to taste. He flicked out his tongue and lapped across her slippery, puckered nub, and she gasped, totally unprepared for the intensity of the feeling. He smiled.

"You're acting like the most experienced whore I've ever met."

She tried to stop the scowl from overtaking her features, but it settled for a moment.

"Don't worry," he continued, "I appreciate your efforts. I just ..."

No! He was pulling away from her. She had to think fast. She slid her hands over her breasts and squeezed her nipples, satisfied at the gleam in his eyes as he watched her. She grasped his cock with both hands and pumped several times, then closed her lips around him and drew him as far inside as she could. Repeating the rapid pulsing rhythm she'd used earlier on his finger, she sucked on him, almost fainting at the heady feeling of his rock-hard cock in her mouth. She cupped her hands around his sac and kneaded gently.

"Oh, God, why are you doing this?" His head fell back and he moaned.

She sucked and sucked until, suddenly, he stilled her head.

"No, I don't want to come in your mouth."

She felt hurt and rejected, but determined not to give up. She licked his nipple and sucked sharply, then laved him with her tongue. She repeated the same treatment on his other nipple.

"Shena, I can't take much more."

"Make love to me, Keern. I want you so badly."

His eyebrows drew together, and the serious look on his face confused her.

"You aren't giving me much choice, are you?" He rolled her over and eased her onto her back.

He held her pinned to the bed, his hands roaming free over her body. His mouth captured one slick nipple, and he began his own torture of her, his gaze spearing hers, suckling with determined precision, drawing a ragged moan from her.

"Is this what you wanted?" he murmured between nipples.

All she could do in response was nod, her head lolling freely back and forth.

He stroked from her shoulder, over her breasts, down to her slick folds, and slipped a finger inside.

"You certainly feel ready." His gaze locked with hers. "Is this really what you want, Shena?"

She nodded.

"You don't have to do this. I'll take you back to Tarun if you want. Still a virgin."

She shook her head. "I want you to make love to me."

He slid the tip of his penis into her slick opening.

She resisted the urge to tense up. She stared into his eyes, knowing she loved him, knowing he wouldn't hurt her.

"You're sure? You're not afraid?"

"Not of you."

He captured her lips in a passionate kiss. His tongue slipped into her mouth at the same time as he eased the head of his cock inside her in a slow, even motion. Her muscles contracted around him. The feel of his hardness nudging into her felt deliriously pleasurable.

He stopped. "Are you doing alright?"

She nodded, keeping her breathing as steady as she could. He leaned down and captured her lips, then surged forward. She jerked and cried out, the sound muffled by his mouth. He gently stroked the inside of her lips as he continued to push forward, slowly, until she held his complete length inside her. He kept his body perfectly still, kissing her tenderly, allowing her body to get used to his rock-hard cock buried deep inside her. Her eyes drifted closed. She relaxed and shifted a little. The feel of his rigid length stretching her inner flesh swept away thoughts of pain and made her insides melt.

He deepened the kiss. A sweet, tender, passionate kiss that took her breath away.

She felt him pull back, and her eyelids sprang open. Was he stopping?

He smiled at her astonished expression and pushed deep within her again. "Don't worry, sweetheart. I don't intend to stop now."

He pushed in again, a little faster this time. Then again.

"All right, Shena?"

"Yes."

He thrust forward again.

"Oh, God, yes."

She arched to meet him. He thrust again and again, driving into her at a steadily increasing pace until all she could feel was the rhythm of their bodies joining, the pulsing beat of their hearts, the impact of their bodies as he led her to the edge of the precipice and threw them both off. Her world spun out of control, and her mind exploded in a starburst of ecstasy.

She clung to him in quiet desperation as she spiraled back to reality, realizing she hadn't allowed a safety net. She had allowed herself no protection for her heart.

* * *

Shena awoke cradled in Keern's arms, her head pressed against his broad chest, his slow and steady heartbeat sounding in her ear.

He nuzzled her temple, his breath sending tremors along her neck.

"You're awake," he murmured.

Sunlight streamed in the window, shimmering across the white sheets. Night was over. Fear quaked through her. Now that morning had arrived, what would Keern decide to do with her? He had said he'd take her back to Tarun if she wanted, but would he stay, too?

Did he still hate her?

"Keern, I didn't tell my father you stole my virginity."

He stroked her back. "Yes, I figured that out."

She turned to face him. "How?"

"One clue was your absolute terror of losing your virginity. You made me believe it was an act the first time, but last time I knew you weren't acting. Another was when you told me your father whipped you. The third was that you said your father would punish you if you lost your virginity. There is no way I would believe you would tell your father anything to give him reason to punish you."

He smiled at her.

"You really do believe me?"

He kissed her lightly. "Yes, I really do believe you."

Breathing came more easily, but tears pushed at her eyes. He pulled her into a warm embrace, holding her close against his chest. He kissed the top of her head.

"Keern, I'm so sorry about your brother."

"Thank you." He eased back and stroked her hair from her face. "I realize now you had nothing to do with Will's death. Unfortunately, I can't say the same thing. Shena, I killed your father."

He stared at her, his tarnished-bronze eyes dark with regret.

She nodded. "I know."

She knew any other daughter would have been grief-stricken when she'd found out about her father's death, but all Shena had felt inside was a cold emptiness.

"You had to avenge your brother and protect your family."

"Do you forgive me?"

She stroked his cheek. "Yes, of course."

He tugged her close again, melting the coldness inside her.

"You deserved better than him, Shena. You deserved love and tenderness. You deserved to be cherished." He kissed her on the lips, tenderly. "If you will allow me, I'd like to make up for what you didn't have as a child. I would like to spend the rest of my life showing you how wonderful you are. I'd like to spend day and night loving you."

She stroked his cheek as tears spilled from her eyes. "Oh, Keern."

He kissed her neck, then tantalized with a trail of kisses sweeping down her chest. "I'll start right now."

He captured her nipple in his mouth, laving it with his tongue, loving it with tenderness. It jutted forward. He licked the hard tip, then sucked deeply. She cried out at the intense feeling.

"Do you want me to make love to you, Shena?"

"Yes."

She arched to him, showing how much she wanted him. Her hand slid down his chest, then curled around his cock. Her fingers stroked the tip, and he twitched in her hand.

He rolled her onto her back and licked one nipple, then the other, then dragged his tongue down her belly to her clitoris, which he dabbed at mercilessly.

She pumped his cock.

He smiled. "Do you want me inside you?"

"Yes. Definitely, yes."

He slid his cock to her opening and eased forward in one long, smooth stroke. Her muscles clenched, holding him in a tight, welcoming embrace.

He stayed like that, buried deep inside, staring into her eyes. He brushed her mouth gently with his own, then nudged her lips open to slide his tongue inside. The effect of his rigid cock filling her, his gentle tongue caressing the walls of her mouth, and his hard male body pressed the length of her gave her a feeling of deep serenity. He owned her, he had complete control of her, but he would never abuse her or his power over her.

"Keern, there's something you should know."

His face tensed. "What is it?" he asked softly.

"I love you."

The tight line of his mouth broadened into a totally devastating smile. He pulled back and thrust into her, making her gasp.

"Do you?"

She nodded. "I have since that first day, when you protected me from the soldiers at the pool. You were so strong and powerful, yet so loving. I had never known that any man could have such capacity for love."

He drew out, then slowly spiraled forward, making her dizzy with swirling pleasure.

"The way you looked at me then, Shena ... I had hoped it was love."

He pulled back and spiraled forward again. She clung to his shoulders, loving how he loved her body.

"I have a confession, too," he said. "In case you haven't figured it out yet, I love you, too."

He drove into her, straight and hard. She felt the waves of pleasure starting.

He pressed his lips to her ear and blew lightly, whispered, "I love you, Shena," and drove in again.

"Oh, Keern." Waves washed over her, flooding her body with pleasure.

"Shena, will you marry me?"

He thrust forward

"Yes."

Then again.

"Yes!"

Harder. Faster.

"Yes, oh, God, yes!"

She splintered into a million different pieces scattered on the wind as Keern tensed and released his seed inside her. She fell back on the bed and held him tight, loving the feel of him still buried inside her.

A warm fuzziness had spread throughout her entire body, and a broad smile spread across her lips. She whispered into his ear. "In case you didn't get that, I said yes."

He nuzzled her neck. "Yes, I think I did hear that."

He nibbled her earlobe, then captured her lips in a passionate, tender kiss.

"I love you, my darling Shena, and I will never let anyone hurt you again."

"Oh, Keern, I love you so much."

Their lips met in a blaze of happiness and passion.

A knock sounded at the door.

They ignored it.

The knocking became louder.

"Keern, it's Jakmerah."

Keern released her lips and smiled. "I'd better let him in, or we'll never get any peace."

A feeling of emptiness nudged through her as his penis slipped out when he pulled away. She wanted to push him down on the bed and capture him again, keep him prisoner in her warm, feminine depths forever.

But she did have forever. He had asked her to marry him!

The knocking continued.

Keern kissed her lightly, then pulled the covers over their bodies. "Jak, stop that infernal knocking and come in," Keern called.

The door opened and Jakmerah stepped inside.

His gaze swept over the two of them. "I take it you two worked things out."

"Definitely." Keern linked his hand with Shena's. "She's decided to let me keep her."

"Really?" Jakmerah raised his eyebrows.

"We're going to be married," Keern continued.

Jakmerah leaned against the doorjamb and smiled. "I knew you'd finally figure it out, my friend."

epilogue

As Keern rode toward the gates of his home, with Shena by his side, he heard the horn sound and whoops from the guards. His name sounded on their lips, along with shouts and hurrahs.

It was good to be home.

As the gates opened and he rode through, people greeted him.

"Keern, you've finally arrived."

"Jacob."

As wonderful as it was to see his cousin again, sadness filled him at the memory of his last homecoming and being met by Will.

He dismounted his horse and helped Shena dismount hers, handing the reins to eager hands. He strode toward Jacob and dragged him into a bear hug, pounding his back for good measure.

"Jordan is here. He wanted to meet this new wife you wrote us about."

Jacob glanced at Shena and smiled. Keern took her hand and led her toward the house, smiling inside at his cousin's obvious interest in the newest member of their family. Keern hadn't missed the fact that Jacob's gaze had briefly settled on Shena's rounded belly.

"Brother, here you are." At Jordan's voice, Keern spun around.

Jordan threw his arms around Keern. "So, my big brother returns, and with a wife in tow." He smiled at Shena. "And a little one on the way, I see."

Keern patted Shena affectionately on the belly. "Yes. I had a long journey to find this woman. Ironic, given she was our closest neighbor."

Shena clung to Keern's hand, uncertain how his family would accept her.

"Neighbor?" Jacob stared at her, his brow furrowed.

"Hello." Shena spoke for the first time. "My name is Shena."

"Shena? As in Shena Wakefield?"

Keern slid his arm around her shoulder, tucking her against his side. "But now Shena Herrington," he responded.

"Keern," Jordan said, "her father killed Will. How can you — ?"

"She is not her father. She is not responsible for the sins of her father."

"Of course, but — "

"No buts. She is my wife and a member of this family now."

Tears welled in Shena's eyes. Keern's heart constricted at the sight.

"Keern, I'm sorry. I don't want to cause strife between you and your family." Shena's quiet words set his protective urges on high.

He drew her closer. "You're my wife and I love you. You will always come first."

"What's going on here?"

Jenna, Will's widow, stood staring at the men. Jordan's wife, Kristinna, and Jacob's wife, Helena, stood beside her.

Keern gave each of the women a hug.

"I introduced my new wife, Shena, to Jacob and Jordan."

"And why have they decided to upset such a lovely young woman?" Jenna asked. Her gaze crossed each man in turn.

"She is a Wakefield." Jacob pointed out.

All gazes locked on Jenna.

"No, she is a Herrington." Jenna opened her arms to Shena. Hesitantly, Shena stepped forward, and Jenna enveloped her in a warm embrace. "Welcome to the family, Shena."

Jordan hesitated, then stiffly stepped toward her and offered his hand. Shena glanced at Keern. He knew she had never had a loving family and this whole situation unnerved her. At his reassuring nod, she shook Jordan's hand. Jenna jabbed Jordan in the ribs, and he cracked a smile, then grabbed Shena and wrapped his arms around her, giving her a sturdy bear hug — gentler than the one he'd given Keern, but solid. Once he released her, Jacob hugged her in kind. A shy smile spread across her face, and Keern's heart swelled at the sight.

The other two women welcomed her with gentle hugs.

That evening, the women arranged a wonderful feast to welcome Keern and Shena. They spent the evening in the glow of warm family conversation. Shena had never experienced the warmth of family, and her heart swelled with the shared love all around her.

"I never thought a Wakefield would be sitting at our table. And such a lovely one at that," Jacob mused. "Now, our lands will be joined."

"And in love, not war," Jenna added.

Keern smiled and kissed Shena tenderly.

"But more importantly," Jordan mused, smiling warmly at Shena, "I never thought I'd ever see my brother so happy. You must be a very special woman, Shena."

"Believe me, she is," Keern responded, hugging her close to his side.

Shena had never felt so much love. She patted her stomach, joy swelling through her at the thought that her child would know the joy of belonging to such a warm, loving family, just as she now did.

The Good Assistant

Cynthia Sax

As I push through the revolving doors and enter Powers Corporation's glass and marble lobby, my phone hums against my hip. It can't be my too-sexy-for-any-woman's-sanity boss. He called me two minutes ago.

I drape the dry cleaning bag over my shoulder, unclip my phone from my skirt's waistband and groan. It *is* my boss. John Powers, billionaire, CEO, and unabashed control freak, is calling me yet again. I sigh. He goes a little crazy whenever I leave the building.

"You have a conference call at 5:30 with Rexton Bass, Mr. Powers," I answer, skipping the formalities. My boss has no patience with small talk. I quicken my pace, my heels tapping against the fine basket weave tile.

"I know where I'm supposed to be." John's growl sends a shiver of excitement rolling down my spine, tightening my nipples and heating my skin. He's the only man who can turn me on with his voice alone. "Where the hell are you, Grant? And where the hell is my shirt?"

John calls everyone by his or her last name. I wouldn't mind this quirk if my last name was at all feminine or sexy. "I have your shirt, sir, and I'll be in your office in five minutes." I avoid the receptionist's pleading gaze as I pass her desk, turning toward the bank of elevators.

Men and women in dark suits crowd around her. All of these visitors want a meeting with my insanely busy boss.

"Get that perky ass moving. I don't have all day," John barks. "I'll be waiting for you in my briefs." The phone clicks. A dial tone buzzes.

My hot-as-hell boss is waiting for me in his briefs. I stare at the small screen, visions of tanned skin, hard muscle, and dark brown hair flooding my overworked, sexually deprived brain.

John doesn't mean anything provocative by his statement. He doesn't see me as a woman. I attach the phone to my waistband and press the button for the elevator. He doesn't see me at all. I'm a resource, an extension of his office like his desk or laptop.

The elevator doors open and I step inside.

"Miss Grant, wait up!"

I hold the doors open and Stacie Moore, the company's newest, most aggressive marketing coordinator, flounces across the threshold, her large breasts jiggling. She's blonde, beautiful, and generously endowed. If she wasn't an employee, she'd be a perfect candidate for John's next one night stand. I select the button for the top floor.

"Is that Mr. Powers' shirt?" Stacie plucks at the dry cleaning bag. "My, he has wide shoulders, doesn't he?" Her blue eyes glow.

I know all about my boss' potent affect on women. I fell in love with him during my job interview. That was three years ago and my obsession with him hasn't dimmed, not one bit. "Mr. Powers doesn't mix personal and business matters, Miss Moore." I jab the button for the marketing floor.

Stacie lifts her eyebrows. "You get straight to the point, don't you?"

I don't say anything as I do get straight to the point. Working for John has trained me to cut through the bullshit.

"I like that." She grins. "So you and Mr. Powers aren't together?" She dances in place, her short skirt hiking up with each wiggle. "You aren't a couple?"

A couple? John and I? I glance at my reflection in the mirrored walls. I remain a plain, flat-chested brunette. I haven't magically become a curvy blonde, a woman worthy of these outrageous assumptions. "He's my boss and that's the extent of our relationship."

Lines appear between Stacie's finely arched eyebrows. "Mr. Powers doesn't look at you like a boss looks at his employee."

I stare at her. "How does he look at me?"

"Like he wants to lock you in his man cave. He's super protective of you." She tilts her head. "But maybe that's because you're his assistant. He relies upon you."

John Powers doesn't rely upon anyone. He built his real estate empire on his own, having no industry contacts, overcoming poverty and a lack of a college education.

"I always speak before I think." Stacie laughs. "Forget I said anything."

She talks about switching jobs and her new roommate and the movie she saw last night, her conversation not requiring any contribution from me.

This is a good thing as all I can think about is her observation about my boss. She has to be wrong. John doesn't want me. He doesn't even lust after the gorgeous supermodels and actresses he dates, his attitude toward the women apathetic.

The elevator doors open at the marketing floor. "This is me." Stacie laughs again. "It was good talking to you, Miss Grant." She exits, her skirt flipping upward, revealing more of her tanned legs.

I gaze at my reflection. The hem of my black skirt suit reaches my knees. I impulsively reach under my jacket and pull my skirt three inches higher.

My cheeks heat. I'm a fool. John won't notice the length of my skirt. I'm his assistant, a woman who picks up his dry cleaning, manages his schedule and arranges his dates.

The doors open, revealing the slick, stylish executive floor. I smile at Nancy, the receptionist, as I pass her antique desk. She wears a headset, her lips moving, her words hushed. Although it is five thirty-five in the afternoon, four men in dark suits wait in the brown leather chairs.

They aren't waiting for John. My boss is attending a charity dinner tonight. His meetings for the day are done.

I hustle along the hallway, my heels falling soundlessly on the pad-ded brown carpet. Gold-framed pictures depicting Powers-owned real estate hang on the beige walls. The desks are spaced widely apart, the corner offices claimed by board members. Every meeting room is filled with corporate decision-makers.

The ultimate decision-maker has his door open, uncaring about his state of undress. I rush into John's personal domain and skid to a stop, my heart squeezing, my body humming with awareness.

My boss stands facing his floor to ceiling windows, gloriously naked from the waist upward, his shoulders broad and his back straight. Silver scars, remnants of his rough childhood, slash his golden skin. His tan is natural, his forearms darker than his shoulders, and his dark brown hair is cropped close to his head. Tuxedo pants hug his narrow hips, his feet are braced apart and a phone is pressed to his ear.

A massive mahogany desk paired with a brown leather captain's chair dominates one end of the office. The shelves lining the interior walls are filled with textbooks, every weighty volume read by my self-educated boss. John's suit, shirt, and tie are discarded over the two guest chairs positioned in front of the desk.

I stride to the brass coat rack and hang his shirt beside his tuxedo jacket. John turns, and his gaze meets mine, his brown eyes dark and smoldering, resembling the richest, most decadent hot chocolate. My stomach flutters.

His profile is sharp, his thin blade-like nose and defined chin striking rather than classically handsome. More scars circle his neck. According to internet reports, a druggie slashed my boss' throat when he was a teenager. Not even that brush with death could slow him down.

My gaze drops and my pulse increases. John's tuxedo pants are undone, the v exposing stark white cotton briefs. A trail of fine brown hair travels downward from the indent at his navel, disappear-ing under the waistband. I lick my lips, wishing to follow this path with my tongue.

"What?" John barks into his phone. "Hell no, Bass." He returns his gaze to the blue sky, his focus on the call. I remove the shirt from the wire hanger. "There has to be profitability in this project. I'm running a business, not a charity."

This isn't the complete truth. Powers Corporation does give money to charity. I tap his fingers. John lifts his arm, his frown deepening, and I slip the shirtsleeve over his hand, his musky male scent engulfing me.

John leans into me, lowering his big body, allowing me to dress him. The soft cotton pulls tight across his wide shoulders, his back muscles ripple and his biceps bulge. He's a man in his prime, strong and beautiful, and I long to drag my lips over his tanned skin, to taste every inch of him.

Good assistants don't taste their bosses. With my slight form positioned in front of my executive's much larger physique, I feel tiny and feminine and needy, so very needy. My fingers tremble as I fasten his black enamel buttons, quickly covering his magnificent chest, his chiseled abs, his heart-wrenching scars, removing the temptation to touch him. My normally keen-eyed boss thankfully doesn't notice my reaction to his near-nudity.

"I know Grant told you that," John rumbles, his voice deep. "What I don't know is why you didn't address my concerns immediately." He spreads his arms.

I reach around his trim waist. His body is seductively warm. I tuck his shirttails into his pants, smoothing the material over his clenched ass cheeks. Dressing John is a test of my professionalism, a test I know I will some day fail.

"I'm a busy man. I don't have time for bullshit."

I wince, having warned Mr. Bass not to waste my boss' valuable time. The young CEO clearly didn't listen to me. I slide my hands around John's hips, over his groin, trying not to touch him, unsuccessful in my quest. My boss is too big, all over.

His cock hardens. In the past, I told myself this was a natural reaction, a man's response to any woman's touch. Now, after the discussion with Stacie, I'm not as certain. Is he reacting specifically to me, to my hands on his body?

"That's what I need to know," John continues his phone conversation.

I fasten the button of his pants. The impressively large ridge in his white briefs prevents me from doing more. I nibble on my bottom lip and glance upward at his face, undecided as to what to do next. John doesn't look at me, showing no indication that he knows I'm standing before him.

Stacie must be wrong. He doesn't want me. He doesn't even realize I'm here. I glide my fingertips over his briefs, flatten my palm along his cloth-covered shaft, and nudge him to the side. A shudder rolls down John's torso, shaking his shoulders.

He knows I'm here now. I smugly tug the metal teeth of his zipper closer together and slowly pull the tab upward, stretching the black fabric of his pants over his hardness. His knuckles whiten around the frame of his phone.

I reach into the right front pocket of his pants, pressing my fingers into his hip as I remove the cufflinks I've stored there, the devil in me teasing him more, seeking to ensure he's aware of me. John's gaze flicks downward, his eyes excitingly dark, tempestuous, holding a warning I won't, can't heed.

I grasp his left wrist, fold the cotton neatly and insert the cufflink, my head bent over my task. John's knuckles are scarred, silver slashes marring his tanned skin, a testament to his rough childhood and his warrior soul. He acts the sophisticated man now but he has fought for every thing he's earned, building his business from nothing.

John transfers his phone from his right hand to his left and I fasten his right cuff, resisting the urge to kiss his scars, to lave the raised skin with the flat of my tongue, to care for him the way I yearn to care for him.

"Breakeven should never be your goal." John bends over, lowering his face to my eyelevel. I retrieve his bowtie and loop the strip of black fabric around his scarred neck. "Grant must have told you that also." My normally direct boss avoids my gaze as he straightens.

Could Stacie be right? I fasten the black cummerbund around his waist. Could John be interested in me?

"She'll set it up."

I hold out his jacket and he shrugs into it. My heart squeezes. Clad in his normal suits, John's appeal damages my control. In a tuxedo, he's downright lethal. I brush my hands over his shoulders and place a folded cloth handkerchief in his pocket, completing his sophisticated ensemble.

"We'll continue this conversation tomorrow." John ends the call, lowering his phone. "Bass wants to meet tomorrow, eleven thirty, half an hour, my office."

John already has a meeting tomorrow at eleven thirty. I maintain my blank expression, not showing my dismay. His schedule will have to be rearranged yet again. "Yes, sir." I extract his keys and wallet from the pocket of his suit pants and I hold them out to him. His fingers brush over mine as he retrieves his essentials.

"Bass is an idealistic kid," my boss declares.

"Yes, sir," I dutifully reply. Rexton Bass is two years younger than John and three years older than I am. "His proposal has legs though."

"So you say," John drawls. "Walk with me, Grant."

He waits for me to exit first and then stalks soundlessly behind me, his tread light for such a large man. My boss prefers that I walk in front of him. I suspect this is to buffer him from overzealous employees.

"Is she meeting me at the venue?" he asks.

Is *she* meeting him? I smother my grin. He doesn't remember his date's name. "Yes, a car has been dispatched for Marcia. You sent her the usual dozen red roses."

"What did you put on the card?" John presses the button for the elevator. "I hope the message wasn't emotional. The last one was a clinger, wanted my direct number." The doors open. He allows me to enter first.

"You wrote the standard 'Beautiful flowers for a beautiful woman.'" I wave my passcard over the sensor and choose executive parking, ensuring the elevator makes no other stops. "Marcia is an actress." I prep him. "She plays a vampire in a TV series."

"I don't plan to talk to her." John frowns, crowding me into the right rear corner. "Have your phone on. We have work to do."

We always have work to do. "My phone will be on all night, sir." I stare at his back, my view obstructed by one massive male.

"Don't sound so grumpy, Grant. I told you, when I hired you, this was a full time job." John glares over his shoulder, his expression stormy as though I've insulted him by wanting a social life. "*I* deserve to be grumpy. I did what you said and tested that damn chair for three days. It's a piece of shit. I don't need the massage mode. I need something I can sit on."

I sigh. Other top executives raved about the chair, claiming it relaxed them. "I'll return it tomorrow, sir."

"And why am I attending this event?" He bumps against me, the contact sending a surge of sweet sensation over my body. "Couldn't we have written the charity a check and be done with it?" He slides a finger between his neck and collar and pulls, loosening his bowtie. "You know I hate these things."

I do know he hates these events, his mood always darkening before he has to make an appearance. "A wise man once told me we all have to do things we don't want to do," I quote him.

He turns his head and narrows his brown eyes at me. "That wise man should be working."

"That wise man should take advantage of this event and hobnob with the Mayor." I give my goal-oriented boss a task to accomplish. "The zoning issues won't fix themselves."

"Are you handling me, Grant?"

"I wouldn't presume to do that, sir." The doors open and I walk in front of him to the waiting limousine. Dave, John's smartly dressed driver, stands by the vehicle. "The Mayor made a comment to the press recently about the absurdity of non-fraternization policies so you might not want to mention that topic."

"I don't want to mention any topic. Small talk is a waste of time." John pauses, looming over me, big and tall and very, very male. "It would be more efficient if assistants could attend these events."

He wants me by his side. A fierce joy fills me. "This is personal, not business."

"For me, it is always business." John's gaze lowers, lingering on my legs. "Your skirt seems to be shrinking." His eyes glow. "You might want to look into that."

He noticed the length of my skirt. "I'll add that to my long list of things to do."

"You do that." John chuckles softly, the sound unexpected, arousing, real. "Don't leave the building without letting me know first. I'll call you." He climbs into the limousine.

I wait, watching as the man I love, the boss I adore is driven away. He'll spend the night being wined and dined by the city's elite, touched and held by one of the most beautiful women on the planet. I'll be alone. Again.

As I trudge toward the bank of elevators, my phone buzzes. The number displayed on the screen belongs to John. I'm not completely alone. I smile, my spirits lifting.

chapter two

"The Mayor wants me to attend his wife's cocktail party tomorrow," John informs me hours later. He was truthful when he said he wouldn't talk to his date. He has been talking to me all night. "You're right about avoiding all talk of non-fraternization policies. The ass was caught last Tuesday sticking his cock into another big-breasted assistant. It cost him a bundle to keep those photos off the internet."

I hear the disgust in my boss' voice. He doesn't believe in mixing business and pleasure, his views well known within Toronto's social circles.

"His poor wife." I sigh. And poor me. John will never see me as more than his assistant. I wiggle my ass into his about-to-be-returned chair.

"The man is a fool." In the background, glasses clink and voices murmur. "What are you doing? Your voice sounds strange."

My boss' skills of observation are frightening. "I'm trying your chair's massage function, sir." Leather hands grope my back. "It's an unusual experience."

"It's creepy as hell." John laughs. "Thank the lord. This dinner is finally wrapping up."

I move the lever in the armrest to vibrate. "Oh my God," I moan, the chair rubbing against all of the right spots.

"Are you okay, Grant?"

"I'm fine, sir," I lie. I'm not fine at all. I'm shamelessly aroused by my boss' kinky chair. The leather smells of his musky cologne. I've heated the seat to match his body temperature. The friction against my cloth-covered pussy is divine.

"Don't leave the office," John instructs. "I'll send the car for you."

"Okay." I'm too distracted by the good vibrations to argue. "Enjoy the rest of your evening, sir." I certainly plan to.

Before he can ask me for anything else, I end the call and set my phone on his desk. He'll be cross with me tomorrow, but this, I need now. I lean back in the chair, swiveling my hips. I need it so badly.

There's too much fabric between my body and the chair. I hike my skirt to my waist, baring my ass. My mons is covered by a skimpy G-string, the bright pink silk already soaked with my readiness.

Once or twice, after a heated encounter with my oblivious boss, I've retreated to the bathroom and touched myself, bringing myself to quiet fulfillment. I've never masturbated in public, in my boss' office, where anyone can catch me, where he can catch me.

John isn't here. He's in the lavish hotel room I reserved for him, cavorting on the luxuriously soft sheets, reaching his own satisfaction, balls deep inside a gorgeous actress.

I'm alone, unneeded. My phone is silent. The rest of the floor is dark. No one else is around. Even the cleaning lady has left for the night.

I can release my inhibitions and not worry about being caught. No one will know. I grind into the vibrating seat, branding the leather with my scent, my wetness. My boss won't realize it's my pussy he smells tomorrow.

I tug on the waistband of my panties, pulling the silk tight against my folds, against my clit. My neatly trimmed brown curls escape their confines. I play with myself, moving the fabric over my sensitive skin, escalating my desire.

I imagine John is behind me, holding me, manipulating my panties, my passion. He'll be as ruthless and demanding with my body as he is with business. The flimsy ribbons crossing my hips snap and the silk falls to the seat.

I'm nude from the waist down. If a coworker, a board member or my boss enters the office, they'll see my pussy. I prop my heels on his desk and spread my legs wide, giving my imaginary audience a better show. Cool air sweeps across my bare skin, driving my arousal upward.

I close my eyes and touch myself, skimming my fingers over my feminine folds, spreading my wetness, my heat. In my fantasies, John is the person touching me, his fingers thick and rough, calloused and scarred. I circle my clit, winding my need, my want tighter and tighter. He'd be hard for me, focused on my body.

I dip one finger into my entrance, the grip snug from sexual neglect. For three years, I've lusted after my boss exclusively, having no interest in any other male. I stroke in and out, in and out of my pussy, working my body, my tempo slow and steady.

The chair hums against my ass, supplementing my intimate caresses. I add a second finger, stretching myself open. The darkness intensifies John's scent and, in my fantasy, I hear him breathing, feel him watching me. He's here with me. I'm not alone, never alone.

John is large, a massive man. Emulating his size requires all four of my fingers. I pump my pussy, the sucking sound of wet flesh against firm skin obscenely loud. My breathing grows ragged, a tight band of emotion strapping around my chest, squeezing my lungs.

"John." I arch my back and lift my hips, rising into each thrust of my hands. I call out his name again and again as I plunge my fingers into my pussy, rub my thumbs against my clit. My juices splatter against my upper thighs, against the leather seat. I work my body faster, trembling, satisfaction fast approaching.

I grit my teeth, pushing myself farther, demanding extra, more stringent with my body than my boss would ever be. My passion builds until I can't take one more thrust, one more second of delicious torment, my need stretched agonizingly tight.

I smack my clit with the heel of my hand. This pain breaks me, and I scream, bucking upward, my pussy clenching around my fingers, moisture flowing over my hands. The darkness bursts with light and color. Sound rushes in my ears. Ecstasy shakes my form.

The tremors gradually ease and I still, sagging against the chair, the tension drained from my shoulders, from my soul. "I needed that." I roll my shoulders.

"We're keeping the chair," a familiar voice rumbles.

"Oh my God." I open my eyes, my body temperature dropping.

"You called me John previously." My boss gazes at me, at all of me, my body spread open to him. I straighten, lowering my feet to the carpet, removing my fingers from my pussy. "Don't move," he commands and I freeze, confused, mortified. He *saw* me.

John rounds the desk, grabs my wrists and raises my fingers. "I have to taste you." He closes his grim lips around my index finger and sucks. The sight of my fingertip in my boss's mouth is the sexiest thing I've ever seen, and the pressure on my skin is exactly right, his mouth hot and wet. My nipples tighten to painful points, my arousal reviving.

His eyelids lower as he leisurely, thoroughly licks every finger clean, the expression on his face blissful. My boss is tasting me, my pussy juices, my skin, everything. I tremble and he tightens his grip on my hands, flicking his tongue over me.

Silence stretches. I can't move, can't escape, can't retrieve my panties, the bright pink silk pooled on the carpet inches away from John's black leather shoes. The cursed chair continues to hum, brushing against my back and ass.

John lifts my hands to his face and he breathes deeply, his nostrils flaring, his eyes as dark as the night sky. He enjoys my taste and my scent. While this thrills me, I don't fool myself into thinking his enjoyment will change my future or ease my punishment.

"You've been a bad assistant, Grant." He pulls me to my feet.

I sway, my legs unsteady. "I know I've been a bad assistant, Mr. Powers." I lower my gaze to his chin, unable to see the disapproval, the disappointment reflecting in his eyes.

"You do not hang up on me. Ever," he bluntly states, holding onto me. "I end our calls. You do not."

"Yes, sir." I squirm inwardly with embarrassment as I wait for him to mention my activities in his chair.

"Now, go. Get me that young pup Bass' file." John releases my wrists. "We have work to complete." He sits down in his chair, the chair branded with my scent, with my wetness.

I gape at him, not moving, not speaking. Isn't he planning on firing me, punishing me, doing *something*? He saw me masturbate, heard me call his name, tasted me.

"The file *now*, Grant," John barks.

I jerk, his voice cutting through all of my concerns, and I rush out of the office, looking for the file.

* * *

We work until the early hours of the morning. I sit in one of the guest chairs across from John, our laptops and the desk separating us. He assigns me task after task after task, driving me as he drives himself, ruthlessly, without stopping.

Around two a.m., I hit the exhaustion wall. One moment, I'm blinking at a spreadsheet, trying to keep my eyes in focus. The next moment, John pushes against my right shoulder, shaking me.

"What? Where? Yes, sir." I raise my head, confused. My curls frame my face and cascade down my back, sticking to my cheeks. I always wear my hair up at work. I can't remember loosening the tight chignon.

"Where is your overnight bag?" John's eyes soften, his expression warm and caring.

I must be dreaming. My boss isn't warm and caring. I rub my hands over my face and his countenance becomes businesslike once more.

"It's under my desk, sir," I reply. He has asked me to always have an overnight bag packed, in case there's an emergency in another city. "Are we going somewhere?" I stagger to my feet and wander into the hallway.

"My house is closer to the office." John follows me, locking his door behind him. "We'll stay there tonight."

We'll stay there tonight. I'm sleeping over at my boss' house. I tug on the bag, my brain remaining fuzzy.

"You're a mess without your coffee, Grant." John takes the bag from me and clasps my hand, pulling me along the hallway.

I stumble forward, holding onto John's arm. His muscles ripple under my fingertips. I barely notice. My eyes feel gritty, my mouth is dry, and I'm tired, my exhaustion bone-deep. "My name is Trella."

"I know what your name is," he drawls, slowing his pace. I'm still dreaming. John doesn't slow down for anyone. "Trella Patrice Grant." He hooks his right arm around my waist, supporting some of my weight. "Who puts their middle name on their resume?"

"You asked me that during my first interview." I tuck my body deeper into his, savoring his heat, his musky scent, his unbending strength. "And again during my second interview *and* once more during my third interview. You were relentless."

"You never did give me a satisfying answer." He presses the button for the elevator. The doors open as though they've been waiting for us. We enter and he chooses executive parking. "You made no sense even then with your fancy degree and your hopeless amount of debt."

"That debt is all paid off now." I hold up one of my index fingers.

"I know it's all paid off." He rests his chin on the top of my head and rubs his fingertips into my hip. "Thanks to this job. What would you have done without me?"

"I don't know," I reply, too sleepy to lie. I can't imagine my life without him. "I love working with you." I love him.

"For me," he corrects. "You work for me. Tonight doesn't change that." He nuzzles into my hair, his tender actions belying his stern words.

We stand, staring at the red digital numbers, John's muscles flattening my curves, his arm around my waist, his fingers splayed over my hip. A companionable silence stretches, broken only by our breathing.

"Are you going to fire me?" I finally ask the question I've been worrying about.

"No, I'm not firing you." He sighs, his chest rising and falling against me. "But next time, lock my door. Anyone could have seen you."

The doors open and we walk to the waiting limousine. I'm steadier, more awake, but I don't pull away from him, relishing this rare chance to touch him, to belong, if only for a moment.

We reach the vehicle before Dave, the driver, wakes. He rushes around the hood, his flat black cap askew. He's too slow. John opens the door for me and I climb inside, inhaling the scent of leather and man. My boss slides along the seat until his thigh presses against mine. Dave takes my bag from him and shuts the door, enclosing the space, creating a private oasis for the two of us.

The limousine moves, the outside noise muted, the tinted windows darkening our already dark surroundings. John stretches his legs out, drapes his arms over the back of the seat, and says nothing. I sit with my knees pressed together, my hands clasped in my lap, very much aware of the big man beside me.

His eyes close, his breathing levels and his body relaxes. He has put tonight's activities out of his mind and I should be glad, ecstatic, relieved. I'm not. I'm irked that I showed him everything, my sexual self, my hidden dreams, a slice of my very soul, and he can forget all of this so easily, purging it from his memory as though nothing has happened, nothing has changed.

I take a deep breath, count to five, and exhale. "I'm tired of being alone, John."

He opens one of his eyes. "Mr. Powers."

"I'm not speaking to my boss. I'm speaking to you." I lift my chin. "I've been alone for the past three years. I won't be alone any longer."

John curls a strand of my hair around one of his fingers. It's brown, plain, unlike the golden hair he favors. "Are you threatening to quit?" His voice is scary soft.

He's worried about losing his assistant. He doesn't care about me as a woman. I swallow hard. "No, I'm not threatening to quit." I turn my head toward the window and gaze at the blackness, not seeing anything other than heartbreak.

"Grant."

I'm Grant, not Trella, never Trella. I grit my teeth. Stacie was wrong. John doesn't want me and I was a fool to think he did. I was an idiot to love him for so long. "It was nothing, sir. I'm just tired."

"Then sleep." John gathers me closer to him, folding me into his hard body. "We have a lot of work tomorrow and I'll require you to think rationally."

I haven't been thinking rationally around him, not from that first interview. Tomorrow, this will change. I close my eyes. Tomorrow, I'll get over John Powers.

chapter three

Getting over John Powers would be easier if I didn't wake in his bed, with his body spooning against mine. I'm wearing a camisole and boy shorts I don't remember changing into. John sports his briefs and he's hard, his cock pressing against my ass cheeks, one of his palms curved over my left breast.

His bedroom, and this must be his bedroom, is massive, filled with dark wood antique furniture, Tiffany lamps, a Rembrandt and other oil paintings hanging on the beige walls. The space is warm and inviting and overwhelmingly masculine, like the man holding me.

I wiggle, brushing against John, and he groans into my ear, squeezing my breast in retaliation, my nipple tightening instantly. I'm wet and ready. If he saw me as more than a convenient lay, as Trella rather than Grant, I'd take him right here, right now.

He doesn't see me this way yet I can't leave him in this uncomfortable state. I care too much about him. "Roll onto your back." I turn in his arms and push on his shoulder.

He frowns, lines furrowing on his forehead. "What are you planning?"

This is John, always wanting to be informed. "I'm your assistant." I reach under the white bed sheet, slide my hand underneath his briefs and curl my fingers around his shaft. He jerks in my palm, his body stiffening. "I'm assisting you."

"Grant." His voice is low and strained. "This action will have consequences."

"I'll accept those consequences." He needs this. He needs me. I move between his spread legs, under the sheets, and I push his briefs downward. "And when I have my hands on your cock, I'm Trella, not Grant." I grip his base, savoring his girth, his length. Short brown hair curls around his base. I pump him slowly, my clasp loose. "Relax and let me take care of you." He can't see my face, can't see who is pleasuring him. If he wishes, he can pretend I'm someone else.

My boss doesn't desire this ambiguity. He needs to know who has his cock in her hands. He pulls the sheets away from us and studies me, his expression grave. I stroke him up and down, up and down, my rhythm constant and controlled.

Silence stretches and my cheeks heats. Does he want this or am I forcing him?

"Harder," he instructs. "Faster."

He wants this. I tighten my grip and increase my tempo. John groans, rocking into my hands, the grooves around his mouth deepening, his lips flattening. I control his satisfaction. With one squeeze of his balls, I can make him come.

I don't want him to come, not yet. His veins pulse under my fingertips. I want to make this encounter last. I've waited years to touch him and I don't know when he'll allow me to touch him again. A dab of pre-cum forms on his tip. I graze my thumbs over him, spreading his essence. His dark skin glistens.

My tough-as-nails executive shakes and a sense of wonder, of womanly power fills me. I'm causing my powerful billionaire to lose his renowned control. He's at my mercy, unable to resist the pull of my hands. I stroke him, watching his face as I work his cock. He gazes at me, his eyes black with need, his focus on me alone.

"Soft," he rumbles. "Your hands are softer than I imagined."

He has thought about my hands. My chest warms. "What else did you imagine, John?" I lick my lips and his cock bobs, his gaze moving to my mouth. "Did you imagine my tongue on you?" I lower my head and brazenly flick my tongue over his tip, tasting him.

He thrusts upward, bumping against my lips. "Yes." John buries his fingers in my wild curls, holding me to him, not allowing any retreat. "Use that ever moving tongue on me, Trella." He breathes my name.

I'm Trella, not the sexless Grant. I lick over his cock head, exploring his slit, skimming his rim, and I lave down his shaft, tracing his hard length. His grip on my hair intensifies and pinpricks of pain shoot over my scalp, exciting me. I play with his balls and explore his body, inhaling his musk, the manly center of him. He pushes his hips upward, silently asking for more.

"Do you know what I fantasize about?" I peek at him through my lowered eyelashes. John watches me, his expression thunderous. "I dream I suck you dry." I push my lips over him and a strangled sound comes from his throat. He wants this, me. I pause, tugging gently on his tip, and he lifts into me, pushing more and more of his cock into my mouth.

My lips are wrapped around my boss' shaft. I sink down on him, the slide slow, sensuous, mind blowing. He's seen me masturbate and now, I'm sucking him off. John might be able to compartmentalize sex and business, separating the two. I can't. Our relationship will never be the same. I'll never view him with detachment.

If this sexcapade ends my employment, I'll ensure I have no regrets. I take as much of his hard, hot cock as possible, drawing him inside my mouth. His scent fills my nostrils. His coarse brown hair tickles my chin. I can't take all of him. He's too large, his tip tapping against the back of my throat. I cover his remaining shaft with my hands.

"Perfect," John groans, massaging my scalp with his fingertips. "You're perfect for me."

I suck, my cheeks indenting around him and he moans, twisting his hands, winding my hair around his fingers, the pain exquisite. His chest rises and falls, his breathing ragged, his body lifting.

I release John and he falls back into the mattress. The muscles over my boss' stomach ripple, a sheen of wetness covering his golden skin, his silver scars. Bracing against his hips, ensuring I maintain the same depth, I bob over him, gliding my lips along his length, varying my suction.

He pushes me down and then pulls me off him, guiding my movements. I allow him this illusion of control as I allow him to believe he sets his own schedule and manages his own time. This is what a great assistant does and I'm a great assistant. I'm also great at sucking cock and I'm applying all of these skills now. He clenches his jaw, a tic of emotion pulsing in his cheek, his eyes black, gleaming with desire.

He desires me. I reach upward and rake my fingernails along his torso, leaving a trail of pink on his tanned skin, marking him. He's mine. I claim him.

John doesn't talk as I pleasure him. My boss doesn't believe in uttering unnecessary words, his guttural sounds and frantic thrusts expressing his pleasure. I long to tell him how I feel, how I've yearned to touch him like this, to taste him, smell him. My mouth is busy, filled with his hard cock. I can only think the words.

My boss' toes curl, his balls hug his shaft and his thighs quiver. If I wish, I can push him over the edge now.

This might be the end of our relationship. I tighten my grip on his base, holding back his release, prolonging this sweet torture. My lips hum and my cheeks ache. Teardrops trickle down my cheeks.

"Trella." John's voice stretches with need.

I look upward, my teeth skim against his shaft, and all hell breaks loose. John shoves me off his cock, his roar temporarily deafening me. I shriek, thrashing my arms, airborne for one agonizing second. The sheets tangle around my body, slowing my flight, and I land dangerously close to the edge of the bed, bouncing on the mattress.

John drives his hips upward. Hard spurts of cum arc from his cock head, splattering on his stomach, his upper thighs, wasted.

I fold my fingers into fists, furious. "What did you do?" I fume.

"Protect." My control freak boss stills, his eyelids lowering.

"I'm clean." I grab four tissues from the box on the nightstand. "I haven't had sex in … a while." Since I started working for him. "And I've been tested."

"I know." John opens his eyes, his gaze meeting mine.

He knows. He wasn't protecting himself. He was protecting me. My anger dissipates. "I would have taken that chance." I dab the tissues over him, cleaning him, caring for him as I always do, with a tenderness no assistant should ever feel for her boss.

"I would never put you at risk."

This almost sounds like he cares for me but I know my boss. He would never put any of his employees at risk. I toss the tissues into the wastebasket.

John pulls me upward, sliding my body over his, and he pushes my face into his heaving chest, his heat, his scent engulfing me, his palms curving over my ass.

I rest against him, listening to the sound of his breathing and the beating of his heart. A Turner hangs near the bed, the painting depicting a ship at sunset, the colors warm and rich.

"You like antiques," I comment, wishing to know more about him.

"Are you making small talk, Grant?"

I'm back to being Grant, his androgynous assistant. I sigh. "It was an observation."

There's a long pause.

"Antiques hold their value," John shares. "If I lost everything and needed to sell them tomorrow, they'd be worth something."

I gaze up at him. "Do you worry about losing everything?" Is this why he works so hard?

"It could happen." His lips are flat, grim. "Anything is possible."

Are *we* possible? I touch the scars around his neck. The grooves are deep. "You'd rebuild." I would help him, forgoing my salary, investing my own meager savings. He'd need those savings. He'd need me.

John catches my wrist and moves my hand lower. "It wouldn't be easy but yes, I'd rebuild."

There's no doubt in my mind he'd be successful. I swirl my fingertips into his chest, watching his muscles ripple under my palms. My boss is intelligent, driven, the type of man who achieves whatever he wants.

"We should work." John reaches for the tablet resting on the nightstand, transitioning into business mode, ending our more personal conversation.

"I should take a shower." I slip out of the bed, not yet ready to resume my duties as his assistant.

* * *

When I exit John's massive bathroom, he's gone. The bed is neatly made, my clothes are folded on a Chippendale chair and my overnight bag is placed between the finely carved chair legs. I dress quickly in a black suit, twist my crazy curls into a semblance of order, and forgo the urge to snoop. My boss trusts me in his personal space. I won't abuse his trust.

I open the door, hear the TV, and follow the noise downstairs, navigating the wide wooden staircase. A huge chandelier sparkles over my head. Every inch of the house is filled with antiques, with warmth, with John's scent.

I find my boss in the kitchen, his black suit jacket draped over a chair. The décor is French country and the tiled floor is immaculately clean. A TV hangs on the far wall, displaying the business network. Coffee drips into a carafe on the counter.

John, clad in a crisp white shirt, blue tie, and dark dress pants, stands between a center island and a gas range. He dices a green pepper into small precise cubes.

I now understand where the specks of color on his cuffs come from. "You cook?" I move beside him, clasp a block of gruyere cheese and the hand grater.

"It's a life skill." His gaze flicks to me and returns to the green pepper. "We need a cup of cheese for our omelets." Drops of moisture glisten on his brown hair. He must have taken his shower elsewhere.

I grate the cheese into a small white bowl. "Did your mom teach you how to cook?" His mom, a single parent, raised him. I know this from the interviews he's given.

There's a long pause. "We didn't have these fancy ingredients."

John slices an onion. "Toward the end, when she was sick, we'd stretch the eggs with water."

I wait. He says nothing more. His mom died from cancer when he was sixteen, leaving him alone. I know all about being alone.

"I taught myself how to cook," I volunteer. "My parents were always working. They didn't have time to teach me." They didn't have time for me. I'd be left to my own devices for hours, locked in our small house, where I'd be safe yet solitary, cut off from everything and everyone.

"My mom had time," he bluntly states. His mom worked two or three jobs, struggling to support them, and she had time for him. She loved him.

"They didn't care enough to teach me," I amend. I suspect my parents had been relieved when I moved out. I hadn't contributed to the household, hadn't been needed.

John steps closer to me, his body heat soothing some of the pain inside my soul. I'm not that little girl any more. I'm not alone and I'm not a burden. My boss might not need me but I do help him. I'm helping him right now.

"That's enough cheese, Grant." John moves the bowl. "The Pittsburgh deal is going forward." He reverts back to business, a safe, emotionally neutral topic of conversation, and I'm glad. I don't want to talk about my painful past. "Read me the specs."

I unclip the phone from my waistband, search for the information and recite the numbers. John tilts his head as he listens. He then asks questions. I find the answers for him. We do this every morning but today, we're in the same room. We're together.

While John cooks, I set the kitchen table, pour the coffee into mugs and address more of his concerns. My mind needs coffee to function. His brain doesn't, his thinking fast and his attention to details keen.

I sip from my mug as I scan through the files. His management team sends me the information. My job is to find it, my boss not having the time to read each document.

"You don't know?" John plates the omelets and places one in front of me.

"I'll ask for the answer, sir." I set the phone on the table. "You'll have it by noon."

He sits beside me, pressing his leg against mine. "I need the answer earlier." John turns his wrist and gazes at his silver Rolex. "This morning has been surprisingly efficient."

Is this what I am? An efficiency? Sexual release and business support rolled into one being? "Are you pleased?" Does this arrangement satisfy him?

John frowns. "It isn't like you to fish for a complement, Grant."

"It isn't like me to spend the night with my boss." I bite into the egg and flavor explodes in my mouth. Hot damn. I moan, my eyelashes fluttering. My billionaire can cook.

John bumps against me and I gaze at him. His eyes are dark with passion. "I'm very pleased." He doesn't sound as though he's talking about business. "I've wanted this for years." My boss reaches over and steals a forkful of my omelet.

I divide the dish into two equal pieces, transfer one half to his plate. "You've wanted me for years?" I do the same with his omelet, placing one half on my plate. My boss prefers to share food with me. It is one of his more adorable quirks.

"Yes." John eats slowly, his gaze fixed on my face. "You're a very desirable woman." His eyes glow. "And I'm a man."

He thinks I'm desirable. Heat spreads across my chest. This is not a vow of undying love but it's a start. "You *are* a man." I allow my gaze to drift down his body, over his shoulders, his arms.

John straightens. "Eat your breakfast, Grant," he instructs, turning his attention toward the scrolling ticker tape on the bottom of the TV screen.

My attention remains on the man I adore. I'm a convenience for him. I might never be anything more. Is this enough for me?

My heart says this isn't.

chapter four

The drive to the office is one long moving meeting. The conference call is streamed into the limousine though speakers embedded in the walls. We can't hold a private conversation as there are mics situated around the interior. Instead, John texts me and I text him back as we sit beside each other.

I listen quietly while John grills the European team, his commanding tone moistening my pussy and tightening my nipples. He's dominant, very much the boss I know, love and desire. I fight the urge to drop to my knees, unzip his pants and —

John pulls me onto his lap, this unexpected action interrupting my fantasy. I squeak, surprised. He covers my lips with his palm and shakes his head. I close my mouth and nod, communicating that I'll remain silent.

He releases my mouth and folds me into his body. As my boss lists his expectations for the next quarter, his voice strong and true, he casually slips his hands underneath my jacket, skimming his course palms along my bare skin, setting off tremors of desire within me.

I tremble, pressing my thighs together. He ruthlessly pries my knees apart, hooking my legs over his, opening me completely to him. I'm at his mercy, unable to speak, unable to move.

John returns his hands to my chest, splaying his fingers dangerously close to my breasts. I wait for him to touch me. He doesn't move, his chin resting on my shoulder, his cloth-covered erection nestled against my ass.

This is a new form of torture. I wiggle. He pushes down on me, forcing me to remain still. Power and heat and musk radiates from him. His management team asks questions. He answers, unaided, the information given to him before this call. John's memory is faultless.

I glance toward the front of the vehicle. The partition is lowered. Can the driver see us, see my legs spread wide, the flash of my red lace panties? I breathe heavily, a band of arousal winding around my chest.

My fingers twitch. I want to touch myself, to find release. John flattens my hands against my legs, silently commanding me to remain still. I swallow my protest and obey, the tension inside me escalating.

As a reward, he cups my small breasts, the roughness of his skin felt through the thin fine lace. My spine bows, his grip decadent, perfect. He squeezes and releases, squeezes and releases. I need more, more, more. I bite my bottom lip, suppressing my cries.

John's voice rumbles as he addresses another concern. I can't grasp his words, all of my attention on his hands, on my breasts, on the need building inside me. He ignores my nipples, spreading his fingers around the sensitive peaks, and I ache for his touch, his neglect crazing me.

He plays with me as though he has all day to claim me. No man has ever concentrated so much focus, so much time on my small curves. But then John is like no other man I know. He flicks the front clasp of my bra and releases my breasts, the skin on skin contact spiraling my need upward. My panties are soaked, my musk scenting the small space, and I shake.

He grazes his scarred knuckles under my breasts and I writhe, fighting to escape, to free myself from his delectable torment. I want to moan, to plead, to demand, and staying silent is killing me. I worry my bottom lip with my teeth until the tang of blood fills my mouth.

John circles my curves with his fingertips, the circles growing smaller and smaller. Tremors roll over my body, the waves of pleasure decimating my restraint, my thinking, everything except my desire. I rub my hands over my lace-covered pussy, seeking release, needing to come.

John's fingertips reach my nipples. He brushes over them once, twice, pushing my closer to the edge. I need more. I need —

He pinches my nipples and I scream, bucking upward, my world exploding with noise and color. I twist and turn, trying to break his hold. John squeezes harder and a second rush of ecstasy flows over me, a dark tunnel forming around me, a spinning vortex dragging me down, down, down.

I fling myself forward and then slam backward. Nothing dislodges his fingers. He clasps me tightly, pressing down on me with his arms, not allowing me to hurt him, to hurt myself.

The pleasure eases, I still, and he releases me. The vehicle is quiet, not moving.

And I remember. "The call." My voice is strangled. Did they hear me moan, scream? My face heats.

"The call ended before you broke," John assures me. "I wouldn't hurt you like that." He swings my legs to the side, turning me to face him and his countenance darkens. "What did you do to yourself, Trella?" He sweeps one of his thumbs over my bottom lip.

I'm Trella again. "I stayed silent." I smile at him, lightheaded, in a post-orgasmic stupor.

"You're a stubborn woman." He captures my face between his big hands and lowers his head. His breath wafts on my cheeks.

My boss is going to kiss me. I tilt my chin upward, eagerly awaiting his embrace.

John licks my abused lips, slowly, tenderly, tasting me, pain mixing with an exquisite pleasure. I want to taste him also. As I think this, my body reacts, my tongue darting between my teeth. We tentatively touch. He growls softly and covers my lips. Skin presses against tender skin as he claims me.

All hope of surviving this relationship with my heart and job intact evaporates with his kiss, the connection between us shifting, strengthening. John surges into my mouth, dominating me as he dominates every conversation, every negotiation. Our tongues entwine, tangle, tumble.

He cups my head, holding me to him, as he plunges deeper and deeper, exploring me. John tastes of black coffee and passionate man and I suck on his tongue as I sucked on his cock this morning, inhaling as much of him as I can. He rumbles into my mouth and tilts me backward, lifting my feet off the floor. I grip his shoulders, off balance physically, mentally and emotionally.

My phone buzzes, dancing across the leather seat, and he pulls away from me. "Who is calling you this early in the morning?" he demands.

He calls me every day at this time. My lips twitch. "You have a meeting in fifteen minutes."

"With New York?" John pushes me off his lap and reaches for his phone.

"With New York." I gather my overnight bag.

"Leave that here," he instructs, opening the door. My boss exits first and then clasps my hand, assisting me. I straighten and he releases me. I conceal my disappointment, feeling like a fool for expecting him to acknowledge our relationship publicly. John Powers doesn't mix business and pleasure.

I stride toward the bank of elevators, my head held high. My boss walks directly behind me. "Do you have their latest numbers?" he asks.

I scan the information and recite the highlights. He presses the button and the doors open. Stacie, the new marketing hire, stands in John's usual right rear corner. "Mr. Powers." Her eyes widen as she sees me. "Miss Grant."

"Good morning." John chooses our floor and claims the spot next to Stacie. I'm surprised and I shouldn't be. She's a beautiful woman, exactly his type. I stand in the left rear corner, a hard knot of jealousy coiling in my stomach.

John moves to the left, standing partially in front of me, his wide shoulders restricting my view. "Do you have historicals?"

"Historicals, Mr. Powers?" Stacie replies.

"I'm speaking with Miss Grant."

His bluntness makes me smile while his returned focus pleases the woman in me. I murmur the comparable numbers from the previous quarters, my voice soft, my words meant for his ears only. The elevator stops numerous times, more and more employees filling the small space, everyone wishing to take the same car as the boss.

John shifts, blocking me into the corner. Soon, all I see is his black fabric of his suit. I whisper the information he should know into his left ear, his head tilted toward me. The elevator doesn't empty until it stops at the floor below ours, and then everyone exits.

"Where the hell are they all going?" my boss mutters. "Isn't that floor being renovated?"

I laugh. He doesn't understand his appeal.

John turns, glares at me. "Are you laughing at me, Grant?"

"I wouldn't dare laugh at you, sir." The doors open and I slide past him, brushing my breasts against his arm. He stiffens and his eyes flash. I scurry into the hallway, wave at Nancy as I pass her desk, the receptionist talking on the phone. Five men and one woman wait in the leather chair.

John trails behind me, his tread silent. "Don't turn off your phone."

"I never turn off my phone, Mr. Powers." I nod at Mr. Zanetti, the company's young CIO. He smiles at me, his white teeth flashing in his tanned face.

John places his palm on the small of my back, the contact sending sparks down my spine. Mr. Zanetti lifts his gaze and his smile fades.

"We have a lot of work to complete today." John's voice has a hard edge.

That my boss feels obliged to warn me says it will be a very long day. He enters his office, I sit behind my desk, and my phone buzzes against my hip. This is the first of many texts, John keeping me completely occupied for hours, requesting information, seeking status updates on projects, asking me to set up meetings.

Nancy calls me at eleven twenty. Rexton Bass, the brass young developer John is considering partnering with, has arrived. I return to the reception area to collect him.

Nancy speaks into her headset, her head turned toward the lobby's leather chairs, her attention snagged by Bass. The budding entrepreneur is oblivious to her admiration. He sits with his back to the wall, his blond head bowed over the phone in his hands. His skin is a perfect shade of golden brown and I suspect this shade doesn't vary over his trim physique, his tan being the product of a salon.

Rexton Bass is young, handsome, Harvard educated, and destined for success. Any other woman would lust after him. I feel nothing, no flare of arousal, no spark of interest. He's not John. He'll never be John.

"Mr. Bass." I stride toward the developer.

He glances upward. His eyes are a startling sky blue. "Call me Rexton, Miss Grant." Rexton slips his phone into his inside jacket pocket and rises to his feet.

Although Rexton's gray suit and black cotton crewneck shirt are well designed and trendy, the garments clinging to his fashionably fit form, they're wrong for this appointment. I hide my grimace. My more traditional boss will view his casual outfit as an insult, as a form of disrespect.

"I'm pleased to see you." Rexton extends his hand, his movements graceful, almost beautiful.

I grip his fingers. His palm is smooth, not one callous marring his skin. He's a baby. John's voice echoes in my mind. I release his hand. "If you'll come with me." I cross the threshold into the main floor and walk along the hallway.

"Powers told me you promoted my project, Trella." Rexton saunters beside me, matching my shorter stride, treating me as though I'm his equal and not merely an assistant. "May I call you Trella?"

I hesitate. No one in the company calls me by my first name. I turn my head, studying Rexton. He gazes at me expectantly. It'd be rude to say no. "Of course, you may."

He smiles, the skin around his eyes crinkling. "Thank you for defending me."

"I defended your project," I clarify, Rexton's gratitude warming me. He welcomes my help. He needs me. I can help him. "Don't repeat anything covered in your previous calls." I lower my voice and slow my pace. "Mr. Powers is a busy man. He doesn't tolerate any rehashing of information."

"That's a good insight to have." Rexton's hand brushes against mine.

I don't like him touching me. At all. I drift to the left, subtly putting more distance between us. "Don't mention his personal connection to the neighborhood," I coach. They are developing the block where John lived as a child. "This is a business decision for him and he won't appreciate it."

"Ahhh ... that's why he walked away during my first pitch." Rexton's lips twist. "I didn't know."

"You should have known." After years of working for John, I no longer have any sympathy for sloppiness.

"I guess." He sighs.

He's a couple of years older than me yet I feel ancient, wise, needed. "Do more research next time." We reach my desk. John's door remains closed. "You can wait here for Mr. Powers." I tap one of my guest chairs. The red light for John's conference call line remains lit. I sit behind my desk, conscious of the handsome man lounging before me.

"Trella — "

My phone buzzes. "One moment." I hold up my right index finger. John wants the sales comparables for the Wilmette project. I search the database and send him the information. "Sorry." I turn to Rexton. "You were saying?"

"Was that Powers?" he asks. I dip my head. It *was* John. "He relies upon you, doesn't he?"

He's the second person this week to say this. "I'm his assistant." I'm a resource for my boss, nothing more.

"I need an assistant." Rexton shifts in his chair. "I tried to hire an assistant through an agency. The people they sent didn't add any value."

"You either have to train an assistant." As John trained me. "Or you have to hire an experienced assistant already at the level of competency you require."

"I don't have time to train an assistant." He holds my gaze.

He can't be asking what I think he's asking. My boss, the man he hopes to partner with, sits in the next office. To pouch his assistant would be rude, a declaration of war. "This isn't a discussion you wish to have." It isn't a discussion I wish to have. Ever.

"We won't discuss it here," he concedes. John's door opens and Rexton leans closer to me. "Are you free for lunch?"

"Bass," John barks and I jump in my seat. My boss' eyes flash, his face hard. He's furious. This doesn't bode well for his meeting with Rexton.

"Powers." The developer leaps to his feet. The men's palms smack together, the skin whitening around their grip. Rexton pulls his hand away first, conceding to John's greater strength, and they move into the office, the door slamming shut behind them.

I receive a text message less than a minute later.

"That fool is asking about you."

I groan. Rexton isn't being subtle at all. He'll cause trouble for both of us. I don't reply, John's statement not needing an answer.

My phone buzzes again. "Why the hell is he calling you Trella?" John asks. I read the anger in his words.

"Because Trella is my name," I type. "I gave him permission to use it."

"I didn't give him permission," my grumpy executive replies. "Send me the notes for the lunch meeting. This fool is wasting my time."

chapter five

My boss' office door opens at noon. A subdued Rexton and a furious John emerge, the silence between them strained. The look on my boss' face tells me this deal is on life support. One more wrong move will kill it.

I suppress my sigh of disappointment and fix a smile to my face. "You'll need this file for your meeting, sir." I hand John a gray file folder with the information he requires. "If you'll wait here, Mr. Bass." I pat my guest chair. I don't dare call him Rexton in front of my boss. "I'll return to see you out." We'll have our talk then.

"Walk with me, Grant." John waves the file, indicating that I should lead the way, buffering him from other employees. I'm not equal. Not at all.

"Of course, sir." I stride toward the west meeting room, my back straight, my hips swaying. "The funding for the software rollout is in the budget but not all members of the team are on board." I give him the insights he needs for the next meeting.

"Bass is a fool." John's mind remains on his previous appointment. "What did they teach him at that fancy school of his?"

"They didn't teach everything, sir." I glance over my shoulder. John scans the area, his gaze shifting from the left to the right. I don't know who or what he's looking for. "He needs someone to guide him."

"I know why he wants to partner with me," my boss growls. "Why do I want to partner with him?"

"It's a good project." I stop outside the meeting room. All of the seats except one are filled, the team eagerly awaiting their leader's arrival.

"There are better projects." John looms over me. "I should exit these negotiations."

John has never cared about what he should do. I tilt my head back and meet his gaze. He wants to be involved in this deal. "Give him another chance, sir." I relay the answer I believe he wants.

"This will be his last opportunity, Grant." John scowls. "Tell him not to waste it." My boss enters the meeting room and the other participants clamber to their feet.

I retrace my steps. Rexton slumps in my guest chair, staring blindly into space, a frown on his handsome face.

He sees me, his head lifts, and his lips curl slightly upward. "It was the small talk, wasn't it?" He stands. Rexton is only an inch or two shorter than John yet he takes up less space, appearing much less threatening. "There's so much riding on these meetings. I couldn't stop talking."

As he can't stop talking now. "You'll have one more opportunity to convince him."

"Really?" His eyes widen.

"Really," I confirm, his reaction making me smile. Was John ever this young and eager? Or was he born tough, cynical, world-wary, the man I now love?

"Then we'll convince him." Rexton beams, his blue eyes sparkling. "Together." He catches my hand. "I need you, Trella." He squeezes my fingers.

I long to be needed, to be included. "I'm loyal to Mr. Powers." I pull my hand away from him.

"Of course, you are." Rexton smiles. "You're a great assistant. Great assistants are loyal to their bosses."

I frown, not liking this assumption. Loyalty is earned. I'm not a dog, blindly following her master.

"I appreciate that loyalty." The developer leans closer to me. "I appreciate you."

John has never said these words to me. Maybe I *am* blindly loyal.

"Have lunch with me." Rexton smiles. "There's a great seafood restaurant next door. We can talk about the development."

I'm not a seafood lover, but I do have to eat lunch and John wants this project to happen. He doesn't give second chances to many people. Mr. Zanetti, the CIO, walks by my desk, his gaze openly curious. This also isn't the place to have a sensitive business conversation.

"I'll walk you out, Mr. Bass." I stride down the hallway. Rexton catches up to me and walks beside me. He doesn't expect me to form a wall between him and others.

"Powers mentioned you went to college," Rexton says.

John talked about me? I blink, stunned by this revelation. "I attended the University of Toronto." I couldn't afford Harvard, couldn't afford to leave Toronto. "Undergrad only." I also didn't have the money for a MBA.

"It's a good school." There's a tinge of condescension in Rexton's voice.

John deals with this condescension every day. I press the button for the elevator. The not-so-subtle insults must have been ego battering while he was building his success. "All my education proves is I can be trained." I tilt my chin upward, quoting my boss.

"You've been trained by the best." The doors open and Rexton follows me inside. He claims one back corner. I stand in the other. If John were here, he'd position his big body directly in front of me. I feel strangely exposed without him, vulnerable.

"I know you're loyal to Powers." Rexton leans against the mirrored walls, his blond hair glowing under the overhead lights. "But he can train another assistant. He has the time and the knowledge to do this. I don't."

If I left him, John *would* replace me both at the office and in his bed. Pain pierces my heart. Months after our split, he wouldn't remember I existed, forgetting about me as my parents forgot about me.

"I need you, Trella," Rexton says all of the right words, appealing to my battered soul.

I force myself to think rationally, to consider the consequences, and as John has taught me, there are always consequences to every decision.

"Mr. Powers would view my defection as a personal affront," I caution. "If you hire me, he won't partner with you on the development. You won't have the benefit of his name, his contacts and his experience."

Rexton pauses for one telling moment. "I'd take that chance."

Part of me is flattered by his high opinion of me. The other part of me thinks he's a naïve fool. John can destroy him, tear his reputation to shreds, freezing all financing, blackballing him with potential partners. The risks far exceed the rewards. "I won't allow you to take that chance."

"Consider my offer, Trella," Rexton urges. "That's all I'm asking. I can't build my empire alone."

I do consider it. I consider Rexton's offer during the walk to the restaurant, while we order our lunches, throughout our strategy session. My relationship with John will end. Will it hurt less if I leave him before he leaves me? I'd save my pride yet sacrifice time with the man I love, the man I will always love.

My phone buzzes. John's number appears on my screen. "I need a moment." I hold up my hand, interrupting Rexton's steady stream of words.

"What can I do for you, sir?" I cup this hand over my mouth, trying to block some of the clatter from the busy restaurant. Rexton and I are seated at a corner booth. Every wooden table is filled with business people and tourists. A tired-looking waitress rushes from the kitchen, carrying platters of crab cakes and dipping sauce, her smile strained, her gray hair frizzy. A bearded man seated next to us wears a plastic bib, a pile of lobster claws piled on the plate before him. The sight makes me queasy, the fishy scent crawling up my nostrils.

"Where are you?" John's words are barely audible which worries me. The softer his voice is, the angrier he is.

"I'm eating lunch at the seafood restaurant on the corner." I don't lie to my boss. Ever.

The phone clicks. A dial tone buzzes. A shiver skitters along my spine.

"You should leave now," I tell Rexton, my voice flat. No longer hungry, I gaze at the yellow lettuce in the shrimpless shrimp salad I ordered.

"Pardon?" Rexton sets his knife and fork down on the red and white checkered placemat, having devoured his grilled salmon in record time.

"John is on his way to the restaurant and he's very, very angry." I poke a grape tomato with the tongs of my fork. "If you're here when he arrives, all of our strategizing is for nothing. You can kiss your partnership goodbye."

Rexton's eyes widen. "I'm leaving." He removes his wallet from his jacket's inside pocket, removes too many bills, and tosses them on the table. "Thank you, Trella." He squeezes my shoulder and dashes away, not looking back.

I remain seated and pick away at my salad, waiting for my boss. I don't have to wait long. Mere moments later, a shadow falls over my table.

"Where the hell is he?" John bites off each word.

I gaze up at him. His face is dark, his fingers are clenched into massive fists and his eyes flash. He's pissed off because I have a life, because I'm not in the office anticipating his next command. My lips twist. "He had another meeting."

"I have another meeting also." John's chest heaves. Beads of sweat glisten on his forehead. Did he run here? "Yet here I am."

Why *is* he here? "Did you need something, sir?"

"What I need is to not have to worry about you, Grant." He rakes his fingers through his hair, mussing the short strands. "I'm a busy man. I don't have time for this shit."

I blink. He worries about me? "I went out for lunch."

"You went out to lunch with that young fool." John sits beside me, trapping me between the wall and his hard body. "And he left you alone and unprotected." He pulls me onto his lap, not caring that we're in public. "You could have been hurt." He runs his hands over my shoulders, arms, chest and hips as though assuring himself I'm unharmed.

He's genuinely concerned about me. I lean back, sinking deeper into his fit form. "This is a family restaurant, sir."

"I almost died outside a family hospital." John rubs his fingers over the silver scars encircling his neck. "And I wasn't as successful then as I am now. I didn't have people targeting me, targeting the people working for me." He sweeps his hands over me once more. "You shouldn't be alone and you shouldn't be sitting here. You should always sit with your back to the wall." He indicates Rexton's vacant seat. "Never allow anyone to approach you from behind."

Had the strung-out junkie who'd slit his throat approached him from behind? The almost myth-like recounts on the internet had been vague. "Would you care if something happened to me?"

"Nothing will happen to you." John tightens his grip on me, pressing his arms against my ribs.

"But if something did — "

"Nothing will happen to you," he repeats. "When you have to leave the office or the house and I'm not available, Dave will accompany you. He's a former marine."

He's assigning his driver to protect me. "I don't need a bodyguard. I'm fine, sir."

"I'm not fine." John pushes me off his lap. "And you clearly *do* need a bodyguard. Your unauthorized lunch break has affected my entire schedule, inconveniencing myself and countless others." He stands, his jaw clenching. "It won't occur again, understand?" He gazes down at me, his eyes hard, his stance unrelenting.

I gulp air. He's still very, very angry. "I understand, sir."

"Move my one and two o'clocks." John places one of his hands on my back and propels me toward the exit.

I unclip my phone, accessing the calendar as we walk. "You have time to make your two o'clock." I find an empty space for the first meeting and send emails, ensuring the participants are aware of the change.

John holds the door open for me. "Actions have consequences, Grant." I step onto the busy sidewalk and pause, the sun's rays blinding me. "This time, I'll allow you to choose the consequences." He guides me toward the side entrance to Powers Corporation. "Choose carefully." He waves his passcard over the security sensor, pokes his head into the building and then gestures for me to enter.

He's ensuring the area is safe, protecting me. I climb the stairs to the second floor, forgoing the crowds waiting for John in the lobby. He walks behind me, guarding my rear, his palm pressing against the small of my back.

Is he protecting me because he's my boss? I step onto the second floor. Or is he protecting me because he cares about me? I rush toward the bank of elevators. Men and women sort the mail into slots, their gloved hands moving quickly. They laugh and tease each other, oblivious to our presence. The brown carpet is worn thin by the heavy carts. A large clock ticks, counting down the minutes of the workday.

My workday never ends. John calls me whenever he likes and he likes to call me often. "I'll work late tonight," I offer.

John presses the button for the elevator. "That's an expectation, not a consequence." The elevator doors open. Faces stare back at us. Undaunted by the crowd, John pushes inside, clearing a path for me. Employees chime greetings. He grunts his replies, maneuvering until I'm positioned between a mirrored wall and his solid form.

"It sure is a beautiful day, isn't it, Mr. Powers?" an eager young employee chirps, his face glowing with hero worship.

"Consequences, Grant," John mutters.

I smother my grin. My boss hates small talk. "This is a great opportunity to talk about the new social media campaign."

John looks over his shoulder and narrows his eyes. I narrow my eyes back at him. His lips twist. He faces his elevator-constrained audience, takes a deep breath and recites the speech he gave to the board last month, his voice rolling over me. His employees gaze at him as though gold gushes from his lips, their admiration almost painful to witness. I rest my forehead against John's spine and relax, my body hidden from view.

When the elevator opens on the top floor, the car remains packed. John ends his monologue and steps into the hallway, holding the doors for me.

"Good afternoon, Mr. Powers, Miss Grant." Nancy smiles. Her greeting is echoed by the three men sitting in the brown leather chairs.

My lips twitch. I doubt any of the men know who I am.

"What are you so happy about?" John growls, pushing me along the hallway. "Consequences are no laughing matter."

"You could dock my pay," I suggest.

"If I docked your pay every time you misbehaved, you'd be working for free."

As we pass Mr. Zanetti, I glare at the young executive. He's likely the one who squealed on me, telling John whom I was with. Mr. Zanetti frowns at me. John growls softly, his hand lowering to my hip. The CIO's eyes widen and he hurries away from us.

I pause near my desk. Half of a grilled Reuben, my favorite kind of sandwich, is set on a plate by my keyboard. I lick my lips, the corned beef, swiss cheese and sauerkraut on rye bread making my mouth water.

"You don't deserve that treat." John propels me forward. "You've been a bad assistant."

My shoulders slump. "Isn't eating in a seafood restaurant punishment enough, sir?" I enter his office, my heels sinking into the thick, soft carpet.

"Bass is a fool." My boss shuts the door. "Everyone knows you don't like seafood." The lock clicks, the sound startling me.

I turn. John's eyes gleam, his expression anything but professional.

"We're at work, sir." My gaze lowers to the pronounced ridge in his black pants. "Everyone will hear us."

"If I was a cruel boss, I'd allow them to hear you." He reaches for his remote control and activates the far screen, increasing the volume. Two talking heads heatedly discuss the Fed's stance on interest rates. "But I'm not a cruel boss." He tugs on his blue silk tie, loosening the knot. "This is your last chance to name your punishment."

He wants to punish me. I watch him remove his tie, the strip of fabric wrapping around his palms. What would it feel like to have his rough skin connect with my tender ass? I swallow hard, aroused by this thought.

"Choose or I'll choose for you," John warns. "You won't like my choice."

"A spanking," I whisper, unable to meet his gaze.

chapter six

John sucks in his breath, his chest rising. "You want me to spank you?" The excitement edging his voice confirms my decision, his response escalating my need. "Are you certain?"

"Yes." I wiggle, having never played these naughty games before. I'm uncertain of what happens next, what I should do, where he wants me.

"Bend over my desk," he commands. I don't have to worry. I'm playing these games with John. He knows exactly where he wants me.

I stride to the desk, my stomach fluttering with nerves, and I lower my chest to the hard wooden surface, stretching my arms out.

John loops his tie around my head, sliding the silk between my teeth. "If you need to scream, bite down on this, not on your lips." He skims one of his thumbs over my abused flesh. I flick my tongue, tasting him, his salt, his warmth. "Behave," he warns, securing the makeshift gag. The TV blasts in the background.

He runs his hands down my back, over my ass. I'm at my boss' mercy and, at the moment, he has none, his body remaining tight with suppressed fury.

"Widen your stance." He kicks my feet apart and I obey him.

"Better." He squeezes my curves, and my nipples tighten. "Your ass is now mine, Grant." He hikes my skirt up slowly, the cool air sweeping along my thighs. "I'll punish you as I see fit."

He traces my lace G-string, following the trail between my ass cheeks, over my mons, his touch delectable. "Did you wear this for me?" He rubs his fingers against me. "It's pretty." I rock into his hand. "But I prefer you bare." He twists the lace. The fabric digs into my skin and snaps. "I want to see your pussy clench."

John smacks my right ass cheek and I cry out, the sound muffled by his silk tie, my inner walls closing around nothing. "That's it." He rubs my heated skin with his course palms and I moan. "Your body wants my cock."

He cuffs my left ass cheek, his movement controlled, using only a portion of his strength, and I jerk under him, the pain exquisite. "But you don't deserve it." He spanks me. "You've been." Smack. "A bad." Smack. "Bad." Smack. "Assistant."

He presses his left hand between my shoulder blades, holding me down. His right hand connects with my ass again and again, the location, intensity and timing varying, keeping me off balance, focusing all of my attention on him.

I scream, plead, cry, my skin heating, burning, scorched by his palm, my protests muted by the gag. Even if John could hear me, I doubt he'd listen. My punishment is set and I don't want him to stop, not truly, my pussy humming with happiness, my soul wanting, needing this.

Actions have consequences and consequences have consequences. If I decide to work for Rexton or I choose to stay with John, John will always have this memory, know this secret kink of mine.

He's the only man I've ever trusted this much, wanted this much. The blows rain down upon my ass, the pain flowing into the sweetest pleasure, my wetness streaming along my legs.

"You're soaked, Grant," my boss comments on my shameful arousal. I squirm, unable to hide from him, every intimate part of me exposed to his all-encompassing gaze.

"You're dripping for me." He slides his fingers along my pussy lips and I tremble. "Dripping for my cock." He spreads my juices over my ass, swirls the moisture into my fiery skin, branding me with my own scent.

John grips my hair and tugs on the tendrils, forcing my head upward. "If I take you now, I won't be gentle." He leans over me, the ridge in his dress pants pressing against me. "I'll be rough."

I ache, needing him, my pussy empty. If I could speak, I'd beg him to take me, to ease this loneliness inside me.

John releases my hair. "Do you want me to fuck you?" he growls into my ear.

I nod vigorously, my entire body shaking with anticipation.

He chuckles. "You've been warned, Trella." A zipper rasps. A package rustles. I glance over my shoulder. He sheathes himself, rolling a condom over his massive cock. "Eyes forward," he barks.

I obey, not wishing him to change his mind or to continue his punishment. The need in me is almost unbearable. I wouldn't survive another sexy spanking. I'll go insane.

"Good girl." He positions himself between my spread thighs, brushing his hips against my burning ass cheeks. "I'll give you what you want." Warm latex-covered skin prods against my entrance. He pushes his tip inside me and I whimper into my silk gag, his girth stretching me painfully wide.

"I'll give you everything I have." John folds his rough fingers over my hips, holding me steady. His thigh muscles flex against me, and he thrusts hard. I scream, my spine bowing, my pussy protesting the invasion. "Yes." He drives even deeper, pressing his base against my feminine folds, shoving his hips against my abused ass.

God, he's huge. Tears drip down my cheeks, leaving salty trails on my skin.

John doesn't allow me time to recover, to adjust to his size. He pulls out to his cock head, and thrusts into me again, pushing me against the wooden desk, the edge digging into my upper thighs. It feels so bad and so good at the same time, pain and pleasure merging, the contrast numbing my brain and spiraling my need upward.

John repeats the action, filling me again and again. We fit together perfectly, as though we are designed for each other. My inner walls hug the bloom of his tip. My pussy lips drag along his shaft. The connection between us intensifies.

My boss shows no interest in our spiritual link. He uses my body, riding me hard, smacking his hips against my sensitive ass, slapping his balls against my thighs, owning my pussy with deep, sure strokes, dominating my smaller form. I can't escape him. All I can do is hold on, submit, accept, enjoy.

The mixture of agony and ecstasy drives me closer to the edge of fulfillment. I grit my teeth, refusing to fall before John does. He bends over me, grunting into my right ear with each thrust, his cotton suit sliding along my suit jacket, the layers of clothing frustrating me.

I yearn to feel his skin against mine, to feel his cum filling my pussy. I want no fabric, no condom, no barriers between us. Damn the consequences. I rock back into him, meeting his punishing rhythm, matching his passion.

"Behave." John growls, scraping his teeth against my neck, and I tremble, tilting my head, giving him access to more skin, to more of me. I ache. I need. I shake.

"You're so wet," he murmurs, his lips vibrating against my earlobe. "Warm. Tight." He pistons in and out of me, dangling me over the emotional vortex and then pulling me to safety. "I knew you'd be like this." He holds onto my shoulders, controlling my movements, propelling me backward, onto him. "Soft and perfect and mine."

I follow his lead, undulating under him. "That's it, Trella. Fuck me," he urges, his pace intensifying. "Fuck your boss like a good assistant." I clench down on his shaft and he jerks, groaning. "Do that again and I'll come."

I smile. This is exactly what I want. When he comes, I can come and I'm desperate for release, mindless with wanting. He withdraws, his cock head grazing my inner walls, severing more of my restraint.

John thrusts and I constrict around him, squeezing him with everything I have, forcing his fulfillment. He swoops downward, bites my suit-covered shoulder, the cloth muffling his roar. As he comes hard, he grinds his hips, the contact plunging me into a spinning black funnel of turbulent emotion.

I scream soundlessly, bucking, writhing, grasping for something, anything, my soul tossed, twirling, ripped from its bearings. He pushes into my release, pinning my hips to the desk, capturing me, securing me.

John holds this pose for three heartbeats, shudders and collapses, flattening me against the desk, covering me with his muscle, his scent, his heat. I'm sore, my ass stinging and my pussy tender, every inch of my physique pulsating from his hard usage, yet I've never felt more desired, more necessary.

He needed this release and I gave it to him. John loosens my gag and removes his tie, the silk damp and frayed. "Thank you." He nuzzles against my cheek and I smile sleepily, warmed by his gratitude. "You *are* a good assistant."

My smile fades. I want to be more.

"Though you misbehave at times." He pulls away from me, his cock slipping from my warm pussy, leaving me empty. "You have such a pretty ass." John bends over and presses his lips to my aching skin. "It's red from my hands." He squeezes me. Pain and pleasure shoots down my thighs. "I've marked you. Everyone will know you belong to me."

"I work for you." I push myself upward, groaning with the effort.

"You belong to me," John repeats. He discards the condom and fastens his pants, becoming my professional boss once more. "No other man will touch you." He grabs a couple of tissues from the box on his bookshelf and crouches beside me. "Spread your legs."

I obey him, my face heating. My reaction is foolish. He's already seen everything, been inside me, felt my pussy milk his cock, my tongue tease his slit.

John leans forward, his breath wafting on my inner thighs. He's looking at me, I know. My boss is examining every inch of me. I quiver, fighting the urge to press my legs together, to block his view.

"You're pink and perfect and mine." His voice is soft. He brushes the tissues over my thighs, my mons, my pussy lips, cleaning me carefully, thoroughly, his touch caring, almost reverent.

John straightens and tosses the tissues into the trash. "You'll attend the mayor's party with me tonight."

Is he asking me on a date? I stare at my boss. "This is a social event. Assistants aren't invited."

"I'm allowed a plus one." John lowers my skirt's hem, smoothes my jacket. "You're my plus one." He brushes a loose curl away from my face. "We'll work to and from the event, make up for the time we lost over lunch."

He's anticipating an evening spent working with me. My joy, revived for a couple of heart lifting minutes, dims once more. "That will be efficient."

"It will be." John smiles.

* * *

John wishes to work the entire night. I know only one way to distract him, the same method women have been using to distract men for centuries.

I stand in front of the full-length mirror in the woman's bathroom, gazing at my reflection, second guessing my plan.

From the front, my gold satin dress appears conservative, bordering on plain. I brush my long brown curls over my right shoulder. John won't be seeing the dress from the front. I turn and the sinfully soft hem of my skirt skims over my bare knees. The back of the dress dips obscenely low, the fabric gathered at my spine drawing even more attention to my ass.

Is this too sexy for a cocktail party? I nibble on my bottom lip. The dress is new, bought on impulse seven months ago and has never been worn in public. I didn't have anyone to wear it for ... until now.

I want to wear it for John. I want him to see me as a beautiful woman, as his date, not as his assistant. His mind won't be on work tonight. I clasp my matching clutch purse and exit the bathroom, my heart pounding.

John leans against the wall, his phone pressed to his ear. He's clad in a black suit, a white shirt, and a plain black tie, his ensemble simple yet classic, complementing his dark brown hair and golden tan.

My fingers twitch, the urge to touch him, to rub my hands over his shoulders, his chest, his hips, tremendous. I want him to want me with this same intensity.

"There's no wiggle room on the Bel Air build." John glances at me. His eyes glow and his lips curl upward. "We have tenants moving in." He stalks toward me. "They're in multiple locations." He curves his left hand around my hip, turning me. "Pushing the date — " His words abruptly stop.

My dress has rendered him speechless. I'm not brave enough to look over my shoulder, to face my boss' reaction. Instead, I walk toward the elevators, my hips swaying, my skirt swishing against my legs, my six inch heels cushioned by the carpet.

John pauses for one moment and then surges forward. "I'll call you back." He catches up to me easily and puts his arm around me, splaying his fingers over my bare skin, one of his fingertips dipping under the satin. "There are other men attending this party, Grant."

"I suspected there would be." I smile at him, his possessiveness lightening my mood. He must care for me a little. "Don't worry, sir. I'll distract them with the dreaded small talk and you can find a quiet place to work."

He presses the button for the elevator and the doors open as though the car has been waiting for us. "You'll be occupying that quiet place with me."

I claim the rear right corner. John stands in front of me, protecting me from no one. I shouldn't find this as thrilling as I do. "Someone has to hobnob with the mayor." I place my palms on his back. He has reapplied his cologne, the scent teasing my nostrils. "Dividing and conquering will be efficient."

John mutters something I suspect I don't want to hear. "There will be no dividing and no conquering. You won't leave my side." He glances over his shoulder, his gaze lowering to my non-existent cleavage. My taut nipples strain against the soft satin, a bra not wearable with my dress. "I don't want men gawking at my assistant." His tone is surly.

"I'm your assistant tonight?" I frown. "If I had known that, sir, I wouldn't have worn this dress." I turn and look at my reflection in the mirror, giving him a good view of my bare back, deliberately tormenting him. "Men will think I've dressed this way for you." I smooth my eyebrows and fix my lipstick. "And they'll assume we're a couple."

John clenches his jaw.

"I'll tell everyone this isn't true, Mr. Powers." I bend over and adjust the straps on my shoes. He sucks in his breath. "I'll let them know our relationship is strictly professional. I'm your assistant. You're my boss." I straighten. John's eyes are as black as his suit. "I have no claims on you and you have no claims on me."

"You're with me, Trella." His voice is soft. "I've claimed you and, if another man touches you, I'll destroy him."

I shiver with excitement. John doesn't make idle threats. He *will* destroy any man who touches me. "Because you care for me?" I press, needing to hear the words.

"Because you belong to me." His eyes gleam.

He can own me and not care for me. My parents taught me this. They claimed me as their daughter yet they never truly cared for me. "Do you need me, John?"

"I want you." He brushes one of his palms over the ridge in his dress pants.

Want and need are not the same things either. A want can be foregone. It is voluntary, a nice-to-have. A need is required, a necessity. If he needed me, I'd be essential for his success, for his happiness. He'd never let me go.

John doesn't need me. He doesn't need anyone. I summon a smile. "I see."

He pivots toward me, facing away from the doors, putting himself in danger. "I don't think that you do see." He cups my chin, forcing me to meet his gaze. Gold sparks flint in his brown eyes. "Your actions tonight will have consequences. Stay by my side."

I gulp air. I suspect these consequences won't be a sexy spanking. "I will, sir."

John searches my face. For what? I don't know. Then he smiles.

"Good girl." He presses a frustratingly quick kiss to my lips and turns toward the elevator doors. "I need the Bel Air numbers."

He needs the numbers but he doesn't need me. I extract my phone from my purse.

chapter seven

During the limousine ride, I perch sideways on John's legs, my ass hanging in the air, my skin remaining tender from the lunch hour spanking. John leans back in the seat, listening to the numbers I recite, his eyelids lowered and his body relaxed. He isn't asleep. His gaze is fixed upon my face. His calloused fingers stroke up and down my thighs, his touch distracting me.

I need him again, always, my workaholic billionaire and sexy boss, the only man I've ever loved, the only man I suspect I will love. Needing and loving him isn't enough. One-sided relationships never last, John taught me that. He has to need and love me also.

He raises one of his hands and drifts his fingertips along my cheek. "Your eyes sparkle like diamonds even when you're sad."

"I'm tired." This isn't a lie but it also isn't the entire truth.

"I've been working you hard, as hard as I work myself." John reaches into his inside jacket pocket.

I stifle a sigh. He's searching for his phone. We have more work to complete. There's always more work to complete.

John removes a black velvet box. "I've kept this for years, waiting for the right moment to give them to you." He opens the lid, revealing the most beautiful earrings I've ever seen. Diamonds cascade down a waterfall of finely woven gold. "Tonight is the right moment."

"You've kept them for years?" I remove my plain gold studs, my fingers shaking.

"Two days after your first interview, I saw them at an auction." John's eyes glow as he helps me with the earrings. They're surprisingly light, as light as his caresses. "They're French and very old and I knew they'd be perfect for you."

I play with the earrings, stunned that he'd give me such a treasure. He must care for me ... at least a little. "That was a risky purchase. You didn't know we'd be working together."

"Didn't I?" John's lips curl upward. "You were quick and clever, refreshingly candid, and you answered every question with that feigned subservience bordering on insolence you have since perfected. I knew I had to have you."

"For your assistant." I gaze at him. If my determined boss had wanted me sexually three years ago, he would have seduced me.

"For everything." John pulls me closer to him, pushing my face into the curve of his shoulder, cradling me against his body. "I knew you'd be mine."

How long will I be his? I discard this worry and savor his warmth, his scent, the quiet, a calm between requests. My billionaire boss is thinking, he's always thinking, and soon he'll need information to confirm or refute his thoughts. I flatten his tie, caress his chest.

The vehicle slows, stops. "Stay by my side tonight, Grant," John warns. The door opens. He exits first, holds out one of his hands.

I clasp his rough palm and allow him to draw me to my feet. Lights flash. Cameras whir. Reporters shout questions. John places his arm around me and guides me through the chaos. Someone asks who I am. Another reporter answers I'm his assistant.

A man in a poorly fitted suit opens the door to the mayor's concrete and glass modern mansion. We cross the threshold and enter a brightly lit lobby. The ruckus dissipates. Strains of a violin drift in the perfume-scented air, the contrast jarring.

We've traveled to a different world, a world where ugliness and assistants don't exist, a world where everyone is rich and beautiful and devoid of emotion. I don't attempt to fit in, to belong, gazing around us with unguarded wonder.

A sharp-edged modern light fixture hangs from the high ceiling. The walls and floors are white. The furniture is sparse, modern, and black. Modern art provides a splash of bright color in the monochrome space, drawing gazes.

Waiters in cheap tuxedos circulate with hors d'oeuvres. Men in dark suits and women in glittering dresses gather in groups of threes and fours, drinking out of champagne flutes and chatting. I recognize many of the attendees, John having met with them.

The mayor and his wife talk with an ad agency partner and his woman of the day. The city's top politician glances toward us, his eyes widen and he whispers into his wife's ear. She looks at John, then at me, and her face hardens. The mayor pulls on her arm. She shakes her head. He shrugs and approaches us solo, an insincere smile on his round face.

"Mr. Powers." The mayor grips John's hand. "And Miss Grant, Mr. Powers' lovely assistant. This *is* a surprise." He lowers his gaze, openly ogling my breasts and legs. "A delectable surprise." He smacks his lips.

I step backward, trembling with disgust. He's the city's mayor, a powerful man and I can't say anything, not without making trouble for my boss.

John draws me into his body, his clasp on my waist tightening. "If you don't show Miss Grant more respect, we'll leave," he warns.

"We wouldn't want that." The mayor meets John's gaze. "I've been waiting for this moment for years, the moment when the great John Powers violates his infamous non-fraternization policy, is caught dipping his pen in the company ink." He smirks.

John never mixes business and pleasure. My body temperature plummets, the wave of cold almost bringing me to my knees. Oh my God. By forcing him to recognize our relationship, I've made him a hypocrite, an object of ridicule. My shoulders shake. I've hurt John, damaging his pride and his reputation in the business world.

"I'm not you, Mayor Whitlock." John's voice is scary soft. "I don't violate my policies on a whim, never thinking of the consequences.

I knew what your reaction would be, what everyone would think. A smart man would ask himself why I'm taking this step."

The mayor's mouth opens and closes and opens again. He's not a smart man.

I'm not a smart woman either. I thought I was clever but clearly I'm not. I've hurt the man I love with my foolishness.

John steers me through the room, and I walk in a daze, not knowing how to fix this situation. Guests turn their heads, tracking our movements, hiding their moving mouths behind their well-groomed hands, their eyes gleaming with speculation.

They're talking about us, about John and his fall from grace. "I'm sorry, sir," I murmur, my head bowed and my shoulders rounded.

"Chin up, Grant," he commands. I obey, lifting my gaze to his. Gold dances in his brown eyes, my boss appearing more amused than angry. "This had to be done." He guides me around three giant haphazardly stacked cubes, the modern sculpture child-like.

"This didn't have to be done." I shake my head, confused by his lack of concern. "You could have asked someone else to be your date tonight. We could have kept our relationship private."

John maneuvers me into an empty corner of the room. "How could we keep our relationship private?" Furrows form on his forehead. "You're living with me."

I blink. "I am?"

His lips twitch. "You are." He grazes his scarred knuckles over my cheek. "You belong to me. I want everyone to know that."

My anxiety melts under his touch. "Tonight will have consequences." I push my face into his fingers.

"Tonight will have consequences for everyone." John curves his palms over my jaw, raising my chin even higher. "This is an opportunity to separate the clever businessmen from the idiots." He smiles.

This is the man I adore, always making the best of bad situations. I gaze up at John with admiration. "I love you." The words slip out.

My boss jerks backward as though I've physically assaulted him, his spine straightening and his muscles flexing.

Oh my God. I've made everything worse. "I mean — "

John presses his index finger against my lips, stopping my sure-to-be inadequate explanation. "We'll talk about this later." He glances pointedly to his right. Two bankers and their wives are watching us, listening to our conversation.

He won't tell me he doesn't love me in public. John would never embarrass me that way. "I'm sorry," I apologize again, turning my head, unable to look at him.

"I'm not sorry." His voice is soft.

A waiter offers us a selection of skewers. John chooses one beef and one chicken, forgoing the shrimp. He hands the beef to me and bites into the chicken.

I nibble on the tender meat, my mind spinning. I told my boss I loved him. There's no taking back this declaration, no pretending I don't feel the way I do. This is scary and also a relief. I no longer have to disguise my emotions.

John switches hors d'oeuvres, finishing the beef, leaving a piece of savory chicken for me. "We've found our quiet corner."

"Are we working?" I ask, hopeful. Business is familiar and safe. If we escaped for a moment, I might be able to deal with the rest of the night.

"We don't have time." John takes the wooden skewer from me and places it on a passing waiter's tray. "We have an incoming fool at twelve o'clock."

Rexton Bass rushes toward us. He's dressed in the same inappropriately casual gray suit and black T-shirt he wore to his meeting with John.

"Mr. Powers." He smiles, displaying perfectly straight teeth and a pair of dimples. "Trella." His blue eyes widen. "I didn't know you were attending this shindig."

"Her name is Miss Grant." John splays his fingers over my back.

"Right, Miss Grant." Rexton winks at me. "You look beautiful tonight."

Is he deliberately taunting John? I glance between the two men. My boss' face is dark and frighteningly hard. Rexton's expression is cheerful, the young man completely clueless. "Thank you, Mr. Bass."

"I asked you to call me Rexton." The developer bumps against me.

"Miss Grant isn't one of your fraternity house buddies," John growls. "She's my assistant and worthy of your respect. You call her Miss Grant. She calls you Mr. Bass." He hands me a flute of champagne, using this action to not so subtly push Rexton away from me. "Did you find the information I needed?"

Rexton answers, using fifty words when one word would do. His constant talking increases my stress levels. I've grown too accustomed to working for the quiet man by my side. John listens patiently to his young protégée. One of my boss' hands rests possessively on my hip. His chest presses against my back. I make mental notes on the information exchanged as I sip champagne, the bubbles tickling my nose, the crystal cool against my fingers.

A tech CEO and his laughing wife approach us. I stiffen, preparing for insinuations and verbal attacks.

"They're friends, not foes," John murmurs into my ear.

They're friends. I relax. They might not approve of John's actions but they won't hurt him. I smile at the wife. She smiles back, no judgment in her eyes.

There's no opportunity to talk with her. As John greets the newcomers, Rexton continues to ramble on, telling me about the issues he's having with a contractor. I listen half-heartedly, hovering between the two conversations, not actively participating in either.

The CEO teases John about fate making fools out of everyone. The wife says she thinks it is romantic. John offers no reply, his silence effectively shutting down the topic. There's a long painful pause and the CEO asks a business question. The two men talk, the CEO's pretty young wife paying close attention to the discussion.

She cares about her husband and her husband clearly cares about her, his arm hooked around her waist, his gaze softening when he looks at her. They're partners, officially in life, unofficially in business. They need each other. They love each other.

John waves away a waiter carrying a plate of bacon-wrapped scallops. Rexton grabs two of the hors d'oeuvres, holding them under my nose. I grimace, the smell making my stomach roll, and my boss tucks me into his body, his cologne partially masking the offensive scent.

We don't move from our chosen spot. John doesn't work a room. The room rotates around him. He holds court in the corner as more and more guests join us. I say as little as possible, content to have him field questions, exchange thinly veiled insults, steer conversations to business, always business.

Very few guests are interested in me. They assume I'm an empty-headed decorative piece, an employee hired merely because she's good in bed. Some of them say as much, comparing me to the mayor's so-called assistant, the redhead he was caught fucking. It's hurtful and ego damaging and I bury deeper and deeper into John's hard physique, concentrating on his voice, his touch, his scent, seeking to ignore the others.

* * *

Two hours later, John stands protectively in front of me, having backed me into the corner. The alcohol has flowed freely and the tone of the party has shifted, the men becoming more aggressive and the women more promiscuous. The mayor's wife has disappeared, conceding defeat after the mayor's redheaded, well-endowed assistant crashed the event.

Peeking around John's big body, I watch, appalled, as this supposed assistant wiggles on the mayor's lap. The married politician paws at her big breasts and she giggles, rubbing against him. She's not wearing panties or a bra and she's very, very drunk, champagne sloshing over the rim of her raised crystal flute.

This is the out-of-control woman-child other guests equate me with. My shoulders slump. Toronto society thinks I'm a slut. They think John is a hypocrite and a liar. Once John and I are alone, he'll tell me he doesn't love me and I'll have to end our relationship, my pride not allowing me to consider any other option.

"I want to leave," I murmur.

John pivots on his heels, stopping his conversation in mid sentence, and he looks down at me. "We're leaving." He wraps one of his arms around me and guides me toward the exit.

I lean against him. If I had known it'd be this easy, I would have asked to leave an hour ago. Guests call out to John. He doesn't stop, ignoring them.

"Trella," Rexton calls.

"Her name is Miss Grant." John tightens his hold on my waist.

The younger developer's face is flushed, his eyes glassy. He's had too much champagne, a dangerous situation for a man who has no discretion when sober. "Have you considered my offer?" he asks me.

I glance up at John. Although he gives no indication, I know he's heard Rexton. I sigh. This day becomes more and more complicated. "Thank you, Mr. Bass, but no, I'm not interested."

I might not have a job or a man by the end of tonight. But saying yes to Rexton would destroy the partnership both men want. I'd rather be alone than hurt John.

Rexton isn't fazed by my rejection. "We'll discuss this." His gaze slides to John. "Later."

"Bass," my boss barks. "She said she wasn't interested. Ask Miss Grant to leave me one more time and I'll be very unhappy, understand?"

Rexton gulps, stopping short. "Yes, sir."

We continue walking. "You knew he wanted to hire me?" I stare at John.

"Of course, I knew he wanted to hire you." His lips twist. "That fool is as subtle as a wrecking ball."

John knew Rexton wanted to hire me and he said nothing. He didn't try to influence my decision. "You don't care if I leave you." I shrug John's hand away from me and I walk faster, my heels tapping on the marble floors. The man in the poorly fitting suit opens the door for me. "You don't need me." The night air cools my heated cheeks. "You'd replace me, hire a new assistant, train her, hold her, sleep with her."

John's limousine waits for us. I stop on the curb. If I enter the vehicle, I'll touch him and all of my resolve will melt away. I look for a taxi.

"Get in the limo, Grant," John growls, pushing me forward. "You're not thinking rationally."

I obey him because I have no other choice. There are no taxis in sight. "I don't think rationally around you. That's my problem." I plunk my ass down on the leather seat and wince, my skin sore from my spanking.

"Come here." John pulls me onto his lap. The door closes. The vehicle moves. I sit primly on my boss' thighs and stare out the window, into the darkness, my chin lifted. Ignoring him is an impossible task. Heat rolls off his big body. His rough fingers brush up and down my legs. All of me is aching aware of him.

"I want to go home." My voice is embarrassingly petulant.

"That's where we're going," John rumbles.

He's taking me back to my tiny apartment where I'll be alone, always alone. He's done with me, with my declarations of love, my messy emotions, my needs. My shoulders droop, my defiance dissipating. He'll allow me to walk away from him as my parents allowed me to walk away from them, not caring if I ever came back.

"Good." I brush my hands over my surprisingly damp cheeks.

John sighs and catches my wrists, bringing my hands to his lips. He licks the moisture off my fingers, flicking his tongue over my skin, his touch rough and wet and arousing. I tremble and press my knees together, determined not to respond to him.

He chuckles, laughing at my pain, and my heart breaks a little bit more. "You're as stubborn as I am, Trella." John says this as though it is an attribute to be proud of. "You would have run that young fool out of his own company within months, weeks. He's not strong enough for you. Why would you even consider working for him?"

"He needs me." I sniff. "And you don't."

"If I don't need you, then I'm a fool also." John nuzzles his face into my palms. "Because I risked my hard-earned reputation for you tonight." I curl my fingers, cupping his defined chin. "I don't have a fancy education or high class connections. My reputation is all that I have."

And tonight, he damaged that reputation by breaking his non-fraternization rule, by publicly acknowledging his desire for his assistant. He did this for me, someone who turned out to be too high maintenance, too costly, to be worth his risk. I lower my fingers, caress the scar around his neck. He flinches but doesn't pull away, allowing me to touch him.

"My parents didn't need me," I share quietly. "They did everything parents should do, providing a roof over my head, food, clothing but I gave them nothing in return. I didn't add to their happiness, to their success, and when I left for school, they didn't even notice I was gone."

"They left you alone," John states.

"They always left me alone." I lean into him and he cuddles me close, rubbing my bare back. John holds me and I almost forget that we're traveling toward my apartment, toward a goodbye I suspect will be permanent.

He breathes in. I breathe out. He breathes out. I breathe in. We share the same air, the same space, the connection between us tight and alive. I don't know how I'll survive without him, how I'll bear our separation. More tears trickle down my cheeks.

"Sleep, Trella," John urges, his voice low and deep, his lips buzzing against my earlobe, making the diamonds in the beautiful earrings he gave me jostle and tinkle.

My eyes burn from unshed tears. The exhaustion presses down on me, a steady weight on my chest. My arms and legs are limp. My ass is numb.

"No, you'll replace me." I force my eyelids to remain open. This might be the last time I feel his arms around me, smell his musk, embrace his heat. I won't squander a second.

"It's not possible to replace you."

I feel his voice, the rumble of his chest. "You could do it." I yawn, the darkness pulling at me. It's been a long day and I'm so very tired. "You can do anything."

"When I'm with you, I believe I can do anything." John wipes away my tears. "Sleep." He skims his palms over my face, closing my eyes. "I'll protect you."

I'm not alone. He's with me. I sigh and slip into the black void.

chapter eight

I'm dreaming. I must be. I'm in John's bedroom with him, not in my small apartment alone. He drags his hot mouth over my shoulder, cups my breasts with his rough palms. I cover his hands with my fingers, forcing him to squeeze harder, pleasure shooting over my form.

He nudges his hard cock between my thighs, pressing his hips against my ass. I wiggle against him, needing more, needing him inside me.

"John," I moan.

"Give me a second." He rolls away from me and cool air sweeps over my back. I huff. This isn't what I need. A package rustles and he returns, wrapping his arms around me, pressing his latex-covered cock against me.

I frown. Why is he wearing a condom in my dream? I want to feel him inside me.

"Open for me, Trella." He pinches my nipples, the sweet pain punctuating his command, erotic bliss flowing down my spine.

I obey him, spreading my thighs, and he pushes inside my slick pussy, stretching me open. This is what I need, this fullness, this connection. When he's inside me, I'm not alone. I'm needed.

I tilt my hips and John buries himself to his base. A rumble of satisfaction rolls up his chest. His skin rubs against mine.

He rocks against me, his pace slow and steady, as though my always busy boss has the entire night to please me. I'm not as patient as he is. I grip his hands, closing his fingers around my aching nipples, clutching my breasts to the same rhythm.

"That's it," he murmurs into my ear. "Show me what you like, love, what you need."

He called me love. I smile sleepily. This is the best dream ever. We move together as one, our tempo gradually building, the bed rocking. John nuzzles, nips, sucks on my neck, the stubble on his cheeks grazing my skin, sending tremors over my shoulders, down my back.

"Yes." I undulate against him, caressing him with my entire body, loving him with everything I have. A wet sheen covers his chest, his arms. I turn my head and lick the moisture off his bulging left bicep, tasting his salt. If all of my fantasies feel this real, this right, I'll survive our separation, living for the nights when I'll see, touch, taste, smell him again.

"Yes," John agrees, his lips humming against my earlobe. He pumps in and out of my tight pussy, and I savor all of him, the bloom of his cock head, the raised veins on his shaft, the coarse curls on his base.

I clench around him and he groans. "I won't last long, not when you grip me like that," he warns. I laugh and clench him again. "You're a bad, bad assistant." He thrusts harder, smacking his hips against my ass.

"Be bad with me, John." I transfer one of his hands to my pussy, pressing the tip of his index finger against my clit. He circles the sensitive spot, winding my passion tighter and tighter around me.

"I won't last long either," I confess, my voice husky with need. "Not when you touch me like that." I push back on him, his fingers making me crazed. "You feel so good." He owns me with each hard stroke of his cock, dominating my body, my heart, my soul.

I pant, John grunts and the headboard thumps against the wall, the sounds of our joining intensifying my desire. There is no thought of the morning, of goodbye. There's only the two of us. In this moment, he's not a billionaire or my boss. He's a man and I'm his woman. We're two beings striving, struggling, fighting for our satisfaction.

I shake, each pleasure-laden tremor shredding more of my control. John takes me harder and harder, smacking his balls against my skin, and my form heats at all points of contact. He taps one of his fingertips against my clit, his touch causing my inner walls to close around his shaft, pushing us both toward the sweet edge of release.

"Please." I reach back and grip his thighs, digging my nails into his skin.

"Come for me, Trella." John teases my shoulder with his teeth. "Come now." He thrusts hard and nips my skin, the pain propelling me over the vortex.

I scream, bucking against him. He tightens his hold on me, capturing my writhing body, as he drives one, two, three more times into me. It's too much, too good, the ecstasy exquisite. I twist as John shudders with fulfillment. He doesn't release me, folding my curves into his muscle, and I surrender to his power, quieting, my eyelids fluttering closed.

"I love you, John," I whisper. This is a dream. I can tell him anything I want. "I've always loved you and I will always love you." I've dated enough men to know John is special, the only man for me.

"I love you too, Trella," John rumbles. "And I need you. I'll always need you." He says the words I want him to say.

I snuggle deeper into his body and smile, wishing I never had to wake up.

* * *

"Double the security detail and clear the area. I won't be alone." John's deep voice rolls over me, a soothing sound I can listen to forever. I lie face down on soft white sheets. The sun's rays stream in the window, warming my bare back.

"I'm well aware of the risks," he says. "We won't stay long."

I turn my head toward him. John sits by the bed, dressed casually in blue jeans and a chest-hugging black T-shirt, his phone pressed to one ear. Although a baseball cap with a tattered bill shades his eyes, I know he's watching me.

"We'll be ready to leave in half an hour." He lowers the phone.

"Are you taking me home?" As he promised to take me home last night.

"You *are* home." John shakes his head as though I'm talking nonsense. "I canceled my meetings for the day. We're going to a site so wear the usual, nothing designer, nothing flashy."

I can't visit a site smelling of sex and him. "I need a shower, sir." I push myself upright, my body naked and sore. There's no time to think about the mess he's made of his schedule, the zillions of meetings I'll have to rearrange, his confusing comment about me being home. "My clothes — "

"They're in the dresser by the window." John watches me as I walk toward the ensuite bathroom. "You have thirty minutes, Trella."

I shower quickly, pull my hair back into a ponytail and don minimal makeup. All of my things have been placed in the bathroom, my hairbrush resting on the vanity's black marble countertop, my bottle of vitamins hidden in the medicine cabinet.

When I emerge, John is no longer in the bedroom. The black velvet box is set on one of the nightstands, my earrings, the gift from John, having been removed while I slept. A pair of jeans, a navy blue T-shirt, and thick gray socks are folded on the foot of the neatly made bed, John having made my clothing decisions for me. My clunky work boots are placed on the hardwood floor.

I dress and rush downstairs with two minutes to spare. John stands by the double doors, a smaller baseball cap in one of his hands. His eyes light up as I descend the stairs. "This should fit you." He tugs the cap on my head. The fabric smells of engine grease and dust.

"Whom did you steal this from?" I pull my ponytail through the back closure.

"I won it fair and square from Ian Smith in the third grade." John grins, opening the door. We step into the bright sunlight.

This was his baseball cap, part of his childhood, and he wants me to wear it. I touch the warped bill, my chest warming with love.

Dave, John's driver, is seated in a battered four-door sedan. He's dressed as casually as we are. Another large man sits in the passenger seat. More sedans idle in front of and behind our vehicle. This isn't abnormal for John. Billionaires are targets for desperate people and he doesn't take any chances with his people's safety, traveling in convoys whenever he visits high risk neighborhoods.

I slide into the backseat. John claims the spot beside me, his arm placed protectively around my shoulders, his thigh pressing against mine. The windows are rolled up, the glass bullet proof.

"What do you need, sir?" I extract my phone from my back pocket.

"I don't need anything." John takes the device from me and tosses it into the vehicle's side compartment. "This isn't a business outing for us and I'm not your boss today."

"I thought everything is business for you." I frown. "And if you're not my boss today, why do you need me?"

"I'll always need you," he echoes the words in my dream. I gaze at him. *Was* it a dream? "And I certainly need you today." John raps his knuckles on the glass dividing the front and back seats. The partition opens and a cup is transferred through the exposure. "Take this." He presses the cup into my palm. "You're a mess without your coffee."

I sip the delectable java and moan with appreciation. "I do love you." I've said it once. It won't hurt our relationship if I say it again.

His lips lift into a small smile, his eyes gleaming. "I know."

I grin. My boss is an arrogant bastard. "Why do you *certainly* need me today?" I pass the cup to John.

He places his mouth where mine had been and he drinks. "That young fool wasn't the first person to approach me about developing the neighborhood I grew up in. I said no to all of the other offers, better offers, from more experienced partners."

"Then why are you considering the partnership with Bass?" I ask, not expecting an answer. My boss doesn't explain his decisions. He makes them and moves on.

"I'm developing the neighborhood now because it's time." John shifts in the seat, clearly uncomfortable with this conversation. "Because it should be done. Because you can help me."

I've never heard him admit he needs help, have never seen him this vulnerable. "How can I help you?"

"You can help me deal." John turns his head and gazes out the window. School-aged boys in black hoodies and low hanging pants stand on corners. Graffiti decorates every vertical surface. A plastic bag blows along the cracked sidewalk. An alarm sounds. "You can help me face this." He waves his hand.

I can help him face his past. "Do you need me to be your assistant, to take on the tasks you'd rather not complete?" I have to be certain, to know exactly what he needs from me.

"You're not my assistant today, Trella. I need your support, not more spreadsheets." His smile holds sadness. "Stand by my side and manage my emotions as only you can. Distract me when it becomes too tough. Slap me when I'm being an irrational ass."

"That's a regular day for me, sir." I force a joke.

John's eyes glimmer. "Exactly."

He needs me as no one else has ever needed me. He also cares for me. Hearing the words is unnecessary. I feel our connection. "Is the neighborhood much different now?" I take the cup from him and finish the coffee, wishing to be wide awake when we arrive, when he requires my assistance.

"Nothing has changed in the neighborhood, nothing substantial." John presses his lips together. "No one has invested here. No one cares."

He cares. I hear the passion in his voice.

"People believe what they see, Trella," John explains. "If they don't see change, they won't believe they can change. If people don't invest in them, they won't invest in themselves."

This is why he constructs buildings, erecting giant symbols of change, of improvement. I slip my palm into his, silently showing my support, my understanding. John folds his fingers around mine, securing me to him. We sit, holding hands, our souls linked, my thoughts focused on the future, his thoughts revisiting the past.

His mood becomes more and more grim as the neighborhoods deteriorate. Tension radiates from him in dark and heavy waves. I can't bear to see him like this.

I search for a distraction. "Was I supposed to wear panties?" I wiggle, brushing my thigh against his. "You didn't set out a pair for me."

John turns his head toward me and blinks. "Are you bare under your jeans?"

"I am." I nod. "And the zipper is rubbing against an interesting spot." I squirm.

"I didn't set out a bra either." John runs one of his palms over my back. He should be feeling smooth cotton. "Trella," he groans. "What are you doing to me?" His mind isn't on his challenging childhood now.

I tilt my head back and meet his gaze. "I'm managing you, sir." I laugh.

John chuckles. "Actions have consequences." He tugs on the bill of my baseball cap. "Remember that, love."

Love. My smile wavers. Does he love me? Before I can ask, the vehicle slows and all of the mirth fades from John's face.

"You won't leave my side today," he commands. "If the situation becomes unsafe, we're leaving, no questions asked."

"I understand." I understand everything. He's showing me a slice of himself, a part he doesn't share with many people, a rare vulnerability. He needs me by his side, to help him through this.

John exits the sedan first, scanning our surroundings, and he reaches for me. His men are positioned casually around us, not so close as to draw attention but near enough to secure the area.

The building looming in front of us is old and depressingly institutional, the address listed on John's comprehensive online biography. Two of the giant gray numbers are missing, their outlines permanently etched in the red brick. Windows are cracked, covered with silver duct tape or clear fixative.

There are no balconies, no flowers, no green space. Every surrounding inch is paved, the patches of black asphalt forming a continual industrial quilt. Squealing children fight over one dirty basketball, playing in the streets around the parked cars. Broken bottles litter the space, the jagged pieces of glass crunching under my boots.

John would have played in these streets also, risked being cut by the glass and hit by passing vehicles. I could have lost him decades ago. I glance at the silver scars around his neck. I came very close to losing him. If he hadn't survived his childhood, I would have remained alone, not knowing love, not knowing him.

I squeeze John's hand, overcome with gratitude. He squeezes back, his gaze on the building, on his childhood home, his lips flat and his expression grim. He doesn't have to say anything. I feel his dread as though it was my own, the feeling growing with each passing second.

"Are you ready?" I whisper, my words meant for his ears only.

"No," John admits. He wraps one of his arms protectively around my waist and takes a deep ragged breath, his chest pushing against my back. "But this has to be done." He surges forward, taking me with him.

chapter nine

Two and a half hours later, I trudge up the stairs. John follows me closely, his right palm resting on the small of my back. One of his men walks in front of us. We don't speak, John having explained to me how voices carry, drawing unwanted attention. Small talk can be dangerous in this neighborhood, and my billionaire isn't taking any chances.

The stairwell is disgustingly dirty, smelling of urine and vomit. Liquor bottles are scattered on every landing. Taking the elevator isn't an option. John claims it has been broken since he lived here.

I can't believe he lived here. This building is so different from Powers Corporation's modern, immaculately clean head office. It hurts my heart to think of him spending his formative childhood years amidst the crime and grime.

The hired muscle opens the door to the roof and a blast of fresh air sweeps over the space. I hasten my pace, my calves burning, my lungs tight.

More men are positioned around the rooftop. Two lounge chairs are placed by a small table. A cooler holds bottles of water. A pizza box is set on the table.

I pace along the perimeter of the roof. Although the surface is as shabby as the rest of the building, the sky is a gorgeous shade of blue and the view is breathtaking.

"This is amazing." I link my fingers with John's and gaze out at the city.

"This place kept me sane," he confesses. "I came here to escape everything else."

I've seen some of his everything else, the tiny, damp apartment with the thin walls, the frighteningly dark hallways, the even more scary common areas. I heard the yelling and screaming, the rustling of rodents running between the drywall. I smelled the oil herb scent of marijuana, felt the grease on the hand railings. I faced this hardship today with John, buffered by his presence. He faced it for years alone, his childhood making him tough and strong.

I lean into the wind. "Up here, everything is possible."

"Yes," John agrees. We stand side by side, not speaking, the quiet comfortable.

My stomach growls and my face heats. "I hope that pizza box isn't merely for show."

"I wouldn't do that to you." My boss chuckles, leading me to the makeshift dining area. He extracts a bottle of water out of the cooler and splashes some of the liquid over his fingers. "Hold out your hands."

The cool water flows over my fingers. "I see this is a fancy joint," I tease, rubbing my palms together.

"Only the best for my girl." John's brown eyes glitter. I *am* his girl. Today has proven this. "Thank you." His voice is soft, sincere.

"Thank me with pizza." I flip the lid open, lightening the mood. The scent of tomato and oregano fills my nostrils, drawing another embarrassing rumble from my stomach.

"Do you need a plate?" John offers me a paper plate.

"For thin-crust pizza? Nah," I scoff. "I'll risk the anger of my fellow Torontonians and eat it New York style." I fold the slice in two and nibble on a corner. "Oh my God." I moan, the cheese melting in my mouth. "This is so good."

"Give me a taste." John bites into my slice.

"Hey, get your own slice." I tug the pizza away from him.

"I want your slice." He lunges forward and grabs my wrists. "And what I want, I get." He forces me to feed him, his eyes sparkling with humor.

"You get what you want with my assistance." I twist out of his grip. "Who has the slice now?" I crow, waving the crust under his nose. He pounces on me and we roll around on my lounge chair, taking bites out of the slice until there's nothing left.

Our skirmish ends with me lying on top of John, his muscles under my curves, his palms resting on my denim-clad ass, both of us breathing heavily. I brace myself upward and gaze down at him. "You like to share meals." It doesn't matter what I'm eating for lunch, my boss wants half of it.

"My mom and I would share slices of pizza, ice cream cones, and any other treats we had." John's face softens. He doesn't say it but I know, having seen his childhood apartment, they shared food because they couldn't afford more.

"And now you share these treats with me." I reach over and grab another slice of pizza.

"I only share them with you." John meets my gaze.

He shares food with me because he loves me. A hard lump of emotion forms in my throat. "Here." I shove the slice into his mouth, covering up my reaction.

My hungry man devours my clumsy offering and I happily feed him another slice. We eat and cuddle and talk, stretching out on the lounge chair, the blue sky above us, the sun's rays warming our bodies.

A companionable silence falls upon us. John strokes my back, drifting his fingertips up and down, up and down. His gaze is unfocused, his brown eyes sad and soulful. He's thinking of his past again.

I touch his face, capturing his attention. "Today took tremendous strength. Your mom would have been proud of you," I assure my billionaire. "I'm proud of you." I cover his lips with mine.

He opens to me, allowing me to control our kiss. I explore his mouth, tasting all of him. Our tongues touch and I retreat. He follows, pursuing me, and we play, finding joy in the middle of a stressful day, sanctuary in an urban war zone.

This is why I happily work fourteen-hour days. When I'm with John, a site visit becomes a date, a slice of pizza tastes better than any gourmet meal, and work becomes a delight.

I wiggle, brushing my denim-covered mons over the hard ridge in his jeans, rubbing my hips over his. John grips me tighter, growling softly into my mouth, the sound flowing down my throat, curling my fingers. We forget about everything, the painful past and the uncertain future, moments passing in a blur of bliss.

A throat clears. John tears his lips from mine, his muscles flexing under my body. We turn our heads toward the sound.

One of his men looms over us, his legs braced apart and his massive arms folded in front of his big barrel of a chest. His expression is deathly serious. "There's been some gang activity in the area, sir."

"Shit." John pushes me to the side and leaps to his feet, his movements fast and fluid. "Call for the cars." He draws me upward and pushes me toward the door, the cooler and patio furniture discarded. "We're leaving."

Another burly employee waits at the entrance to the stairwell. His right hand rests on his gun holster, his biceps bulging. I gulp. This is serious business.

John pivots me around to face him. "Follow Tiny," he instructs. I blink up at him. The bodyguard's name is Tiny? "I don't care what you hear or see. You stay behind him. He'll protect you."

Who will protect him? Before I can ask this, John pulls me into a fervent embrace, pressing his lips against my forehead. This feels like good-bye. My heart pounds.

"Now, go." John flattens his palm between my shoulder blades and propels me forward.

I focus on his touch as I pelt down the stairs. As long as John's palm rests on my back, I know he's behind me, he's safe. I'm not worried about my own life. My body is sandwiched between the two larger men's physiques, shielded by broad shoulders and hard muscle.

John would die for me. I realize this now. And I couldn't live without him. The men descend silently and I try to mimic their light treads, the smack of my boot heels against the concrete obscenely loud.

My thighs burn. A trickle of perspiration drips down my spine. My lungs ache, my breathing ragged. I fix my gaze on Tiny's shoulders and concentrate on moving my legs, on not falling.

A shot fires and I flinch, my left boot connecting with a beer bottle on the landing. As I watch, horrified, unable to do anything, it rolls off the edge, falls, shatters against the concrete. Tiny exhales, this soft sound expressing his disgust, and he draws his gun.

John grips my hip and squeezes. We move even faster, a feat I didn't think possible. His hold steadies me, reminding me of my goal. We must move my billionaire to safety.

We reach the bottom of the stairwell and Tiny motions for us to stop. He opens the door, gazes to the left and to the right, flicks his fingers forward. I exit the building, John following me. Children no longer play in the streets, our surroundings eerily empty, freakishly still.

Tiny ushers us into the waiting car, the second of three vehicles. I enter first. John slides into the seat beside me and pushes my face into his lap, bowing his body over mine, covering me. The floor rumbles under my boots. We must be moving. All I can see is denim-covered thighs.

Shots were fired. We could have died. I shake uncontrollably.

"You're safe, love," John murmurs, straightening. "I have you." He rubs one of his hands over my back, his touch soothing me. He's alive, unharmed. I'm alive, unharmed. I breathe in, breathe out, breathe in, breathe out. The tremors ease and I slowly relax.

"Is everyone okay?" I whisper.

"Everyone is okay." John removes my baseball cap and releases my hair, threading his fingers through the curls. "I can't promise you that everyone will always be okay."

I turn my head and gaze up at him. His eyes are hard. Grooves are etched around his lips. "No one can make that promise." I caress his chest, seeking to distract him from his concerns. "I've read that the most dangerous place in the world is the bathroom."

John lifts one of his eyebrows. "Are you handling me, Grant?"

For the entire day, I've been Trella. Now, I'm Grant. He's retreating once more into business. Although I'm disappointed, I understand why. Today has been an emotionally challenging day for both of us. Business is easier on the heart.

"I wouldn't presume to handle you, sir." I return to my own seat.

John doesn't allow me to move this far away from him. He hooks his right arm around my waist and pulls me to his side, tucking my curves into his muscle.

I sigh with contentment, savoring his heat, his musky scent. This is where I'm meant to be, with John. He rests his chin on the top of my head and gazes out the window. The neighborhoods become brighter, cleaner, wealthier.

There are plenty of opportunities for development in these less volatile communities. Some of these opportunities are more lucrative, allowing John to easily expand his empire without risking his personal safety. But these aren't the actions of the man I love. The man I love invests in areas, in people other businessmen won't. He gives hope to the hopeless.

"I love you, John." I press my lips to the silver scars around his neck.

"I know," my arrogant man replies, a hint of humor in his voice. "Enough small talk." He reaches into the side compartment and hands me my phone.

"Are we working, sir?" I ask, knowing the answer. There are two thousand and forty-four new messages in my mailbox, countless more voicemails. I swallow my groan.

"We're always working, Grant." John squeezes my hip, his touch softening his blunt words. "Ask Bass what type of temporary low-cost housing is available for the existing tenants. He should have also researched government grants."

My boss' voice rumbles, his list of must-knows long, almost never ending, as though he has been storing these requests in his overactive brain all day.

He likely has. He could have easily asked others for the answers. Instead, he waited to funnel the questions through me. I smile, feeling included, needed, loved.

* * *

We return to the house and work all afternoon. I reschedule John's cancelled meetings. John makes call after call, driving his management team relentlessly, throwing himself into a frenzy of activity. I recognize it for what it is — an attempt to control his emotions, to distract himself from the trials of his stressful day.

I also realize it isn't working. He doesn't need to be the boss right now. I set my phone aside and slip onto his lap. He needs the release only I can give him. I untuck my T-shirt and slide one of his hands underneath the faded cotton. He needs me.

I arch as his calloused palm covers my left breast, my nipples tightening, aching for him, for this. John hardens, the ridge in his jeans pressing against my ass.

"Send the information to Grant by the end of the day." My boss tosses his phone against the brown leather couch cushion. "We're taking a break." He pulls my shirt over my head, my crazy curls tumbling down my back, and he cups my breasts, pinching my nipples.

I wiggle, grinding my ass against him. "Can I assist you, sir?" My voice is husky with desire.

"I have the matter well in hand, Grant." John pinches my nipples and pulls, elongating my sensitive flesh. I cry out, clenching his thighs, the pain delectable, the pleasure exquisite.

He sucks on my neck, his mouth as wet and hot as my pussy, his lips firm. I undulate against him, brushing my ass over his groin, tormenting him as he's tormenting me.

There are too many barriers between us. Huffing with frustration, I unfasten my jeans, fold the denim back, and slip my fingers inside, skimming my fingertips over my private curls, dipping them into my wetness.

"Are you slick for me?" John asks, his breath wafting over my neck. He tightens his grip on my small breasts, molding my curves with his massive palms.

I reach deeper inside me, working my pussy. "I'm slick for you, sir."

"Show me."

His command sends a tremor down my spine. I hook my fingers and remove them, drawing moisture from my core. My scent fills my nostrils. I lift my hand, showing him the evidence of my arousal.

John closes his grim lips around my fingers and sucks, the tug of his mouth exciting me. He growls his approval, taking more of me into his heat, his tongue darting over my skin, my billionaire boss savoring every drop of my pussy juices.

"Oh my God." I turn my head. He kisses me and I taste myself on his lips. "You know how to drive me crazy."

"You showed me how to drive you crazy." John slides one of his palms over my stomach, my mons, cupping me. I allow my head to loll back, submitting to his sure handling of my body. He holds me to him, not allowing me to move, as he taps my clit with his index finger, his slow, steady tempo making me wild. "I paid attention."

"You paid too close attention," I moan, my legs trembling.

"Don't come until I'm inside you," he orders, pushing me to my feet.

I turn around. His eyes are black with passion, the ridge in his faded jeans pronounced. My boss wants me. Badly.

"Then I suggest you come inside me quickly, sir." I slide the denim over my hips and shimmy until my jeans fall to the Persian rug.

"Soon, I'll come inside you." John's eyes glimmer. He pulls his shirt over his head, revealing golden skin and silver scars. "I'll feel you, fill you, put our baby inside you."

I inhale sharply. "You want to have a child with me?" I rub my hands over my breasts, between my thighs, waiting for him to touch me, to claim me completely.

"Baby making isn't on the agenda for today." He plucks at his button-fly. "We'll do this properly, getting married first."

"Doing this properly means asking me to marry you." My lips

twitch. My arrogant man assumes I'll marry him, assumes I'll wish to have his children.

"Asking a question is unnecessary if I already know the answer." John scowls. "You love me. I love you. We'll get married. Have those three kids you want."

My hands still. "I mentioned that once, over two years ago."

"You could have mentioned it a hundred years ago and I'd remember." John shrugs. The muscles over his stomach ripple, distracting me. He is one hot man.

"Enough talking." He lowers his jeans and briefs with one hard yank, freeing his cock. My nipples tighten to the point of pain. He's also one generously endowed man. "I have to fuck you, Trella."

"Where do you need me, sir?" I sway.

"On the couch." His eyes gleam. He does enjoy being in control and I enjoy allowing him this illusion. "On your back with your legs spread."

I recline on the soft leather couch cushion and open to him, giving him a clear view of my glistening pink folds, my empty entrance. As he sheathes himself, I roll my nipples between my thumbs and fingers, my body humming with anticipation, with desire. He gazes down at me, stroking his cock, sliding his hands up and down his shaft.

"I'm ready, sir." I lift my hips, wanting him to take me.

"I see that." He drifts his cock head over me, spreading my wetness, teasing my pussy. I swivel my hips, silently pleading for more. He refuses to be rushed, his lips curling into a smug smile. John knows what he's doing to me.

He plays with me, spiraling my lust upward. I grit my teeth, determined to obey him, to not come until he's inside me.

"You're a good assistant." John's praise warms me, the approval in his eyes making my chest swell with pride. I need this, him, and he needs me. I'm not alone. I'll never be alone again. "Good assistants earn the right to touch their bosses."

There's no need for John to repeat himself. I lunge forward and eagerly wrap the fingers of my right hand around his shaft. My boss' smile fades, his body stiffening. "Thank you, sir." I cup his balls with my left hand. A trickle of sweat drips down his cheek. "I want to please you." I pump him slowly, my grip tight.

"You do please me." John groans, rocking into my hands. "You please me too much. Guide me into you."

"Yes." I position him at my entrance and he pushes into me, stretching me open, filling me as only he can, my pussy designed for his cock, my soul fitting into his. Our gazes meet as he takes me, his focus on me, on my face, my pleasure.

I shift under him, cradling his hips between my thighs, and he slides deeper, his weight reassuring heavy, his chest flattening my breasts, pressing my smaller form into the leather cushion.

"I'm claiming you, John." I drag my fingernails down his back and he shudders.

"I claimed you three years ago," he admits. "I've been waiting for you to claim me, to be ready for a forever commitment, because what I claim, I keep, Trella. Always."

"I know." I smile, my heart and pussy full. My boss keeps his word. He will never let me go. "I want forever. I want you." I explore his back, the dip near his spine, the swell of his muscles, the scars on his skin.

John moves over me, nudging forward and easing out, his unhurried pace coaxing my passion higher and higher. I lick the scars around his neck, laving the marred skin, acknowledging the pain of his past, paying tribute to his strength. He tastes of salt and man and love.

John increases our tempo, driving into me harder and deeper. I wrap my legs around his waist, hooking my ankles over his ass, and I hold on, clinging to his shoulders. He crushes his lips against mine, swallowing my ragged breaths. I sigh my surrender, conceding with no hesitation, and he surges his tongue into my mouth, captivating me body, heart and soul.

This is my man, my future. I lift into each thrust, meeting John halfway, as equals, our forms smacking together, a wet sheen covering our skin. My nipples ache and my legs shake. I dig my nails into his back and John jerks, growling into my mouth, his rhythm growing erratic, his lovemaking fierce.

And this is lovemaking, John's expression warm, almost reverent. He breaks our kiss and presses his cheek to mine. "Grip me with that hot pussy," he urges. "And come for me." He drives hard into my softness and grinds against my clit.

I scream and buck, clenching down on his shaft, breaking. John bellows my name and pushes even deeper, the couch skidding across the carpet, rattling the lamps on the end tables.

The room spins around me, a blur of color and light. I rake John's back, clasping him, my only anchor in a storm of emotion. He shudders and shakes, pinning my hips to the cushion, the movement of muscle under tanned skin, power restrained, enthralling me.

My world stills and John falls, capturing me under his body, covering me with his warmth, his musk. "I love you." I skim my hands over his back, soothing him, easing the pain I've caused, seeking to erase the marks I've left.

"I love you too, Trella." John braces himself upward by his elbows and gazes into my eyes. "I don't know what I'd do without you."

"You'll never be without me, sir." I smile up at him. "I'm your assistant for life."

"I'll need you longer than that." My billionaire boss covers my lips with his.

The Geek Job

Eve Langlais

4

chapter one

"I don't work the evening of or morning after a full moon." She began the negotiations with an aloof smile, casually seated in a leather covered club chair, her steel toed boots propped on top of a marble topped desk.

The dark haired vampire with full sensual lips and dark eyes — handsome if she could ignore his walking corpse status — touched his fingertips together to form a steeple and leaned back in his chair. "The job I have in mind will be occurring this coming weekend, so that won't be an issue. What else?"

Lexie couldn't hold back a cocky grin as she recited her list of demands. "I work alone. While you can have other guards discreetly stationed, they are not to approach me or interfere with my target. You will provide a cleanup crew for any messes that occur during my protection of the target. In case I'm injured while protecting my assignment, you will ensure I receive immediate and first class medical care. I will study the file and provide an additional list of requirements, at your expense of course. As for my fees, it'll cost you fifteen thousand for the weekend, consisting of no more than seventy two hours. That number could go up if the subject proves difficult. I expect to see the full amount deposited to my Paypal account no later than eight a.m. the day I begin the task. Oh, and I also want four, front row tickets to the next UFC match in Vegas." She threw that last bit in just for fun.

The vampire arched a brow. "You think highly of yourself, don't you?"

She leaned forward and her leather jacket gaped open to flash the cleavage clearly visible through the gaping neckline of her tank top, a calculated ploy that grabbed her prospective employer's attention. *Dead or not, all men are the same.* "For what you're asking, I think you're getting my services cheap. I mean, guarding some science dweeb is all well and good, but to pretend to be some normal human ditz and shack up with him as his girlfriend, which I might add will require me putting out ... Damn, given what a high class call girl goes for these days, I should be asking for more."

Frederick Thibodeaux, the vampire who'd called her in for the job interview, gave her a pained look. "You'd better be worth what you're asking for, Lexington. Do you know how many strings I'm going to have to pull to get those tickets?"

Lexington, who preferred to go by her nickname Lexie, smirked. "That's the price you pay if you want to engage my golden pussy and talent. So, do we have a deal?" She'd worked with Frederick before and knew he'd cave to her demands. He just liked to beat around the bush and fake hardship before he sealed the deal.

"Let's make sure you've got the details of the job straight. You are to befriend the good doctor as he arrives for the conference. In other words, finagle your way back to his room. Once you've got him pussy whipped, you are to stay glued by his side the entire length of the conference, doing whatever you need to keep him happy and oblivious. I want him returned without any holes or scratches he didn't own already. Your task ends once he gets into the limo for the airport, taking him back to my property and his lab."

"Wouldn't this whole task be easier if you told him what we were, thus allowing us to guard him openly?" Lexie didn't have a problem with the fact she needed to sleep with the guy. The nerdy types tended to work harder for it in bed, and not take as long doing it. However, she found it hard to bend her mind around the fact Frederick had a geek working on a solution to the vampire sun allergy issue without letting the nerdazoid know vampires were involved. How the hell was that supposed to work? Not that she cared, but curiosity made her ask.

Frederick made a moue of annoyance. "Unfortunately, our resident scientist has proven skittish in the past. We let our secret slip by accident once before with almost catastrophic consequences."

Lexie snorted. "He caught one of you guys munching on someone, didn't he?"

Frederick smiled coldly. "We don't take kindly to trespassers. Unfortunately, given the bloody methods we use to set an example, our scientist had a minor gibbering meltdown when he came across it during one of his nocturnal walks, walks that I might add we've since banned. We managed to wipe that unfortunate incident, but as you well know, too much messing around in a humans brain, and ... poof. He'll end up a vegetable. And given how close he is to solving our dilemma, his remarkable brain must be protected at all cost."

"So why even let him go to that conference? Can't you just like, forbid him or something as his boss?"

"We've tried to dissuade him; however, because of some scientific paper he wrote, he was asked to act as a speaker. Some great honor apparently. He was quite adamant about attending."

Lexie stopped attempting to dissuade her employer. She rather looked forward to the assignment even if she had to put up with a few minutes of groping and grunting. Besides, she needed a vacation and what better time or place than at a five star hotel with free food, money and the UFC tickets she coveted. "What kind of opposition can I expect?"

"The usual — rival clans looking to steal him, even more so since an ex-employee leaked secrets about his work. The Fae also want to eliminate him because they fear us embracing the day, and then there are the assassins, like yourself, who have probably been offered a bounty to capture him, dead or alive."

Lexie whistled. "Sounds like fun." And she wouldn't mind the exercise to her skills. "Now, while I'm working as his shadow, I am going to assume you'll have men stationed throughout the conference area scanning for suspects."

"Correct. You won't see them, but they'll see you." The leer on the vampire's face made her roll her eyes.

"If he's as geeky as you say, then they won't see much because I doubt it will take more than a minute to please your little scientist and put him to sleep. And besides, you seem to forget, nudity is my preferred state." Werewolves scoffed at the hang ups other beings held about the naked body. Given how the change tore through anything they wore, many shifters preferred to wear little to no clothing and didn't care who saw them in their natural state.

"So we're agreed then?" Frederick asked as he stood.

Lexie also got to her feet and held out her hand. "Consider me your geek's new girlfriend." They shook and sealed the deal.

Time to pack.

She left the vampire's mansion with a folder tucked into her knapsack, additional information on her target. She straddled her sport bike and put on her helmet, not because she feared injuring herself, but because human cops could be dicks about their stupid laws.

The half-moon teased her in the sky and made her inner wolf rumble knowing the full one soon approached. Until she could run wild through the woods, the night air ruffling her fur as she hunted, she'd make do with the speed on her bike.

She started the engine, enjoying the rumbling vibration of all that power between her legs. Put a cock on the seat and she'd probably enjoy herself more than she managed with a man. With a chuckle to herself, she gunned the bike and, with a squeal of spinning tires, took off for home.

As she weaved her bike in and out of the sparse traffic that flowed this time of night, she pondered her assignment. It wouldn't be the first time she had to seduce a target. Her nonchalance about it was one of the reasons her services were in such high demand and fetched a pretty penny. She refused to look at it as whoring herself, more like scratching an itch while getting paid. She saw no shame in admitting she had needs only another body — preferably male — could take care of. What that male looked like didn't truly matter in the scheme of things, that's what light switches and paper bags existed for. As long as he had a dick and a tongue, any man could do the job. She wasn't one to get hung up on girly notions of love and relationships. She truly was a lone wolf compared to the other bitches of her kind.

Most female wolves were submissive, rolling over and showing their belly to the first interested male. Lexie, however, possessed alpha tendencies. She refused to cower for any male, not exactly a popular trait for a female in a society where packs were ruled by men. So, she'd left rather than kill the annoying males who'd thought to cow her into their preconceived notion of a she-wolf. And she wasn't invited back despite her poor mother's pleas. The male wolves she'd maimed were apparently still pissed at her for showing them, with violent means, that no meant no.

Alone, without a pack or family to support her — her father disowning his unnatural daughter — she struggled to make ends meet with job after job. She discovered there weren't many career opportunities for a girl like her. Well, not ones that paid the money she needed to live comfortably. She fell into her calling quite by accident, saving the daughter of a business man who'd just joined the vampiric ranks. He rewarded her and began throwing jobs her way along with referrals which was how she encountered Frederick.

Security work fit her perfectly because she had the muscle, the brains and the cunning to make a great bodyguard. As her special status became known among certain groups, they'd added to her repertoire of uses — killer, spy, personal guard, and undercover agent. She did it all in the name of her dream retirement — all that was, except the killing of young'uns and the innocent. Her perverse moral code wouldn't allow her to stoop that low. But ask her to stake a rogue vamp gone wild and she was there in her leathers. If a rabid wolf required putting down, she owned a shot gun loaded with silver shot for the job. No matter the task, she prevailed, and she loved every minute of it.

This newest assignment, which she'd nicknamed to herself *The Geek Job*, sounded almost like a vacation compared to her usual stuff, a much needed weekend of relaxation. She just hoped her target wasn't paper bag ugly because she hadn't enjoyed dick in a while and her pussy had no qualms complaining about the fact it was long overdue.

Arriving at her townhouse, she flicked the button on her key fob dangling from the ignition and the garage door opened. She slid in and dismounted her bike after flicking the kickstand forward. She strode into her home and tossed her backpack on the kitchen island. She stripped off her leathers, hanging them over a chair, not stopping until she got down to her panties. She kept the place warm so she didn't even shiver in her almost nude state. She only kept her bottoms on to preserve her couch. Coochie stains on the furniture just didn't scream class.

She unzipped her knapsack and brought the folder along with a beer into her bedroom. She flopped onto her king-sized bed and began to read. Frederick had provided a thorough background on her geek, and she sipped her beer as she perused the file.

> *Name: Anthony Dominic Savell*
> *Born: September 19, 1979*
> *Height: 76 inches*
> *Weight: 95 kg*
> *Hair: Brown*
> *Eyes: Blue (wears glasses)*
> *Orientation: Heterosexual*
> *Other info: Graduated high school with honors at the age of fourteen. Went on to university with scholarships and obtained numerous degrees in the fields of biology, medicine, science, chemistry. Went to work for a private research corporation in 2005. Offered a lab with anything he wanted, on site residence in 2008.*

Lexie fought a yawn as she read through the dull biography. Boring. It sounded like her geek didn't have a life outside of his work and research. She rifled through the rest of the papers looking for anything interesting about her target, but found nothing, not even mention of a girlfriend. Mind numbing as she found the info, she needed to study it and his reason for going to the conference. While she planned to play the part of seductive science groupie, she would still need to know a little bit about him. At the very bottom of the pile she finally found a picture, more like an employee mug shot, but it gave her a face for her nerd. He sported shaggy, brownish un-kept hair, dark rimmed glasses and a slightly startled look which seemed at odds with his square chin and sensual lips. *Well, at least he's not butt ugly.*

His height and weight also put him on the larger size, which would work out in her favor. *Nothing worse than breaking a fragile human when you're trying to get them off.* The human boy she'd accidentally maimed in high school eventually regained use of his legs, and she became more careful with her affections when dealing with humans. A shame because she really did enjoy going wild and unrestrained in the bedroom — biting and scratching totally turning her on — however, only another Lycan or supernatural could handle her passion when she let loose. Unfortunately, shifter lovers tended to try and mark her, making them unsuitable for bedding. Although few tried that anymore since word had gotten out about Derrick. She still wasn't allowed anywhere near Tennessee, where one-eyed Derrick ruled the packs since his father's demise. She'd warned him though, not her fault he refused to listen.

As she snuggled into her comforter, she made a mental list of the things she'd need to pack for her trip — slutty business suits, thongs, flats so she didn't tower, nylons and garters, her Browning High Power loaded with silver bullets, her stakes, ooh and her vibrator in case her geek came before the main event.

With a snicker at her last thought, she slipped into sleep.

chapter two

Anthony pushed his glasses back up on his nose as he stepped from the cab that deposited him outside the hotel housing the conference. He couldn't believe he'd made it. For the last three years, he'd buried himself in his work at Mr. Thibodeaux's lab. He'd shown little interest in leaving the property given the fascinating project he worked on, a project he'd reluctantly left to attend this conference, yet, how could he refuse? They'd selected his paper on DNA abnormalities where he'd theorized that a simple twist of a DNA strand could make a person's condition seem unreal, supernatural even, like Mr. Thibodeaux for example. The man exhibited a fatal allergy to the exposure of UV rays and required vast amounts of iron and blood transfusions to keep his body healthy. In times past, the superstitious masses would have condemned his employer as some unnatural creature, a vampire. Ridiculous, of course. Mr. Thibodeaux suffered from an allergy which came about as a result of some warped DNA strands. A genetic anomaly was the culprit here, not mystical nonsense.

With science, he would prove monsters did not, in fact, exist and if all went well, he would cure them. Then —

A body jostled him as he stood woolgathering on the pavement; a feminine form whose tantalizing perfume made his saliva glands work overtime. How strange, given both his mind and body knew a woman didn't provide bodily sustenance.

"I'm awfully sorry for bumping into you like that."The sultry voice slid around him and, to his mortification, his cock twitched. *Surely it hasn't been that long since I've taken care of my bodily needs that my penis would show a sexual interest just from a voice?* He'd have to rectify his neglect later in the shower before he embarrassed himself.

Anthony had to look down to see the owner of the voice, his freakish height as always making him stand out, which made her not seeing him so odd. But he forgot all about her clumsy nature when he saw her.

Tall herself, even in the flats she wore, she gazed up at him in surprise.Anthony lost his train of thought, drawn into her soft green eyes flecked with brown. His gaze took in her lustrous brown hair caught up in an untidy chignon, and her proper, yet sensual, attire which consisted of a fitted cream jacket over a crimson blouse tucked into a pencil thin, black skirt. Her smooth, lightly tanned skin provided a perfect contrast to her pink glossed lips.

Humor glinted in her expression and her mouth tilted into a partial smile.Anthony struggled to regain control of himself and blushed as he realized she'd caught him staring. His heart sped up as he strove to find his voice in the face of the most beautiful woman he'd ever encountered."Uh, no harm done. I guess I shouldn't have been blocking the sidewalk."

"No, it's my fault for not looking where I walked," she replied, her gaze not wavering from his, sending a shiver racing down his spine.

Her close proximity not only affected his lower regions, it made his pulse race. Anthony knew he needed to escape and regain his composure, then he'd need to figure out why one pretty woman flustered him so. "Um, well, I should get inside and get signed in." His genius in the lab, as usual, didn't extend to his banter.

"Are you also here for the conference?" she asked in a low tone that set his body tingling and made the blood in his brain rush elsewhere.

"Uh, yes. I'm actually one of the speakers." Anthony flushed at his boast.

"Really? How fantastic," she purred. "I'm here for just one of the speakers. I'm just dying to hear Anthony Savall talk. I read his paper on DNA and myth and just loved it. He is so brilliant."

Anthony's body suffused with heat and he wanted to reply, but his lips refused to move, mostly out of fear he'd say something dorky and scare her off. The confidence he enjoyed among his peers evaporated in the face of his immense attraction to her.

She didn't seem to notice anything amiss; although, he surely looked like the world's biggest doofus standing there like a mute.

"I guess I'll see you around." She smiled before she turned and strutted off with a wiggle that made Anthony close his eyes, hoping the blood in his penis would return to his brain. Thank science he wore baggy trousers and a long jacket.

He cursed his social ineptness at the prime opportunity, now lost, to introduce himself and ask the gorgeous woman to dinner. In a fantasy world, where he didn't turn into a stammering schoolboy, he would have swept her off her feet with his witty banter and smarts. He would have wined and dined her, all the while charming her with his intellect. At the end of the repast, she would have come back to his room where he would have worshipped every sun kissed inch of her body while she moaned his name.

Could have, should have. Anthony sighed. He was a researcher not a suave Casanova, and it didn't take a genius to realize his reality sucked.

* * *

Lexie checked in at the front desk, her room conveniently situated next to the giant scientist, a string that Frederick had pulled to ensure the ease of her task. As she waited for her room card, she pondered the geek she needed to protect. Turning part way, she could see him through the glass front doors, still standing outside. His dumbstruck expression warmed her.

While Anthony Savall looked the part of nerdy scientist with his pale complexion, large glasses and untidy hair, his height took her by surprise. Sure the report listed him at seventy-six inches, but for some reason she hadn't clued in that it would make him tower over her. In her world, geeks were supposed to be short and round shouldered, not freakishly tall next to her five foot nine. *And I didn't pack heels.* Expecting a shorter stature, slouching target, she'd packed her flats so as to not appear too imposing. *I wonder, if I can order up some heels?*

Another surprise was the fact her wolf showed an interest in the human, waking and staying attentive during their conversation. Strange, because her lupine side usually waited for blood and violence to rouse itself. She paid it no mind though. Who knew what intrigued her beast. Maybe it had scented the fact her skittish geek was prey — a male red riding hood to her big bad wolf. Lexie bit her lip so as to not snort at that last thought.

The desk clerk handed her a key card, his expression fawning. Lexie growled and giggled when the youth blanched.

With a wiggle she knew would turn heads, she made her way to the elevator. A sideways glance showed Anthony, who'd finally come in with bright cheeks, watching her. *Don't worry, my giant geek. You'll be seeing me again real soon.*

Lexie found her room and slid her key card in the slot. She stepped in and dropped her luggage. She quickly went to work, unlocking the door that adjoined her room to Anthony's in case of an emergency. She performed a rapid check of his quarters to ensure nothing dangerous waited to surprise her target, but saw nothing more menacing than a pillow mint, which she ate — her sweet tooth just couldn't resist. She didn't have time to sweep for bugs, but assumed their presence.

She slid back into her room, closing the now unlocked barrier. She unpacked her things as she waited for the next stage in her plan, using this moment of free time to hang her suits and arrange her toiletries. She also stashed her weapons around the room and used her keen sense of smell to scout out the cameras Frederick would have installed. Dead in body didn't mean dead in libido. She'd known the pervert would want a peek. He'd placed one in the bathroom and one by the bed. She left them for the moment. Forewarned, she could control what he'd get to see. Besides, an audience always added an extra element to sex.

Done with her preparation, she waited for her moment. With her enhanced shifter hearing, she had no problem making out her geek's actions next door. He unpacked, the sound of his suitcase zipper loud. Drawers opened and closed. Hangers rattled as he hung things. He left the bathroom door open as he peed, and then washed his hands. *A nerd with manners.*

He returned to his room and she strained to hear him. He mumbled to himself, something along the lines of "... she's just a pretty woman. No reason why I can't talk to her or ask her to dinner."

Lexie smiled. Apparently her first impression had stuck — good. So far her plan unfolded smoothly, not that she'd had any doubts. Men and their dicks were so predictable.

She ditched her jacket and slipped the top button of her blouse out of its loop, creating a shadowy vee. She waited to hear the sound of him opening his door into the hall before stepping out of her own room, and of course, turning with surprise etched on her face to greet him.

"Hi, there. What a coincidence meeting you again," she said brightly.

He looked startled — kind of like the deer she'd run down on her last run through the woods. It was kind of cute.

"Um, hi."

She could judge by his reddening cheeks that he'd meant to say more, but shyness rendered him mute. "I was just going down to check into the conference. You know, get my name tag and a schedule of events. Then I was going to get some dinner. I know this is presumptuous, but I don't know anybody here and well ... " She trailed off and gave him an expectant look.

"W-what?" he managed to stammer.

Lexie smiled at him coyly and restrained a giggle as she batted her lashes for good measure. "Would you have dinner with me?"

His jaw dropped, his surprise at her invitation clear. "I — uh-um. That is — "

Lexie dropped her eyes and schooled her features to look disappointed. "I knew it was silly of me to ask. You probably have plans already. I'm sorry to have bothered you." She started to turn slowly.

"No," he almost shouted. "I mean, yes, I would love to have dinner with you."

She pivoted back and beamed at him. "Oh, thank you. Shall we both go down then to get checked in? After, we can go straight to dinner? I'm *famished*." She inflected her last word and saw his eyes dilate behind his lenses. She didn't wait for him to answer this time. She wasn't sure he could, and honestly, it turned her on, her erotic effect on him strangely contagious. Something about him drew her, made her want to rip those glasses off his face and kiss him. *This job might turn out to be a lot more fun than I expected.* And apparently her body needed some exercise given its rousing interest in a geek whom she usually wouldn't have given a second glance.

She linked her arm around his — and found it surprisingly thick. A nerd who worked out? She couldn't wait to unwrap him later and find out.

At her urging, they made it to the elevator and rode it down in a thick silence. She could tell he wanted to talk, but every time her gaze met his, he blushed and looked away — and the bulge at his groin grew. His bulky clothes couldn't quite hide from someone with her developed powers of observation the fact her presence titillated him. It made her own panties dampen as her cleft reacted with pleasure. For a moment, she naughtily wondered what would happen if she were to press herself against him, right this very moment. *Probably faint,* snickered her mischievous mind.

She gave him a break and let go of his arm when they reached the lobby. However, she did nothing to control the wiggle in her walk as she made her way over to the sign in table. She waited until he was almost behind her to bend over and sign her name, thrusting her bottom out to accidentally bump him in the groin.

His strangled moan and rigid poke against her ass made her smile. She straightened and turned to face him, pretending she hadn't just felt his erection against her backside. She peeled her nametag off the wax backing and slapped it on her silk covered breast, holding in a smirk as his eyes couldn't help following her every movement. She rubbed the tag for good measure and saw him swallow. *Poor guy doesn't stand a chance.* "Your turn."

She moved aside and pretended to look around with interest. He signed in and only when he placed his name tag on did she exclaim, "Oh my god. You're Anthony Savell. Why didn't you say anything?"

Again his cheeks heated, but he managed to speak — finally. "I didn't want to appear like I was bragging."

"Why ever not? That piece you wrote in that journal a few months ago was brilliant. I can see we're going to have a fantastic time at dinner. I can't wait to pick your brain."

The smile he bestowed on her warmed her and, to her shock, tightened her nipples. The man had a killer grin when he used it. "Thanks for saying so. It's definitely an exciting field."

"And I can't wait to hear all about it over dinner and drinks."

She linked her arm in his again as they made their way to the hotel's restaurant. Phase one of the geek job was well underway, and it looked like phase two which involved getting into his room via his pants would actually be more fun than anticipated.

* * *

Anthony wanted to pinch himself. *I'm hallucinating.* He could think of no other explanation for how and why this beautiful woman ate dinner with him. Talking animatedly one minute, listening attentively the next, she managed to melt some of his shyness at her obvious interest in him, even if she tied his tongue in knots every time she touched him. Her hand kept reaching out to squeeze his, and each time it felt like she'd wrapped her hand around something else, something hard and throbbing, thankfully hidden by the table. He still didn't understand why she affected him so deeply. Never before had attraction to the opposite sex turned him into a blushing idiot, but at the same time, he loved it.

Logic stated that the woman's pheromones must be unusually developed or of a variety that truly appealed to him, but his dick didn't care about the biological science of it. It just wanted to bend her over the nearest table and pump her to orgasm. Anthony bit back a groan at the mental image and dug the tines of his fork into his leg, the pain reining in his raging, baser desire.

Lexie, his gorgeous dinner partner, didn't seem to notice a thing amiss. She chattered away, inane talk that thankfully required little thought or input from him. Their waiter brought their entrees, and he looked forward to something to occupy him other than imagining how she'd look on her knees, peering up at him.

Anthony took a bite of his pasta then forgot to chew. Heck, he forgot to breathe, he became so caught up in watching Lexie enjoy her meal. She took a bite of her juicy, rare steak and closed her eyes with a groan. Her pleasure in her meal, the way she licked her fork, masticated with sensual satisfaction — it was the most erotic thing he'd ever watched and yet had nothing to do with sex.

She caught him watching and smiled. "I do so love a properly cooked steak." She gazed at his mostly uneaten meal. "Mmm, that pasta of yours looks yummy. Mind if I have a bite?" She reached forward and wrapped her hand around his. She drew his laden fork to her mouth and sucked the food off before releasing his hand. Anthony had no idea what his meal tasted like, but he regained interest after her lips covered his fork. Just knowing the tines had touched her mouth turned him on. *How pathetic am I?*

As the food on their plates — well, mostly hers — dwindled, a new waiter approached them with an open bottle of wine. Lexie, short for Lexington as she'd informed him, frowned at the man. "We didn't order this."

The waiter smiled with a lot of teeth that, for some reason, sent a chill down Anthony's spine. "It's a gift from an admirer," said the waiter with a heavy accent.

It was Anthony's turn to frown. *Is someone trying to hit on her?*

Understandable given her beauty, but he didn't like it, which in turn, baffled him. He had no claim on her, so why the jealousy?

The waiter poured the ruby colored wine into their glass goblets, and then stood, as if waiting for them to try it. Anthony picked his up by the stem and inclined his head at her. "To not eating alone." He held his glass out in a toast.

She smiled and leaned forward to grab her own glass, but fumbled it instead, splashing the liquid across the front of her blouse. Lexie jumped up from her seat and grabbed a napkin to wipe with while the waiter fled, probably to get a cloth for cleaning. Anthony put down his wine and snatched up his own napkin, then, not thinking, began dabbing at her too. It only took him a few swipes to realize he was brushing her breasts and he snatched his hand back as if burned.

Mortified, he stammered. "I-I'm so sorry. I didn't mean — that is, I — "

She stepped close and shh-ed him. She grasped his hand and brought it back up, pressing it against her chest, her pebbled nipple evident through the wet silk. "I don't mind. Actually, can't you tell I enjoyed it?"

Anthony's cock tented his pants and he wanted to pull away in embarrassment, but she wouldn't let him. Instead, she pressed in even closer and lifted herself on tiptoe to brush her mouth across his. Anthony stopped breathing, afraid she'd realize she kissed a nerd.

"I need to get out of these clothes," she murmured against his mouth. "Care to help me?"

He didn't trust himself to speak aloud, not when his mind spun with pure gibberish, so instead, he nodded. She kissed him lightly on the lips again before sliding an arm around his waist. It seemed only natural he slide his arm around her back. Entwined like lovers — if he didn't fuck it up between here and the hotel room — they walked out of the restaurant to the elevators and he thanked the fact he'd signed to charge the dinner to his room at the start of the meal. He wanted nothing to interfere or delay his time with Lexie.

He feared breaking the spell tentatively spun between them,

certain it would only take one word to make her change her mind. But as soon as the elevator doors closed, she proved her interest as she pressed her body against his while her mouth hotly latched onto his. He met her with a passion usually reserved for science, his body afire instead of his mind. He circled his arms around her, only mildly surprised at the wiry strength he felt in her frame.

The elevator arrived at their floor with a ding and they broke apart, both panting. Anthony couldn't believe the smoldering look in her eyes. *She wants me?* She licked her swollen lips and grabbed him by the hand, tugging him down the hall. She unlocked her door and dragged him inside. He'd no sooner shut the door behind him than she was on him, her mouth eagerly tasting his, her hands tugging at his belt.

Events began moving at the speed of light. He wanted to tell her to slow down. Her passion overwhelmed even as it flattered him. He didn't say a word, couldn't with his tongue caught in a tangle with hers. Although, he did grunt when she freed his cock and wrapped her hand around it. She stroked him, sliding her hand from tip to base and Anthony fought to keep control, a lost cause because she dropped to her knees and took him in her mouth. All he could do was moan as his fingers clutched at her hair, still tied up in that sexy upsweep.

Sweet gods of science. It didn't take her long to get him off, a few wet sucks and he bucked into her mouth, his hot cream spurting in record time to his embarrassment.

He expected her to laugh at him, make some comment about his premature ejaculation and he prepared to flee with his shame. But truly, the woman was a goddess because instead, she said, "Been a while, huh?" He nodded, too humiliated to reply out loud. "Don't worry, now that we've gotten that out of the way, it's going to make round two all the better."

Anthony's eyes widened. *We're not done? I must be dreaming.*

She stood up and plucked his glasses from his face. "We wouldn't want to accidentally break these." She placed them on the small table by the door before she stepped back from him. Slender fingers reached up to her hair and released a clip, letting it tumble about her shoulders in a silken dark wave. She then unbuttoned her wine stained blouse, and flung it back to drape over the lamp by the bed. She revealed firm round breasts unfettered by a bra. Even his less than perfect eyesight couldn't miss how her nipples puckered and as he watched with a watering mouth, they shriveled even further.

"Suck them," she said huskily. "I want to feel your mouth on me."

His cock twitched back to life at her demand, a fact he'd have found fascinating and worthy of study any other time. He forwent taking notes on this amazing phenomenon to cover the few feet that separated them in a daze. He placed his hands on the taut skin of her waist and drew her body up. Electricity sizzled at the contact and she sucked in a breath, her startled eyes meeting his. She raised her hand and ran her fingers down his cheek, tracing his lips. She inserted one between his lips and he sucked it, enjoying the way her eyelids drooped and her body swayed towards him.

"Mmm," she moaned. "Do that to my tits."

He didn't need further urging. He'd have walked on fire at this point for her. He bent down until he could grasp one of her nipples with his mouth. He inhaled it slowly, each suck bringing more of her breast and nub into his mouth. She cried out in pleasure and gripped his hair with her hands, pulling him tighter against her. He switched breasts, paying the same attention to the other. She growled, a soft primal sound that should have sounded stupid, but instead, spurred him on. He bit down on her puckered berry and she mewled, her hips arching forward against him, the soft skin of her tummy butting against his already rigid cock.

"I want you to do that to my pussy," she purred pushing him away. She moved towards the bed and stopped at its foot. She undid the side zipper to her skirt and let the fabric drop to the floor.

Anthony almost joined it in a boneless puddle when he saw she wore no panties. He definitely swayed as she stood there clad only in nylons and garters. When her hands went to untie them he spoke in a gruff voice he didn't recognize. "Leave them on. Please."

He saw her body shudder in reaction to his words and his

confidence soared. *This woman wants me.* Logic, sense and science had no meaning here, only a primitive lust like he'd never known.

He stripped his shirt off as he moved towards her, enjoying her look of surprise. She ran her hands over his toned upper body with wonder. "A big cock. A lickable chest. What else have you been hiding, my giant scientist?"

He answered her with a kiss, suddenly glad he spent an hour every day in the gym to keep himself fit — she didn't need to know that he used his mindless exercise time to puzzle out problems in the lab. She wrapped her arms around him and toppled them backwards onto the bed. He tried to brace himself so as to not crush her, but landed on her body anyway, not that she seemed to mind. Her legs wrapped around his waist, trapping his cock against her lower belly.

She kissed him, her lithe tongue sliding along his until he feared coming again, so erotically did she touch him. He pulled away, determined to give her pleasure. He embraced her body, worshipped it with his mouth and tongue as he slowly made his way down to her mound. He flicked his tongue against her still hard nipples and bit them just to hear that growling cry that sent a shiver through him. He laved a circle around her flat navel, fascinated by her toned physique, so different from his previous — if sparse — lovers. He caressed her body as he moved down to the neatly trimmed pubes and the treasure below. The proof of her desire glistened on her plump pink lips and he could even smell it. Her evident arousal awed him for he couldn't deny, nor could logic argue, this woman wanted him. It emboldened and enflamed him.

He knelt on the floor and grasped her thighs to draw her towards him, aligning her sweet sex with his mouth. Then he tasted her. At the first touch of his tongue against her pussy, she let out a keening cry and her back arched. He licked her again, a long wet swipe of his tongue between her lips up to her clit. She bucked and moaned.

"That's it, taste me. Suck me. Then fuck me."

Her crude demands fired him. He held onto her thighs and went to work, determined to pleasure her like she had him. It made his cock throb the way she trembled at his oral tease of her sex. He groaned at the way she tasted so sweet in his mouth. He flicked his tongue faster and faster over her swollen nub, her quickening cries goading him on. When her body tightened, he moved over her, sheathing his cock inside of her.

"Oh fuck," she growled, her low tone touching him in a primitive place that drove him wild. "Fuck me. Fuck me hard."

Anthony needed no urging. He pistoned his hips, thrusting himself in and out of her velvety moistness, holding back his release even as her pelvic muscles clamped him so tightly. He pumped harder, his hands on her waist, driving her down onto his cock. Deeper. Faster. Her fingers dug at his shoulders, her nails biting into his skin; the pain of it though, spurred him to plow her even more vigorously.

She screamed when she climaxed and her whole body bowed up off the bed. Anthony held on tight as her orgasm milked him in waves, and came seconds after her with a hoarse shout.

He collapsed beside her on the bed, breathing heavily, utterly blown away by the most extreme pleasure he'd ever experienced. She rolled against him, snuggling into him. He curled his arms around her, hugging her back.

"Spend the night with me," she whispered.

His answer of "Sure" sounded stupid and inadequate to him, but it seemed enough for her because her breathing evened out as she fell asleep.

I don't know how I got this lucky, but please, don't let it end.

Anthony was convinced he'd never fall asleep beside this goddess. In truth he feared doing so. *What if I wake and discover it was all a dream?* But, two orgasms in quick succession soon had him drifting into a pleasant dreamland where Lexie featured front and center — naked.

chapter three

Lexie inched out from under her geek's arm, not because she wanted to — which surprised her and she'd analyze the why later — but because she heard stealthy movement from the room next door, the room her dear Anthony hadn't gone back to.

Getting him to stay with her — again part of her master plan to protect him — had gone off without a hitch and came with a fabulous orgasm. Who knew her unimposing scientist hid a gifted lover with a decent body and a large cock? While his pale skin seemed to indicate a life mostly spent indoors, his body had the general tone of a man who hit the gym daily, a fact she appreciated.

Later, she'd explore his body and his skills further. Time to earn her paycheck.

She briefly thought of getting dressed. Her nudity didn't bother her, and if the waiting assailants were male, it could give her the leverage needed. She did, however, grab her gun and Anthony's key card from his pants pocket. She glanced over at him and saw him still sleeping soundly. Hopefully, she could take care of the problem quickly and quietly before he woke. She peeked out through her peephole into the hall first.

Seeing nothing, not surprising give the time of three a.m., she opened her door on silent hinges and took the few steps over to the room beside hers. She decided against the adjoining room door because the time and noise needed to swing open the double barrier would have alerted them something was amiss. Better to let them think Anthony staggered back after a night of debauchery.

She slid Anthony's keycard into the electronic lock which disengaged with a snick. The motion inside the room halted as she'd expected. She swung the door open and sauntered in. Her nude body caught the waiting vamp by surprise, and he stared at her hungrily for only a moment before she shot him between the eyes. It wouldn't kill him, but it would incapacitate him long enough for the cleanup crew she'd call to take care of him.

Two more figures rushed at her from the darkness of the room and she shot another one before the third slammed into her.

The vamp tried to hug her, grope her and bite her all at the same time. Males, even dead ones, could be so predictable. She brought her knee up as hard as she could. The vampire folded with a pained gasp. She dropped to her knees and twisted his head until his neck snapped.

Round one taken care of and her geek safe for the moment, she made a quick call to Frederick's cleanup crew. All vampire families had one for situations like these that required discretion and, most of all, ensuring the humans remained oblivious.

She then sent a quick text to her employer mentioning the attempted poisoning at dinner — a plan foiled because of her sharp scenting skills. She also mentioned the nocturnal visitors and the fact his scientist now slept in her bed. Like he didn't know. She'd covered the lamp where the camera hid with her blouse, but their audio would have clearly picked up the sounds of their fucking.

Lexie slipped back into her room and crawled into bed with her giant geek. She still refused to examine why she smiled when, in repose, he threw his arm over her and drew her back into his body. She also ignored her wolf who whined in her mind, wanting something that Lexie didn't understand.

She buried everything that bothered her in the pleasure she

roused by wiggling her bottom against his dormant cock. Lucky her, it didn't sleep for long.

* * *

Anthony woke alone. He sat up and looked around, but couldn't tell if this was his room or not. Hotels tended to lack imagination when it came to decorating. *Did I dream it all up?* Had he just passed out on his bed after he checked in?

The sound of running water came to him from behind the closed door of the bathroom and he looked about wildly for some clothes. Anthony didn't enjoy nudity, on him at any rate. However, he could have stared at Lexie naked all day long. But he was pretty sure she wouldn't feel the same way about him. Sure, he went to the gym and maintained a decent physique, but more for his general health than for looks. His pasty skin and hairless chest in the light of day weren't exactly his best attributes. He needed to cover up before she realized it too. He'd just found his glasses and snagged his pants when the bathroom door opened.

"Oh, goody, you're awake."

Anthony straightened, holding his pants to his chest and stared at Lexie as she sauntered from the bathroom wearing the tiniest towel imaginable. "Um, g-good morning," he managed to stammer. How this woman managed to make him sound like a simpleton, he still couldn't figure out. What happened to his calm and confident demeanor? His ability to analyze and respond appropriately to situations?

"It's a wonderful morning," she said with a smile. She approached him, her eyes glinting and he swallowed hard. "In the mood for some *breakfast*?"

A suave man would have said "Yes, now get your sexy ass on the bed so I can eat." Anthony just nodded his head.

"Excellent. I took the liberty of opening the doors between our rooms. I thought you might want to grab a shower and fresh change of clothes before we went down to eat. Then, I figured we could check out the conference events starting in an hour."

Anthony would have actually preferred pulling off her towel, throwing her on the bed and seeing if plowing her body really felt as good as he remembered. Instead, with a blush and his trousers clutched to his groin, he fled through the adjoining door, her husky laughter following him.

At least it wasn't the derisive kind he'd come to expect. He jumped into the shower, the hot water hitting his back and making him hiss. The sting of the scratches across his shoulders and upper back reminded him of her passionate response to their coitus. *She marked me.* The realization made him grin. As he showered his mind couldn't help turning over the fabulous turn of events that had occurred in the last twelve hours. He, proven geek and flop where woman were concerned, not only had a drop dead gorgeous woman seduce him — and suck him off — she still wanted to spend time with him. Even better, the sex had been amazing, the best he'd ever had, and more astonishing was her response to him. She hadn't faked her desire or her orgasm — he knew what a pulsing channel meant. And he suspected his middle of the night dream of taking her from behind while spooned in bed probably occurred as well.

Just thinking of her lithe body made him rock hard. He couldn't help gripping his cock and fisting it. He also couldn't help the low moan as he thought of the way he'd felt when she wrapped her lips around his shaft, sucking him while her hand cupped his balls.

The shower curtain rustled and his eyes shot open. Shock at getting caught masturbating made him want to swirl down the drain, until he saw her face. Lexie stood in front of him, the steam from the shower pearling on her skin, the expression on her face hungry, and not for food.

"I'm sorry," she murmured. "I just couldn't resist joining you." She wrapped her fingers around his hand still on his cock. "I hope you don't mind."

Anthony didn't mind when she bent over for him in the shower exposing the most perfect pink pussy. He didn't mind that the water made her tighter when he sheathed his cock into her. And he didn't mind at all that she screamed when he fucked her until they both came.

If his stomach would have stayed quiet, he would have suggested skipping the morning's events in favor of going back to bed, or the table, or wherever she preferred. However, he knew without some form of nutrition, no matter how his mind felt, his body would never keep up, and he was determined not to disappoint her. Even if the copious amount of sex with her made his dick raw, he had no intention of saying no.

* * *

Lexie tried to pay attention to their surroundings and the possible threats to her geek sitting across from her, but dammit, she kept remembering how he'd taken her in the shower, which in turn made her so fucking horny. All she could think of was how fast she could get him somewhere private so she could screw his brains out again.

She didn't understand her insane reaction at all. Usually she got the itch, she fucked, and then she went on. Sure, this time she'd gone without scratching for longer than usual, but she'd gone through sexual dry spells in the past and never had a problem before. This out of control, raging desire to have this man in front of her — a geeky scientist and not her usual steroid body builder — baffled her. Sure he was cute in a nerdy kind of way. He sported a decent bod, nothing like her usual play toys whose abs could bounce quarters. His technique, while enjoyable — really, really enjoyable — was nothing new. So why, oh why, did she sit in drenched panties wondering if anyone would notice if she slipped under the table to give him a blowjob?

She must have stared at him for too long because he blushed and dropped his head. For a brilliant scientist, he took shyness to a new level, and she couldn't figure out why. After what they'd done together, she expected him to overcome his tongue tied demeanor. Or did he blush for another reason?

"Penny for your thoughts," she said. His color deepened and she smiled. No need for a penny, his face read like an open book. "If it's any consolation, I wish we were back in the room with my lips wrapped around your cock, too. But you came here for a reason, so

I'm going to be a good girl, for now, and clamp my thighs tight and think of the lectures as foreplay."

He couldn't stifle the small moan which, in turn, made her squirm as more liquid heat seeped from her cleft.

Despite her good intentions — and the fact she wanted to have him out in public long enough to see if she could spot any more assassins/kidnappers — she couldn't stop fidgeting during the lecture given by the boring nerdazoid in the bow tie. She tried to focus on the speaker's words, but she couldn't help comparing the balding, short individual with her giant sitting next to her. She doubted she'd have wet panties had the dull, droning midget at the podium been her target.

She sighed as the lecture went on and on, absolute torture for an outdoorsy type like herself. Large fingers laced around hers and she darted a glance sideways to see Anthony with his lips in a half tilt. "What do you say we go for a walk? Somehow I think we'll learn more from the fresh air than this pompous idiot."

"Oh, thank god." She immediately stood, surprised at his initiative, but at the same time delighted.

They made it out to the vestibule and she wondered for a moment if their walk would take them back to her room — not that she minded. But Anthony, still on a take charge kick, strode with her towards the front door of the hotel.

"Where are we going?" she asked. She hadn't planned on leaving the building, and given her intimate relationship with her geek, not worn any weapons lest he find them and question their presence.

"There's a park one block over. I thought we'd go for a walk and then maybe hit an outdoor café for lunch?"

Lexie chewed her lip for half a second as she thought furiously. Given the bright sunlight, she wouldn't have to worry about vamps. The Fae and other creatures, who could walk by day, might see their excursion as an opportunity to move. The smart thing would have involved her plastering her mouth to his and convincing him to return to bed, but her animal side craved the fresh air and sunlight. She'd have to hope that Frederick's goons watched and followed. If she kept them to public areas where assassins would require subtlety if they attacked, she could handle the rest.

Her giant scientist kept a hold of her hand as they crossed the road and walked the short distance to the park. She found the intimacy of it odd. As a rule, she wasn't a hand holding, or cuddling for that matter, kind of girl. Her domineering presence and attitude tended to scare off a lot of men. Actually, if she weren't currently playing a role right now of cutesy science slut, she'd probably have sent Anthony running, too. It wasn't that she eschewed femininity, she just had a dominant persona that most men couldn't handle.

They reached the park without mishap, although she kept her eyes peeled as she breathed deep of the air that wasn't entirely fresh given the exhaust of passing traffic. But it sure beat recycled hotel air.

"Do you spend a lot of time outdoors?" Anthony asked as they strolled along the cobbled path.

"You might say that." While she lived in the city during the week, on weekends and vacations she went to the woods where she ran wild and lived off the land.

"I love the outdoors." At her pointed look, he laughed, the most carefree sound she'd heard him make thus far. "I know. I've got the coloring of a lab rat. But, before I got caught up in my research, I used to spend a lot of time outdoors."

Lexie found herself listening attentively to the first freely given personal information from him. Where his sudden relaxation came from she didn't know, but she encouraged it. "Do you love the whole research thing?" she asked.

"It obsesses me. It's like having a puzzle with a few extra pieces and knowing if you can just figure out which one fits, you'll get the whole picture. But, enough about me. What do you do?" he asked peering down at her. "You never did say."

Lexie's prefabricated lie of working as a college professor's assistant got tossed aside in favor of a partial truth. "I do odd jobs for those who require finesse and subtlety."

"You know that doesn't tell me anything."

She grinned up at him. "I know. My jobs all have confidentiality agreements. Let's just say I'm good at what I do and well compensated, which, in turn, allows me a lot of freedom for things like this conference."

"I almost didn't come. I'm getting real close to a breakthrough on my current project. If it weren't for the fact my paper got selected, I would have probably stayed in my lab." He squeezed her fingers and smiled down at her. "I'm glad now I didn't."

Guilt stole her tongue and made her drop her eyes. She didn't understand it. She'd gotten her geek job right where she wanted him — eating from the palm of her hand and safe with her. But why did she want to beg his forgiveness for misleading him, and even worse, want him to keep looking at her with that smile in his eyes? *Don't get attached, Lexie. You know humans and werewolves can't be together,* not if she wanted him to live a long and healthy life. The reminder didn't cheer her.

chapter four

Anthony cursed himself for being an idiot. He'd spoken the truth about how happy he was to meet her and Lexie couldn't look him in the eye since then. She kept her hand laced in his though, so maybe all wasn't lost. *Idiot! Why not drop to one knee and declare undying love? Why not try a little harder to make her run by acting clingy?*

He blamed his runaway tongue on the insane feelings she roused in him. Lust yes, but more than that, she captivated him. He sensed some of her sweet girl routine was an act, hiding a woman who tended to dominate, a woman used to wielding power and having people around her obey. The fact she couldn't talk about her job intrigued him, and at the same time made his whirring mind wonder if she had an ulterior motive in befriending him. But he squashed that thought. She'd made no attempt to pump him for information, on the contrary, the only pumping involved mutual pleasure. He wanted to trust her interest in him was genuine, but he couldn't help a nagging fear that she wanted something from him.

When their walk turned silent as they passed through the woods, he found himself watching her. She looked everywhere in the miniature city forest, everywhere except at him. Watching out for possible muggers during daylight or avoiding him? He decided to see if lunch would rouse her. He led them out of the park and a moment later she relaxed and smiled up at him.

"So where are we going next?"

"You'll see," he replied enigmatically. He directed her to an outdoor bistro he'd noticed on his way in to the hotel. It offered a roof top patio with fabulous views which he hoped would make her forget his tacky declaration earlier.

The elevator up with others forced her against him, not that he minded, especially when she slipped her arms around his waist. Of course, he could have done without the inevitable reaction of his cock and her knowing laugh.

The metal doors slid open and spilled them out onto a rooftop partially covered by a canopy. A hostess halted the group that crowded out in front of them. Anthony, seeing the many buzzing tables, worried that he hadn't made a reservation first, but luck remained with him. Although the large group ahead of them was forced to wait, the hostess quickly bustled them off to a secluded table for two around the back of the elevator. Screened with potted plants, Anthony could almost imagine he and Lexie were alone.

She broke the silence. "What a fantastic place! How did you find out about it?"

Anthony shrugged. "My employer mentioned it to me. Said if I happened to bump into a gorgeous woman, I should make the effort to take her here for dinner. He recommended I do it at night, but I thought you'd enjoy the sunshine more."

"You were so right." Her smile at him warmed him more than UV rays of a thousand suns, and he managed to bask in her pleasure without blushing for once.

The silence broken, the conversation flowed lightly as he made sure to stick to easy topics like the weather and movies.

Lunch passed uneventfully, unless he counted the way she kicked off her shoes and stroked a foot up his calf to settle it on his lap before rubbing him with it.

He was ready when she announced, with a vulgarity he enjoyed way too much, "Let's get out of here and fuck." He threw some bills down on the table and wished he could fly when the elevator took too long to arrive. By the time they reached her room, he was just about incoherent.

Sensing his need, she yanked up her skirt and bent over. He retained enough control to know he wouldn't last long enough to give her what she needed. He dropped to his knees and then just about came anyway at the sight of her soaked panties, proof of her own arousal. He dragged her undies down and ran his hand over her cleft.

She growled, "Don't fucking tease me. Give me your cock, now!"

He obliged and to his surprise, she came first, although he followed closely in second.

* * *

Lexie straightened Anthony's tie instead of tearing it off. She ran her hands down his chest and his jacket smoothing it. "You look dashing," she declared.

His lips quirked into a smile. "If you say so. I don't think the audience will care. We science geeks tend to be more interested in facts and argument than clothes."

"And that's what sets you apart. You're head smart and dressed smart. I can't wait to see you in action, well, somewhere other than the bedroom that is. We both know you rock there already."

What only a day ago would have set him to blushing, now made his eyes twinkle behind his lenses. He kissed her, his shyness of before gone with the confidence he'd gained in her presence — she blamed her wet panties from lunch for that. If she'd found the shy geek cute before, she found this more self-assured side even sexier.

They went down to the conference area, splitting up at the door as he went to the front to ensure everything was ready for his coming presentation. She took a seat in the back and carefully watched everyone who entered. They'd spent a quiet, attack-free day, and she didn't trust it at all. Two attempts on their first night and then nothing? She knew the best attempts were yet to come. She needed them to come so she could remind herself she was here for work and not pleasure. Despite all the men her mother had thrown at her, all the males who'd tried to claim her and the humans she'd toyed with, none had affected her like Anthony did. She still hadn't figured out why, nor did she intend to. Once she completed this job, she'd move on, like she always did.

As the time for Anthony's speech neared, the room began filling and she moved forward until she sat in the first row. Let Anthony think her eager, she wanted the proximity in case she needed to protect him. He glanced at her from time to time, not having forgotten her presence, and his quick smiles warmed her even as she chastised herself for acting so stupidly girly.

The lights in the room dimmed and the crowd hushed as Anthony stepped to the podium. She'd expected him to appear flustered, or hesitant, but when he spoke, she shivered. Apparently his shyness was reserved only for her. In front of his peers, the man was a genius and he knew it.

He spoke, and even though he used words she didn't quite understand at times, she found herself riveted for he spoke of her. Well, not her directly, but her species, werewolves, and not just shifters, but vampires and even the Fae, too.

The more he spoke, the more Lexie grasped just how dangerous her geek truly was. Not dangerous in a Rambo gun toting way, but even more lethal because his research was allowing him to unravel the truth of their existence. With his understanding of their DNA, he could possibly cure their state of supernaturalness, or even scarier, improve it.

Of course, he still believed the DNA he examined came from a human, a human with mutated genes. It was even possible his theory was true, that in fact, beings long thought special or paranormal were in truth a simple birth defect, a twisted DNA strand in the original human strain. It humbled and at the same time frightened her. She finally grasped just why so many factions might want him — dead or alive.

Holy fuck, what if he does find a way to twist the vampire strain in a way that makes them impervious to sunlight? What if he expands his research and discovers a way to make shifters invulnerable to silver, or strips the Fae of their powers? A lot of 'what ifs', but Lexie didn't doubt for a moment that Anthony would succeed. *He's just too smart for his own good.*

At the conclusion of his oration, the silence hung thick, then the questions came fast and furious from the nerds in the crowd who dared question his brilliance. Anthony handled them all with aloof aplomb. This was his element. He had the facts on his side and he used them against the naysayers.

Lexie didn't raise her hand, how could she when she was one of the monsters he considered still human, if special. *I wonder what he'd think if he knew the woman he was fucking turned hairy on the full moon or when I get really freaking pissed?*

But knowing how he'd turn from her in probable horror and disgust — or even worse, with a clinical eye towards experimentation — didn't stop her from wanting him. As the crowd thinned, she stood up and caught his eye. He broke off from the group around him and strode towards her, his face flushed with triumph. He grabbed her and kissed her, more forcefully than all his previous embraces. She melted under his touch.

He pulled back and smiled at her. "Come on. I'm starved."

So was she, but not for the five course meal being served. Nevertheless, she wouldn't take his moment of glory from him for selfish, sweaty sex. She did, however, make him a promise for later. She leaned up and whispered in his ear. "That was so fucking hot, and I'll show you later just how much it turned me on." Then she nipped his ear with her teeth.

* * *

Anthony almost went crossed eyed at her words and his cock immediately went rock solid. Screw dinner, she was the only feast he wanted. *Now.*

He dragged her into the side chamber where they kept the presentation equipment stored. He kicked the door shut and shoved a chair under the handle.

When he turned back to face her, he saw her panting. She licked her lips as she watched him with bright eyes and flushed cheeks. She threw herself at him, her hands grasping at his hair as her hot tongue found the seam of his mouth and slipped in. Anthony groaned and clasped her tight to him, squeezing her perfect ass.

"God, you were so fucking hot up there," she panted.

"If you say so. The entire time I could only think of how I wanted you to spread those legs so I could see if you wore panties." His brazen words spilled from his mouth, but he forgot to get embarrassed when she grabbed his hand and guided it up her skirt. He touched her moist flesh and groaned.

"You are a goddess," he murmured as he rubbed his thumb against her clit. She clutched at his shoulders with a gasp and threw her head back.

The closet he'd dragged them into didn't exactly have a bed or open spot for him to take her. Although, it did have a bare section of wall. Anthony pushed her back against it and fumbled at the closure for his pants. Lexie helped him to unbuckle and shoved his pants and briefs down far enough for his cock to spring forth.

She'd grasped his plan and wrapped her arms around his neck as he palmed her ass cheeks. A little heavier than expected, he still hoisted her up and she aided him by wrapping her legs around his waist, drawing his cock into her moist pussy as she did so.

Anthony hissed at the feeling. He pressed her back against the wall and thrust into her. In and out, he claimed her sweet flesh, feeling her mounting excitement in the way her moist sex clamped his cock.

A rattle of the doorknob to the closet distracted him for a moment, but instead of shriveling his desire, knowing that people passed just outside the flimsy wall excited him. He plowed her faster and she urged him on.

"Oh, yes. Fuck me. Fuck me hard," she murmured squeezing him tight.

His fingers dug into her ass cheeks as he bounced her faster on his shaft. His balls drew tight under him as he slammed into her over and over. He feared getting too rough in his enthusiasm, but the harder he went at her, the wilder she grew. She must have remembered their public location at the last minute because instead of screaming like she did in their room, she leaned forward and sank her teeth into his shoulder.

Thank science for his jacket, which took the brunt, because she nipped him hard, but the pain mixed with the pleasure catapulted him into his own orgasm. He gasped as his knees trembled with the force of his climax, his hot cream jetting into her still quivering sex.

She unwound her legs from his waist and slid down with a contented sigh. "You just keep surprising me, don't you? And here I took you for a bedroom only type of guy."

Funny, that's what I thought too until I met you. And he loved it.

chapter five

They emerged from the closet furtively like teenagers afraid of getting caught; not that anyone remained in the conference hall when the bar was open and serving drinks next door along with a buffet.

On impulse, she twined her arms around Anthony's neck and kissed him. "Thanks."

"For what?" he asked.

"For showing me science can be passionate instead of boring." She recognized her error when his brow knitted. Her statement clashed with her first day claim of loving his paper in the journal. To distract him, she kissed him again and when she had him properly flustered, she dragged him out into the corridor where conference goers milled. They made their way hand in hand to the hall, where the buffet sat on a long train of white cloth covered tables. Some of the dweebs from Anthony's conference swarmed him, firing questions. Anthony answered them whilst squeezing her hand as if to remind her she wasn't forgotten. But Lexie had a more pressing problem and it was leaking down her legs.

She leaned up on tiptoe to murmur. "I need to go visit the bathroom. I'll be right back." She kissed the corner of his jaw and slipped away.

Lexie didn't like leaving him alone to go to the bathroom to deal with her sticky thighs, but surrounded by a herd of nerds, she figured him safe for the few minutes it would take her to clean up.

She did her business quickly, washing herself off with a silly grin at his impromptu act. Who'd have imagined he'd garner the nerve to haul her into an oversized closet and fuck her against a wall? She couldn't deny her corrupting influence in this case.

Crotch wiped down, hair brushed and her makeup repaired, she re-emerged into the hall, her eyes immediately zoning in on Anthony, his height a definite advantage among these odd looking trolls. Finding him safe, she scanned the hall for danger as she approached, but saw nothing, which didn't reassure her. When she got within fifteen feet, with her enhanced hearing, she caught the conversation swirling around Anthony and growled under her breath.

"So Savell, where did you go and hide last night? We kind of expected you to join the meet and greet or were you too chicken to hang out with real scientists?"

She saw Anthony's body tighten and she clenched her fist, not liking the tone of the taunt. "I was otherwise occupied," her scientist replied enigmatically.

The short nerd whose lecture she and Anthony had skipped out on sneered. "Oh, please. Admit it, you were afraid we'd rip you a new one and shred your theory to bits."

Lexie had heard enough. She slid up behind Anthony and wrapped her arms around his waist. "Hi sexy," she murmured. She nudged his arm and he raised it so she could slide around his body to press against his side. She smiled at the gaping nerd crew.

"Well hi there, boys. I do hope you'll forgive me taking up so much of Anthony's time. The man is a tiger in bed, and well ... " She ran her hand up his chest. "I just hate to waste good hotel sex time."

Anthony coughed behind a hand and his body shook.

"Uh. Ah. Gee." The little geek who'd dared ambush her giant scientist blushed and stammered.

She turned into Anthony's arms with a pleased smile. "Let's dance, lover," she purred.

Only once they hit the makeshift dance floor did Anthony's shudders turn into laughter. She peeked up at him. "What's so funny?"

He grinned down at her, his smile so natural and filled with mirth it made her heart stutter. "Anyone ever tell you that you're amazing?"

"Shut up." Lexie ducked her head as her cheeks heated over his compliment. Blushing, a new thing for her, and she didn't like it one bit. It made her feel…vulnerable.

He chuckled and she rubbed her face against his chest, enjoying the rumbling sensation. They continued to dance in slow circles that allowed her to see in a three sixty angle if anyone looked out of place. In this room full of dweebs, geeks and nerds, the suave gentleman in the immaculate suit stood out like a sore thumb.

Lexie pulled back from Anthony. "I could use a drink, something sweet and nonalcoholic."

"Sure."

"I'll be standing by the exit door," she said pecking him on the lips. Or meant to. He crushed her to him, lifting her until she stood on tiptoe so he could thoroughly plunder her mouth.

With a cocky grin, he left her at the edge of the dance floor and made his way to the bar. Bolder and bolder, her geek job had not only grown a backbone around her, he'd also grown some balls. *How cute.*

Lexie pretended to wander aimlessly, but all the while she noted the thug in black. As expected, he went after the supposedly easier target — her.

She allowed him to grab her and bustle her out the exit door. Once outside she played innocent a while longer. "Wh-what do you want?" she cried, clasping her hands.

"I need to talk to your boyfriend."

"Anthony? Whatever for?"

He pulled a revolver out and pointed it at her. "Just do as I say and no one will get hurt."

Lexie dropped the fragile human routine and laughed. "Seriously, does that line ever work?"

The lackey's brow creased. "Shut up before I shoot you."

"Go ahead. It wouldn't be the first time." She didn't want to ruin her dress though, or her evening. She hiked her skirt drawing his eyes down to her legs and the foot that swung up to connect with his chin. The loud crack preceded the thug's eyes rolling back in his head. He sank to the ground in a slump and Lexie scoffed at the ease with which she'd taken him down.

Too fucking easy. Shit.

She scurried back inside in time to see Anthony with a puzzled brow being escorted out of the hall. She darted back out the side door and ran around to the front of the hotel. She skidded around the corner, glad she wore flats instead of heels, and quickly walked to the front doors. She slowed, smoothing her dress, and strode in just as Anthony and his expected captors appeared.

"Darling, there you are," she gushed. "I'm sorry I wasn't waiting for you by the door, but I got so hot, I just had to get a breath of fresh air." She could see the panic in his eyes and his not so subtle hint via head shake that she needed to go away. She wanted to kiss him for his attempt to protect her.

"Are these friends of yours?" she asked with wide eyed innocence. She stuck out her hand. "Hi, I'm Lexington, Anthony's girlfriend."

The goon on the left threw a puzzled look at his partner on the other side. With a shrug, he thrust his hand out grabbing hers, but when he squeezed and would have pulled her into him, probably as a hostage for Anthony's good behavior, Lexie returned the favor — harder.

The man yelped and his buddy, sensing a problem, began to tug Anthony towards the door. "Oh dear, did I catch you with my nails?" she smirked at the fellow on his knees. "I'll have to talk to my manicurist. Were we going somewhere, darling?" She turned to the other fellow who pulled a now struggling Anthony.

"Lexie. Run," Anthony finally yelled. "They've got a gun."

"But that's illegal," she said still playing the part of innocent. She sensed movement behind her and thrust her elbow back connecting with a sickening crunch. "Oops. Sorry about that."

The click of a gun cocking made her sigh and she raised her hands as the barrel poked her in the back. The jig was up. She'd now have to kick some serious ass and as a consequence, probably forgo one last night of great sex because there was no way Anthony wouldn't clue in if he saw her take down these thugs without breaking a sweat. She coiled and prepared to unleash her nasty side as Anthony's face struggled through a myriad emotions — disbelief, fear for her and finally anger.

What her geek lacked in finesse, he made up for in size and adrenaline. He stomped down on the foot of the assailant holding him and then shoved him hard sideways. While Anthony was occupied, Lexie donkey kicked the idiot behind her catching him in the nuts. He crumpled and she flew into Anthony's arms.

"Oh, Anthony. Are you okay?" she asked, keeping his attention on her as hotel staff finally came running to deal with the commotion. Not that they did anything as the wanna-be kidnappers, with their cards played, fled out the door.

Anthony appeared dazed and looked around in confusion. "I — What — How?"

"We're safe. Those petty thieves are gone. You saved me." And she even managed to keep a straight face as she said it.

"I did?" The stunned look in his face made her want to smother him in kisses.

"Oh, yes, you did," she smiled. "Come on. Let's get out of here and go up to our room so I can properly thank you for being my hero."

"But shouldn't we call the police?"

"What's the point? We're fine. They're gone. Besides wouldn't you prefer to spend our last night naked in bed rather than in a boring police station?" She coaxed him. When the staff would have stopped them with questions, she pretended to faint. Anthony caught her slumping body and took charge. He swept her up into his arms.

"Sir, we need you to give a statement to the police."

"About what? Your gross incompetence where the safety of your guests is concerned?" Anthony sounded really pissed. "Thankfully, the miscreants where chased off with no help from this establishment. They didn't actually manage to steal anything, so what exactly would you like me to accuse them of? Showing how feeble your security truly is?" Lexie bit her tongue so as not to giggle as she imagined her geeky lover facing down the hotel staff. "Idiots. Get out of my way so I can get my girlfriend back up to our room."

Feigning unconsciousness, Lexie didn't know what she found sexier — his domineering manner with the hotel staff or the fact he called her his girlfriend. Both made her tingle all over.

He carried her into the elevator and punched the button for their floor. Once the doors closed, she nibbled his jawline.

"I thought you might be faking it."

She laughed. "I'm horny and they were getting annoying. Nice job getting us out of there."

"Care to tell me what happened?" he asked tilting his head to look down at her.

"What do you mean?"

"Those guys. They wanted to kidnap me, not rob me."

"Are you sure?"

Anthony sighed with exasperation. "I'm not that oblivious. Just like I know you did something to get them to let me go."

Lexie widened her eyes. "Me? I didn't do anything. You saved me."

Anthony narrowed his gaze. "Don't toy with me, Lexie. I might have taken care of the one thug, but you did something to the other one. And how did you know to come around to the front of the hotel to intercept us? Who are you?"

"Nobody."

He snorted.

Lexie sighed. "Fine. You caught me. Remember how I said I'm kind of an odd jobs kind of girl? Well, sometimes the things I do can get a little dangerous, so I've had to learn how to protect myself. When I came out of the bathroom and saw those thugs carting you off, I couldn't just do nothing. I couldn't make it through the crowd in time so I let myself out a side door and ran around to the front. I'll admit, I did act a little pretending to not grasp the situation, but I didn't want those guys to see me as a threat. When I grabbed the one fellow, I used some pressure points I learned to temporarily incapacitate him. But you took care of the other on your own," she reiterated pressing herself against him and slipping a hand down to cup the growing bulge at his groin.

"I did, didn't I?" His smile emerged, banishing his doubts for the moment. Lexie knew she'd squeaked by with her feeble explanation, and given time, when he'd thought it over more fully with that fabulous brain of his, he'd probably have more questions. So, she'd just have to make sure to keep his focus distracted until the limo showed up to take him away in the morning. She'd ply him with erotic pleasures to keep him occupied the rest of the night. *The things I do for my work — numerous orgasms and pleasure. What a way to end the job.*

They arrived at their floor and she took charge. She grabbed him by the tie and tugged him after her. "I've got a special reward for my hero, that is, if you want it?"

His lips quirked when he replied. "Depends. Are you going to use some of those pressure point moves on me?"

She used his tie to reel him into her and she stood on tiptoe to murmur against his mouth. "Oh, definitely. Did you know about the one on the head of your dick? It's guaranteed to bring you to your knees. Maybe I'll just show you with my tongue how deadly it is."

His eyes lost focus behind his lenses and she felt his body temperature rise. He didn't answer her with words, but he did use his mouth. He kissed her fiercely, pushing her back up against her door and Lexie returned his embrace as her hands fumbled to yank out her key card to unlock the door.

They staggered into the room, and Lexie kicked the door shut before she stepped back to look at him. He met her gaze boldly. His adrenaline over his aggressive act downstairs and his arousal submerged his shy side, not that she'd seen it much lately as his confidence with her grew. She yanked his tie off and looped it around her neck for later. She slid his jacket off his broad shoulders and, in her impatience, she gripped the linen of his shirt and pulled the material apart, popping his buttons. He sucked in a breath at her rough handling, but she knew by the tenting in the crotch of his slacks that he enjoyed it.

She raked her nails down his bared chest, pinching his nipples as she made her way down to his belt. She unbuckled him and then undid his pants. His black briefs barely covered his erection and she slid her hand down the front of them to grasp him. She made a sound of satisfaction, a cross between a growl and a rumbling purr that made him groan. She pushed him back towards the bed, tumbling him onto the mattress. Her wolf rode her hard, pushing for control and Lexie closed her eyes lest their glow give her away. She breathed deep, reasserting her control over her suddenly anxious beast.

She straddled his waist, her skirt riding up and pressing her moist pussy against his stomach, her cleft still pleasantly swollen from their earlier tryst. When he would have grabbed her, she growled again. Her control held on by a thread and she didn't trust herself not to hurt him if he touched her. She snagged his hands and exerting some of her strength, she pulled his arms above his head and using the tie she'd saved, tied them to the head board.

His body stilled and he regarded her with a touch of trepidation. She whipped his glasses off to get the full effect of his stare — and to blur his vision so that he wouldn't clearly see anything like, say, her not so human side which fought to come to the surface. Besides, he had the most beautiful blue eyes and she hated to see them trapped behind his ugly lenses.

She grasped his tied wrists and leaned down to brush her lips over his. "Don't worry my giant scientist. I am about to help you discover the joys of bondage along with a good dose of tease."

She leaned back from him and in one fluid movement, stripped her dress off, leaving her bare except for her garters which she knew he loved. Under his avid gaze, she cupped her breasts, rolling and pinching her nipples between her fingers.

"Are you trying to drive me insane?" he muttered.

Lexie smiled. "What? And waste your beautiful brain? Never. But I'm going to make you come like you've never imagined. Eventually ... "

She laughed at the way his breathing hitched and his eyes lost focus. She especially enjoyed the way his hard cock twitched behind her, pressing against her backside as if alive and seeking the moist core it longed for.

She raised herself and moved back, pushing his thighs apart to rest herself between them. Having Anthony at her mercy calmed her wolf somewhat, but a wildness to possess this man, to ensure he never forgot her took its place. *I'll ruin you for all other women.* She didn't examine why the thought of him with anyone else made her claws pop and a low rumble emerged from her throat.

She dragged the sharp points of her nails down his muscled thighs and his body tensed. But even better, his cock jerked. She leaned forward, her face hovering over his appendage while her hair tumbled to tickle his groin. She blew on him, soft warm breaths that made his dick strain. She didn't touch it though, not yet. She puffed up and down its length as her hands cupped his balls, kneading them between her fingers.

He groaned and his body tensed up on the bed.

"Tell me what you want me to do?" she whispered. Could she make her geek talk dirty to her?

"I — ." He swallowed hard.

She blew on his tip and watched a drop pearl, waiting for her tongue. "Tell me, Anthony."

"S-Suck me."

She peered up at him and saw him looking down at her. A sheen of sweat coated his face while a reddish hue heightened his cheeks. "Like this?" She took his swollen head into her mouth, the salty taste of him on her tongue, making her moan. She gave him a hard suck then let him go with a wet pop.

"Yesss," he hissed.

"I'll suck you, but is that all you want? Do you want to come in my mouth?"

"Yes. No. I want you to ride me. Suck me, then fuck me."

Lexie's body quivered as he mouthed the dirty words. They sounded so strange coming from his lips, but they excited her. With a mewl of pleasure, she went to work, her lips sliding down the length of his shaft, taking all of him down until her lips touched the root.

His hips bucked, but she held on tight. She sucked him, her cheeks hollowing as she inhaled tightly. She slid her mouth back up his cock, swirling her tongue around his head, then she plunged right back down. He thrashed as she deep throated him, over and over. She kept her pace slow, methodical, knowing it would drive him crazy. The balls she kneaded drew tight and she let them go. She also released his cock with a wet sound and sat up to regard him.

He sat on the edge of bliss, right where she wanted him. Now for her turn before she took him over that abyss. She sidled up his body and held her mouth just above his. He strained to kiss her, but she kept out of reach, the slow tease and denial exciting her.

She moved again until she straddled his face, her pussy hovering over his chin. He stuck his tongue out and managed to flick the very tip against her slit. Lexie shuddered.

She lowered herself an inch. He laved her again and she moaned. But, she had another plan in mind. She flipped herself so she faced back toward his cock. She crawled forward on her forearms, leaving her cunt over his face while bringing her own visage above his prick.

Sixty-nine: her favorite number and position. She dipped her head down as she lowered her pussy. *Let the oral pleasure begin.*

Anthony latched onto her sex eagerly, his tongue probing between her lips to stab at her core. Lexie keened around the cock in her mouth, using her concentration on sucking him to distract her from the fantastic things Anthony did to her clit. He swirled his tongue around it, then rubbed it before sucking it between his lips. She felt the moisture seeping from her, soaking him and coating his tongue. She didn't remember ever getting this aroused for anybody. Wanting someone so much she ached.

She'd initially planned to get off on his tongue and make him gush into her mouth, but she suddenly wanted to see his face as he came, imprint this special man into her psyche, a rainy day memory for the future.

She pulled her sex away, but he fought to keep her, his mouth tugging and giving one last suck to her pussy lips. She released his cock as well and turned back to face him, panting. She impaled herself on his shaft in one swift stroke unable to wait any longer. She cried out and he bucked under her, his tilting hips driving him even deeper. She closed her eyes at the ecstatic sensation, but opened them again once fully seated. He watched her with bright eyes and she shivered at the desire in them. *Why couldn't he be wolf so I could keep him?*

The astonishing thought made her lose control for a second and she found herself battling her wolf for supremacy. The bitch had lain in wait for a moment of weakness, but while Lexie sensed her she-wolf didn't mean harm to her geek, she didn't understand what she wanted.

Her hips began to move and Lexie, only partially in control, realized her wolf wanted to feel a part of this, to enjoy the pleasure found with this surprising man. Lexie closed her eyes knowing that even with his myopic eyesight that Anthony might find it odd that her eyes glowed. She rocked on top of his cock, the pressure on her clit making her channel squeeze the hard rod inside.

Faster and faster she moved, while the wildness grew in her. The urge to mark this male, to keep him, grew stronger and stronger.

A part of Lexie knew she should get off before she and her beast did something stupid and irreparable, but selfish pleasure won out, and she could only pray she wouldn't hurt him.

* * *

Anthony stared up at Lexie, her luscious body undulating on top of his, and realized something illogical and mind blowing. He loved this woman. He'd known her less than two days, but irrational as it seemed, emotionally and sexually driven as it was, he'd fallen for her. He wanted to say something, or at the very least clasp her to him, but with his arms tied, he could only buck under her as she used her pelvic muscles to clamp down on him tight.

Then he forgot what he'd wanted to announce because she opened her eyes and stared down at him, her usual green eyes changed somehow, and even more uncanny, they glowed. His mind refused to accept what he saw and he shut his eyes, blaming the change in her eyes on hotel lighting and on the fact he didn't wear his glasses. People's eyes did not reflect light like a nocturnal animal.

Her hands came to rest flat on his chest, her sharp nails biting into his skin. She growled, a low sound that made his balls tighten. She buried her face in the curve where his neck met his shoulder and sucked at his skin as she continued to ride him. Anthony panted, trying to hold on for her, but she nipped him, her sharp teeth pinching his skin and he bellowed as his orgasm hit, shooting his seed deep inside her. The biting teeth squeezed harder and he winced at the pinching pain. She came with a shudder and a drawn out moan, the muscles of her channel flexing over and over, until Anthony, his dick so sensitized from her sensual play, thought he'd pass out from overload.

Her body collapsed on his, the tension of their lovemaking receding to leave her relaxed on him. Her warm breath tickled his skin and made up for some of the ache he felt from her bite. *She's certainly enthusiastic.* He didn't mind, although this level of roughness in the bedroom was new.

Her hands crept up and massaged his neck, pressing against his muscles. "I'm sorry," she whispered her face still buried in the crook of his shoulder. He meant to say for what, but his mind went blank.

Anthony woke hours later to find himself untied with Lexie snuggled into his side. *I can't believe I fell asleep on her like that.* He blamed it on the intense lovemaking they'd enjoyed. He stroked her hair, brushing it back from her face. So much mystery surrounded her. He knew she hid something from him, an important facet of herself. Yet despite that, he couldn't help wanting to be with her. She made him feel like ... a man. And not just a man, but a virile one who could sweep a woman off her feet and also be her hero.

How strange for a geek who'd always dedicated himself to the sciences. Anthony hadn't even known he owned an ounce of courage until he'd seen her threatened by that thug. Funny, because when those same assailants ambushed him, he'd let them drag him out of there without a fight. However, when they threatened Lexie, fear for her safety triggered a sudden rage in him. In that moment, he'd acted, not caring for himself, just knowing he had to do something to save her, to rescue her from harm.

Great, I have hero potential, but I think the more important thing here is the fact someone wanted me in the first place. Mr. Thibodeaux always insisted on absolute secrecy and guarded the grounds which included the chateaux and his lab, with a vengeance. *And violently.* For a moment an image flashed of one of the nighttime guards, his chin dripping with blood. As quickly as he recalled the thought, it disappeared and Anthony crinkled his brow. What an odd thing for his mind to conjure, especially given he wasn't prone to watching horror or gore flicks.

Back to his previous problem — why would anyone want to kidnap him? And who? His project in Mr. Thibodeaux's lab, while exciting, was scoffed at by many in scientific circles. Could it be that someone other than his employer believed in and understood what he was about to accomplish? Anthony knew his research sat on a threshold that would possibly catapult him into the spotlight and worldwide recognition. If he looked at it from that angle, it made sense that someone other than his employer might want to steal that kind of knowledge and glory for themselves.

But surely, if he was in danger, Mr. Thibodeaux would have never let him leave, especially without a guard. Or had he.

Lexie stirred against him and Anthony stroked her hair pensively. Perhaps, had he spent more time out and about instead of making love to Lexie, he would have seen some familiar faces spread unobtrusively throughout the hotel, keeping an eye on Mr. Thibodeaux's investment.

His train of thoughts was broken by a hand that skimmed over his stomach and grabbed hold of his dick. "You're thinking too loud," she complained against the skin of his chest, before kissing it.

"Sorry. I was just thinking about the attack."

"I've got something better for you to do," she murmured, squeezing his cock.

A few minutes later, Anthony could barely remember his own name let alone what bothered him about the attack. Thankfully, he remembered her name and he shouted it as he came inside her velvety softness.

chapter six

The next morning, Lexie packed as Anthony showered. The night had been chaotic with her making love to Anthony and then rendering him unconscious as she dealt with the factions trying to kill and/or kidnap him. She'd prevailed of course, but it pissed her off. *I'd kind of hoped we could just fuck like wild animals all night long.*

She'd managed a few pussy clenching rounds in between ass kicking, the final one occurring less than fifteen minutes ago while under the hot spray of the shower. At least while they were fucking, she didn't have to think of what she had to do next. She dreaded the imminent goodbye. Stupid, since she should have celebrated her fat bank account. The geek job hovered on the edge of completion, successfully so, so why did she wish Frederick would call and extend her use?

Just the fact she even thought of it made her lips tighten. Anthony was simply a target that required protection and no matter the fun they'd had — and orgasms she'd enjoyed — he didn't belong in her life, and she didn't belong in his. Even if he could look past the fact she'd initially seduced him as part of her protection plan — a hard thing to overlook for any man with pride — her very heritage made it impossible for her to contemplate a future with him. Already, she had to fight her urge to love him more roughly. Hell, she'd almost lost it the night before and counted her lucky stars she'd only bruised him. Never before had she needed to fight her wolf like she did currently. Her inner bitch paced restlessly even now, urging her to bite and mark Anthony as if he were a shifter, a fucked up conundrum indeed. She needed to get away before she lost control and treated him like her body increasingly urged. Her violent brand of love was not something she recommended given his fragile human status. She'd maim him at the least, kill him at the worst.

The best thing she could do for him was walk away. Now, if she could only find the words to make him understand.

I am, of course, assuming he'll have an issue about us parting ways. Heck, for all I know, I was just a fun conference fuck. But she knew better. She saw how he watched her and came to life when she was near.

With a curse, she zipped her suitcase shut as Anthony strode out wearing just a towel around his hips while he used a smaller one to dry his hair.

"Thanks for letting me use your shower," he said softly. "Weird how the plumbing in mine got all messed up. So, what's the plan?"

It was her turn to end up tongue tied. "Um, my cab is coming in about 20 minutes, so I need to get downstairs."

Anthony peeked at the clock. "Shoot, my boss's limo will be arriving in 15. I better get a move on. Wait for me, we'll go down together."

He dashed through the adjoining door and she heard the sounds of him rapidly packing, their last sweet love making session this morning having put them both behind schedule. The minutes to their departure crept by quickly, and it was in silence that they left their rooms with suitcases rolling behind them to the elevator.

Anthony wore what she liked to call his 'pensive face', his head slightly dropped as he tumbled a thought over in his mind. When the elevator doors closed behind them, on impulse she dropped her suitcase handle and pressed herself against him, her mouth seeking his hotly. He returned her embrace fiercely, his timidity of the first day, completely vanished.

The bell dinged and the doors slid open. Lexie broke off the kiss and grasped her suitcase before she stepped out. She immediately noticed Frederick's men — Lycans like her — waiting by the glass doors and her stomach plummeted. The geek job was officially over.

Her throat tight for some strange reason, she gave Anthony a smile that shone perhaps a tad too bright and managed a low, "Thanks for everything. Bye."

She turned and began to walk. Of course, escape wasn't that easy.

"I want to see you again."

Lexie froze mid step. Despite her half-baked theory this was just a weekend thing for him, she'd — hoped — expected this. With his simple statement, he dangled temptation before her, and for a moment she reacted; her body tingled in pleasure, her heart stuttered and her mind screamed 'Yes, I want to be with you, too'. Then reality intruded as she reminded herself, he was simply a job. Fun as the sex had been, they both had their lives to return to. He to his lab, and her to, well, doing whatever paid the bills in between full moons.

She turned back to face him, steeling her face and resolve. "I can't."

"Why not? I-I thought we had something going." His face showed bewilderment.

"The sex was great, thank you." Her cheeks warmed as did her pussy. "Very fun, but really, you can't tell me you expected this to continue beyond the conference? You've got your work you need to get back to and I've got a life, too."

She hated the hurt and confusion clouding his blue eyes, but he'd get over it. And once she got back to her home and day to day world, she would as well.

"But — "

"It was nice knowing you." She turned to walk away and, to her shock, her eyes brimmed wetly. However, tears and a strangely aching heart didn't prevent her from scenting the danger. She recognized the distinct odor of Fae.

She whirled back around screaming, "Duck." But her sweet geek regarded her with incomprehension, so she did the only thing possible. She dashed toward him, and when the Fae assassin stepped from behind the column in the lobby, she dove in front of Anthony whose eyes widened even as he still didn't recognize the danger.

The missile hit her upper chest, splitting open her flesh with barely a sound, but the arcing blood made up for it. The fiery touch of the projectile immediately sent her into convulsions. Damned Fae and their poisons. She hit the floor hard, not that she noticed, having already blacked out.

* * *

Anthony stared in horror at Lexie's convulsing body, and his stomach roiled at the messy hole in her chest. Blood oozed from her wound, spreading in a deadly stain that spurred him into action. He dropped to his knees feeling helpless without his lab and equipment. He pressed his hands to her chest attempting to stop the gush. Around him he could hear shouting and the sound of return fire as his bodyguards, who'd waited by the front doors, finally sprang into action. *Too late.*

"Hold on, Lexie. I'll get you some help. Why the hell did you do that?" he cried. Anthony wasn't so oblivious that he'd failed to recognize she'd saved his life, taking a hit meant for him. He just didn't understand why, especially when she had no problem walking away from him in the first place.

If you didn't care, why throw yourself in front of me? Why? Tears blurred his vision as the hot liquid continued to seep sluggishly from her chest, staining his hands and cuffs.

Meaty hands grabbed his upper arms and lifted him. Anthony tore his eyes from Lexie to stare in incomprehension at the gorillas on either side of him, guards he recognized from the compound housing his research facility.

"What are you doing?" he yelled as they toted him out the hotel doors as if he weighed nothing.

"Bosses orders. We need to get you to safety," one replied, his cold eyes darting from side to side looking for signs of more danger.

"But we need to help her." Anthony tried to twist in their grasp, but they didn't relent and rushed him outside to toss him into a wait-ing limo. Anthony scrabbled to get out, but they slammed the door shut and the car took off with a lurch.

Anthony lost his temper, a rarity. "Stop this car right now. We've got to help her."

The dark gaze of his guard settled on him. "She's beyond our help."

A cold dread settled on him. "No. You can't mean — No, she's not dead."

But the grunt from his guard with the flat, "Sorry," hit him with the weight of a freight train.

Anthony sank in on himself, horrified he'd caused Lexie's death. Appalled that even though she didn't think enough of him to want to pursue a relationship, she'd obviously cared enough to risk and lose her life for him.

I am so unworthy. That thought followed him on the car ride to the airport and during the flight on his employer's private jet back home. It dogged his footsteps as he dragged his ass up the stairs lead-ing into the compound facility where the top floor served as a pent-house suite for him. It rang over and over in his mind as he ignored the flashing red button on his answering machine and didn't bother checking his email.

He stood with his shoulders slumped in the middle of his living room, lost and in pain. He raised his hands to rub them against his burning eyes, his tears having dried up hours ago. The rusty color staining his hands and cuffs made him gag as he finally noticed it. He stumbled into his bathroom and retched into his toilet. Once he'd emptied his stomach, his body heaved with harsh sobs. *Oh, Lexie.*

He showered, the dried blood caking his skin, running down the drain along with his tears. His bloody clothes he left on the floor, unable to deal with their disposal with his grief so raw. He tried to box away his emotions for a woman he'd known only two days. He attempted to not replay over and over her last heroic act. He wished he could forget, but Lexie had touched him in her brief stint in his life. *How can I forget the first woman who showed me what love was?*

He buried himself in his pillows, trying to erase the mental image of her death, but sleep refused to give him escape. He tossed and turned, his nightmares rehashing over and over those final moments. He couldn't help blaming himself and not just for the assassination attempt on him, which he didn't understand. He hated the fact he'd not told her how he felt, that he loved her. He lamented, even more, the fact that despite all his knowledge and brain power, all of it meant nothing when the need for action arrived. Helpless as a newborn, useless as a tit on a bull, he'd stood and watched as the woman he'd come to love saved his life, and as if that weren't emasculating enough, all his medical knowledge couldn't stop her from dying. He also cursed the guards who'd dragged him away, the ones who'd used their strength to force him from her side.

If only I were stronger or had that commanding presence like Mr. Thibodeaux, then maybe I could have saved her. Or at least, not let her die alone on the floor.

In the morning, things still appeared bleak. He wanted to do something, anything to remember the most amazing woman ever, but it appalled him to realize that he not only didn't have a picture, but he'd never even gotten her last name.

No wonder she thought it was just a fling. I never made much of an effort to get to know her. And now he had nothing. With that depressing thought, he dragged himself into the bathroom and noticed his bloody clothes lying on the floor. A light bulb went off. Blood meant DNA.

Anthony scooped up the stained clothing. He skipped his morning ablutions and breakfast and took the elevator down to his lab.

He flicked on the fluorescent lights and didn't pause to admire the vast space filled with state of the art equipment, all ridiculously expensive but needed for his DNA research. And now even more useful to get a DNA imprint, the only thing left of Lexie.

He separated flakes of her blood onto slides and deposited more into test tubes with various solutions. He ran her essence through a barrage of tests on autopilot. *Don't worry, Lexie. I'll find some way to keep part of you alive.*

chapter seven

Lexie groaned as she woke. Her head pounded like she'd downed several bottles of tequila, something she'd sworn never to do after her last hangover when she woke up next to a buck toothed shifter. Along with the pulsing ache in her brain, her limbs felt weighted down. *What the hell did I do?*

Memory flooded back to her and she gasped. *Anthony!* Her eyes shot open to discover she lay in her own bed back in her house. And fuck did her chest hurt.

She lifted the covers and noted a bandage covering the area where the Fae bastard shot her. She peeled the tape and looked under. The skin appeared pink and tender, the violence of the wound taking longer to heal due to the use of poison. What a fucking pain, but still better than the alternative. Anthony and his frail human constitution would have never stood a chance. Speaking of whom, had he made it back to his lab safely? She'd never find out lying in bed.

She winced as she sat up, wondering how she'd made it from the hotel back home. A knock preceded a head peeking around the door.

With a sigh, Lexie leaned back onto her pillows as her mother approached with a tray of food. "Hi, Mom." Just her ill luck, her mother had come to tend her.

"About time you woke, Lexington. You had me a tad worried there." Her soft spoken mother arranged the tray on her lap and then perched herself on the edge of the bed.

"I'm fine, or I will be. Damned Fae," Lexie grumbled as she grabbed the piece of toast slathered in jam. "How long was I out?"

"Three days."

Lexie winced.

"I really wish you'd find a different line of work," her mother broached.

Lexie rolled her eyes. *Here we go.* "Mom, not this again. I'll have you know this last job netted me fifteen thousand in two days. Know of any other jobs that pay that well?"

Her mother's lips tightened into a flat line. "If you had a mate, then money wouldn't be an issue."

"Yes, well, I tried that and it hasn't worked out so well, has it?" One, she had issues kowtowing, and two, she had yet to meet a wolf she couldn't take down. If she was going to tie herself down for the rest of her life, then she'd prefer someone who could actually handle her. *Although, I didn't mind handling Anthony.*

She snapped out of her sudden daydream of her geeky scientist and realized her mother still spoke. "The only reason it doesn't work is because you refuse to act as a woman."

"Mom," Lexie growled in warning.

"Fine. But who's going to come and care for you when I'm not here anymore?"

Lexie didn't have an answer to that, so she kept quiet as her mother bustled around her room tidying up. She ate all the food and drank all the juice knowing anything less would have her mother haranguing her again. *What is it about my mother that makes her able to boss me around, no problem, but act like a submissive bitch around dad?* To give her dad credit, though, he did treat her mother like gold. What a shame more wolves weren't like him, or as big and tough. Even though he'd disowned her, Lexie still respected him, most of the time.

"I don't suppose you know if my target made it back safely?" Lexie tossed that out nonchalantly, but her mother whirled with wide eyes.

"Since when do you care about your targets after a job is done? If you ask me, that little human didn't deserve what you did for him. Unless ... " Her mother's mouth open and shock spread across her face. "Don't tell me you care for that-that — "

"His name is Anthony, Mom. And no, I don't care for him, I was just curious if he made it back. No biggie." Lexie lied with a straight face, but her mother's lack of information made her heart flutter. She needed to find out if he was okay, but first she'd have to get rid of her mother before she had an apoplectic fit. "Mom, just forget I said anything. You know what I could really use is some ice cream. You know the cookie dough kind like you used to get me when I was little." Lexie truthfully hadn't eaten the stuff in about fifteen years, but her request worked like a charm.

"You must have run out because I didn't see any in your freezer. Why don't you just lie here, and I'll run down to the store and get some."

"Thanks, Mom." Lexie snuggled down in her blankets and closed her eyes, pretending to go back to sleep. She kept one ear cocked and tracking the movement of her mother as she gathered her purse and keys then went out the front door. Only when she heard the sound of her car driving away did Lexie dive out of her bed and go looking for her phone. With her mother the neat freak around, it took her a few minutes to find it stuffed in a drawer along with her gun.

Lexie grabbed both and returned to her room. She slid the revolver under her pillow and then scrolled through her phone book until she found the number she wanted.

She dialed and stared at the ceiling as she waited for an answer.

"Ah, so the she-wolf survives," Frederick Thibodeaux's smooth voice would have been sexy if he weren't so freaking dead.

"I'm not easy to kill. So listen, I don't recall anything after that Fae bastard shot me. What happened?" In other words — had Anthony made it back safe and did he miss her?

"My incompetent guards let that Fae bastard slip through their fingers. They didn't live to regret it. Lucky for us, after you used your body as a shield, no further attempts were made on my scientist, and he's now back to work under my watchful eye."

"Oh. That's good." Relief infused her at the knowledge Anthony was safe. Now if only it would take care of her longing to see him again.

"Not really. You made quite the impression on Anthony. Since he thinks you died — "

"What!" Lexie yelled. "What do you mean he thinks I died?"

"What else would he think when he saw a hole blown in your chest? A human would have succumbed in minutes." Frederick replied matter-of-factly.

"You have a point," she grudgingly conceded. "And it's not like we'll see each other again."

"Don't be so sure. My enemies have grown bolder, and with my daytime guards executed for dereliction of duty, I find myself somewhat shorthanded."

Lexie wanted to scream, *I'll be there in half an hour,* but sanity prevailed. Much as she wanted to see him again — and her wolf paced in her mind eagerly at the thought — it was a bad idea on several levels. First, even if he got over the fact that she survived a deadly wound, he'd end up discovering their weekend tryst was nothing but a sham. Lexie wasn't sure she could handle his anger and condemnation. Although, on the other hand, perhaps it would help her to stop thinking of him. But then again, what if he forgave her and wanted to resume, did she have the will power to say no and even worse, how would she ever keep her wolf leashed? Even now, just knowing he missed her made her beast push at her control. What if she slipped and accidentally hurt him?

"Sorry, but I'm kind of busy." She blurted the words out quickly before she changed her mind.

"A shame. You would have been well compensated."

Lexie closed her eyes and gritted her teeth. "Well, thanks for the offer. Let me know if I can be of service again in the future." She hung up her phone and flopped back on her bed.

Anthony's okay. The geek job is over and I'm home. Time to forget him and his sexy blue eyes and get on with my life.

Thankfully her mother arrived with a huge container of ice cream to help with the healing process.

* * *

One week later ...

Frederick Thibodeaux watched with irritation as his once brilliant scientist sat with slumped shoulders in his lab, staring off into space, something he'd done in equal measures with moping, since he'd returned from the conference. Had the self-pity resulted in work getting done, Frederick wouldn't have cared. However, his resident geek had not managed more than a few minutes of work, so intent was he on his misery.

Unacceptable, especially with summer fast approaching. Frederick had walked in darkness for nigh on three hundred years and he'd grown damned tired of it. Anthony and his brilliant mind offered the first ray of non-burning light and hope since Frederick had succumbed to his curse. Frederick could handle the teeth, the pale skin, the hunger for blood, and even the hunt to feed, but he damned well missed the hot kiss of sunlight on his face. *And now, because that damned she-wolf blew him better than a practiced whore, my chance to day walk is shriveling faster than a cock in ice cold water.*

He'd tried to reassure Anthony that Lexie indeed lived, but his geek just turned disbelieving eyes to him and said no human body could have survived what she did. It occurred to Frederick to tell him that Lexie was as human as him, but somehow he expected that to meet with even more disbelief from his fact loving scientist.

It galled Frederick that he couldn't just mesmerize his pet geek, but playing with human minds was a dangerous endeavor, and a chance he just couldn't take.

Frederick growled and cursed — killed a few trespassers to blow off steam — but ultimately, he recognized there was only one solution to his dilemma and it arrived wearing skin tight leather on her sport bike. Frederick had to grudgingly admit her appeal. If he didn't treasure his life, or unlife as it was, he would have attempted to seduce her. However, life as a eunuch didn't appeal and wouldn't resolve his moping geek problem.

He'd chomped down on his pride and called Lexington for help. Initially she'd just hung up on him. Her brazenness made him see red and gave him a massive hard on. Defiant women were his weakness. Eventually, he got her on the phone and managed to spit out the terms for a new job. She agreed for a high price, higher than her previous demands because, as she'd told him on the phone, "Anthony's going to be pissed, and I'm really not into the drama." But at ten thousand a day, even she couldn't refuse.

Frederick drummed his fingers as he waited for his manservant to bring her to him. She arrived in his office, filling his space with the rich scent of her blood and a musky perfume. A lovely she-wolf indeed, and such a shame she'd probably rip his balls off if he told her. Haughty as she acted, Frederick had to restrain a snicker because regardless of her thoughts on him, she'd actually made him come quite a few times. While she'd covered the camera in the hotel room, thus denying him a view of her naked body, he'd enjoyed himself grandly, listening to the sounds of her fucking Anthony. He'd never expected her to be a screamer and he'd shafted his cock numerous times to the exquisite music of her orgasms.

Lexington paid him no mind and strode over to his screens, staring down with a tight expression at Anthony, slumped on a stool. "This is such a bad idea," she murmured.

"Well, maybe next time I ask you to play the part of temporary girlfriend you could do so a little less enthusiastically," Frederick replied dryly. "The man is crushed by your loss." And if he wasn't mistaken, the she-wolf appeared affected as well. How unexpected.

"Let's get a few things straight about this new job. I am here to protect Anthony this time, not fuck him. So you can forget about the naked entertainment. With the full moon fast approaching, be reminded that I will require red meat for both lunch and dinner, or I might start chewing on your staff. Also, you'll need to have Anthony put under lockdown starting at six p.m. the day of the full moon as I won't be of any use until the following morning."

"I've already spoken with the chef and he's put in an order for a few cows, so feeding you won't be an issue. As for the full moon, I've got a special code already in place that will automatically shut the place down tighter than a nun's thighs."

"Do you ever take anything seriously?" she asked in an exasperated tone.

"Very, but I've lived a long time and find humor helps pass the time. Now, please follow me if you will, so we can get you started. After all, there's no time like the present to reunite lovers and watch the fireworks."

Lexie growled and Frederick chuckled. Emotions would definitely run high in the next few moments, but it beat the depressing pallor of the past week.

Frederick led the way through his chateaux and underground tunnels to the building housing the lab and Anthony's apartments. He didn't warn his scientist of their impending arrival, preferring instead to surprise him. The human had a strong, healthy heart. He could stand the shock of seeing his dead lover come back to life.

Lexington strode alongside him, her body tense. Frederick could sense both anticipation and trepidation rolling off her. What a pity his feeding involved blood and not emotions like the psychic vampires who fed off extreme feelings. But even if it wouldn't feed his dark hunger, he'd greatly enjoy the live action drama.

He pressed his hand against console after console, each allowing them access deeper into the building.

"Quite the setup you've got," she remarked.

"Worth every penny if Anthony manages to reverse the curse of sunlight."

"Funny, I would have thought that not having to eat people for lunch and dinner would have been a higher priority." She threw him a questioning glance.

Frederick shrugged. "While eating from the source is more

satisfying and fresh, blood is easily obtained, both the real and synthetic version. How much of a monster I choose to be is completely up to me. The sunlight factor, however, is deadly. Even the tiniest sliver of skin exposed to that brilliant beauty is enough to turn me into a puddle of steaming goo."

Lexington shuddered. "Okay, I see your point. I still say, though, that Anthony knowing what you are, a real vampire, would help him. How can he fully understand what he's curing otherwise?"

Frederick clasped his hands behind his back as he walked the length of the last corridor before the lab. "I'm beginning to believe you might be correct. However, it is not something I can just dump on him. His fragile human psyche couldn't handle it."

"I think he's stronger than you give him credit for."

"And that is why you are going to tell him you are a werewolf?" Frederick stopped in front of the door and faced her with an arched brow.

The she-wolf, who feared nothing, actually fidgeted and dropped her gaze. "Yeah, well, no. I hadn't actually planned to do that." At Frederick's chuckle, her chin shot up and she attempted to defend her position. "I mean, it's not like he needs to know what I am to fix me."

"But he will need to know if you are to become a couple."

Lexington scowled at him. "We are not going to be a couple. Humans and wolves, while they can play, do not stay together."

Frederick shrugged. "If you say so. But just so you know, if you do break him by accident, I could always turn him. He wouldn't be wolf, but he'd be strong and able to heal."

"Don't you dare," she growled.

Frederick flashed her a grin replete with fangs, then smacked his hand on the console which slid the door open and forestalled her rebuttal.

Anthony didn't even turn to see who'd arrived. He sat hunched on a stool, staring at a screen full of squiggly lines.

"How's the work coming?" Frederick asked moving to stand beside him while Lexington hovered by the door.

Anthony shrugged.

Frederick peered at the screen and pretended he didn't know what he saw. "Whose DNA is that?"

"It was supposed to be Lexie's, but I must have contaminated the sample somehow because it keeps coming up twined with a secondary strand."

"Forget staring at a screen. Try turning around and saying hello to the real thing instead."

"What?" Anthony lifted his head as Frederick spun the stool.

Then he had to catch his resident geek as he fell off it in a dead faint.

chapter eight

"You asshole." Lexie swore as she knelt down beside her prone geek.

"What? You had a better way of announcing you'd come to visit from the dead?" Frederick drawled, leaning back against the stainless steel counter. "Why not kiss him and see if he awakes like a true sleeping beauty."

"Just get out and let me take care of this."

"By all means. Feel free to do so naked. I would dearly love a video to go with my soundtrack." Frederick chuckled as he walked away, then cursed as she tripped him and he smashed to the floor. "Evil bitch."

"Dead dick walking," she retorted. She ignored the leaving vampire as Anthony stirred, his eyes blinking behind his large lenses. She knew when he saw her because they widened and he sucked in a breath.

"Lexie?" He reached a hand up to touch her face and she couldn't stop herself from leaning into his touch. He sat up and before she knew it, he'd pulled her to him and latched his mouth to hers. Startled, she didn't immediately pull away, and that gave him a chance to ignite the heat she remembered all too well. Moisture pooled in her cleft, her nipples tightened and when he groaned against her mouth, she almost threw him on the floor to ravage and mark him.

With a soft cry, she broke the embrace and stood to move away. She heard the sound of him getting to his feet, then approaching. When he would have touched her, she sidled sideways, but turned to face him.

"Hello, Anthony."

"You're alive? But how? And shouldn't you still be in bed? What stupid hospital released you already?"

He fired questions at her and she took a steadying breath to feed him the lie she'd concocted. "It wasn't as bad as it looked." Feeble, but the best liars knew to keep it simple and to the point.

His brow creased. "Not as bad as it looked? You had a hole in your freaking chest!"

Lexie shrugged. "Not the first one, either. I heal fast. What can I say?"

She could see a storm of questions in his eyes, but given her pat answers, he bit them back in favor of, "Why are you here? How did you find me?"

Finally, the moment of truth had arrived, in one respect anyway. "Frederick called me."

"My employer? But how did he know where to find you?"

"I do odd jobs for Frederick." She could see the confusion on his face as his mind and heart refused to put the obvious together. She gritted her teeth as she spelled it out. "I work for your boss. I just recently completed a job for him as a matter of fact." She couldn't mistake the moment all the pieces fell into place — his face tightened and his blue eyes turned arctic cold.

"You were paid to be with me," he spat.

"Paid to protect you, which I did," she amended, her voice husky as she fought the choking tears at his obvious anger. She didn't understand her reaction. Why did she care if the truth upset him?

"Paid to be a whore," he yelled.

"If needed," she cried back. "My primary objective though was to keep you safe, which I did in case you've forgotten. The rest ended up being a bonus."

He gaped at her. "A bonus? You used me. You made me believe you cared for me."

"No, I never led you to believe the weekend was anything other than two people having mutual fun." The fact she'd grown to care for him had been an unexpected snarl, but she kept that to herself.

"I don't believe this. Did you have a good laugh about the easy geek when you got home?"

"I was a little too busy trying to recuperate from getting shot," she snarled. "And for your information, I would never have laughed at what we did. I didn't fake those orgasms, or were you too caught up in your own pleasure to notice?"

Anthony moved to stand behind a counter, his hands fiddling with the equipment there. "Fine. You enjoyed it. I enjoyed it. You survived and got paid. What are you doing here now?"

"Frederick is concerned for your safety. He's hired me to act as one of your bodyguards, seeing as how some of the others had to be let go."

"No." Anthony said the word flatly and refused to look at her.

"You don't have a choice."

He swung his head up and his gaze froze her. "Why are you doing this? Are you enjoying torturing me? Just this morning, I thought the wonderful woman I'd grown to care about had died. And then she shows up, very much alive and I find out everything I thought and felt was a lie."

"I do care for you, Anthony."

"Shut up. I don't want to hear your pity for the nerd who fell for your act."

Tears brimmed in her eyes. "I didn't mean to hurt you. And of all the things I felt and still feel for you, pity was never one of them."

Anthony snorted and dropped his head again.

Lexie stood, indecision swamping her. He'd made it clear, he didn't want her around, but Frederick seemed very concerned about his safety. Sure, she could step aside like Anthony wanted and let someone else take her place guarding him. However, no one would guard him as well as her, and given how much he hated her now, she wouldn't have to worry about hurting him with her brand of affection. Much as her wolf howled in her mind, and despite the ache in her heart, his rejection of her was for the best, the safest thing for him.

God, I hate it when I don't even believe the lies I tell myself.

* * *

Anthony's hands trembled as he tried to come to grips with the torrent of emotions swamping him. Anger at her subterfuge and a rare loss of control made him want to hurt her. She'd made him think she liked him, but she'd lied and played him for a fool. He'd fallen for an act. His eyes burned at the shame of knowing she'd never found him attractive, that she'd seduced him as part of her plan to protect him. *How could I ever have believed she did?* But even knowing she'd fucked him because she'd been paid, he couldn't forget she'd almost died saving him. A part of him even dared believe that while she'd beguiled him as part of her agenda, she'd enjoyed their lovemaking, make that their fucking. *Love was never involved.*

As if those emotions weren't enough to deal with, relief that she'd survived also invaded him. He'd suffered thinking she'd died because of him. Despite her treachery, it made him glad to know she lived.

Anger at her actions, relief at her survival, he could handle, but it was the last emotion that flabbergasted him the most and embarrassed him. Even now, knowing he'd meant nothing to her, his cock still wanted a piece of her. His whole body did, and he found that unacceptable.

"You need to leave." He pushed his glasses back up on his nose before raising his head to face her, trying to keep his expression placid.

She chewed her lip and didn't immediately answer. In that moment, Anthony finally really looked at her, the shock of seeing her return from the dead and the truths imparted now settling. What he saw made his erection thicker. Gone was the woman in sexy business suits and hot cocktail dresses. Vanished was the seductress in garters with a naughty smile. Facing him now was a babe dressed in skintight leather pants that molded her round hips. She wore an unzipped, waist length leather jacket, open just enough to reveal the low cut, snug fitting tank top that outlined her breasts and clearly displayed her erect nipples. Anthony swallowed hard, even more attracted to her now in her bad girl getup than before.

"I'm sorry my presence is pissing you off, but you're in danger. If you want to live, you'll suck it up and let me do my job."

Anthony closed his eyes and counted to ten trying to rein in his temper. Her words, though, had the effect of dousing his libido. "Whatever. You know what? I don't care. Just stay out of my way." He pretended not to see the hurt in her eyes. *What does she have to feel hurt about? I'm the one she played for a fool.*

"I'll be just outside the door if you need me." She turned, displaying a perfect ass encased in leather, and Anthony's resolve almost crumbled. Thankfully she left, the door sliding shut behind her.

"Fuck!" Anthony grabbed a glass beaker and whirled, throwing it at a wall covered in writing. It smashed, the glass shards flying while the liquid rolled in heavy lines down the wall. Chest heaving, he stared at the mess and wondered when his well-ordered, fulfilling life had gotten so messed up. Even odder, how had he allowed it? *There's a reason I love science. It never disappoints me.*

He dropped his gaze and focused on the screen displaying the genome results which made no sense. The twirling 3-D image mocked him and intrigued him because he'd never seen anything quite like it, never even imagined it was possible. He'd run the DNA sequence on Lexie's blood several times now, and each time it ended up the same. Two strands of different codes wrapped around each other in a complex double helix that fascinated him and actually stirred his brain with an idea that might work with his dilemma concerning Mr. Thibodeaux's genetic makeup. Tapping a few keys, he ran a sub routine to separate the strands and then run them through his database for comparison.

He wondered if Lexie would give him another sample of blood so he could see if the anomaly persisted or prove a simple contamination was to blame. Somehow he doubted she'd just roll up her sleeve for him to plunge a needle in the name of science. Although, there were other ways of getting DNA ...

If she intended to stick around — an idea that excited him more than he liked or wanted to admit — then she was sure to leave traces of her passage in the form of hair, or even saliva. He preferred working with blood, but his curiosity didn't care at this point. Alive in body and mind, an invigorating feeling after the previous days in his catatonic state, he attacked his work with an eagerness he didn't examine. *It has nothing to do with her and everything to do with this discovery.* Or so he tried to convince himself.

While the computer ran the analysis on Lexie's DNA strand, he pulled up his genetic files on Mr. Thibodeaux, whom Lexie familiarly called Frederick. Just how close was she to his employer? Anger flared in him and he didn't understand its source. Why should he care if Lexie and his boss knew each other intimately? His hand clenched tightly around his pen and it snapped under the pressure.

Sweet gods of science, don't tell me I'm jealous? But he knew no other explanation for his extreme dislike at the thought of Lexie with his employer, or any other male for that matter. It seemed even though his mind wanted nothing to do with the deceitful woman, his subconscious and his body weren't quite ready to let go.

A yawn crept up on him and he peered at his watch realizing the late hour. He'd gotten used to starting his work later so his boss could come speak to him, his sun allergy keeping him out of sight until sun down. But Anthony, while willing to compromise, still couldn't work wholly at night. He needed sunlight even if he didn't always get a chance to enjoy its warm embrace.

Leaving his machines running simulations that would take hours to compile, he made his way to the door only remembering as he opened it that Lexie waited on the other side.

She lifted her head as he appeared. Without a word, her face an indecipherable mask, she straightened herself from the wall she leaned against. A twinge of guilt suffused him as he realized he'd left her waiting out in the corridor without even a chair to sit in, but she said not one word of recrimination.

"I'm going to bed now," he announced, then his cheeks heated as he realized how it sounded. "Um, so I guess I'll see you tomorrow."

Lexie smirked. "Lead the way. As your new bodyguard, you're not allowed out of my sight."

"I assure you this building is quite safe."

"No, it's not. It's decent, I'll grant you, but to someone like me, still too easy to infiltrate."

Anthony held his tongue at her statement. *What does she mean when she says "someone like me?" Just what is she capable of?* Deciding an argument would get him nowhere, Anthony led the way with his lab coat flapping, much too conscious of the fact she followed. He pressed his palm on the scanner for the elevator and the doors slid open.

"I'll have to look into getting added to this system," she mused.

"I can do it for you," he offered.

She turned amused green eyes toward him. "Yes, you can do it for me," she purred. She laughed when his face heated even hotter.

He didn't understand her game. Why flirt with him anymore? He was glad when the elevator arrived at the penthouse, the close proximity of the cab making him too aware of her, the subtle scent of her perfume wrapping around him and firing up his senses. He walked into his apartment and whirled to say good night, but she stalked around him, scanning the room.

"What are you doing?"

She didn't turn to face him when she answered. "Checking for danger, of course." She flowed through his space, her body moving with a fluid grace that dried his mouth. She looked like a dark predator in her leather, moving from room to room, her eyes scanning every nook and cranny, and even stranger, he could have sworn she inhaled the air, as if tasting it. The whole thing disturbed him even as it raised his body temperature and cock.

She finished in his bedroom and whirled to face him, because like a stupid puppy, he couldn't help following her. "All clear."

"Thanks, I guess. See you in the morning."

"Night." She flopped into the armchair by his bed and closed her eyes.

He watched her, puzzled. "Eh, what are you doing?"

She opened one eye and peered at him. "Guarding you, of course." She closed her lid again and Anthony ogled her.

"Can't you guard me from another room? I need to get undressed and go to bed."

Lexie sighed and forgot feigning sleep to regard him. "How am I supposed to guard you if I'm not with you? It only takes seconds for an assailant to kill you. Now stop protesting and do what you have to so we can both get some sleep."

Anthony gritted his teeth as he grabbed a pair of track pants and headed into the bathroom. No way was he undressing in front of her and making a spectacle of himself. He stripped in the bathroom and stared at his hard dick. Regardless of his thoughts on the matter, his cock appeared more than happy to have her stay.

Unwilling to embarrass himself further by walking out with a stiff prick, Anthony turned the shower on and jumped in. He stood under the hot spray and let it pound against his skin, relaxing his muscles, well, all except the rock hard one. He knew of only one solution to that dilemma.

He wrapped a soapy hand around it and fisted it back and forth. He tried to picture anything but Lexie as he pleasured himself; however, nothing in his past could compare to the ecstasy he'd enjoyed with her. His breathing hitched as he recalled a previous shower where she'd bent over for him, her round ass perfectly tilted to display her pink cleft. She'd watched him over her shoulder, her eyes heavy with passion as he slid into her, the tight walls of her channel clamping down on him. She'd come before him, the ripples of her climax triggering his, and now, like in the memory, as he stroked himself, he came again.

His body shuddered with minor aftershocks as the water washed away the traces of his climax, nothing like the quakes that rocked him when Lexie made him come in the flesh. He finished washing himself, trying once again to block her from his mind and thought he was doing a great job until he stepped out into his bedroom wearing a t-shirt and sleep pants and saw her splayed in the chair.

She'd kicked off her boots and let down her hair which framed her in a dark silken fall. She'd also removed her jacket, leaving her clad in her leather pants, which had to be uncomfortable, and a tight top that delineated her bust to perfection. His cock twitched and he almost ran to his bed to hide under the covers.

He tossed and turned in the large bed, unable to sleep knowing how wretched her current location was. He opened his eyes and looked over at her. As if sensing his stare, she opened her eyes and stared back.

"Is everything okay?" she asked.

"Yes." He sighed. "No."

"What's wrong?"

"I can't let you sleep in the chair."

Her gaze narrowed. "I already told you, I'm not leaving."

"I got that part. This bed is huge. It would be selfish of me not to share it."

Her lips twitched. "Why, Anthony, I never thought you'd have the nerve to ask."

He blushed at her innuendo. "That's not what I was implying. I wasn't asking for sex. I just can't in good conscience let you sleep in the chair when this bed has more than enough space for both of us. And, if you need something less confining to wear, I've got some shorts and track pants in the top drawer of my dresser."

"Thanks. I think I'll take you up on the offer. Frederick's goons apparently didn't bring my shit up." She moved to rummage through his drawer pulling out a pair of his jogging shorts, then, instead of going into the bathroom to change, her hands went to the button of her pants. Anthony shut his eyes and turned his head as she yanked her leather bottoms down, her amused chuckles making him heat and not just in the face.

He rolled himself over to his edge as she climbed into the bed. He held his body stiffly and he heard her sigh. "Good night, Anthony. Don't worry, I promise not to bite."

She said the words as if disappointed, and truthfully, Anthony was too. He'd quite enjoyed the way she'd nibbled him in the past. But as his mind reminded him, *she needed to get paid to fuck the geek.*

Holding onto his anger — and hurt — he fell asleep.

* * *

Lexie woke to find herself plastered to Anthony with an arm and a leg thrown over him. She immediately scooted away, appalled at her lack of control. She didn't allow the excuse of slumber to placate her. She couldn't allow herself to get involved with him, especially not this close to the full moon. Her wolf roiled restlessly in her mind and her pussy throbbed, the pair of them arguing against her plan of action, or in this case, inaction.

Too bad. Anthony is a human and deserves better than me. She used the bathroom while he slept, leaving the bathroom door open so she could hear if anything untoward happened. She quickly peed, showered and brushed her teeth with a spare toothbrush she found in the vanity. When she emerged, the bed lay empty with her geek nowhere in sight. Dressed only in her tank top and panties having forgotten her pants by the bed, she dashed out into the main apartment, sniffing the air and locating him along with coffee. She stalked into the kitchen, bristling.

"Don't you ever sneak off on me again," she growled, chastising herself for taking too long in the bathroom.

Anthony, already dressed for the day in chino's, a white shirt and a fresh lab coat, arched a brow as he held out a mug of coffee. "Good morning to you, too. Are you always this grumpy in the morning?" As soon as he said it, she could see him recall their previous mornings together where they'd woken in a more intimate fashion wearing smiles of pleasure.

She couldn't resist teasing. Why not, she already knew she was going to hell when she died. "I prefer your previous method of wake up involving hot sausage."

He flushed and he turned around to busy himself, but not before she caught his pants tenting. *I'm playing with fire. Good thing I heal quickly.* She sat down and watched him, unable to stop herself. It took him a few minutes, but eventually he turned around again holding two plates and his composure. He slid a plate in front of her before sitting down.

She grimaced at the scrambled eggs and microwaved bacon. "Are you trying to kill me?"

Anthony, seated across from her, regarded his own plate with a frown. "My cooking skills don't extend to the kitchen, but ask me to whip something up in the lab and I'm your man."

"Oh, I'd say the lab isn't the only place you can cook." Lexie wanted to slap herself as once again she flirted with him, but it wasn't entirely her fault. She got a kick out of seeing him flustered, and it didn't hurt her pride either to know that despite what she'd done, he still couldn't help desiring her.

Bad wolf. Stop baiting the human. Lexie couldn't wait until the full moon came and went so she could put her wolf to sleep. This close to the forced change, her wolf sat too close to the surface, just waiting for a chance to take over. *Not happening, my inner bitch, so settle your furry ass down. Anthony is off limits.*

Lexie choked down the breakfast using her coffee to wash it down. Thank god, she'd requested red meat for lunch and dinner. She'd starve if she had to rely on Anthony for sustenance, well, other than the wiener type.

Appalled that she couldn't keep her mind out of the gutter, she stood and didn't remember her lack of pants until she noticed Anthony's gaze riveted on her crotch, and of course, said crotch immediately got wet.

"I'd better finish getting dressed," she mumbled turning to leave. As she walked back to the bedroom her keen hearing caught the sound of him groaning and a thump as if he'd banged his head on the table. She couldn't help the smile that tilted her lips.

She slipped her pants back on, making a mental note to herself to find out where the hell her bag with her change of clothing had gone. Her shower had refreshed her, but without clean underwear, she felt scummy.

She jammed her feet into her boots and grabbed her jacket. Then she retrieved her revolver from under the pillow and slid it in the special holster inside her jacket. She also patted her pants and coat sleeves to check that her silver blades were present. It never paid to go to work unprepared.

She returned to the main living area to find Anthony standing by the large floor to ceiling window. She cursed under her breath.

"Do you have a death wish?" she barked.

He turned with a puzzled frown.

"The window? Like, hello, would you like to paint a larger target on yourself for any snipers that might be outdoors?"

He gaped at her for a moment, then her geek found the nerve to laugh.

"This isn't funny, Anthony," she growled.

He snorted. "Yes, it is. I mean, seriously, snipers? First off, Mr. Thibodeaux has excellent security, and second, these windows are bullet proof. Apparently, you aren't the only paranoid one around here.

"Laugh all you want, my giant geek, but bullet proof glass doesn't stop everything." That shut him up and she slapped her hand on the console to call the elevator.

"You need to be put into the system for it to work ... " He trailed off as the light turned green and the door opened.

Lexie bared her teeth in a smile that made him flinch. "You might be good at what you do, but I'm wicked at what I specialize in. Now get your ass in this elevator." She hated scaring him, but he needed to understand she was in charge; that, and she couldn't keep allowing him to tempt her. Shyness was one thing — she found it cute. But fear? Fear brought out the monster in her.

They travelled down in silence, and when Anthony entered his lab, she followed him. When he darted a look at her, she again bared the smile that freaked him out. "Don't mind me. I've decided, given your inability to follow common sense where you safety is concerned, I'd better stick close by."

He grunted in reply and then proceeded to ignore her as he flicked on monitors and read the screen results.

"Impossible," he mumbled.

Curious, Lexie wandered over to see what had his briefs in a knot. "What's up?"

"The results of your DNA test."

Lexie froze. She'd heard mention of her DNA the day before, but ignored it because she'd figured she misunderstood. "Where did you get my DNA?"

Anthony flashed her a brief look she didn't understand before concentrating on the screen again. "I came home covered in it when you got shot."

"And, what? You just decided to use it?" Panic fluttered in her breast. The decision to tell him or not about her alter ego was no longer a choice. Her secret was about to see the light of day because of bloody science.

He shrugged. "I thought you were dead. It was my way of preserving a part of you. Anyway, the how and why I got it aren't the interesting parts. What I'd like to figure out is why your DNA is twined with that of a wolf's?"

"A wolf's?" Lexie's laughter sounded brittle even to her. "That's crazy."

"Exactly, and yet … there's no denying it. Somehow my samples got contaminated with wolf genes and, even stranger, they merged with yours in a most fascinating double helix."

"Wow, that is weird." Lexie walked away lest her relief at his obliviousness become too obvious.

"It's weird alright, but at the same time, it gave me a fantastic idea on how to deal with Mr. Thibodeaux's condition."

And with those words, her geek went to work, bustling from work station to machine, to computer then back. Lexie perched on a stool and kept one eye on him as she used her BlackBerry to check on emails and other items that required her attention. She also tapped back into the lab's security network, checking for anomalies and weaknesses in the system. During her middle of the night check, she'd easily hacked into the main system using some blackmarket hacker apps and added herself, along with a few surprises.

A few hours after their arrival in the lab, a buzzer sounded and Lexie jumped up, glad to have a reason to move.

Anthony peered over at her and smirked. "That's just the lunch bell."

"Oh." She scowled at him. "Well, come on then. I'm hungry."

"And if I say I'd rather stay and work?"

Lexie's stomach rumbled and shredded her patience. "Unless you want me to embarrass you by carrying you over my shoulder to eat, then you'd better pause whatever you're doing."

"Oh, please. Like you could carry me."

"You'd be surprised at what I can do," she muttered under her breath. Thankfully, she didn't have to show him because he typed a few keystrokes then came toward her. She ignored how cute he looked with his hair standing up wildly in Einstein fashion, and how his blue eyes shone with excitement. She clamped her desire down tight and followed him as he led the way to a secure room setup as a dining area, replete with a dining table and another large window overlooking the grounds.

Lexie sat him at one end of the table and then positioned herself square in the middle facing the view outdoors. She wanted a direct line of sight just in case.

Dishes covered in silver domes waited amidst cutlery and napkins. Lexie slapped Anthony's hand away and lifted the covers, sniffing the food for traces of poison.

Anthony assumed she smelled for a different reason. "Smells like chef outdid himself, and look, no mini assassins are waiting on my plate."

Lexie shot him a dark look even as her lip curled at his sarcastic humor. She'd enjoyed shy Anthony at the conference, then the confident one, but this new sarcastic side intrigued her. It proved he had a backbone hidden somewhere inside his geeky body.

Seated in front of olfactory heaven, Lexie dove in. The chef thankfully knew how to prepare his beef and Lexie groaned as she chewed, her tongue and taste buds dancing as they met red meat heaven. Anthony stared at her as she devoured her meal and after a few bites she stopped. "What?"

Shaking his head as if startled, he dropped his gaze. "Sorry, just wondering about a few things."

"Such as?" She asked feigning disinterest as she resumed her meal.

"Do you live around here when you're not working?"

"Kind of. I've got a place in the city, but it's more a crash pad than anything else."

"What about family?"

She stopped eating again and gave him a pointed look. "What's with all the questions?"

He shrugged. "Just making polite conversation and wondering how your parents feel about renting yourself out."

The jibe stung and, as if ashamed of his comment, Anthony ducked his head, but he couldn't hide the red creeping up his neck. She bit back a smile. *My geek has more backbone than I keep giving him credit for.* "My mom keeps waiting for me to settle down, but I'm not the type." Her mom also lamented the fact her daughter had a brain and wouldn't do her duty to the pack. As for her dad, he just muttered that she'd settle down once the right wolf came along who could beat the stubbornness out of her. And they wondered why she avoided coming over to visit.

The conversation stalled, and Lexie concentrated on filling her belly. She scraped the last bite off her plate and leaned back with a happy sigh. "That chef is a bloody genius."

Her happy belly held her as Anthony spent the next few hours in the lab. Boredom set in quickly as she watched Anthony bury himself in his work. To keep herself entertained, she did yoga, stretching her limbs and arching her body in complicated poses which relaxed her.

"Must you do that," he sputtered after a while.

Lexie, pretzeled into a yoganidrasana position, grunted. "I'm bored and I need exercise."

"Fine, then we'll hit the gym. I need a break anyhow."

Unfolding herself carefully, Lexie's keen sight didn't miss the tent in Anthony's pants. *I guess it wasn't what I was doing that bugged him, but the fact he wanted to do me.* Her nipples tightened at the thought.

He brought her to a new part of the building which housed a state of the art gym. Her geek stripped his coat and dress shirt off, leaving him clad only in his slacks and a t-shirt. He set the treadmill and began to run, his eyes closed in concentration. Just as eager to ignore him, Lexie hit the weights, exerting her muscles as a way of ignoring her other bodily needs.

After a while, a prickling sense let her know he watched her.

"What?" she asked through gritted teeth, hefting the weight.

"Um, you're awfully strong."

Determined to give herself a good workout, Lexie hadn't paid attention to the fact she bench pressed more than the average body builder could. Honestly, she hadn't really expected Anthony to notice or know the difference.

"It's all about technique," she lied, getting up off the bench and heading towards the punching bag.

"Why is it I get the impression there's more to you than meets the eye?" he murmured aloud.

Lexie didn't answer. Anything she said other than the truth would have probably sounded false.

* * *

They fell into a routine over the next few days, one wrought with tension — the sexual kind. She knew he masturbated nightly in the shower, and wished she dared do the same, but she didn't want to risk rousing her passion any more than it already was. The imminent full moon pressed on her and she knew she wasn't completely successful at hiding her hungry gaze around Anthony. And stupid human that he was, he didn't run away.

She successfully fought off her urge to tear his clothes off and fuck him, but the tension in her body took its toll. Even worse, she could tell he fought the same battle.

She had no idea what he did hour after hour in the lab, but she knew he'd made some kind of progress because he worked at a frenzied pace, muttering to himself and working late into the night. Of Frederick, their employer, she saw neither hide nor hair, although she did catch glimpses of his guards and minions. They wisely made a wide berth around her, knowing her reputation — smart because, in her current frame of mind, any wrong move, look or word would have been deadly.

The day of the full moon, Lexie paced restlessly and Anthony looked up from his work long enough to notice. "Are you alright? You're acting like a lion in a cage."

Lexie almost snorted. Change the lion to wolf and he'd hit the problem dead on. "Listen. There's going to be a bit of a change tonight. I've got to go out for a while."

"Going on a date?" Anthony tossed the words at her casually, but she could see the tension in the tight way he gripped his pen.

Jealousy — how yummy. Lexie mentally shook herself. "No, I've got some business to take care of. I want you to lock this place down tight when I leave."

"But how will you get back in?"

"Don't worry about me."

"You know, it's been three days since you arrived and more than that since the attempted kidnapping and shooting at the conference. Don't you think you and the boss are being a tad paranoid?"

She stalked toward him, her wolf side growling when he backed up from her. She crowded him and leaned in close, close enough to smell his fear — and excitement.

"Listen here, my giant geek."

"I really wish you wouldn't call me that."

Lexie lost her patience. She grabbed him by the lapels and pulled him close. "You. Are. In. Danger. Just because you're not seeing the violence directed at you doesn't mean it's not happening. In the days since I've been here, we've intercepted one bomb, two assassins and one really ugly shirt. So do not tell me you're not in danger."

"Uh, if you say so."

This close to him, her emotions swirling, she couldn't stop herself from leaning in the last inch that separated them and pressing her mouth to his. He hesitated at first as she slid her lips along his, her tongue coaxing him to open wide. Lexie, no longer quite in control, pressed herself closer, and gave a grunt of satisfaction at the feel of his hard cock pressing against her belly. It only took a few seconds more before he relaxed, giving her access to his tongue as his arms came to wrap around her.

A fever caught hold of her and she felt her claws and canines extending as her wolf pushed, make that demanded, she claim this man. She wanted to shred his clothes from him and ride him hard, as she sank her teeth into his skin and ...

With a snarl, Lexie pushed away from him. She turned and gave him her back, knowing she couldn't hide the changes in her body from him. She didn't dare look at him lest she completely lose her mind and do what her pulsating body demanded. *Fuck him. Mark him. Keep him.* Her wolf's needs and desires came through crystal clear. Lexie fought her inner bitch, but she could feel the tide of the battle shifting away from her, putting Anthony in danger.

"Get up to your apartment, now." She held herself stiffly as she faced away from him.

"I wasn't done with my work here."

She whirled with a growl. "Don't make me knock you out like I did our last night at the conference."

He sucked in a breath and regarded her incredulously. "I didn't pass out like I thought, did I?"

"Pressure points, baby. Now get your sweet cheeks moving before I show you some less pleasant ones." Lexie didn't curb her tone. She needed him to move now. Even though night had only just started to fall, her wolf side pushed at her. Called her to shed her humanity and revel in her animalistic heritage.

She watched him flee and couldn't help pursuing him, his prey-like action clashing with her desire to possess him. She stalked him down the hall as he scurried to enter the elevator. He paused at the threshold. He turned around and tossed her a strange look — *was that defiance I saw on his face?* The doors slid shut before she could chase him down and reiterate the need for him to stay away from her and remain safe behind as many locked doors as possible. Assassins and enemies of their boss weren't the only danger to him tonight.

She loped down the hall towards the emergency stairs. She slapped her hand on the console and for a second feared her elongated nails would fuck up the reading, but the electronic portal whisked open and she barreled down the stairs, her need to run wild pulsing just below her skin.

Two more hand scans and she made it outside. Quickly, she whirled and keyed in the lockdown code — the new one that her geek didn't have access to. She didn't trust him to not try and disable it to return to his lab.

Silvery fingers of moonlight tickled across her exposed skin and Lexie turned to drink them in. She let her jacket slide from her shoulders to drop to the ground. She kicked off her boots and shimmied out of her pants. Her top and panties quickly followed suit. Naked, she strode forward, ignoring the niggling warning that she should move to the back of the building where there were fewer eyes.

But her wolf drove now, and it had no shame. It rejoiced in the call of the moon. Paced with a frenzy as the time to run — to be free — fast approached.

Bathed in moonlight, Lexie let out a long sigh as she gave up the fight to hold her inner self back. Her skin rippled, a painful thing that made her cry out, and then scream as her limbs cracked and shifted, reshaping her. Her screaming cry of pain transitioned in pitch until she stood there on four feet and howled.

Time to hunt.

chapter nine

A nthony rode the elevator up to his apartment trembling. Part of it was fear if he were to be honest with himself, but the rest had to do with what he'd just seen. Something possessed Lexie, or had always been a part of her if he could believe the tests he'd run.

With her living in such close proximity to him, it proved ridiculously easy for him to snag DNA samples in the form of saliva from her toothbrush and hair from her pillow with follicles still attached. Each test, no matter which way or how many times he ran it, came back the same. Lexie's genetic code was not one hundred percent human. His discovery of the double helix of human DNA twined with wolf belonged to her. He'd assumed the anomaly was a dormant portion of her genetic makeup, until a few moments ago in his lab where she'd *changed*.

Even as clueless as he usually found himself around women and their moods, he'd noticed a strange energy imbuing Lexie all day, an almost sizzling current that emanated from her, strong enough it made the hair on his body stand on end. He'd watched her with wary eyes, unable to help himself, intrigued — and in lust — with the wild animal magnetism that rolled off her while she moved about his space with predatory grace. Anthony feared her coiled tension and leashed violence, almost physically visible beneath the veneer of her indomitable will, but his trepidation wasn't the only thing flooding his senses. Her dominant persona drew him, made him want to beg her to share that passionate energy, to touch him and let him taste it. When she finally did, with a kiss so scorching he'd expected to implode, he'd almost come in his pants. Then just about crapped them when he'd felt her change.

When she'd kissed him, he'd felt, to his shocked disbelief, how her canines had elongated, and the way her nails seemed to suddenly sharpen into razor points. Even more astonishing, he'd seen the way her eyes glowed. She hadn't needed to threaten him to get him to flee, he was ready to do that on his own as myths he'd scoffed at tumbled around in his mind, making a mockery of his assertions that creatures of the night didn't exist.

He attempted to cling to disbelief, to wrap tight around him the rules governing science. Perhaps in his fear of her strange mood, he'd imagined or exaggerated some of the things he'd perceived. People couldn't grow fangs and their eyes definitely didn't shine with an inner light, and the woman he'd once made love to most assuredly wasn't a werewolf, even if her DNA seemed to want to say otherwise.

Then why did I run away?

Anthony moved across his darkening living room and leaned his head on the glass overlooking the front of the building, the soft glow of the moon bathing him in a pale radiance. His eyes fluttered shut as he sought to control his rampaging imagination, but a motion outside caught him before his lids fully closed.

Peering down, he saw Lexie. He forgot to breathe as he watched her strip until she stood naked, her body a thing of beauty. Head held high, she walked forward, away from the building, the light from the moon along with the security lights behind her illuminating her bare shape. And then despite all his scientific knowledge, despite everything he believed in, he saw the impossible.

Her whole body rippled as if alive. His stomach churned at the sickening movement on her flesh that brought to mind alien movies he'd watched in his youth because, just like those horror movies, it appeared as if something tunneled under her skin and fought to escape. Under his riveted gazed, her skin darkened as fur sprouted spontaneously while, at the same time, her limbs contorted. As if that weren't horrifying enough, through the tempered glass he could hear her strident screams, her rapid change from woman to beast an obviously painful ordeal.

When the agonized cry transformed into a howl, the truth hit Anthony like a freight train, refuting every logical assumption he'd ever made. Lexie was a werewolf just like her DNA touted.

He slumped to the floor in disbelief as the woman he'd made love to bound off into the darkness of the trees his boss kept on the premises. An eternity passed as he stared out into the night, his mind a clean slate as his psyche adjusted to his sudden, new reality. Shock could only last so long before his brain and common sense kicked in. *So what if I've discovered that the impossible is real. This is a moment to celebrate, to explore a new frontier.* How many scientists could boast they'd been given the chance to research a live werewolf? And yet, here he sat like a dolt, staring at nothing.

Eagerness to not let this opportunity escape made him spring from the floor and head to his bedroom to change. He dressed in dark clothes and found a navy colored hat. Snatching his digital camera, which he set for night-time photography, he moved to the elevator and slapped his hand on the console. The light flashed red and a message scrolled onto the screen.

System Lockdown.

Lexie had locked him in. Or so she thought. Anthony didn't spend much time attempting to get around her lockdown code. Why, when he already had an alternate escape route for the times he needed to spend time alone without guards or cameras watching him.

The fire exit to his apartment hid behind a large pantry in his kitchen. He'd hidden it early on in his tenure and programmed it to run on its own network. He slid the heavy furniture to the side, revealing the door and security panel. When he tapped his hand to the scanner, the light turned green and Anthony grinned.

He jogged down the dark stairs, excitement bubbling in him. He reached the bottom and with another slap of his hand, opened the door to the outside. Hidden behind dense brush, Anthony fought his way through until he stood in the clear. It was only as he viewed the dark tree line that he wondered how he'd find Lexie. Mr. Thibodeaux's property spanned over a hundred acres, a good portion of it wooded. He refused to allow discouragement to bring him down. Somehow, he'd find her.

Anthony searched the darkness for some of the guards that usually lurked, but not seeing any, he sprinted across the grounds to the shelter of the forest. The white light from the moon didn't reach under the dense canopy of branches and Anthony stumbled for some time through the underbrush like an idiot before halting.

How the hell am I going to find her? At this rate, I'm more likely to twist an ankle than document her. The easy and probably smart solution involved him returning to his apartment and confronting Lexie in the morning. However, Anthony grew tired of always taking the safe route. All his life, he'd followed rules whether of science or society's making. Tonight, for the first time in his life, he realized that rules didn't need to apply, not if he wanted to live life to the fullest and truly discover things. In order to open his mind, he needed to leave his comfort zone and confront the unknown, starting with one intriguing werewolf in the woods.

His enthusiastic inner pep talk held him for a while as he tread through the forest; however, the further he went, the more the icy grip of fear tried to clutch him. His neck prickled as if eyes watched him. His skin grew cold and clammy as the gloom hugged him tight and mocked him for his inability to see further than a few feet in front of him.

He stood still, his heart racing, and listened to the sounds of the night, but he had to admit, he had no idea what the heck he expected to hear. The outdoors wasn't exactly his strong point and he grew tired of tracking her, if his feeble attempt could be termed such. It occurred to him that while he couldn't discern her presence, with her probably heightened senses, she could more aptly find him, especially if she were made aware her charge had escaped the building she'd imprisoned him in.

Taking in a deep breath and ignoring his manly pride, which at this point was mostly swallowed by fatigue and fear, he bellowed for her. "Lexie!"

A hush seemed to descend over the forest, and he shivered as he reminded himself there was nothing to fear. The woods on Mr. Thibodeaux's lands were not truly in the wilds with any number of feral creatures; although, Lexie's assertion that his life was in peril came back to haunt him. In leaving the lab to satisfy curiosity had he painted a target on himself? And now, by bellowing like some idiot, pinpointing his location, was he signing his own death warrant?

Fear descended on him, a blanketing cold that amplified every noise, from the crackle of underbrush to the slight whistle of the wind through the branches. His heart rate sped up as the darkness became cloying, and he whirled, sensing more than one predatory gaze on him, yet he saw nothing. He started to walk, his steps noisy compared to the quiet that had fallen because even the whirring of the insects ceased. Soon, his slow steps turned into a paced jog, then a full out run. Something roamed out there in the shadows. Irrational as it seemed, Anthony could sense it there, a dark hunter watching him hungrily.

Anthony crashed through the shrub, almost losing his balance several times in his headlong flight. Around him, the sounds of chase erupted as those stalking him dropped their pretense of hiding. His breathing hitched and sweat poured all over his body as he pumped his legs faster, cursing his own stupidity in not listening to Lexie. She'd warned him about leaving the building. Warned him that things waited for their moment to harm him, but like the stupid blonde in the movies, the one he used to mock, he'd not obeyed. And now, like the victim of a horror flick, he ran for his life.

He saw the welcoming glow of building lights, closer than expected, and he didn't take the time to hear his mind mocking him over walking in circles; in this instance he thanked his ineptness as it meant safety loomed nearer than expected. He strained harder to reach the haven he should have never left. He hit the edge of the woods and stumbled out into the cleared area. The nightmare followed him with snarls.

Anthony reached the main door to his lab and slapped his hand on the console only to have the lockdown warning flash.

"No," he whispered. He'd forgotten about Lexie's extra security. He whirled around to move to his secret exit, but froze as he encountered a line of beasts moving toward him.

Anthony backed against the door, riveted in fear as three large wolves stalked towards him, their eyes glowing balefully. He could hear their low growls and see their raised hackles as they approached. He scanned them, desperately looking for Lexie, whose pelt, he recalled, gleamed a solid black; however, she didn't appear to number among the approaching wolves.

Standing and waiting to get eaten wouldn't save him. His only chance at survival involved him making it to that damned exit. He shuffled his feet and almost tripped over Lexie's clothing. His foot nudged a hard lump and he chanced a quick look down. He almost gibbered in relief when he saw the revolver. Quickly, he stooped to grab it and pointed it with shaking hands at the encroaching beasts.

"Stop," he whispered. Then louder, "Stop it, or I'll shoot." Why he assumed the creatures would listen he didn't analyze. Perhaps it was the cunning intelligence in their eyes that made him realize these wolves hadn't sprung forth as a cubs, or their immense size which made it seem more likely he'd found more werewolves. If they understood, then they chose to ignore his command. Squeezing his eyes shut, Anthony pulled the trigger. The loud crack of the gunshot rang loud, and Anthony pried an eye open to see if he'd scared the beasts.

Nope. They still approached, but now he could swear he saw disdain in their eyes. Given he couldn't shoot worth a damn, Anthony went to plan B — *run*.

Before he could weigh the pros and cons of that action, he moved, sprinting across the front of the building. He might as well have waved a red cape. Vicious snarls erupted as the beasts charged him. Anthony pumped his legs harder, even as he knew he'd already lost the race.

A heavy weight hit him in the back, and he fell, his knees meeting the ground painfully. Teeth snapped as Anthony rolled, trying to move away from the creature determined to kill him. Sharp, burning pain raked his left arm as something latched on. Anthony gasped at the fiery agony. He tried to pull away, but a heavy weight sat on him as the jaw holding his arm shook it back and forth, toying with him.

A piercing howl caught his attention, but not for long considering the more pressing problem of the wolf trying to chew his arm off. Another howl erupted, its chilling challenge even closer. The creature using his arm as a chew toy bounded off his back and Anthony waited for the attack to resume on a new body part; however, while he heard snarling, it seemed to have moved away from him. He turned his head, the waves of pain radiating from his arm threatening to pull him down into darkness. He blinked at what he saw. The three wolves who'd cornered him were fighting a fourth with sleek black fur.

Lexie. She'd arrived to save him, and now, fought for her life. Anthony struggled to his knees, his wounded arm hanging limp and useless at his side, his glasses cracked and sitting skewed on his face. He watched as she snapped at the other wolves, her sharp fangs drawing blood and yelps. Her fluid movements mesmerized him, for not only did she show no fear, she was savagely beautiful. And even more astonishing, gaining the upper hand.

The wolves attacking her got wise to her tactics and circled her. Anthony wanted to yell when they charged her all at once, but he feared distracting her. Horrified fascination froze his gaze on the battle, and anguish pierced him as her fur became matted with blood. *Useless, I'm freaking useless.* Even if his arm weren't a throbbing piece of ruined flesh, he'd have had nothing to offer help-wise. He didn't have super strength or teeth or anything to help her, but he also couldn't kneel there like a coward watching her fight alone. *Hold on, I do have something to even the odds. The gun.* He'd dropped it in his tussle with the wolves, but he quickly spotted it on the ground. He grasped it and staggered to his feet, gritting his teeth at the cascading pain.

Once on his feet though, he ran into a dilemma. He couldn't shoot well enough to aid her; although, even the poorest shooter could score if close enough to its target. Refusing to analyze the stupidity of his action, Anthony staggered over to the snapping furry melee and aimed a kick at one of the attacking wolves. As kicks went, it sucked, but it served its purpose in getting that particular wolf's attention. It turned to face him with a snarl and Anthony aimed the gun. He fired, the loud crack not stifling the yelp as he hit the damned wolf. He didn't get a chance to see the damage though, as the recoil from the fired shot sent him reeling.

Anthony hit the ground, and ended up splayed flat on his back, staring at the spinning sky. As he lost the battle with the darkness creeping over his vision, he prayed Lexie survived his stupidity.

* * *

Lexie paced Frederick's office, the metal shutters pulled tight against the encroaching dawn light. Her employer hung up his phone and glared at her. "You almost allowed my asset to die."

"Me? It was your fucking minions who tried to take a piece out of him. If you can't control your dogs, then maybe I should put them down permanently." She allowed her anger to fill her. It beat the alternative of anguish when she'd seen Anthony fighting for his life.

"I thought you were supposed to have him locked up tighter than the president's daughter?"

"Apparently, our resident geek had a secret exit, one he wiped from the building schematics housed on the computer." *Brilliant fucking idiot.*

"I don't pay you for excuses," Frederick snarled.

"Fine. Then don't pay me at all." Lexie couldn't believe she'd said that, but once spoken, she didn't take the words back.

"What? You're quitting?"

Lexie braced her hands on his desk and leaned forward, her lips curled in a sneer. "You wish, dead dick. I'm still going to guard, Anthony, because the idiot needs me, not because you're paying me."

Besides, she'd made enough in the last few days to cover her for a few months, that and she felt guilty for failing Anthony. While she'd technically done her job to the best of her abilities, she'd fucked up. She should have known about the secret exit and, even with the moon change, never left off guarding the perimeter of the building. If she'd stayed closer instead of haring off on a run to clear her mind, Anthony's attack could have been averted.

"Well, in that case then, do whatever you wish. I'm not going to argue a free bodyguard." Frederick leaned back in his chair and crossed his arms, the smirk on his face begging for a slap.

"You're still feeding me though," she grumbled as she stalked out of his office and back to the building housing the lab and apartment.

She walked with quick steps, her mind whirring with the developments of the last twelve hours. First and foremost, she'd discovered she loved the damned geek. Sure, she'd realized she cared for him, even liked him, but when she'd seen him, struggling to stay alive as he hovered so close to death, it hit her hard — *I love the stupid, human nerd.*

Not that it changed anything. She was still a werewolf and he a fragile human. Even if she pretended she could control herself, she knew it was only a matter of time before she forgot herself and killed him in the throes of passion. Her nature just wouldn't allow her to play nice forever.

And even if she thought she could make her bitch behave, she also assumed Anthony wouldn't want to come near her after discovering her furry side. For all she knew, he'd left the safety of the building to escape because she'd stupidly allowed her wolf to take charge in full sight of the building. Perhaps a subconscious act on her part to relate the truth?

At least now, if he still wanted her after discovering her hairy problem, he'd understand what she meant when she told him they couldn't be together. Now, if only the thought of his rejection didn't fill her with sorrow.

She arrived at his apartment and relieved the guard inside. The human doctor whom Frederick kept on staff to tend his sheep, straightened from Anthony's bedside.

"How's he doing?" she asked, her eyes anxiously scanning her geek's pale face. She winced at the thick bandages wrapping his left side.

"He'll live, but whether he keeps the arm or not is anyone's guess. I've done the best I can, stitching the flesh up and cleaning it. I've also dosed him with painkillers and antibiotics."

She gnawed her lip, not encouraged by the doctor's blunt assessment. "When will he wake?"

The doctor shrugged. "When his body feels ready. I've left some drugs for the pain on his nightstand. I'll be back in about eight hours to change his dressing."

Lexie nodded and saw the man out before she returned to keep vigil. As she stared down at Anthony, lying so still, she wished there were a way to impart her shifter healing powers on him. However, unlike legends, werewolf status was something her kind were born with, not a mutation caused by bites. *How I wish it were different. If I could make him a werewolf, not only would his arm heal, we could also be together.* Wishful thinking though wouldn't change reality.

Lexie paced at the foot of the bed, waiting for Anthony to regain consciousness so she could tear him a new one. She thought back on the harrowing moments of the night before. It still amazed her that Anthony had found enough courage even after his injury to take on one of the wolves himself. Lexie would have prevailed in the long run, but when the number of assailants suddenly dropped to two, she dispatched them quickly. But that ended up only the start of a long night. She'd stood over her geek's prone body, guarding his nerdy ass from Frederick's resident shifters who had poor control of their beast side and also from the younger vamps who'd smelt the blood and come running.

Finally, someone not out to try and fight her or eat him showed up and she led them to Anthony's secret entrance. Frederick himself had arrived as Anthony was placed on his bed and tended the wounds himself, totally grossing Lexie out. Frederick had licked the bloody gashes, the coagulant in his saliva stopping the bleeding and at the same time releasing agents to speed the healing process, an inborn vampire defense mechanism that fooled victims in doubting they'd been attacked. However, all the vampire spit in the world couldn't heal the deep, bloody gouges covering Anthony's arm. The doctor arrived and went to work with his needle, but Lexie knew enough about wounds to guess that Anthony's arm would require a miracle to remain attached.

It wasn't until early evening that he finally stirred with a groan. Acting on intuition, she knelt at his side and supported his head up, offering him a straw to sip water. He swallowed, his eyes shut as his throat worked, pulling the liquid. He spat the straw out when done and she lowered his head back down to his pillow. She stood and watched as he fluttered eyes with thicker lashes than she'd noticed before.

It took him a moment to focus and she waited to see what he'd say. Hopefully, nothing along the lines of, "Argh, werewolf!" That would probably crush her.

"Lexie," he whispered.

"Yes, Anthony."

"You're safe. Thank the gods of science." He closed his eyes with a smile.

Lexie snapped. "Don't you dare go back to sleep, Anthony. I want to know what the fuck you were thinking, leaving the apartment yesterday after I expressly told you not to."

He opened one eye to peer at her. "I wanted to take pictures of you."

"Of all the stupid things," she muttered. "And it couldn't wait until I came back?"

He shrugged, then winced. "Ow. I guess the part about my arm getting chewed on is real, too. Why didn't you tell me you were a werewolf?"

She wanted to slap him for having a one track, curious mind. "Shouldn't your first question be how bad is your arm?"

Anthony gave her a wan smile. "I know it's bad. My guess would be if infection sets in, I'll lose it."

"And that doesn't bother you?" Lexie wanted to check him for a fever. She expected hysterics, sobbing, denial even, but this calm acceptance freaked her out.

"I'm more worried about you. You took a beating from those wolves. Are you okay?"

Lexie gaped at him. He'd lost his fucking mind in the attack. That had to be it. "I'm fine. See." She lifted her shirt and whirled, flashing her already closed wounds, the red weals the only remaining sign of the attack.

"Wow. That's impressive. I don't suppose I'll turn into a werewolf now that I've gotten chomped on?"

He sounded so hopeful. She sighed. "Sorry. Legend only. Werewolves are born, not made."

"I see." He seemed to ponder this for a moment, and she thought he'd gone back to sleep when he said, "So, is it the fact I'm human that keeps you from being with me?"

"What makes you think I even want you?"

A flush crept up his cheeks. "My mistake. I assumed the tension between us was sexual in nature."

Lexie thought about lying, but she just couldn't do that to him anymore. "You weren't mistaken. I don't know why, but I want you." Before he could speak, she held up her hand. "But it can't happen. Our time at the conference was wonderful, I won't deny that. However, that gentle side of me isn't the norm. Having sex with humans requires me being careful, and I can have fun, but while it scratches the itch, it doesn't cure the problem. It can actually compound the urge."

"So things get a little rough."

She glared at him. "A little rough? I am stronger, faster and tougher than you can imagine. If I were to forget myself for even one minute in the throes of passion, I could kill you."

"But what a way to go," he replied wistfully.

"You're fucking nuts," she muttered. "Or the drugs are making you spout stupidity."

He struggled to sit up using his good arm. "Why is it stupid to want to be with you? I feel things for you I've never felt before. I want to be with you."

"It was just good sex."

"Fantastic sex and more. You intrigue me with your smarts that you hide under a tough girl veneer. Your courage and audacity awe and inspire me. Your presence makes me happy."

Tears pricked her eyes at his speech and she turned lest he see them and use them against her. Even if drug induced, his words touched her and made her long for something she couldn't have — him.

chapter ten

Lexie shot him up with drugs and then left the bedroom, but Anthony didn't mind. She'd given him plenty of food for thought. Over the last while, he'd begun to wonder if their attraction to each other existed only in his hopeful mind. Sure, she'd kissed him the day of the attack, and ended up snuggling him nightly even if she scurried away every morning as if afraid he'd catch her. *Like I wouldn't notice the woman of my dreams molding her curves to me.* Discovering her werewolf status should have sent him screaming in the other direction, but instead he felt as if a great weight had been lifted. Their biological differences kept them apart, not him and his geeky nature.

However, knowing she wanted him but was afraid of killing him didn't bring them any closer to a solution. Actually, the way he saw it, there were only two options — cure Lexie of her werewolf side which he got the impression she'd probably protest, or he needed to change himself.

The bigger question though, was could it be done? The answer awaited him in his lab where twelve lab rats injected with various nanos — a forbidden technology that Mr. Thibodeaux readily encouraged — would tell him if the genetic disorders he'd located in both his employer and Lexie could be replicated, or reversed.

But how to get to his lab? In his current condition, Lexie wasn't likely to let him go waltzing down to check on his test subjects. At the same time, the more time he waited, the more likely he'd lose his arm. Given the grave consequences, he could deal with her anger.

A great plan, if he hadn't fallen asleep, the effects of the drug drawing him down.

When he woke, he sensed someone watching him. Opening his eyes warily, he saw Mr. Thibodeaux sitting by his bed. "Ah, the scientist awakes. How are you feeling?"

Anthony forwent answering for a question that had come to him while he slept. "Are you a vampire?"

His boss chuckled, and Anthony's cheeks flushed, wondering if he'd perhaps assumed wrongly.

"About time you figured it out. I began to wonder if you were as smart as I'd hoped."

"Not so smart, apparently, given I fell for a woman who was paid to like me." Anthony meant it as a snub. He still hadn't quite forgiven his employer for the subterfuge, even if he'd meant well and had only his personal safety in mind.

"Ah, the luscious Lexie. She's quite the woman isn't she? Or should I say bitch?" At Anthony's glare, Mr. Thibodeaux raised a hand. "Down boy. I referred to her animal status, not her actual attitude. I like kick ass women myself. I do apologize for the girlfriend ruse though. But honestly, you can't tell me you didn't enjoy it?"

"Don't ever do that again. It's demeaning. How would you like it if you found out a woman only had sex with you because she was paid?"

"Fine. I'll concede that point to you. You must be ecstatic now then, that she's refused payment to remain your guard." Frederick finished speaking and watched him, waiting for a reaction.

"What?" Anthony's brow creased as he tried to make sense of his boss's words.

"Lexie told me after your accident there last night that she no longer wished to be paid to be your guard."

"She's leaving?" Panic clawed him. She couldn't leave, not until he'd had a chance to see if he could solve the problem keeping them apart.

Mr. Thibodeaux sighed. "You know, for a smart man you are awfully dense. She's not getting paid, but she's staying. Or in simple terms, since you don't get it — she's staying with you because she likes you, not because of the obscene salary I was paying her."

Anthony's head spun. Despite her objections and assertion they couldn't be together, she didn't want to leave him. Anthony felt like jumping out of the bed and dancing. He couldn't stop his silly grin when she walked in and with a scowl, she growled, "What's so funny?"

He and his boss laughed as she grumbled about men and their little heads doing their thinking. Mr. Thibodeaux left after assuring him he'd get the best medical care possible for his arm, and a hint about the progress of his sun allergy research. Anthony ignored the blatant probing even though he knew the solution possibly already waited in his lab.

Lexie slammed a tray down with dishes. "Dinner," she announced unnecessarily.

"I need to go to my lab."

She crossed her arms over her chest and smirked. "Not likely. Now eat."

"Just for an hour. I need to check on some mice I injected and run a few tests, else my progress will be moot."

"Eat and we'll see."

Sighing, Anthony picked up a spoon and ate the stew the chef had prepared. Truthfully, the food energized him enough that as soon as she whipped the tray away, he swung his legs out of the bed and stood. He'd forgotten about the drugs though. He swayed as the pain medications made him woozy. Arms wrapped around him, steadying him, and he breathed deep of her scent, his cock twitching at her proximity.

"Idiot," she grumbled.

Given her closeness though, he'd actually have said more like genius. "I ate, now please can we go to my lab. Just for an hour. I promise to do the tests and observations sitting."

"I want it known that I disagree totally with this, and when you faint and I carry you back like some pansy, I'm going to laugh at you."

Anthony didn't take offense. He finally understood her mean verbal attacks were a way of hiding her feelings. And besides, he'd gotten what he wanted.

She slid her arm around his waist and draped his good arm over her shoulder. Anthony didn't really like having to lean on her for help — he did have some pride left after all — but if his fervent wishing came true, soon, she'd be able to lean on him.

The trip down the elevator and up the hall to his lab made his stomach roil and a cold sweat broke out all over his body. A glance over at Lexie showed him tight lips and a furious look in her eyes, but she got him into his lab and seated before she spoke.

"This better be important or I will beat you worse than those wolves did," she growled. "Now, where are those mice?"

Anthony pointed at a door and she wheeled his chair over. They entered and she wrinkled her nose. "Eew. Stinks in here." She peered at the cages and made a moue of disgust. "Mice. Nasty things. I don't know how you can work with them."

"Since they gross you out, why don't you wait outside then? I just need to take some notes. I'll call you when I'm done."

She threw another glance at his test subjects and shuddered. "Fine. But if they get out, don't expect me to catch them. I'm a wolf, not a fucking cat."

She left and Anthony focused his attention on the animals in the cages. The results astonished him.

He grabbed his clipboard off the metal counter and verified the serial numbers he'd assigned for the different serums. Cage 00011 — the two mice injected with an untwisted version of his boss's DNA were unrecognizable, their bodies misshapen, but the horrifying part was their elongated teeth which they'd apparently used to feed off each other in a frenzy before dying. *Okay, reversing the vampiric condition is not a feasible option at this time.*

He went on to the next cage, 00014. Inside, the two mice peered at him with red eyes. He leaned forward and the critters suddenly hissed, displaying pointy fangs as they flung themselves at the bars. *Interesting. I'll have to test and compare their DNA mutations to Mr. Thibodeaux's. If I can provoke the vampiric condition then there must be a way to suppress or eliminate it.*

He'd left the most important cage for last. Inside, only one mouse appeared, grooming itself. Anthony could see pale scars as if the creature had hurt itself, and yet, he knew the previous day the mouse had been unmarked. Excitement began to build in him as he perused the cage for the other specimen. He opened the cage and kept a watchful eye on the live mouse, but it just regarded him placidly. Anthony grabbed the plastic house and upended it. He recoiled at what tumbled out, mostly because of the blood and the deadly wound gaping in the creature's neck. However, fascination had him look past the gore to see the miracle he'd created — a miniature wolf with white fur. Apparently its death had frozen its state. How interesting that even though the moonlight hadn't touched it, the mouse, injected with Lexie's wolf DNA, still changed.

Even more fabulous, it worked. Logic dictated he run some tests, that he duplicate his trial run, that he exercise caution; however, the fiery pain in his arm and the shooting red streaks he could see creeping across his hand let him know time was running out.

Done in here, he debated how to get to the fridge where he'd stored the surplus nano imbued serums. Lexie wouldn't just let him shoot himself up, so he'd just have to get her out of the way for a few minutes.

"I'm done in here," he called.

Keeping her eyes averted from the cages, she strode in and pushed the wheeled chair back out into the main lab area. When she continued towards the door back to the hall, taking him away from where he needed to be, he spoke, "Wait. I'm not quite done. I need you to take cage number 00014 and place it in the solarium. I need to verify the next stage of the sun serum for Mr. Thibodeaux."

She didn't pause. "I'll come back and do it after I get you back to bed."

"No." He almost shouted the word and his vehemence made her

spin the chair to face her and her narrowed eyes. "That is, I still need to enter a few things on the computer while you do that. It will only take you a minute and it's just down the hall. Plenty of time to run back if I need you."

She didn't look certain and bit her lip. "Fine. But, you better be done by the time I get back or I'll haul you over my shoulder and carry you off cave girl style."

Anthony wanted to snap at her to stop treating him like a weakling, but he could easily imagine her mocking reply. Like, love or not, she currently held the upper hand when it came to strength.

Not for long though if this works.

He pretended to type one handed as she entered the specimen room. She emerged with her nose wrinkled, dangling the cage. Anthony knew he doomed his mice to death given the sunlight that would arrive in the morning, but their demise was a small price to pay. The door no sooner clicked behind her than he pushed away from his workstation with his one good arm, sending his chair skidding over to the glass door of the fridge. He pulled it open and fumbled through the vials, but the one he wanted was at the back of the tray. He lifted the tray onto his lap and located his prize. He snapped the ampule onto the syringe he'd stashed in his pocket. He didn't think, he didn't contemplate the insanity of his actions, he just jabbed his leg with the needle and depressed the plunger. Unsure if the small dosage he'd given the mice would be enough, he grabbed a second and third vial, injecting each in quick succession.

It was only as he slid the tray back into the fridge that he noticed the third vial wasn't the one for Lexie's Lycan gene, but his boss's vampiric one. Then it was too late to think, as his body went into convulsions and the blood coursing in his veins caught on fire.

chapter eleven

L exie dropped the cage in the solarium and made a face at the ugly mice inside. They returned her look with baleful red eyed ones of their own. Then they hissed, showing elongated, pointy fangs, and she sucked in a breath.

"Holy fuck, Anthony. What did you do?" Because she somehow knew Frederick hadn't wasted his time turning a pair of mice into little bloodsuckers. She peered at the glassed panels of the solarium and then back at the little critters. Realization bloomed — *he tricked me.*

She took off running back up the hall, a faint crash making her curse and pick up her speed. She slapped her hand on the console and waited for the door to open, each second an eternity. She slipped inside and scanned the room, not immediately seeing him, but she could hear movement. She peered behind the first counter of equipment and vaulted over the second, stumbling in her shock at what she found.

Anthony trembled on the floor, his body in the grips of a seizure. His eyes were rolled back in his head while spittle foamed at his mouth.

"Fuck. Fuck. Fuck." She cursed nonstop as she whipped a pad of paper off the counter and slid it between his teeth so he wouldn't bite off his tongue. She straddled his body, one of her knees pinning his good arm. For his injured arm, she pinned his hand. But that didn't stop him from banging his head off the floor.

She held him down with her body and spotted the vials on the floor along with the syringe.

"What the fuck did you do?" She whispered the words even as understanding dawned. He'd experimented on himself like the mice. *But what will he become, if he survives?*

After what seemed like an eternity, his body ceased thrashing and he lay still under her. She slipped off him and knelt at his side. She debated fetching the doctor, but at the same time, she didn't want to leave him alone. She tugged his glasses off, and smoothed his hair back.

A tremor ran through his body, then another. Her nose prickled as his regular scent changed into something unique. He reminded her of wolf, and yet, he also emitted a disturbing element she'd only noticed around Frederick and other vamps. And yet … Anthony lived. *Not for long, because as soon as he wakes up I'm going to kill him for being stupid.*

He moaned, a low, deep sound that rolled into a growl.

Lexie shivered as the noise touched her and roused her wolf. A flare of lust ignited inside her to her mortification given Anthony's prone state. She stood and walked away to gain some distance and perspective. She heard a whisper of sound and whirled only to find herself captured in arms of steel and pushed back up against a wall.

Startled at the speed of the attack, it took her a moment to register who held her. Anthony peered down at her with eyes that glowed a brilliant blue.

"You smell good," he grumbled. Then he dipped his head to kiss her.

She'd always enjoyed her embraces with Anthony, the heat he could engender. But this? This was like a match igniting the driest of timber. His mouth claimed hers with a passion and power that actually made her knees weak. She clung to him as his hard lips slid over hers, sucking and pulling on her flesh. He thrust his tongue into her mouth and the taste of him made her moan.

He apparently enjoyed her reaction because he ground his hips against her lower belly, his solid erection pressing against her. She clutched at his shoulders, knowing somewhere in the back of her mind that she should be pushing him away, questioning his wellbeing; however, caught up in a maelstrom of lust, she could only burn.

His hands slid down her back to cup and squeeze her buttocks as his mouth moved lower to suck at the tender skin of her neck. She whimpered when he nipped her and wanted him to do it again, but instead he moved his head back to stare at her possessively. She licked her lips and a tremor went through his body.

Before she could ask him what he'd done, or berate him for his foolish experiment, he moved, tearing her skimpy top with his bare hands and baring her flesh. It was her turn to shudder.

"Mine," he growled. She could only gasp as he ducked his head and his mouth latched onto her bared nipple. He took her tight bud into his mouth and swirled his tongue around it and Lexie cried out in pleasure. While his mouth tortured her nub, his hands got busy unbuckling and tugging down her pants. Her snug bottoms caught around her knees and he stopped yanking them to slide a hand between her thighs, stroking her moist flesh.

He stopped his decadent pleasure of her breast to whirl her around until her backside pressed against his fat dick. A hand in the middle of her back pressed her forward, bending her over and she heard the sound of a zipper lowering. Before she could utter a word — or two like "fuck me" — he'd shoved his hard cock into her.

Lexie yelled as his swollen flesh stretched her, seemingly larger than before. His hands caught her around the hips and he plowed her, his body slapping back and forth against her ass as he drove himself into her. She didn't mind his rough play though. It was just what her body craved. She gasped and panted as his quick thrusts quickly brought her to her peak, and then shoved her over it into a quaking orgasm.

With a bellow that sounded more animal than man, he jetted

into her. When she felt the rigid tension leave his body, she opened her mouth to ask him what the fuck just happened, but she heard the sharp crack of a slap before she felt the burning pain on her ass cheek.

"Get upstairs, woman. We're not done."

She just about came again at his domineering words and tone. But he was mistaken if he thought she'd give into his orders without a delicious fight.

* * *

Anthony laughed when she threw an indignant glare at him over her shoulder. He slapped her ass again just because he could, and besides, even if she tried to deny it, he could smell the fact she enjoyed it.

The scent of her lust was actually what drew him from the earlier agony of his body's change. His nano injected serums had coursed through his body like wildfire, mutating his body at a molecular level. While he couldn't be sure the extent of his new abilities, he'd definitely noticed an enhancement in his olfactory sense. Like the most evocative of perfumes, her arousal had woken him and driven him to his feet to claim her. He'd opened his lenseless eyes, to discover a sharpened sight beyond anything he'd ever imagined.

As he'd captured her in his arms and with his mouth, he'd vaguely noticed the speed with which he moved, but he'd found himself more intrigued by his dominating need to fuck her, to claim her body.

A distant part of him recognized this new aggressiveness was probably a side effect, but Anthony didn't fight it or care. He'd always wished he could be more assertive, but fear had held him back. Now he feared *nothing*.

Lexie moved away from him, trying to yank up her pants which made her breasts bob enticingly. Anthony stalked toward her and noticed how her breathing hitched.

"Take them off," he ordered.

"Like fuck. What the hell happened to you? I came back to find you doing the worm on hot asphalt dance and now you're acting like you're hopped up on steroids and Viagra."

Anthony let a slow smile creep across his face and he made sure she noticed his new dentition. Her eyes widened and he chuckled. "You said you couldn't be with me unless I was like you. Guess what, darling? I'm now just as much wolf as you are."

She shook her head. "That's impossible. Lycans are born, not made."

"Lycanthropy never counted on a geek who wanted to bang his woman."

His words made her eyes dilate and once again, the waft of her desire tickled his nose. "I want you," he said softly. *And not just in my bed, but in my life forever.* He didn't say those words aloud, knowing she wasn't ready for them — yet.

She shook her head. "You're not just wolf though. If I didn't know better, I'd say you've got some vampire in there, too."

Anthony cocked his head. "A regrettable error. Or not. I'll admit, I panicked when I realized my gaffe, but now..." He used his right hand to tear the bandages off his left revealing smooth skin with only faint red lines to remind him of his maiming. He flexed his healed arm, his muscles bulging, and grinned. "Now, I think that cocktail was just right."

"Shouldn't you be running some tests on your condition?" She moistened her lips with the tip of her pink tongue and Anthony took a step forward, determined to claim those lips for himself.

"The only test I'm running tonight is how many times I can fuck you before we both pass out from exhaustion. I suggest, if you want to do it on a bed that you get your sweet ass moving this instant or you're going to find the floor awfully chilly."

Lexie regarded him for one silent moment before kicking her boots off and shoving her pants down to her ankles. She stepped out of them and kicked them away. She stood there naked, her nipples pebbling, desire rolling off her in a thick wave he could almost grasp. She cocked her hip as she placed a hand on it provocatively. Anthony's cock hardened and he took a step forward.

"Come and get it then if you think you can handle me." She moved fast, darting away from him and leaping over the metal counters. Her hand slapped the console to unlock the door and she exited, sprinting. Anthony grinned as he gave her a five second head start. Then he took off after her.

And when he caught her, she was so fucked.

chapter twelve

L exie ran up the hall to the elevator, not really trying to escape Anthony, but, given his suddenly dominant attitude, she wasn't just going to roll over and give him her belly — even if she couldn't wait until he took her cunt.

He gave her a head start, but it wasn't enough, not with his new super speed. He caught her before the elevator, swooping her up with one brawny arm that had grown since his change. She shrieked as he threw her over his shoulder then moaned as his hand slid between her thighs to rub against her wet folds.

She noticed he'd shed the remains of his clothing before catching her, and she let her fingers trail over his taut buttocks. She still didn't understand how he'd managed it, but somehow her geeky scientist had not only made the change into wolf — with some vamp mojo for extra speed and strength — but he'd also transitioned into an alpha. Her wolf was beside herself in her mind, yipping and barking about claiming him as their mate.

But Lexie, despite her body and wolf's longings, determined he'd have to pass the same test as the others. If he could best her, then he could have her. She creamed herself at the prospect.

They entered the elevator and Anthony's finger slid into her and she gasped as he found her g-spot and stroked it. He withdrew his hand, to her disappointment, and growled.

"What?" she murmured.

"They're watching." He shifted his weight to balance up on the balls of his feet and a crunching sound filled the cab as Anthony destroyed the camera.

"Frederick won't like that."

"Frederick can kiss my ass if he wants to see sunlight ever again."

Lexie almost giggled. Somehow she didn't think Frederick would be as impressed with this new take charge Anthony. She, on the other hand, found his new persona even more titillating than his previously shy and geeky one.

She didn't make her move until they reached his apartment. She twisted and flipped herself over his shoulder, landing on her feet. She ran and bounded over the couch before she turned to face him with a grin.

"What are you doing?" he barked.

"I have this policy when dealing with male wolves. If you want to have me, first you have to best me."

A slow, wicked smile spread across his face and he took slow measured steps toward her. "Sounds like fun. How do I know when I've won?"

"If you can bite me at the moment of orgasm, marking me, then I'm yours. But keep in mind, Lycans mate for life. So be very sure before you do this. Once you claim me, there's no turning back."

Her words didn't slow him, but they did make his cock thicken and bob in a distracting manner. "Perfect. Prepare to become mine."

"Cocky geek," she taunted.

"Confident master," he retorted making her knees tremble in a way she'd never expected any man to accomplish.

In the blink of an eye, he went from almost eight feet away to standing in front of her. She just managed to evade his hands, dashing into the bedroom. Again though, his speed overtook her and she found herself swept up into his arms, cradled against his chest. She expected him to fling her onto the bed and have his wicked way with her, but instead he headed for the bathroom. What a letdown.

"What are you doing?"

"Washing my dinner."

Said meal clenched tight. She waited until he put her down in the hot shower before she attempted to escape him again, a failed endeavor, as he caught her before she even set one foot out of the stall. He upended her over his shoulder again, one arm holding her legs firmly as the other spread the lips of her cleft and let the water pour against her sex.

Lexie squealed and pounded at his back and buttocks as he manhandled her with ease. She'd already gone past the point of no return, but she still planned to make a good show of it, loving the way he handled her with ease.

They were both dripping wet and squeaky clean when he carried them back to the bedroom. He dumped her on the bed, but before she could spring up, his body covered hers. Lexie moaned at the hot and heavy feel of his form plastered to hers. His mouth clashed with hers in a fiery kiss that sent electric tingles to her cleft. When she would have twined her arms around his neck, conceding his superior strength, he gathered them in one of his and pushed them above her head. For a moment, she panicked and pulled at her trapped hands, but they didn't budge.

Submission to a male was a new thing for Lexie, and to her surprise, it made her cream.

He grunted against her mouth and moved his lips away to rub his unshaven jaw against her skin. "I can't wait to sink into you."

"Then what are you waiting for?" Lexie gave up fighting. Anthony was who she wanted, and now that the barrier of their species had been torn down, she found herself eager to have him claim her. And to claim him in return.

"You are going to beg me to fuck you," he said before nibbling his way down her neck.

His cocky words made her taunt him. "Then you'd better shut up and get to work."

He nipped her skin in response and Lexie arched as a jolt of desire shot through her body. He sucked at her flesh, pulling at the skin, leaving a hickey for sure, but he didn't attempt to bite her although he teased her with the edge of his canines. Using his tongue to trace his way, he moved down her body a bit, laving a path between her breasts. He didn't let go of her hands as his mouth brushed over her nipples. He blew on them, his warm breath tightening her nubs. Cream pooled in her cleft as he teased her. Around and around, he kept moving, circling her nipples, never quite touching them. Lexie bit her tongue before she begged him to suck them — or even better, bite them.

He did neither. Yanking her hands down, he pinned them to her stomach as he crawled backwards, his chin brushing against her trimmed pubes. Her cleft quivered, anticipation coiling it tight as she waited for him to eat her like he'd promised. He didn't. He pressed his mouth to the soft skin of her thighs, nipping and kissing, left then right.

Lexie panted with need, but she refused to ask. As if sensing her inner war, he chuckled, his warm breath feathering across her moist lips, unleashing an involuntary moan from Lexie.

"Tell me what you want," he murmured, his lips a bare hairsbreadth away from her core.

Lexie clenched her eyes tight, fighting his allure out of pure stubbornness. She shook her head, unwilling to give in so easily.

He flicked his tongue against her clit, a swift, scorching motion that made her cry out. "Admit you want me to touch you. To lick your sweet pussy until you come on my tongue."

She made the mistake of opening her eyes and gazing down at him. His magnetic blue gaze caught hers and his lips tilted in a seductive grin. She caved to her needs and the pleasure he promised.

"Make me come."

Apparently those three words were enough. He swiped her with his tongue, a long wet lick that made her shiver from head to toe. He spread her lips and jabbed into her core, lapping at her cream. While his one hand held her own down, a prisoner to his delightful torture, his other roamed freely. He used the pad of his thumb to rub her clit while his mouth sucked and tugged on her lips. Lexie's head thrashed and she moaned as he pleasured her. His tongue took the place of his thumb, flicking her clit in a rapid back and forth motion that had her hips bucking. He slid fingers into her sex — one, two, then a tight third. In and out they pumped, as his mouth worked her swollen nub.

After the past few days of abstinence, her climax came fast and hard. Anthony grunted with satisfaction as her pelvic muscles clamped his digits tight.

The tremors hadn't ceased when he moved, his body covering hers. His hands yanked hers back up above her head in a move meant to show he still held control. She loved it.

He settled himself between her thighs and the tip of his dick rubbed against her cleft. "Beg me for it," he growled.

Lexie didn't play any more games. "Take me. Fuck me and mark me. Please."

With a groan, he thrust his swollen cock into her, triggering after-shocks that had her keening mindlessly.

"Now for my turn," he said.

* * *

Buried to the hilt in her shuddering moistness, Anthony gritted his teeth not to come. Pleasuring her, holding her prisoner and making her beg, all those things combined put him on the edge of his own orgasm. But he well remembered her words. To claim her, and keep her forever, he needed to bite her at the moment of orgasm.

With that thought in mind, he moved slowly in her, setting a steady pace. She looked so beautiful and soft beneath him, her cheeks flushed and her lips curved in a sweet smile of pleasure. However, he wanted to see her eyes, read them.

"Look at me," he ordered.

Her green eyes flickered open, her lids heavy with passion, and her gaze aglow with emotion. Staring into her visage, he increased his pace, noting how her breathing hitched and the smell of her arousal clung heavy in the air. He deepened his stroke and her lips parted on a sigh. Her hips gyrated in time with his thrusts, tilting to take him further inside her. He felt his orgasm building, but he strained against it until he felt the walls of her sex begin tightening around him.

"Mine," he growled. He buried his face into her shoulder, licking the skin there, biting only when the tremors of her orgasm rippled along his cock. He sank his teeth into her soft skin and heard her scream his name, her climax suddenly tripling in intensity and launching his own bliss.

The metallic taste of her blood hit his tongue and suddenly a deep hunger invaded him, and he gulped hungrily at her essence. Caught in the throes of a pleasure so intense, he only vaguely noted her cries of pleasure, so intent was he on marking and feeding from her. What seemed like scant seconds later, a growled warning from the newly acquired pet inside his mind made him release her flesh reluctantly. As sanity returned, he suffered a moment's guilt and horror at what he'd just done. *What have I become?* Then he saw the silly smile on her face, and all doubt fled. He'd do and become anything if it meant keeping Lexie.

"I love you." He uttered the words without thinking, and her eyes shot open in shock.

Uncertainty tried to grab him like it had so many times in the past, but he fought it. He loved her, and even if she didn't know it yet or wouldn't admit it, she loved him — and even better, according to the vivid bite-mark on her neck, she belonged to him.

"I — " She never got to finish her sentence, because the sudden cracking of glass had them both diving off the bed. He stood in front of her protectively, while she went for the jacket on the chair where she pulled out a gun.

"We're under attack."

It was an unnecessary statement on her part because, with his enhanced hearing and senses, Anthony could hear the sounds of battle. He also saw a prime opportunity to try out his new powers.

He ran at the window and dove through the shattered remains.

Lexie's scream of, "No!" followed him as he dropped through the air and hit the ground in a crouch without the slightest jolt or pain. *Cool.*

The wide expanse around him overwhelmed him for a moment with sensory overload. His brain quickly went to work sorting what his five senses noted, and zoomed in on the most important — danger. He sniffed the air, inhaling deep, then turned his head sideways to peer at the darkness. A figure stepped from the shadows and Anthony growled as he recognized the bastard who'd shot Lexie at the conference.

He noticed something else too — the guy had pointed ears.

"What the fuck are you?"

The Spock eared assassin didn't reply, but he raised his gun. In a flash, Anthony reached the attacker and flung his paltry weapon away before grabbing him in a headlock. Then he bit him.

Anthony didn't have time to savor the new unique flavor of the thug turned victim. Movement from the trees coalesced into more sharp eared freaks.

Anthony thrust the limp body away from him and wiped his mouth before giving them a feral grin. "Who's next?"

Wielding a variety of weapons, and in some cases, just themselves, the invaders rushed him. And then stopped to look for him. With his new found speed, Anthony moved amongst them lightning quick, punching, kicking and tearing at the bastards who'd tried to kill him and almost managed to kill Lexie. His intrigued scientific side noted that while he kept downing them, the bastards kept getting back up.

He also discovered that while newfound strength and powers were great, they didn't prevent injury — even if said wounds healed quickly — and against great numbers, he began to question the wisdom of his decision in facing them alone.

A pointy eared, green skinned creature that made Anthony think of a goblin lunged at him, only to stop with a stunned look before falling face first on the ground. A silver blade stuck out from the back of his head. No sooner did he note this than the crack of a revolver boomed. Anthony looked up to see Lexie had arrived and judging by the glint in her eyes, she was pissed. But not as pissed as he was when he realized how many male eyes had swiveled and regarded her naked form.

And thus did he truly begin to battle in earnest.

chapter thirteen

Lexie used up the ammo in her gun, shooting the attacking Fae in the heads with silver bullets, the only way to bring the sly bastards down and render them out of action for a while. To truly kill one of the immortal ones, she'd require an axe, gas and a lighter. Hopefully, Frederick kept some marshmallows in stock.

Adrenaline pumped through her body, more from the way Anthony dove out of the window than the battle. As she worked her way toward her new mate, she noticed the vamps, including Frederick, had come to join the battle. The Fae risked a lot attacking in such large numbers, not that she could blame them given what she knew of Anthony's success. Unfortunately for them, she was on his side, and as such, they needed to die for trying to harm him.

She got distracted several times by the sight of her geek-turned-alpha fighting. What he lacked in training and finesse, he made up for in raw power. With no prior instruction, he'd managed to bring forth his claws and he used them with devastating effect along with his fangs which she still wasn't sure were vampire or wolf in origin.

She worked her way toward him, taking out the goblins who got in her way — nasty slimy creatures. She hated them as much as mice.

When she got within a few feet of Anthony, she yelled. "Don't you ever dare scare me like that again."

Without pausing in his ass kicking of the pair of trolls attacking him, he snarled back. "Get inside, and get some damned clothes on."

She laughed. "Like hell am I leaving you to fight alone."

"How am I supposed to protect you if I'm distracted by your naked body?" he growled as she took aim and fired at one of his assailants between the eyes.

"Get used it to, lover. You're part shifter now. Just wait until I take you to meet my parents. You'll get to see lots of naked people."

He stopped fighting to turn and face her with a pleased look. "You're going to take me to meet them?"

She shot the goblin sneaking up on him before answering. "Well, duh," she said, rolling her eyes. "It's what a girl does when she meets the man of her dreams, falls in love and mates with him."

And that quickly, she found herself swept into his arms. "You love me?"

"Of, course I love you. I wouldn't have let you mark me if I didn't. Which reminds me, we got interrupted before I returned the favor."

"Well then, shall we adjourn?" He stepped away and crooked his arm at her. Lexie arched a brow and looked around at the dying battlefield.

"Um, don't we need to finish up here?"

Anthony chuckled. "Nah. Let Frederick do the rest. We took care of most of it already. Besides, we've got more important things to do."

They left the scene of chaos, but never made it to bed. Anthony thrust her up against the elevator wall, and as he pounded his dick into her soaking sex, she bit him. She sank her fangs in deep, marking him to show the world that this geek — the most wonderful, sexy and lovable man ever — was all hers.

Forever.

epilogue

The swish of the apartment door opening had Anthony bounding from bed, stark naked. Lexie didn't immediately follow, opting first to dress herself before going out to rescue Frederick. Anthony held him pinned to the wall by the throat and, while the vampire strived to pry the choking fingers off, he wasn't making any headway.

"Anthony, put him down."

Her lover and mate peered at her over his bare shoulder. "I will, once my former employer and I come to an agreement."

"Former?" Frederick sputtered, his undead face turning red.

"Yes, former. From here on in, we'll be partners."

"Easy for you to say since I'm the one who's expended the funds to set this place up. And if I'm not mistaken, you've taken advantage of the research you were doing for me to enhance yourself."

Anthony dropped Frederick and moved to stand by the large window, unashamed of his body as he stood proudly and stirred her just-sated hunger. "With what I've discovered," her lover said. "You'll make your investment back plus some."

Lexie blanched as his words sank in. "You can't mean to sell the serum. The world couldn't handle that kind of influx of shifters or vamps."

Anthony whirled and shook his head at her with a smile. "Of course not. But what I've discovered will allow us to make money with the big pharmaceuticals healing humans. My nano technology, and what I've learned about the DNA helix, will revolutionize healthcare."

Frederick's eyes brightened and a predatory smile emerged. "We'll make billions. A fantastic plan, but what about my ability to sun walk? I thought you told me that you almost had a solution."

"I do. Lexie, fetch the cage from the solarium."

Lexie, more worried for Frederick's safety than Anthony's at this point, hurried to fetch the cage. She returned with the cage and shook her head as she placed it on the floor in front of the two men. "I think your solution needs more work," she said. "Only one of them survived."

Anthony snorted. "Only one was supposed to. Both were vampire mutated, but only one held the solution to survive direct sunlight."

Frederick's face tightened with such longing Lexie actually hoped Anthony could help him. After all, the vampire was the reason she'd found her one true love. He deserved some kind of reward for that.

"How soon before you can run some more tests?"

Anthony shrugged. "I can start today. I'll even videotape the results. When you're satisfied, come to me and I'll administer the serum."

Anthony actually didn't make it to the lab until much later on — first he required breakfast, followed by dessert. Once they did make it down to his lab, Lexie had a smile plastered from ear to ear and a deliciously sore pussy.

* * *

True to his word, Anthony worked hard the next few days. Becoming an alpha werewolf with some vampire tendencies hadn't diminished his smarts, but rather amplified them.

Frederick took three days before he returned, arriving just before dawn broke. He hesitated before holding out his arm. "How can I be sure, you won't kill me?"

Anthony smirked. "If I wanted to kill you, I'd do it with my bare hands. Lucky for you, I kind of like you. Now stop being a wuss."

"Bossy geek," Frederick muttered as Anthony pricked him, probably harder than necessary, with the needle.

Lexie waited for him to go into convulsions, scream or something, but other than turning more pale than usual, Frederick did nothing untoward.

"Ready to get your first sunburn in a few hundred years?" Anthony asked with a grin.

"I swear, if I melt into a puddle of goo, I'm going to haunt your ass," Frederick grumbled.

"It'll work. Come on."

Lexie held her breath as Anthony opened the door to outside and stepped into the crisp morning air. Dawn was cresting and its soft rays bathed him in a fiery light. She saw Frederick swallow hard, still hidden in the gloom of the hall. With a courage that had to take every ounce of his strength, Frederick straightened his shoulders and took brisk steps to join Anthony, his only hesitation came at the doorway, then he plunged outside.

Lexie followed, a smile breaking free as she saw Frederick, a rapturous expression on his face, twirling in the UV rays that were deadly to every other vampire alive — make that undead.

"It worked. It worked!" Frederick shouted.

"I told you it would," Anthony replied, rolling his eyes. "But, there is one side effect that you should know about."

Frederick stopped his spinning and narrowed his gaze. "What?"

"I couldn't quite cure your vampiric state."

"I should hope not. I like being a vampire. I just didn't want to be stuck in the dark."

"Good. Well, the serum I gave you will not affect your night time vampire abilities, but as for the day ... "

Frederick grabbed Anthony and tried to lift him, to no avail. "What did you do to me?" he shouted instead.

"In order to allow you to walk by day, I needed to make you human again." At Frederick's inarticulate cry of rage, Anthony shrugged. "Just when you're in direct sunlight. As soon as you get out of the UV rays you'll go back to your regular vampire self."

As if to test this theory, Frederick ran back into the darkness of the building. Lexie pivoted to watch him and saw his eyes flare red from the shadows.

Anthony laughed. "Hey, it's not that bad. And just think, you'll be able to enjoy regular food again so long as you eat it on a patio."

Frederick stalked back outside and growled. "I liked you better when you were a geek."

Anthony smirked. "You mean when I was a pushover. Tell you what, if you really hate it, then I'll take it away. But take a few days to think about it first. Go, enjoy the sunshine, but try not to get sunburnt."

Frederick leaned his face back and closed his eyes against the rising sun. He sighed. "I still hate you." With those words, he stalked off in the direction of his house, the sunlight making his black hair glint with blue highlights.

Lexie shook her head. "That wasn't nice, lover. You should have warned him about the side effects beforehand."

"Bah," Anthony scoffed. "He would have done it anyway. If you ask me, it's the best of both worlds. Although, I probably should have mentioned the need to start carrying condoms around because another tiny issue is the fact his sperm becomes viable if he makes love by sunlight."

Lexie tried to stifle her laughter, but it bubbled out, and seconds later Anthony joined her. Her cell phone chirped on her hip, and still giggling, Lexie answered it. "Hi, mom. I was going to call you. I'll be coming by this weekend for dinner with my mate."

Her mother's voice squeaked. "What? How?"

"Well, remember that geek job I got injured on? Turns out, a nerdy scientist was just the man I needed to steal my heart." She hung up her phone while her mother was mid squeal and took a step back, preparing to flee, because judging by the look in her mate's eye, she was about to pay for using her nickname for him. *Lucky me.*

author notes

Opal Carew

I write erotic romance. Since 2009 when I was named "Fresh Face of Erotic Fiction," my books have won the Award of Excellence and the Golden Leaf Award, and they have been finalists for the National Readers' Choice Award, HOLT Medallion, Laurel Wreath Award, Gayle Wilson Award of Excellence, and Passionate Plume Award.

I love crystals, dragons, feathers, cats, pink hair, the occult, Manga artwork, and all that glitters. I earned a degree in Mathematics from the University of Waterloo, and spent 15 years as a software analyst before turning to my passion as a writer. I live in Canada with my husband, two sons, and two cats.

To learn more about Opal, visit her website at www.opalcarew.com, or contact her at OpalCarew@BestRomanceAuthors.com

Other books by Opal Carew

From St. Martin's Press:
Total Abandon
Pleasure Bound
Bliss
Forbidden Heat
Secret Ties
Six
Blush
Swing
Twin Fantasies

From Samhain Publishing:
The King and I
(Celestial Soul-Mates series)

From Red Sage Publishing:
Crystal Genie

From Sinful Moments Press:
Christmas Angel

Through Smashwords:
Three

———————

Lauren Hawkeye

I never imagined that I would wind up telling stories for a living, but I was always the kid who read all the time and made up stories about my favorite characters once I'd finished a book. I once spent an entire year narrating my own life internally. No, really. But where I was just plain odd before publication, now I can at least claim to have an artistic temperament.

I live in the Rocky Mountains of Alberta, Canada with my husband, toddler, pit bull, and idiot cat, though they do not live in an igloo, nor do they drive a dogsled. In my nonexistent spare time, I can be found knitting (the husband claims that my snobby yarn collection is exorbitant), reading anything I can get her hands on, or sweating my way through spin class. I love to hear from my readers!

Sign up for Lauren's mailing list to receive new release alerts at http://eepurl.com/OeF7r

Or find her online: Twitter: @LaurenHJameson or www.laurenhawkeye.com or www.laurenjameson.com

Other books by Lauren Hawkeye
Three Little Words
Love Me For Me
Love Me If You Dare
Spring Fling
A Bride For A Billionaire
Surrender to Temptation

———

Eve Langlais

A true romantic, I am a believer in love at first sight. I also think there is life 'out' there — hopefully as sexy as the aliens I've created in some of my books. As the author of more than 50 works, I have plenty of other stories sure to entertain, from rough around the edges werewolves to super sexy aliens. I even have a few cyborgs! If you're the adventuresome type, then you might want to check out some of my bestselling ménage series, where the erotic focus is always on the heroine — to her screaming delight. To learn more about Eve, visit her website at http://www.EveLanglais.com or contact her at eve@evelanglais.com.

Other books by Eve Langlais

From Amira Press
Alien Mate 1-3
Defying Pack Law
Betraying The Pack
Seeking Pack Redemption
Broomstick Breakdown
Mated To The Devil

From Liquid Silver Books
Lucifer's Daughter
Snowballs in Hell
Hell's Revenge
Last Minion Standing

Other Books
Bunny and the Bear
Alien Abduction Series
Delicate Freakn' Flower
Jungle Freakn' Bride
A Demon and His Psycho
Date With Death
Wickedest Witch
Aramus

Cynthia Sax

I live in a world filled with magic and romance. Although my heroes may not always say "I love you," they will do anything for the women they adore. They live passionately. They play hard. They love the same women forever.

I have loved the same wonderful man forever. My supportive hubby offers himself up to the joys and pains of research, while we travel the world together, meeting fascinating people and finding inspiration in exotic places such as Istanbul, Bali, and Chicago.

Please visit Cynthia on the web at www.CynthiaSax.com

Other books by Cynthia Sax

From Avon:
He Watches Me
He Touches Me
He Claims Me
Flashes of Me
Breaking All the Rules
Sinful Rewards

From Ellora's Cave:
Warlord's Bounty
Alien Tryst
Lust by Moonbeam
Menage Lost